PAINTED
LIVES

CHARLOTTE VALE ALLEN

PAINTED LIVES

RANDOM HOUSE

TORONTO · 1 9 9 0

Published in Canada in 1990 by
Random House of Canada Limited, Toronto,
and simultaneously in the United States by
Atheneum, Macmillan Publishing Company.

This is a work of fiction.
Names, characters, places, and incidents either
are the product of the author's imagination or
are used fictitiously. Any resemblance to actual events
or persons, living or dead, is entirely coincidental.

Canadian Cataloguing in Publication Data
Allen, Charlotte Vale, 1941–
Painted lives
ISBN 0–394–22136–2
I. Title.
PS8551.L52P34   1990   C813'.54   C90-093162-0
PR9199.3.A55P34   1990

Book design by Chris Welch

10 9 8 7 6 5 4 3 2 1

Printed in the United States of America

for my fine friend
and traveling companion
Nina Ring Aamundsen

PAINTED
LIVES

One

Sarah came out to the verandah saying, "There's a call for you."

"Who is it?" Mattie asked irritably.

"She says her name's O'Connor."

Reluctant to take her eyes from the view, Mattie growled, "I don't know any O'Connors."

"She says she knows you."

Mattie lifted the receiver from the extension on the table beside the rocker. "What is it?" she barked into the mouthpiece.

"Mrs. Sylvester," began a young voice, "I'm Ellen O'Connor from the *Boston Globe* and I . . ."

She didn't get to say anything more. With a look of disgust Mattie slammed down the receiver. "Jesus Christ, Sarah! Haven't I told you repeatedly to screen the calls! You keep letting these goddamned journalists sneak up on you."

Sarah stood calmly, accustomed now to the old woman's sudden explosive fits of temper, and simply listened.

"If you can't figure out how to keep those hounds away from me, I'll have to get rid of you. I can't have those people bothering me. How many times do I have to tell you?" she roared, her anger formidable and frightful.

"Sorry," Sarah said quietly. "She said she knew you."

"It's the oldest damned trick in the book. Haven't you figured that out yet?"

Sarah let her go on, having learned early on that when the old woman didn't get any kind of reaction, her anger fizzled out pretty quickly. Already Sarah could see Mattie's eyes starting to shift back to the view.

"Tell Bonnie we'll have lunch late today. I want to walk."

With ever impressive energy, Mattie levered herself out of the rocker, picked up her sunhat and dark glasses, and made her way across the wide verandah to the steps leading down to the lawn. Sarah watched the tall, stately figure move across the grass, headed for the beach. Mattie was, she knew, going to spend an hour or more now immersing herself in the view that so held her attention hour after hour, every day of the week from early morning until after sunset. Even in bad weather the old woman sat in the rocker and gazed at the beach. They'd been on the island for seven weeks and the routine had been established the day after they'd arrived. And it didn't vary significantly from the routine Sarah had come to know during the winter at the Connecticut house. Another beach view, another verandah, another rocker. The only difference Sarah could discern between the winter and summer routines was the number of hours the old woman spent out-of-doors in each place. Sarah had started the job the previous February, after having endured one of the most bizarre interviews of her life.

First she'd been preinterviewed by the agency and then, after several telephone calls, Mattie had agreed to an evening meeting. The old woman had stood framed in the open front door as Sarah had pulled to the top of the circular driveway in the rental car, and the first words Mattie spoke were, "Good! At least you're punctual. Come inside."

She'd led Sarah into the immense living room where she'd seated herself in a wing chair, waving Sarah to the sofa opposite. It had taken every ounce of Sarah's self-control not to let her eyes go roving over the paintings that took up all the available wall space, or the silver-framed photographs grouped atop a fringed shawl on the grand piano. She'd seated herself on the sofa, then looked boldly into Mattie's large, very bright, blue eyes. Those eyes, Sarah had thought then and still did now, absorbed everything, missed nothing. Remarkable, famous eyes. They were exactly as they'd been in paintings done by Gideon Sylvester thirty and forty years ago: direct, daunting, tremendously intelligent; Mattie's eyes were the windows into which she defied people to dare look. It wasn't easy, Sarah had discovered at the outset.

Mattie sensed a lie before it was spoken; she could see dishonesty forming in the distant recesses of someone's mind. You couldn't fool Mattie, and if you tried, her capacity for anger and that deep booming voice could scare the hell out of you. Until you got used to her and realized the anger was as much an art form to Mattie as her husband's work. Everything about the old woman was on a grand scale—her height, her eyes, her vocal range, her emotions.

"If you're some kind of writer thinking to get inside my home for the sake of a story," Mattie had said, "I'll know it soon enough. And I'll make you regret the day you ever imagined I'd be so simpleminded that I couldn't tell an honest-to-god secretary from someone with secret ambitions. If I wanted the world to know about my life with Gideon Sylvester, I'd have told about it long since. I plan to go to my grave being the only one who lived my life. Everybody else can go live their own lives. No one's going to get even the smallest vicarious thrill from any of my late husband's exploits. They'll have to make do with what's on the record." She delivered this speech like a set piece, but with galvanizing gusto.

Sarah had nodded, then waited.

"So what can you do?" Mattie had asked her. "And if you don't do it well, don't bother telling me about it. I loathe mediocrity."

"I can type seventy words a minute. I don't do shorthand, but the agency said you don't require that. I can file, and keep books. I can also cook, and even clean, if it comes to that."

Mattie had listened with her eyes slightly narrowed, taking stock. "You're young," she'd said accusingly. "You're looking for a husband."

Sarah had laughed. "I'm not that young. I'm forty-one. And I've had a husband, thank you very much."

"Oh?"

"Yes, ma'am. It lasted about twenty minutes one Friday afternoon."

To Sarah's pleasure and relief, Mattie had laughed hugely, her eyes approving. Then she'd asked, "What else?"

Sarah had to take a moment to decide how best to reply. This wasn't a woman who'd tolerate answers designed to please her. She was after truth. "I need to be somewhere," Sarah had said finally. "I'm tired of working for men who aren't half as competent as I am but who make twice the money. And I'm tired of wondering what I'm going to be when I grow up." Mattie's eyebrows had lifted, and Sarah added, "I'd rather be useful to someone I respect than waste my time working to pay rent for rooms that'll never be mine."

At this point Mattie had removed a cigarette from a silver cup on the table at her side and proceeded to light it with a wooden kitchen match. She drew hard on the cigarette, then crossed her very long, still attractive legs, and stared through the smoke at Sarah.

Again Sarah had waited, aware of the absolute silence of the house, and of all those tempting paintings surrounding her. She'd expected less, of everything. She'd imagined the reknowned Mathilda Sylvester would be less vital, less healthy, less alertly suspicious, and far less attractive. Her idea of a seventy-seven-year-old woman as someone ailing and frail couldn't have been farther off the mark. Mattie looked considerably younger and was anything but frail. Sarah thought that if she set her mind to it Mattie could probably lift a small truck. She exuded strength. She was slender; her hair was still abundant, although faded from its once vibrant red to a tame silvery gold, and she wore it haphazardly but most attractively in a topknot secured by several silver combs; her posture was exemplary. Sarah straightened, squaring her shoulders, her eyes remaining on those of her potential employer.

Mattie smoked her cigarette for a time then said abruptly, "Whatever goes on inside my home is strictly private, not for public consumption."

Sarah had nodded once more.

"I've had more young women traipsing through here than I can count. I'm tired of that." She'd extinguished her cigarette then looked at her hands as if for traces of ash. The diamond bracelet on her left wrist sent a number of tiny rainbows onto the walls, ceiling, and thickly carpeted floor. "Are you reliable?" she'd asked wearily, as if fatigued beyond measure by the onerous task of conversing with a stranger.

"Yes," Sarah had said simply.

"All right." Mattie had stood up from the chair and started toward the foyer. Sarah had no choice but to follow. "Bring your things tomorrow," she'd said, opening the front door. "There are three on staff: Bonnie, my cook, who's been with me twenty-seven years; Carl, my driver and handyman, who's been with me twenty-two years; and Gloria, my housekeeper, who's been with me eleven years. I doubt I'll live long enough to keep you employed for so long, but I'd like to think you'll want to stay until the end."

It was a chilling statement, but Mattie had allowed Sarah no time for a response. She'd extended her long cool hand, and Sarah had shaken hands with her, saying, "Thank you, Mrs. Sylvester. I'll do my best for you."

"Call me Mattie. And I'd prefer you did your best for yourself. I've found pleasing one's self usually results in pleasing others."

With that, Mattie had closed the door and Sarah had found herself staring at the heavy brass lion's head door knocker. Mattie, she'd discovered, didn't waste time on hellos and good-byes.

That had been just over six months ago, Sarah thought, watching Mattie make her stately progress along the beach, the breeze causing the gauzy fabric of her dress to flatten against her long body. Sarah told herself she was going to have to be more careful. That O'Connor woman was the third journalist who'd managed to talk her way past her, and it drove Mattie wild.

She returned indoors and went to the kitchen where Bonnie was seated on a high stool at the counter, placidly shelling peas into a white enamel colander.

"Mattie wants to have lunch late," Sarah told her, opening one of the cupboards for a mug, then moving to the coffee maker.

"What about you?" Bonnie asked. "You wanna wait and eat with her?"

"Uh huh," Sarah answered, getting the cream from the refrigerator. "I've got a few more letters to do."

"She down walking on the beach again?"

"Uh huh."

Bonnie smiled down at her lapful of peapods and gave a shake of her head.

"What?" Sarah asked, leaning against the counter and taking a sip of the coffee. Bonnie made the best coffee, not to mention the finest food, Sarah had ever consumed.

"She's been tracking something on that beach for the last six years. I figure she's going back over the whole of her life, step for step. Been doing it since the Mister passed on. Same thing at the winter house. She sits out-of-doors, tracking it all, step for step."

"You know that for sure?"

Bonnie looked up and smiled. "What else d'you figure it'd be?" she asked reasonably. "Haven't you seen the way she can't hardly wait to get rid of folks so she can get back out there to her tracking?"

"What did she do before?"

"Ah," Bonnie sighed. "She never had a minute's time to sit still. He kept her going good," she said with some satisfaction. "He had her on the run from morning to night. I never saw two people keep each other so on the go like the two of them. And fight! God almighty! You wouldn't believe two old folks would have the energy for it, but they'd be at it night and day. God! Their fights! I sure do miss that man. There won't never be another one like Gideon Sylvester. And that's the truth."

"How did he die?" Sarah asked casually.

"Stroke." Bonnie set aside the colander, gathered her apron together over the spent pods, and went to dump them in the trash bin. Straightening, she stood with a hand on the counter. "Right in the middle of a fight so bad we could hear them all the way in here."

"Where were they?"

"Down to the beach. Shouting away at each other like always, then there was this sudden quiet. And I thought, That's strange, so I went out the back door here, around to the front of the verandah, and after maybe five minutes she come running like hell back up the lawn. I knew just from the look of her. So, I rushed back in here and phoned Doctor Bob, told him to come quick. Only took him a few minutes. He was pulling into the driveway when she'd finally got her breath back. She grabbed hold of him by the arm and led him off back down to the beach. I just knew. You know? She wouldn't've left him down there if he wasn't dead. She'd've stayed there, breathing for him if she had to. So I knew."

"What d'you mean?"

"It's the way they were." Bonnie shrugged, as if what she was saying was clear as day and Sarah was being dense.

"I don't follow," Sarah said. "How were they?"

"Close," Bonnie said. "Two people living inside one head, kind of. All them arguments, all that fighting, that wasn't any kind of fighting like you and me might know about. It was more like one person thrashing out the pros and cons of a situation. You know? They didn't never really disagree, it seemed to me. They were just keeping the spark alive." With pride, as if she was privileged to be one of the few who knew, she said, "They were *special*. And the ordinary rules never did apply to the two of them." She gave Sarah a sudden smile and said, "I'll tell you a little something. It wasn't only fighting they were up to all the day and night."

"Oh?"

"Uh-uh. They were at each other like newlyweds right to the last."

"You're joking!"

Sobering, she said, "The missus wouldn't even sleep in that bed for six months after he passed on. I couldn't say for a fact she slept at all those six months. Then one night she just went back to her bed, and that was that." Bonnie looked at the clock on the stove and said, "You'd better get outta here now, do those letters you were talking about. She'll be back in half an hour, forty minutes, and she'll want her lunch."

"Thanks for telling me," Sarah said.

"How's that?"

"It helps," Sarah told her, then set her empty mug in the sink before heading off to the upstairs office at the front of the house.

Keeping an eye on the clock, she fitted on the earphones and started transcribing Mattie's dictation from the old Dictaphone. The machine was a relic, and the dictation sleeves were no longer even available. But Mattie had a big box filled with them, and had told Sarah, "When we get to the end of these things, I'll buy a new system, one that takes cassettes. I don't see the point of throwing away something that still works perfectly well."

Sarah listened through the headphones. More declines to invitations; more refusals to galleries. No personal letters today. This was, without question, the least taxing job possible. Half a dozen letters on average daily; fielding telephone calls; paying bills and making bank deposits; writing the staff checks, including her own; and generally keeping herself available should Mattie want her for some reason.

So far, aside from expecting Sarah's company at meals, Mattie had made few demands. She'd also said very little. When they sat together in the dining room three times a day, Mattie scarcely spoke. Occasionally, she'd comment on Bonnie's culinary offerings, or on the weather. For the most part, though, the old woman seemed as distant and distracted as she did during those hours she spent scanning the shoreline. Sarah wondered if it was always going to be this way. And if it was, would she be able to endure the boredom? She'd imagined Mattie would converse with her, even if on inconsequential matters. Sarah did talk to Bonnie fairly regularly, and apparently to Gloria, too. Carl was a huge taciturn man in his mid to late forties who apparently never spoke to anyone. He was always busy mending something in or around the house, or leaning beneath the upraised hood of the ancient Lincoln town car, doing this or that to the engine. Whatever it was he did, he kept the car in perfect running order. Black and dignified, like an elderly family retainer well past his prime, it stood ever at the ready should Mattie decide to go somewhere. Since Sarah had been in her employ, Mattie had gone out only two or three times, and then it had been on some undivulged errands.

She'd imagined glamour. It had always seemed to her an integral part of the lives of the famous. There was unquestionably glamour in the trappings of Mathilda Sylvester's life, but none elsewhere. The woman ate, slept, and gazed into space. It seemed to be the sum total of her existence. Sad and a little dreary and not in the least enviable. It was hardly an appropriate life-style for the widow of one of America's greatest painters. Or was it?

Sarah was awakened by a tapping at her door, followed by the unmistakable sound of the doorknob turning. When she opened her eyes it was to see Mattie, spectrally lit from the rear by the landing light, approaching the bed.

"I'm sorry to wake you," Mattie said in what, for her, was a whisper. "I wondered if you'd mind sitting with me for a bit."

"Is something wrong?" Sarah sat up reaching for her robe.

"Not a thing," Mattie said, already on her way to the door, confident Sarah would follow.

The door to the master suite was open and Sarah stepped inside. Mattie was outside on the balcony. Sarah went to sit in the companion chair, taking stock to assure herself there really wasn't anything wrong. Mattie had a cigarette lit and was smoking methodically.

"Would you like me to get you something?" Sarah asked, her eyes drawn to the vast star-speckled underside of the black umbrella she thought of as night.

"Nothing."

"It's a lovely night," Sarah observed.

"There was a splendid lightning show an hour or so ago. I thought it might rain, but it was only heat lightning."

"Have you been out here long?"

"A while," Mattie answered. "Some nights I don't sleep. And God knows I don't sleep anywhere near as much as I did when I was young. Don't need it, I suppose." Her shoulders rose then fell. She took another draw on her cigarette, then with an elegantly lazy gesture brushed stray ashes from the lap of her long nightgown. "I'm still not used to the nights," she said, her voice lighter and almost youthfully regretful.

"Do you miss him?" Sarah risked asking.

"In a sense."

"It must be hard, after so long with someone you love."

"Love?" Mattie's voice hardened. "You've been gossiping with Bonnie," she declared knowingly.

"We've talked," Sarah conceded. "Nothing like gossip."

"Love," Mattie repeated scornfully. "Gideon had that woman utterly bamboozled."

"You didn't love him?"

Mattie gave a low bitter laugh. "I despised him," she said forcefully. "I don't miss that bastard. I miss the battle. I intended to win, you know." She looked over at Sarah. "I had every intention of winning, but the goddamned son of a bitch dropped dead on me."

"But . . ."

"But what?" Mattie snapped. "Oh!" she said, as if able to read the lines and shadows on Sarah's face. "Bonnie also told you about the bed linens." She smiled and looked up at the sky. "All part of the fifty-year battle. I had my weapons, he had his. Mine were talent and intelligence. His was sexual skill. Are you shocked?" she asked, looking hopeful.

"A little," Sarah said truthfully.

"Why, because it's nothing like the magazine pieces?"

"Partly. And partly, I guess, because I can't understand why anyone would spend fifty years with someone she hated."

"Oh, my dear." Mattie smiled, showing still-strong teeth. "You never met Gideon Sylvester. He'd have charmed you out of your underwear in no time flat. God knows, he did it to me often enough."

"You sound as though you enjoyed it."

"Enjoy isn't quite the word. There was a time when I relished it, savored it. Whatever." She gave a long sigh, realized her cigarette had burned down to the filter and dropped it into the ashtray, at once reaching for another. "You appear trustworthy, Sarah. You've lasted longer than most of the others." As she struck one of the kitchen matches on the underside of the table, then held it to her cigarette, her face was grotesquely illuminated. "Repeat a word of this to anyone," she said, "and I'll make sure the remainder of your life is a complete misery."

"Don't threaten me," Sarah said unemotionally. "In the first place, there's no one for me to tell. And in the second place, who'd believe me?"

Mattie stared at her for a long moment, then laughed. "I'm beginning to like you very much, Sarah Kidd. You don't take any crap, not from anyone."

"That's right. I don't."

"Good," Mattie said with satisfaction. "Good. Because I'm starting to feel like talking again."

It was about time, Sarah thought. What was it Bonnie had said? That was it. It had been six months after Gideon Sylvester's death that Mattie had gone back to sleeping in the master bedroom. It was now six months since Sarah had come to work for her. Was it significant? she wondered.

"I was also thinking," Mattie said, "about starting to paint again."

"You paint?"

"Of course, I do!" Mattie spat.

"I didn't know that," Sarah said rather dumbly.

"Naturally not. There are only a handful of people alive who know."

Unable to stop herself, Sarah yawned. Mattie saw and said, "Go to bed. You're tired." Then, her voice softening, she said, "Thank you for your company."

It was the first time Mattie had thanked her for anything. Moved, Sarah said, "I like being with you."

Mattie didn't choose to respond.

Sarah got up, said, "Good night, Mattie," and went back to her room.

"Yes," Mattie said absently, some moments after Sarah had gone.

Two

Gazing out at the star-dappled horizon, Mattie found herself being drawn, as so many times before, to a consideration of those years that had culminated in her disownment by the family. As before, she seethed at the outrageous unfairness, the blind rigidity, and overweening morality of those two people who'd given her life and had then sought to direct and rule over every aspect of it.

Even the fact of her own motherhood didn't alter her hindsight view of those two insufferably stupid people. If anything, having been a mother herself—and never mind her success with one and her failure with the other—only heightened her anger, because she knew from firsthand experience that it hadn't had to be the way it was.

From the moment her hands were sufficiently coordinated to hold and direct a pencil, Mattie had taken her thoughts and emotions to paper. While her two older sisters fussed over ribbons and beads, Mattie was sketching doors and windows, jugs of flowers, misproportioned horses drawing lopsided carriages; she labored to reproduce an image of the doll's house that occupied a corner of the nursery, or of the pair of porcelain dolls her sisters had abandoned once they'd come to consider themselves too sophisticated to waste time with toys.

At the beginning she'd gone to show Mama and Papa her work, but their vague smiles and lack of interest, beyond a distracted, "That's very nice, dear," from her mother, brought her to the realization that they saw nothing of value in her efforts. It didn't stop her. She simply quit trying to get them to see.

No one in the house on Seventy-first Street had the least interest in the youngest child's scribblings; not the cook, or the two maids, or the housekeeper. The family itself seemed perpetually preoccupied with preparations for some forthcoming social event to which, as members in good standing of the well-to-do segment of New York society, they had entrée.

By the time Mattie was six, the world had been at war for two years. During the early evenings in the drawing room, she heard her parents and their friends discuss the latest war news. But their voices were so calmly moderated, their comments so mildly stated that she had no sense of war as being something unpleasant. And since, by 1918, when Mattie was eight, that often-discussed war came to an end, she assumed it was something unspecified, that took place far away, and that started and finished so unceremoniously that most people never even knew it had happened.

Of course, later on she was to look back on that childhood notion with dismay. But at the time, satisfied with the conclusions she'd drawn, she returned her attention to the books she was now able to read, and to the stealthy pleasure of seeing the pictures she drew attain cleaner lines and more realistic proportions. The family was quite content to see her tucked into a corner of the drawing room or on the floor of the nursery, head down, hands busy, because when she was engaged in her doodling, she was wonderfully quiet. The rest of the time, Mattie was more trouble than both her sisters put together. She was disobedient, untidy, and had little regard for authority, whether parental or otherwise; she was overly energetic, disputatious, and altogether unnatural. Her height was the subject of numerous whispered conversations between Mama and Papa, as was her flamboyantly carrot-colored hair. Yes, there had been a member of Papa's family with these features. But how on earth had they turned up so unexpectedly and distressingly in his youngest child? Mama was as mystified as he and was halfway willing to believe Kathleen, the Irish cook, who once ventured to observe within Mama's hearing (albeit unknowingly) that Mathilda Harrison might very well be a changeling, so far as she, Kathleen, was concerned. Mama was fairly scandalized by this remark, and would have liked to take issue with the cook, but since she had, in fact, been eavesdropping—a pastime of which she was guiltily fond, but upon which well-bred ladies tended to frown—she could only go on about her business wondering if there could possibly be some truth to this notion. Heaven only knew, she'd never in her life encountered a child less inclined to do as she was told.

Mattie had been a trial even before her birth. Mama's pregnancy, unlike the previous two, had been frightfully obvious, so that she'd been miserably housebound for close to four months at the last. And when the pains had come, Mama had stoically settled in for a lengthy, painful labor, glad not only of the prospect of being rid of the restless weight of this third, unwanted, baby, but also of the gift of jewelry Papa would undoubtedly purchase as her reward for her extended suffering. But instead of the protracted agony that had accompanied the two prior births, Mama had barely opened her thighs before the infant began its emergence into the world. And unlike her predecessors, Mattie hadn't responded to the administering physician's smack on her bottom with mewling cries but had instead (the physician dined out for years after on this, swearing it was the God's honest truth) behaved like a miniaturized, deeply offended matron; her tiny body going rigid while her silent red features twisted disapprovingly.

Mattie started out in life an improbable twenty-four-and-one-half inches long and grew at an appalling rate, so that by the time she was twelve she towered over her mother and sisters, and by fifteen had succeeded in surpassing her father's five feet nine inches. Her growth finally stopped in her sixteenth year, to everyone's relief except the dressmaker who'd had a dozen highly profitable years sewing garments for the girl. Mattie gloried in her seventy inches, although she quickly wearied of the witless comments people ceaselessly felt compelled to make; observations having to do with the weather up there, and skyscrapers, and with the peculiar smallness of her feet, which should have been, they opined, far larger for someone of her exceptional height.

In the years between eight and sixteen Mattie was fortunate enough to be able to have drawing lessons at school, which made the study of other, less interesting subjects, tolerable. Her teachers were by no means serious artists, but rather dilettantes with a gift for pretty pastels or for line drawings who had some basic knowledge of form and perspective and color. Each of them in turn was impressed by the child's ability, and each in turn sent home letters recommending Mattie be encouraged to pursue this interest by means of private teachers or through attendance at one of the city's specialized schools. These recommendations were consistently dismissed by Mama and Papa, who believed Mattie would grow out of this odd interest and become as biddable and, indeed, as marriageable as her two sisters—one of whom married when Mattie was twelve, and the other who was affianced to a most acceptable young man the year Mattie turned fifteen.

For her part, Mattie found her sisters boring and feckless, definitely not worth emulating. Not that Mattie lacked interest in the opposite sex. Rather, she'd decided to pursue a career in art, and one simply couldn't be engaged in tedious matters of domesticity and hope to produce anything of artistic merit. She needed to be free in order to continue doing the one thing she'd found that gave her any consistent degree of pleasure, along with a profound sense of accomplishment.

At sixteen, determined to win over her father, she visited him in his study one evening and, using every last bit of her skill with words, as well as her knowledge of what he wanted to hear, she vowed if he allowed her to attend an art school she'd behave in exemplary fashion henceforth; she'd be obedient, respectful, and less untidy. She swore tearfully to do absolutely anything they required of her if only he'd consent to her applying to the school of her choice.

She was, she knew, impressive in her impassioned pleading. She was wise enough to seat herself so that she remained at all times lower than her father; she summoned tears to advance her cause; and she expressed remorse at her failures heretofore. She'd rehearsed her speech for weeks in the bathroom adjacent to the nursery, and delivered it impeccably.

With obvious misgivings, her father said, "Well, Mattie, if it means so much to you, I don't suppose any harm can come of it," and gave his consent.

She restrained herself from falling at his feet in gratitude, and instead allowed her now-genuine tears to overflow. She thanked him several times, said, "You won't be sorry, Papa," then flew to the nursery for the application she'd long-since prepared. In moments she was back in the study saying, "All you have to do is sign, Papa." He did so, with his customary flourish. And thus began her formal art training.

Her first year at the Academy was—and remained so in her memory— the single happiest time of her life. She drew, and studied, and painted in watercolors and oils; she did line drawings and pen-and-ink studies; she devoured art history books and volumes of paintings by the Italian, Dutch, French, and English schools. She absorbed details, saw how the Masters effected light and shadow, discovered the magic of India ink crosshatching; she was taught to etch, to illuminate, to make prints. But primarily she was provided with an endless number of models and of still life arrangements of which she might do anything from one-minute sketches to full-blown paintings.

When she wasn't at school, she had the entire city from which to select her subjects. She went from the Bowery to Harlem with her pencils and sketchpads and sat on park benches, or the front stoops of brownstones, or leaned against the pilings at the piers in the West 40s while she made hundreds of renderings of everything that caught her eye.

She kept her promise to her father for the better part of the year. Happy, she was able to hold her impulses in check. She avoided family arguments quite simply by paying little attention to whatever was said over the dinner table. The nursery, now her studio, stayed in fairly good order because she discarded many of the books and toys that had cluttered the space for so long.

Things were going swimmingly, and during the summer before her second year at the Academy she put in her time with her mother and the staff at the summer house at Lake Onondaga, showing up promptly for dinner but otherwise occupying herself with washed watercolors of the lake and its environs. When her father came up on weekends, Mattie smiled affably and listened as he narrated the unrelentingly dull details of his business week.

Papa was a lawyer. Business had never been better. Nineteen twenty-seven had been his most lucrative year yet, and he was anticipating (almost rubbing his hands together) 1928.

Primarily Mama and Papa's conversation revolved around the mentioning of names. Papa would say, "I ran into Kipper Adamson," and that would be enough to set Mama off for half an hour, working her way through the ranks of the Adamson family. Then, when she paused, Papa would supply her with yet another name, and off she'd go again. Mattie found it hard to stay awake when they commenced what she thought of as the "I saw so-and-so game." Her parents played it with unflagging dedication, especially Mama. Mattie would sit at the table, suitably attired in something prim, wondering what point there was to the lives of two so utterly insipid people as her parents. The only thing they'd ever done for which they deserved credit, she thought, was having created her.

During the course of the summer there were visits made by her two sisters, their husbands and offspring (a repellent group of overweight little trolls Mattie couldn't abide). Then the group around the table indulged in the Game with a vengeance. Any one of the participants might go for hours recounting names, dates, and places. Mattie drew invisible images on the tablecloth with the blade of her knife, waiting to escape upstairs to her second floor bedroom where her supply of reading matter and her art supplies beckoned.

Upon returning to the city at the end of August, Mattie promptly took herself off into the streets, looking for subjects. And it was on one of those outings that she first encountered Avery Moon.

She was outside Grand Central Station on Vanderbilt Avenue, sketching the station entryway when she became aware that someone was standing close by, watching her. When she looked up to investigate, she saw an attractive man who looked to be in his early thirties. One quick glance and she'd absorbed every detail, from his Panama hat to his immaculate white kid gloves.

"You're very good," he said, in a voice that from the outset captured her complete attention. "Very good indeed."

"How can you tell?" she challenged him.

"Oh, easily," he said with a confidence she came to learn never abated. Avery Moon never doubted himself. His belief in himself was so absolute, so well entrenched, that nothing was able to shake him. "Your eye is keen," he went on to say, "and your lines have no hesitation. You're a student?"

"I am," she replied with hauteur. "What are you?"

He laughed, made a bow, as if to say *touché*, and introduced himself. "Avery Arkwright Moon," he said, "would-be poet and ne'er-do-well gentleman of leisure, at your service."

"That's a contradiction," she said, tapping the end of her pencil against the top of her sketchpad.

"Which part?" he asked with an amiable smile.

"I don't believe you can be a ne'er-do-well and a gentleman," she replied.

"Oh, I assure you I can."

"You assure me, do you?"

"Indeed, I do. I don't suppose you'd care to partake of some liquid refreshment?" He asked with another winsome smile.

"A cup of tea would be agreeable," she said, curious to know more about this most interesting man.

"Wonderful!"

He took her to a nearby restaurant and, once seated with his Panama hat carefully set aside, he ordered tea for them both, then asked, "How old are you?"

"How old are *you*?" she countered, enjoying herself.

With a laugh, he said, "I do believe you're a ne'er-do-well young woman."

"Possibly," she allowed. "I'm seventeen. I haven't really had a chance to explore my full potential."

"Ah! At thirty-three," he said, "I've had a really splendid chance to explore mine."

"Is your poetry any good?" she asked.

"Atrocious," he said promptly. "But I'm fond of it. You're a symphony of color, aren't you? The reddest hair, the bluest eyes, the whitest skin. And majestically tall."

"Thank you. You have nice teeth, and I like your eyelashes. In fact, I covet your eyelashes."

"Were they mine to give away, you'd have them," he said with another laugh. "Are you spoken for?" he asked.

"That's quaint. No, I am not spoken for. I have no intention of being spoken for, either." Boldly, she asked, "Have you got a wife?"

"That's a perplexing question," he said, offering her a cigarette which she waved away. "I have a wife, so to speak. She prefers not to consider herself wedded to me. In fact, she is at this very moment attempting to extricate herself from the legalities that bind us together."

"Do you always talk that way?" she asked. "If you do, your poetry probably really is atrocious."

"You are too sublime!" he declared as the waitress came with their tea. "You must agree to meet me again. I'd hate to think I've been lucky enough to find you only to lose you before I've had any real opportunity to get to know you better."

And so it began.

They took to meeting once or twice a week in the late afternoon when she left school. He'd take her to tearooms or small restaurants, and they'd talk for an hour or so, then he'd see her uptown in a cab, on the way setting the date for their next meeting.

She liked Avery Moon. He was rather silly, but he wasn't boring. And when in mid-October he ventured to kiss her in the cab on their way uptown, she found she liked that, too. He had a good mouth, firm well-shaped lips, and kissed very nicely. She liked Avery Moon and his kiss so much that she kissed him again, and felt as if her body was going to burst into flame when his tongue slipped between her lips and his hand squeezed her knee.

"Next time," he said before she left the cab, "let's meet at my place." He gave her a card, said, "Four o'clock, Tuesday," and told the cabbie to drive on.

In the intervening five days, Mattie spent a lot of time inspecting herself in the bathroom mirror, and daydreaming about the things that could possibly happen on the following Tuesday. Her knowledge of sexual matters was all but nonexistent, based solely on her recent reading of Elinor Glyn, Theodore Dreiser, and Upton Sinclair, among others. The Glyn novels were strictly taboo and she had to read them in the dead of night when she could be sure her parents were soundly sleeping. She didn't think she had "it," that Glyn quality ascribed to certain of her racier heroines, but Mattie was definitely curious. She had little doubt that Avery Moon intended to kiss her some more if and when she went to his apartment.

It turned out to be more, and much less, than she'd hoped. Avery Moon talked far more effectively about making love than he actually performed it.

Upon her arrival at his apartment, a small place in the East 40s not far from where they'd first met, he locked the door, drew the curtains over the windows, then, without a word, took her into his bedroom.

"I think it's time," he said, his hands at her waist, "you discovered the true depths of your potential."

"You do, do you?" she said, not completely sure she wanted to go through with this, but prompted by her overwhelming curiosity to see what would happen.

"Yes, I do," he replied with that phenomenal confidence.

His hands went from her waist to the sides of her face and he gave her another of those open-mouthed kisses that so elevated her body temperature. Finding her compliant, he proceeded to go about the business of removing her from her clothes. When she was standing before him wearing nothing more than her stockings and shoes, he walked in a circle around her, with a smile, stating, "I will write several epic poems to commemorate your dainty breasts and exquisite haunches."

He then matter-of-factly took off his own clothes and posed before her, doing a slow turn.

"You have a good body for someone your age," she said, having been exposed to quite a number of nude models at school.

"I'm pleased you like it," he said, then took her by the hand and directed her to the bed. "I hope you like the rest of it just as well."

She did, and she didn't. The preamble was most stimulating. His hands moving over her body was quite pleasurable. When he touched her between the legs, it made her squirm. Fortunately, she thought, that odd aspect of his investigation didn't last long. Evidently satisfied with what he'd discovered between her thighs, he positioned himself on top of her, spread apart her legs, and began pushing himself into her.

"Wait a minute!" she objected. "Are you supposed to be doing that?"

"Oh, indeed!" he said, somewhat red in the face from his exertions.

"Oh!" she said, and was quiet, thinking she ought to write a letter to Elinor Glyn accusing her of being a bold-faced liar. This just wasn't worth writing books about. And, besides, it hurt like the dickens.

When he'd finished, Avery Moon pulled himself out of her offended body and flopped down beside her, panting and sweaty. She lay very still thinking she couldn't imagine a circumstance when she'd care to do any of this again. It was almost as tiresome as her parents' dinner table conversation. She really was furious with Elinor Glyn. Her belly ached and so did her bottom. She was soaking wet and her thighs were coated in sticky white fluid.

"I have to go home now," she announced, rousing Avery Moon from his doze.

"Pity," he said, and leaned on his elbow watching while she got dressed. "Monday, at four?" he asked.

"I'll see," she told him, gathering up her belongings.

Of course she didn't go on Monday. Avery Moon would've wanted to take off all her clothes and bounce on her again, and it was the last thing she wanted to do. She was sore for days after, and was grateful she could stand for most of the classes at school.

She returned her attention to school and scarcely gave Avery Moon another thought. She'd never given him her address. He only knew she lived on Seventy-first Street, but he had no means of contacting her. Perhaps it was unkind not to let him know she didn't intend to see him anymore. She had enjoyed their conversations, and the terrifically arch way he had of speaking. But he was far too old for her, for one thing. And, for another, if her parents found out she'd been seeing him there'd be hell to pay.

Two and a half months later she understood she was pregnant. In a panic, she went after school to Avery Moon's apartment, but he was gone. A middle-aged frowsy woman came to the door and asked, "Who're you looking for?"

"Mr. Moon."

"Oh, him. Far as I know, he's gone back to his missus. Mind you, I can't say for sure. It's what they told me when I rented this place."

Mattie went home and tried to think what to do. She wasn't close to either of her sisters and if she tried to tell one or the other of them about her condition, they'd go straight to Mama and Papa to tell them. There wasn't a single person she could think of who might help her.

All she could do was try to hide what was happening, and pray for a miracle.

While she was praying for the miracle, she made a point of going along Vanderbilt Avenue every day after school, hoping to run into Avery Moon. She believed he'd help her, if she could only find him and talk to him. But she never saw him again.

Everything ended the last week in April of 1928. Mattie was soaking in the tub one evening when for some reason she never discovered, her mother opened the bathroom door, took a long look at Mattie (her eyes going so round, Mattie thought they might very well pop right out of their sockets) and let out a small shriek. Her face the very picture of horror, she ran off bellowing for Papa while Mattie climbed from the tub and began pulling on her clothes.

Three hours later, after an extraordinary amount of high-volume screaming done by both her parents, Mattie was out on the street, with two suitcases, her father's check for five hundred dollars, and the declaration ringing in her ears, "Don't ever show your face here again, you tramp!"

Mattie stirred and blinked. The sky was starting to go light at the very edge of the horizon. She got up, went inside, and lay down on her bed. As she settled, her bones creaked audibly. "Christ!" she muttered. Old age was absurd.

Three

A t breakfast, almost a week after their conversation on the balcony, Mattie announced, "My children will be coming on Saturday."

Sarah said, "You must be looking forward to that."

Mattie snorted and struck one of her kitchen matches to light a cigarette. "There are," she said, "one or two things you should know about my sons. Matthew, the youngest is, I swear, the reincarnation of my father. He's strait-laced, pedantic, and unutterably boring at times. He is also the oldest forty-seven year old I've ever encountered. If you accused him of being staid, he'd be flattered. He's not a bad man; he's simply lacking in imagination.

"Now Giddy," she said, pausing to take a puff of her cigarette, "is something else entirely. Giddy, much as I adore him, is a prancing queen. And seems to become more blatant annually. Not that I have anything against homosexuals, you understand. I just cannot abide blatancy. I've never been able to fathom why such a large segment of the homosexual community feels it necessary to behave effeminately. Giddy's just ridiculous at times. He's very dear, but his judgment leaves a great deal to be desired. He'll spend most of Saturday waiting to get me on my own, hoping I'll commiserate with him over his latest tragedy." She took another puff. "He took up last year with a biker. A biker, for Christ's sake. Who ever heard of a faggot biker? I ask you! Well, the biker loved to bash poor Giddy over the head with frying pans and whatever else came to hand. It all came to a disastrous end with Mr. Biker pounding poor Giddy to mush and then, while Giddy was at the hospital getting himself patched up, the scoundrel took off with all Giddy's ready cash and jewelry. But the worst of his crimes . . ." She had to stop, overtaken by laughter. After mopping her eyes with her napkin, she said, "Mr. Biker stole all Giddy's Fiesta Ware." Again she laughed. "What I want to know," she said when she'd regained control of herself, "is how did he carry it all off on his motorcycle?"

Sarah laughed until she, too, was blotting her eyes with her napkin. Bonnie came in, cleared the table, refilled their coffee cups while casting speculative looks at the two women, then returned to the kitchen with her laden tray.

"Well," Mattie finally picked up the thread, "that's what Giddy will want to talk about." She shook her head, lit a fresh cigarette, then drank some of the coffee. "You're welcome to join us for lunch. I know it's your day off and perhaps you have plans. But I think you might find it amusing to meet my sons."

"What do they do?" Sarah asked.

"Matthew is an attorney. He plows through mountains of corporate bushwah for reasons completely unknown. He seems to enjoy it. Giddy has a nightclub. Quite entertaining. All these drag queens put on shows, mime records, that kind of thing. And Giddy, of course, is the star attraction."

"He performs?"

"Not actively. He holds court at a table beside the bar. His name, naturally, has a certain cachet."

"I would guess so," Sarah said politely.

"You *guess*?" Mattie frowned. "My dear," she said imperiously, "there are few people anywhere, excluding third world countries, who don't know the name Gideon Sylvester."

She said this proudly, and Sarah wondered how the old woman could claim with such commanding energy to have despised the man and yet refer to him with such proprietary pride.

"Matthew and Giddy will come together. Matthew's idea, to save money. Giddy will foot the bill, of course. He's far too generous."

Sarah was thinking that when Mattie said she was ready to talk she meant it. And she seemed to find Sarah a suitable audience, which made Sarah feel very flattered.

"Why do you look the way you do?" Mattie asked with abrupt rudeness. "There's no need for someone as attractive as you to make herself so dowdy. Don't you *care?*"

"Not very much," Sarah admitted.

"Well, you should!" Mattie insisted. "I've always believed a woman should make every effort to look her best, for her own sake."

This was patently the truth. Mattie did her hair and made up her eyes and mouth every morning, and she was always dressed as if for company. Sarah, on the other hand, thought as long as she was clean and neatly dressed, with her hair brushed away from her face, that more wasn't necessary. There was no one she wished to impress, and clothes and makeup were a waste of money.

"I'm not unhappy with the way I look," she said, although Mattie's observation had made her instantly self-conscious.

"You should be," Mattie said peremptorily, rising from the table. "The way a woman presents herself to the world states loudly and clearly how that woman feels about herself. You might want to think about that."

"Are you telling me you don't like the way I 'present' myself?" Sarah asked testily.

"You could make an effort," Mattie said, and sailed off.

"Well, hell!" Sarah said under her breath. "Thanks very much."

Mattie popped back into the room saying, "Don't be oversensitive. In half an hour I'd like to see you in the attic."

"Right," Sarah said as Mattie went off again. "Oversensitive," she repeated to herself.

Sarah hadn't been up to the attic before, so she was surprised to open the door at the top of the stairs and find a vast skylit space, kept cool by a large air conditioner set into the far wall. Blank canvases leaned against the walls. A big paint-spattered easel stood beneath the skylight, and at its side was an old wooden table covered with dusty tubes of oil paint, brushes, palettes, palette knives, tins of linseed oil and turpentine. Mattie was at the far end of the room, going through the drawers of an old dresser. She straightened, looked over at Sarah and said, "I'll give you a list. Write everything down."

Mattie rhymed off a considerable number of items, all of which she wanted ordered from an art supply store in Manhattan, to be collected by Carl, who'd make the trip to the city.

"Wouldn't it be easier and faster to have them send everything by U.P.S?" Sarah suggested. "Have someone on the mainland take delivery, then call to let us know when it's arrived. Then Carl would only have to go over on the ferry, pick up the stuff and bring it back instead of spending about ten hours driving back and forth to New York."

"Fine!" Mattie said. "Take care of it." She waved Sarah away and went back to rummaging through the dresser drawers.

Sarah retreated, somewhat offended by the brusque way Mattie so often dismissed her, as if Sarah was of no importance whatsoever. She reminded herself that Mattie treated just about everyone this way, regardless of who they were. In the months of her employ, she'd heard Mattie shriek at several gallery owners and curators over the telephone; she'd also been present when Mattie had demonstrated overt impatience with two old women friends who'd come to visit at the Connecticut house. When the women had gone, Mattie had poured herself a drink, all the while shaking her head and loudly exclaiming, "Silly goddamned old women! I wish to hell they'd stay away!"

It would have been all too easy to dislike Mattie, Sarah thought, settling at her desk in the office to make the call to New York. Mattie was abrupt, intolerant, and given to voicing her opinions without regard for the feelings of those to whom she spoke. And yet one couldn't help being drawn to her for any number of reasons. She was fiercely intelligent and well-informed; her sense of humor was unexpectedly sharp; she still retained a substantial measure of her good looks; and she was the only one left alive—aside from their two sons—who'd known Gideon Sylvester intimately. Mattie had tales she could tell, and Sarah very much wanted to hear them. She longed to know about the life the Sylvesters had lived.

After placing the order with the store, Sarah went in search of Carl to give him the details. She found him in the downstairs bathroom, replacing the toilet float.

"There's a delivery coming for Mattie on Thursday," she said from outside the door. "They're going to call from the mainland when it's in."

"I'll go over on the noon ferry," he said without looking up.

She waited, but he said nothing more and after watching him work for another minute or so, she went to the kitchen to get some coffee. No one was around. A bit disappointed, she got her coffee, then went out the kitchen door to the verandah and along to the front of the house.

As usual, the morning was hazy and cool. When they'd first arrived, she and Mattie had sat together at breakfast and Mattie had told her, "It's always overcast in the mornings. It burns off by midday. You'll get used to it." She was used to it now, but there was something faintly oppressive about days that began with a grayish mist that obscured the view and made her feel, no matter which room of the house she was in, as if she were underwater. The bulky cardigans she wore, and to which Mattie had taken exception, were to Sarah's mind a necessity against the chill breezes that came off the ocean.

She'd thought she might swim since the beach was only a couple of hundred yards away, but the water was so cold it turned her feet numb just to walk along the sand barefoot. Bonnie had told her that by August the water was a good ten or fifteen degrees warmer, but even at that Sarah guessed it wouldn't be much more than seventy degrees. So much for her thoughts of swimming. For exercise, she took long walks up the beach in the late afternoons, almost never encountering anyone else. Aside from the fact that it was Mattie's privately owned beach, this end of the island was fairly deserted and got the worst of the weather. The other end actually had a year-round population of several hundred people, and a summertime population that swelled to over a thousand. It was the summer people who kept the local businesses going, who paid the astronomical rents the locals laughed about, and who kept their boats and private airplanes on the island airport and marina. There were legendary macabre tales about small planes attempting night landings and winding up in the harbor, or about the luxury yachts making a day trip to the mainland, staying too long, then getting lost at sea in the dark on their attempted return.

Sarah had never dreamed a place like this existed, that wealthy families from Manhattan and various parts of Connecticut but primarily Hartford had, early in the century, built enormous summer homes on a narrow strip of land some six miles out in the Atlantic Ocean. But they had, and the houses had passed down from one generation to the next until, by the late sixties, they'd become so expensive to maintain that the families could no longer afford to live in them for an entire summer. So they rented out these engaging white elephants to people from Manhattan or Boston for huge sums for two of the three summer months. They got to spend one month per year altogether in the houses themselves, two weeks in June getting the places ready for the tenants, and two weeks at the end of August before finally closing up their inherited albatrosses for another year.

There were only eight or ten houses that still belonged to the original families. The rest had been sold. One had been turned into an inn. Several had burned down when the local volunteer fire brigade had been unable to arrive in time to set up their pumps and douse the burning wood structures with either available seawater or water from the swimming pools. There was one famous case which Bonnie had recounted about a house fire quite nearby.

Halfway up the island, some of the summer people were one year holding yet another of the dozens of cocktail parties that went on throughout the season, and the guests' cars parked on both sides of the main road had reduced that thoroughfare so drastically that the fire truck had been unable to get through. By the time all the cars had been moved, the house had burned to the foundation. "That's why the cruiser's always traveling up and down out there," Bonnie had explained. "They'll tow you soon as look at you. There are notices everywhere warning people not to park on the highway. Hasn't cut down the number of cocktail parties one bit, though. Folks coming from the south end just come together, five or six to a car, instead of two each in three cars. Some genius figured that out."

While Sarah stood on the verandah drinking her coffee, Carl came out of the house and went toward the garage, wiping his hands on a piece of rag before jamming it into one of his back pockets. He walked over to the Lincoln, grabbed the rag and polished a spot on the chrome grille. Then he disappeared into the dark recesses of the three-car garage. A few minutes later came the roar of the lawn mower starting up, and he came back into view cutting a neat swath along the side of the garage.

Without thinking, she sat down in the chair beside Mattie's rocker and watched the brawny man take the mower back and forth across the wide expanse of lawn. The air filled with the nostril-tingling scent of grass cuttings mingled with faint traces of gasoline. As she watched Carl work, she wondered who he was and how he'd come to spend what she estimated to be half his life with Mattie. The one time she'd seen Mattie talking to him—she'd happened to look out the office window and catch sight of the two of them near the garage—Carl had heard Mattie out in his typically taciturn fashion and then, when Mattie had finished, he'd given the old woman a smile that shone with affection. Mattie had patted him on the arm before turning away, and Carl had stood looking at her until Mattie was inside the house, the screen door slamming after her like a fired bullet.

Mattie found the journal, saw that its wrapping hadn't been disturbed, and, satisfied, returned it to the dresser. Then she walked through the attic, ignoring the canvases leaning against the walls, to inspect the brushes and to check the condition of the tubes of paint on the table. One or two still gave to the touch and so were usable. The rest she tossed into the metal trash can. The majority of the brushes, except for a number of sable watercolor ones, were still good. Drawing in a deep breath, she turned to survey the room from the near end, then descended to the kitchen to ask Gloria to go up and give the attic a thorough cleaning.

"You goin' back to work?" Gloria asked with a smile.

"I believe so. Don't forget to take the ladder, if you can manage it, and Windex the skylight. I'll get Carl to go up on the roof and wash down the outside of it. Oh, and dig out my smocks, will you, and put them through the wash."

"Okay, Mattie," Gloria said. "Happy to do it."

Coming out the front door, Mattie saw that Carl was busy with the lawn, and there was Sarah, sitting watching him as if in a trance. As the screen door slammed, Sarah started and looked over guiltily.

Lighting a cigarette, Mattie settled into the rocker, with a smile, asking, "Find him interesting, do you?"

God! Sarah thought. The woman was omniscient. "I was just wondering how he came to work for you."

"Why not ask him?"

"I got the impression he doesn't talk much."

"Not without invitation, no," Mattie allowed. "But he's not uncivilized. Ask him a question and he'll most likely answer it. Without frills, mind you. But he will answer."

"Maybe I'll ask him," Sarah said, her eyes returning to the man.

"He didn't have a home," Mattie said flatly. "It was something I understood."

"What do you mean?"

"My parents threw me out when I was seventeen."

"That's awful! Why?"

"Avery Moon gave me a baby," Mattie said, as if confident Sarah would know to whom she referred. "I couldn't find him, and didn't know what to do. I was incredibly ignorant then. Things were very, very different. None of the sex education youngsters get today. I was taking a bath one night, and my mother came in. She took one look at me, knew at once I was pregnant, and went screaming for my father. To make a long story short, I'd been a thorn in their sides from the day I was born, and this was all they needed. After denouncing me as a trollop, they gave me money and ordered me out of the house.

"So there I was, five months pregnant, with nowhere to go, no one to call upon for help." Mattie exhaled, then held the cigarette to her mouth without taking a puff.

"What did you do?" Sarah asked.

"What did I do? I went to a hotel for the night. In the morning, I bought the paper and found a room to rent near Gramercy Park. I got my bags from the hotel and spent the night in my new rented room trying to think what to do. The only thing I could think of was to go back to school. My tuition was paid for the year. And I'd made friends with a few of my classmates. I thought perhaps one of them might be able to help me. But when I looked at them I knew there wasn't one who'd be of any use. That's when I started looking more closely at my instructors.

"There was only one who seemed likely: Nicholas Harvey. He was an actual artist, unlike most of the other instructors. Nicholas Harvey was then perhaps thirty-one or -two, a thin, intense young man who was not only a fine watercolorist, but an outstanding teacher. I learned more from him than from anyone else, ever. Soft-spoken, soft-eyed, slight, and bearded. I can see him as clearly as if it were yesterday. After watching him closely for a week, I was certain he'd be sympathetic. For one thing, he believed I was gifted, and so worked extra hard with me, telling me, for example, when I'd been too facile with a line, too presumptuous about a curve or an angle. I had a tendency to take liberties, embellish what I thought I'd seen. He'd stand by my side in class and say, 'Look harder, then do it again. It comes too easily to you, Mattie. Work to make it truer.' He'd be right every time. What would've gone unnoticed by the other instructors, he saw. He knew I had a tendency to take one long look at the subject and then draw from memory instead of looking again. Nicholas Harvey taught me to *see*. He never had the success he deserved," she said sadly. "Even now I think he was one of the most worthy artists this country has ever produced. But he was alive at the wrong time. It happens," she said with a shrug. "Timing is extremely important, and watercolors weren't in vogue at that time. Where was I?"

Sarah reminded her.

"Yes, well," Mattie sighed. "I'd been praying for a miracle, and I got one, of sorts. Not quite what I'd had in mind, but still . . ." Her eyes locked on the now visible shoreline, she went silent.

Sarah waited, hoping she'd go on, but Mattie's silence grew lengthy and, at last, Sarah quietly slipped away.

In her room Sarah gazed into her closet, knowing she could never again, with any degree of complacency, put on a single item hanging there without hearing Mattie say, "There's no need for someone as attractive as you to make herself so dowdy." It was the "dowdy" that rankled. Because it was true. She shoved the closet door closed and marched back downstairs to the verandah.

"My mother died when my sister and I were eleven and six," she said loudly enough to cause Mattie to turn toward her with lifted eyebrows. "Two years later my father married a woman who hated children. So Pru and I were treated like garbage. Nobody told us how to dress, and whatever clothes we got came from secondhand stores because our stepmother didn't want to waste good money buying clothes for two children she detested. If it's all the same to you, I'd like to take the afternoon off tomorrow to go to the mainland, shopping. God knows, you can't have me sitting around here looking *dowdy*!" She turned to go.

"I didn't mean to hurt you," Mattie said gruffly. "Why do you take everything so personally?"

"Who were you talking to this morning if it wasn't me?" Sarah asked hotly.

"By all means go to the mainland," Mattie said. "And if you're going to buy yourself some new clothes, why not see a hairdresser, too? All that long, limp hair doesn't do a thing for you. Every time I see you I have the feeling I'm looking at some documentary from the early seventies."

"Anything else?" Sarah asked sarcastically, her face flushing.

"Write yourself a check for however much you think you'll need," Mattie said, and turned back to the view. "It'll do you a world of good," she said, reaching for her cigarettes.

Her anger effectively defused by Mattie's generosity, Sarah wet her lips, found she had no comeback, and went inside. The old woman defeated her at every turn, and Sarah wished she hadn't said any of that embarrassing stuff about her childhood. All she'd done was humiliate herself by dredging up that pathetically Dickensian melodrama.

And Mattie hadn't told her what the miracle had been.

She went back once more to the verandah. "You didn't tell me," she said. "What was the miracle?"

Without looking around, Mattie said, "I had a miscarriage."

"Oh! I'm very sorry," Sarah apologized, although she wasn't sure for what exactly she was sorry.

Four

In just half a year the seventeen-year-old Mattie had discovered previously undreamed of things about her own body. The most unpleasant and alarming was the miscarriage.

She was asleep on the Friday night of her first weekend alone in the dreary little room when the pains started. They quickly became so powerful they awakened her. Throwing back the bedclothes, she saw the blood. She did know that it took nine months for a baby to be born and since it had been only five, something was definitely wrong. She had no idea what to do. She was far too uncomfortable to remain in bed so she got up and removed the stained sheet from the mattress, then stood holding it, feeling the pain ripple through her belly. It was only a small mound but she could feel the whole of it shift beneath her hand, and she had a strong desire to push down against the pain, as if, if she pushed hard enough, she might manage to drive everything inside of her out.

Taking off her nightgown, she saw rivulets of blood trickling down her thighs, and was terrified. Perhaps she'd die. If she died it would be on her parents' heads. The way they'd screamed at her, the names they'd called her! They'd treated her vilely, warning her against contacting any other members of the family. As if she would have! She loathed them all, every last one of them. If they all dropped dead playing the Game over the dinner table, she'd be delighted.

The pain robbed her of her breath, made her dig her fingernails into her palms, as her belly contracted and shifted, contracted and shifted, the downward pressure intensifying. The baby was going to come out of her. There was nothing else it could possibly be. And how was she going to take care of it? What would she do with an infant? She was so frightened she couldn't think. She stood there naked on the sheet she'd dropped, almost dancing from one foot to the other between the times of pain. She didn't dare call Mrs. Webster, the landlady, to come help. What good would an old woman be anyway? She'd only make a fuss because Mattie had ruined one of her sheets. Lord, the pain!

It went on and on, and she grew so exhausted she could no longer remain upright, so she sat naked and shivering on the cold wet sheet with her hands on her abdomen pressing against the mound that was inexorably moving down, down, until the instinct to push overwhelmed her. She sat on her haunches and ventured to feel between her legs, gasping at the sight of her blood-drenched hand. As long as she lived she'd never let another man touch her! she vowed, frantically wiping her soiled hand on the sheet. If this was what happened when a man touched you, she'd die before another one ever got a chance to come near her.

Weeping, she pushed each time the impulse came to her. Her thighs aching from the strain of squatting for so long, her ears throbbing, she finally gave one lengthy violent push that nearly made her faint. And all at once her body let go and a small bloodied mass slithered out of her body. With a cry of revulsion, she scrambled backward, frenziedly covering the thing with the sheet. Then she stared in disgust at the sheet and the lifeless monstrosity it contained, her horror absolute.

The pains were considerably diminished, reduced almost to an echo of their former strength. Completely worn out, she went reeling to the hand basin in the corner and washed herself. Then with a clean rag between her legs, in a fresh nightgown, she lay down directly on the itchy mattress ticking, pulled the blankets over herself, and slept.

She didn't awaken until early afternoon on the following Sunday. And when she did open her eyes, the first thing she saw was the sheet, exactly where she'd left it.

Weak and dizzy, she dressed, wrapped the sheet and its contents in several layers of newspapers, tied the package with twine, then put on her coat and went out to find a trash can. Feeling like a criminal, looking around to be certain no one was watching, she shoved the package into the can, then hurried away as quickly as she was able.

She stopped to buy some food at a nearby store, then returned to her room, hating the world and everyone in it. If she ever saw Avery Moon again, she'd kill him. She drank some milk, ate a hunk of bread with a piece of cheese, then lay down again, fully dressed, on the bed. She dreamed of the thing that had come out of her, dreamed she'd crept closer to look at it, only to see that what she'd expelled from her body was a perfect tiny version of Avery Moon, complete with bloodied Panama hat and white kid gloves. This miniature incarnadined Moon grinned up at her and, in a fury, she ground it beneath her heel.

That weekend she made the transition from girl to woman. Angry, upset, betrayed, and without prospects, she felt herself harden inside. She was going to have to find some means of supporting herself, which meant giving up her studies. Since she had no marketable skills, she needed help. And the only person she could think of who might help was Nicholas Harvey.

She waited for him at the end of his class the next day and said, "I have to talk to you."

Without hesitation, he replied, "Of course," and left the school with her, observing, "You look under the weather, Mattie."

"I'll be all right."

They went to a tearoom near the school where he ordered tea and sandwiches, then invited her to talk to him.

"My parents have disowned me," she admitted straight out. "I have a little money but not enough. I've got to find some kind of work."

He had the wisdom not to ask what it was she'd done, but turned his attention to her immediate needs. "Have you got someplace to stay?" he asked, and when she said that she had, he said, "Well, that's something. I'm going to have to think about this, Mattie. Can you give me a few days?"

She said she could, then told him, "If I could find some kind of work that would leave me free . . . I'd really like to finish out the school year."

"You should, if it's at all possible," he agreed. "I'm sorry for your trouble," he said earnestly. "There's no hope of a reconciliation with your parents?"

"None."

"Leave it with me," he said. "I won't promise anything, but I'll see what I can do."

"I'm very grateful."

"Well, yes," he said a little uncomfortably. "I suggest, for now, you continue with your classes."

Four days later he held her back after his class to say, "I think I've found something for you," and gave her a slip of paper. "This is a company that does limited editions of fine quality books. They need someone to work on marbled endpapers, and I know you did especially well with that last year. The only catch is it's a full-time job. But I'd be happy to work with you one or two evenings a week and at the weekends."

"I'll never forget what you've done for me," she declared.

"It was nothing. I just asked around."

"No," she disagreed strongly. "It's everything."

"Mattie, keep up your drawing and painting. You're too good to let it go. I mean that. If the job pans out, take your sketching equipment with you and go out on your lunch hours, and after work. And remember to *look*."

The publisher was housed in a deep but narrow building in the West 30s near Ninth Avenue. His first words, expressed with misgivings, were, "I didn't expect you to be quite so young."

"If I can do the work, does it matter?" she asked.

He considered this, then gave her a smile. "Let me show you around. I'll give you a two-week trial. I pay good money and I expect quality work."

"I do good work. How much is good money?"

His smile growing wider, he said, "I'll start you at twelve-fifty a week. If you're as good as you say, I'll raise you to fifteen after the two weeks."

"Fine."

The building smelled of ink and glue and paper, but was very clean. And the nineteen other employees looked happy. The area where she was to work was at the rear of the building, spacious and well lit, near the fire exit. At first sight of the large containers of ink and the supply of heavyweight paper awaiting the marbling process, she felt a small inner surge of combined excitement and challenge.

Her new employer, Mortimer Sternholt, said, "The majority of the endpapers are traditional. But if you care to experiment and you come up with designs I like, I'll give you a bonus. For the modern poetry and short story collections, I'd be willing to try something more contemporary, with brighter colors." Picking up a beautifully bound volume that was sitting on the worktop, he ran his fingers over the leather binding with its gold embossing, and turned the book carefully to show it to her, opening the cover to display the endpaper. It was, as he'd said, a traditional Italian design, with muted colors that ran in evenly spaced Florentine ripples from side to side, top to bottom. "We do the best work in the city," Sternholt said proudly. "Every one of my people, from the typesetters to the embossers, are artists. Books are forever," he said solemnly. "They should invite you to pick them up, open them, and begin to read. We do a small number of volumes by living authors. The majority of our stock is classics, for private libraries and collectors. Do you like to read, Miss Harrison?"

"Yes, sir, I do."

"And which authors, if I may ask, do you prefer?"

"Classic or contemporary?" she asked, liking this man with his courtly manners and old-world charm.

"Whichever."

"Dickens, Wilkie Collins, Trollope, Stendhal, Stevenson, Kipling," she rhymed off. "Sinclair, Dreiser, Colette, Fitzgerald, and practically everyone else *except* Elinor Glyn."

He burst out laughing. Returning the volume to the worktop, he said, "I think I'm going to like you very much, Mathilda."

"Please call me Mattie. I think I'm going to like you very much too, Mr. Sternholt."

"Good. You'll come Monday morning at eight, and we'll get you started. Oh," he added, "you'll want to invest in a few smocks to protect your clothes."

And so began her career with Stern's Editions.

True to his word, Sternholt raised her to fifteen dollars after two weeks and by the end of her third month, she'd earned seventy dollars in bonuses for four new designs. She liked the work, found the other employees congenial, and, as Nicholas Harvey had suggested, spent her free time either out-of-doors sketching or at home in her room working on new paintings. Twice a week, on Wednesday evenings and Sunday afternoons, she took her latest efforts to Nicholas Harvey's apartment in the Village where he made comments, offered criticisms, then set her to work on some new project. She insisted on paying him, and when he protested, she said, "It's only fair. I'd probably be a streetwalker by now if it wasn't for you. So you take the money!"

He acquiesced, grateful for the extra three dollars a week. His wife was expecting their second child, his job at the Academy paid very little, and he rarely was able to sell any of his work.

Upon receiving her bonus from Sternholt, Mattie insisted on purchasing a watercolor of Nicholas's she particularly liked. It was a view of the East River at sundown she'd long admired.

"I can't let you pay for this, Mattie," Nicholas argued.

"I want it," she said, "and I believe in paying for things." With that, she pressed twenty dollars into his hand, said, "I'll see you Wednesday," and went off to take the picture to a framer. It was the first significant acquisition of her life, aside from some items necessary to brighten her room, and she hung it in a place of honor where it could be seen immediately upon entering.

Fearful of ever again finding herself dispossessed, she tried to set aside five dollars every week, keeping her savings in a small locked metal box she kept hidden under a loose floorboard in the closet.

Thirty dollars of her bonus went into the box. The remaining twenty she spent on food, a new lamp, some pretty blue and white cups she found in a secondhand store, and a haircut.

The hairdresser looked with dismay at Mattie's nearly waist-length hair and said, "Honey, you don't want to cut all this off. It'd be a cryin' shame to do that to such a gorgeous head of hair."

"I want it bobbed!"

"You could sell this hair," the woman said, still doubtful.

"Fine! I'll take it with me. Or do you want to buy it?"

"I'll tell you what. I won't charge you for the cut, and I'll give you five bucks for the hair. How's that?"

"Make it ten! Now bob my hair!"

Mattie was still out on the verandah late the following day when Sarah returned from the mainland. Wishing she didn't care about Mattie's opinion, she went out to present herself to the old woman, asking, "What d'you think?"

It seemed an actual physical effort for Mattie to tear herself away from whatever it was she saw out there, or was thinking about. Her head turned, her eyes reluctantly surrendering the view, her hand automatically reaching for a cigarette.

"What is it?" she growled.

With her hand, Sarah indicated her hair and the new outfit.

"Better!" Mattie said, lit her cigarette, and turned away. "Now try some makeup!"

Sarah wondered why she'd bothered. She was never going to gain Mattie's approval. And why was she seeking it? she asked herself as she put away her purchases, all of which she'd paid for with her own money. Anyway, the haircut was an improvement, she decided, studying herself in the mirror. Cut to just above her shoulders, with a side parting instead of the center part she'd worn for at least fifteen years, she looked younger, she thought, and definitely not dowdy.

Reluctant but determined, she took what she considered the worst of her old clothes from the closet, bundled them into a plastic bag and consigned them to the trash. Mattie probably wouldn't like the new things any better than the old ones but there wasn't much she could do about that. She liked what she'd bought, and that was what mattered.

In the office, she found Mattie had left a fresh sleeve for transcribing. Sarah sat down, fitted on the headphones, pushed the foot control, and waited to hear what Mattie had dictated. There was the usual rushing sound of dead air, and as always, Sarah wished Mattie would get herself a modern new dictating machine. Then Mattie came on saying, "You're stubborn and too emotional. You know that? And you have this penchant for rushing in and hurling the truth at people, then expecting them to dish up exactly the response you want. You're not going to get that from me, Sarah. I like to think about most things before I decide how I feel. There are plenty of people with wicked stepmother stories. If anything, it ought to have given you more grit than you seem to have. Now . . ." Mattie audibly took a breath, then there was the sound of rustling paper. "Type up a reply to this idiot in Santa Fe, and tell him if I wanted to consign my collection to his gallery upon my death, I'd have been to Santa Fe long since to see just what kind of gallery he's got there. Tell him, politely, of course, to take a hike."

The rest of the sleeve was taken up with more letters, the majority business replies, one to her personal banker at Chase Manhattan, and a note to some woman in Hartford saying she was sorry to have read in the *Times* about the death of her husband. The name didn't mean anything to Sarah, but then Mattie had an enormous range of friends and acquaintances, and she often sent off notes on the occasions of births and deaths, even engagements. Mattie was scrupulous about replying to every piece of mail she received, even if the letters sometimes had her nearly spitting with anger. A very few personal letters she answered by hand, sitting up in her bedroom on the chaise longue with a writing board across her lap and a box of her embossed Tiffany stationery close to hand.

Every last piece of correspondence was retained and filed. Sarah had, in the course of keeping the files up to date, found letters dated as far back as 1928.

There were letters from a lot of famous people that were probably worth a fortune. In the unlikely event Mattie ever needed money, the sale of even half those letters at, say, a Sotheby's auction, would bring her in a very tidy sum. But for a woman who could sell just one of her late husband's paintings for upward of half a million dollars, it was doubtful she'd ever have to resort to selling any of the letters from people like Nathanael West, for example, or Max Ernst, or Giacometti.

Almost without exception these letters were in reply to congratulatory remarks Mattie had made to authors, musicians, painters, photographers, playwrights, even actors. Clearly if Mattie saw something she heard or liked, she let the creator of the work know. Almost without exception, the return letters from these people were filled with appreciation of her kindness.

Initially, Sarah had been surprised to discover her employer was an enthusiastic audience in almost every artistic avenue. But when she thought about it, it made sense that Mattie would have no compunction about committing words of praise to paper. In a very real way it was infinitely safer to write a letter than to enter into a conversation. There was little possibility of being misinterpreted when one took the care to set one's thoughts down in pen and ink. In conversation, there were always the potential liabilities of one's voice, one's facial expression, even one's physical language. These things could belie the contents of one's speech. And, God knew, Mattie's manner could be most offensive.

The correspondence finished, Sarah slid the letters and their envelopes into the leather portfolio and carried it downstairs, with a pen, for Mattie's signature.

Mattie looked over asking, "Well?"

"You're absolutely right," Sarah said, handing her the portfolio and pen. "I shouldn't have said anything about my family. I hated myself the minute the words came out of my mouth."

"So, don't do it anymore," Mattie said, quickly scrawling her thick bold signature across the letters. "Never do anything that makes you dislike yourself. The haircut's a big improvement. And the dress is rather sweet. Now!" She shut the portfolio and set it aside. "Care to take a walk with me before dinner?"

Five

○nce the supplies were put away, Mattie walked several times around the attic, then sat down in the old armchair in the corner with a cigarette and stared at the easel, wondering what the point of starting back to work again would be. She'd stopped when Gideon Sylvester had dropped dead on the beach, but lately her need had been growing progressively stronger. She longed for the smell of paint, the slide and density of it under her brush; she yearned for color, for the streaks of yellow melding with blue producing that first ripe hint of green; or for the crimson folding into the outside of a wormlike coil of cobalt blue, creating a child's paintbox purple; she had a craving for the blend of yellow, white, and red rendering up flesh tones. She had scores of images inside her head, like tidy files of negatives waiting to be printed and hand-tinted. But maybe she'd lost it. Six years at this point in an old woman's life was a very long time. Perhaps after so long away from her beloved brushes and tubes, her hand and eye had lost their hard-won complicity. She wondered if, like some faded diva long-since retired, she'd approach her art only to find her voice had gone, never to return. The thought of it frightened her. It hadn't, until now, occurred to her that she might be sacrificing her gifts by failing to use them. But now, with everything at the ready and beckoning to her like an infant howling to be nursed, she was very afraid to step up to a blank canvas for fear of discovering that as a result of her delaying for so long the baby had died.

It struck her as terribly ironic that when she was finally free again to commit her personal visions to canvas she was actually afraid to try. Goddamned Gideon Sylvester had managed, it seemed, to take her to the grave with him. The question now was whether she'd voluntarily bury herself. Getting up, she descended the stairs to the master bedroom and went out to sit on the balcony, depositing her burned-out cigarette in the ashtray and at once lighting another.

Matthew loved to preach at her about her smoking, warning her of all the diseases caused by cigarettes. Too late to worry about any of that now, she thought, taking a good hard drag. Old age was as likely to carry her off as any of those pernicious ailments. She'd always been healthy as a horse, and the only times she'd ever stayed in hospitals had been to give birth. She'd never broken a bone, never even had influenza. And while all her friends were crumbling under the onslaught of advancing age, falling victim to arthritis, rheumatism, shattered hips, strokes, heart attacks, and sundry other ailments, she went right along in a state of good health, suffering only from the irritation of bones that creaked and skin that had long-since lost its elasticity and now hung in revolting folds over her bones. She didn't care a bit for the sight of the flesh that hung suspended from her hips like badly pinned laundry on a loose line on a windless day. The same was true of her slack underarms and inner thighs. Her once haughty behind looked like nothing so much as a pair of overused, deflated balloons appended to the base of her spine. There was a damned good reason why old people died: to spare youngsters the sight of them. Who the hell wanted to know at twenty that they'd one day look like a quirky assemblage of shapeless rubbery parts tacked any which way to a set of crumbling bones? She herself had never believed for a moment that she'd end up one of those ancient ruins that were such a source of embarrassment to the arrogant young. Her brain wasn't a day older than it had been sixty years ago, and as long as she avoided mirrors or inadvertently looking down at herself while in the bathtub, she could quite happily ignore the fact of her age. But since a lot of things died hard, including a certain vanity and pride in maintaining one's appearance (as she'd told Sarah), she was obliged to approach her image every morning to liven it up with a bit of dark eye shadow, mascara, cheek color, and lipstick. Naturally, she was careful not to overdo it, like a number of her friends who emerged daily looking all set to attend some perpetual Halloween party. Christ, those women with the overmade-up faces were appalling! And would they listen when one suggested going at the makeup with a lighter hand? Of course not. They'd been doing their faces that way for half a century. Why change now? She refused to be seen in public with them, which was why she invited them to come to the Connecticut house, or here. At least that way she was the only one, aside from her staff, who had to look at them.

She could remember most vividly how she'd looked during those years she'd worked for Sternholt. She could still see herself crossing Madison or Park, knowing the men in automobiles waiting for the lights to change were admiring the healthy bounce of her bobbed hair, the shimmer of her legs in silk stockings. She'd been in fine form, sure of herself and of her prospects, and relatively content with her life.

By the end of her first year with Sternholt, she was earning seventeen dollars a week. She'd sold him a total of seven new designs, and had started collecting, at the employee's price, a number of the Stern's editions. Her money box was healthy and she was painting well. Even Nicholas Harvey was impressed by the energy and directness of her images.

Through the Harveys she'd come to know a number of their friends, most of whom were also painters. The Harveys entertained often, holding open house with the understanding that everyone who came would bring along something edible. There were evenings when a meal at the Harveys consisted of six desserts and no main course, so people happily tucked into apple cobblers and blueberry pies. Mattie looked forward both to her lessons with Nicholas and also to their Friday night open houses. There were always interesting people who willingly sat on the floor, balancing plates of food on their knees, as conversations ranged over everything from the latest trends in modern art to the pros and cons of local politicians.

Mattie was the youngest of the regular guests and one of the few women. She'd spend a fair portion of the evening helping Juliet Harvey with the children, or in the kitchen, developing a great fondness for the tiny, harried woman who seemed to become pregnant within minutes of giving birth. By April of 1929, she was pregnant again, and a favorite lament of the Harveys was their desperate need for more space. Their three-room apartment simply wasn't big enough for four of them, much less five. But they couldn't afford to move.

Still, it was a happy time. A fair number of the open house guests were putting most of their money into buying stocks on margin, and making big profits. And one evening in June, it was unanimously decided that everyone would make blind contributions to a kitty that would go toward moving the Harveys into a larger apartment. The Harveys protested, but they were summarily shushed, and envelopes and a hat were passed.

"You folks have got to move," declared Otter Stoughton, one of the oldest members of the group and the most affluent. "The Harvey Regulars need more space."

This was met with cheers from the other eight people who most often showed up for the Friday night potluck dinners.

As the hat came around each person got up and went out into the hallway to make his or her contribution, then returned to pass the hat to the next Regular. Then the hat was presented to Juliet because, Otter said, "This woman deserves better than this scrawny hick from Kenosha can provide."

"I don't know," Juliet said, with a red-faced smile. "I'm a hick myself, you know, even if I didn't come from as far away as Wisconsin."

"No one," said Danny Briggs, who was a beat reporter for the *Tribune*, "who hails from Brooklyn could ever be considered a hick. Shame on you, Juliet Harvey. On behalf of all those good people across the bridge, consider yourself thoroughly chastised."

The envelopes in the hat, when opened, contained a hundred and twenty-two dollars and fifty-two cents.

"Who's the bastard who put in fifty-two cents?" Esther Loftus, a likable painter of incredibly ugly paintings, wanted to know.

Sheepishly, Hughie Dickinson, another of Nicholas's students, raised his hand. "It was some dollars *and* fifty-two cents," he told the group. "I kept some change back for carfare."

"Don't pick on dear Hughie," Juliet said. Then, overcome, she thanked them. "You're all such good friends," she said, wiping her eyes with the back of her hand as the baby started to squall in the bedroom.

"Now all we've got to do is find the right place for these people," said Otter. "Who's going to volunteer to do some looking?"

Esther promptly said, "I will," and looked around at the others.

"I guess I could help out," put in Golly Gordon, the most serious and most successful of the painters.

"I could help after work," Mattie said.

"Me, too," said Hughie Dickinson.

"Golly and I should be able to swing this," Esther said, "but if we need you, Mattie, we'll let you know at Stern's. And Hughie, same goes for you."

And so it was that the Harvey Regulars found a good-sized three-bedroom apartment on Sixty-eighth Street off Columbus Avenue, and then moved the Harveys into it. Everyone pitched in to help pack and load the borrowed van, and made a party out of the event. All the artists went to work on the new place, using the walls as large-scale canvases. Everything else got a couple of coats of white paint before the furniture was set into place. After the last boxes had been carried up to the third floor and the van returned, ten wearied Regulars settled into the living room to eat the spaghetti Juliet had prepared while they worked.

A week later the first open house took place in the new apartment. And Otter Stoughton brought along a friend named Gideon Sylvester.

"This guy went to grade school with me up in Avon," Otter said by way of introduction. "Then he had the temerity to show up at St. Paul's. And do you think I could get away from him by going on to Yale? Not a chance. Lucky for me, Gideon left after the freshman year. Then, there I am going about my life, happy as all get-out, and who should turn up trying to flog his paintings, but this young bastard." Otter laughed, an affectionate arm around the taller man's shoulders, and after introducing everyone said, "Now, these are my friends, Buddy. So behave yourself."

Mattie wasn't particularly impressed by this latest addition to the group. But then few people impressed her, especially men. When they displayed any interest in her, as happened now and then when Regulars brought friends along to the open houses, she used her height, and her deep voice, and a calculated air of indifference to discourage them. It wasn't that she didn't like most of Nicholas Harvey's friends, it was just that she was determined to remain uninvolved and, therefore, safe.

So when Gideon Sylvester brought his plate of food over to the sofa and sat down beside her, Matty was pleasant, but not encouraging. It didn't appear to bother him one bit. He launched into a long, really quite funny, monologue about his childhood that had her laughing in spite of herself.

"My three older sisters were pretty damned miffed," he said, "when I finally stood my stocky little ground and said they weren't going to put me into one more dress. Shook my fists in their faces and called them every dirty name I could come up with. Horrendously insulting things like 'stinky road apples,' and 'sissy-shits'—that one, I thought, was particularly choice—and, my very best of all, 'bum farts.' I'd just shouted 'bum farts' at the top of my lungs when my mother came in to see what the fuss was about. All she had to hear was 'bum farts' and never mind that I was standing there in Emily's party frock, she grabbed me by the ear and took me out to wash my mouth out with Lifebuoy. Jesus God! If ever there was a truly disgusting experience, having a Lifebuoy gargle has to take the cake.

"Anyway, the girls, thinking they'd got off scot-free, were having a good old laugh and congratulating themselves when mother swooped in and somehow performed a triple Lifebuoy washout on the three of them. And then it was my turn to have a good laugh, even if I was standing there in a white organza party frock with ruffles."

Gideon Sylvester was six feet four inches tall, with sandy brown hair, a high rounded forehead, and even, well-placed features. Mattie supposed some women might consider him handsome, but she didn't think about men in those terms. He had the kind of rangy body upon which all clothes draped well and looked good. His teeth were big, white, and strong. His hands and feet were almost laughably large.

But the best thing about him, in Mattie's opinion, was his narrative skill. He had the ability to recount a story with such a wealth of detail, and so humorously, he was quite irresistible once he began to talk.

"And what about you?" he asked, finally turning his brown eyes to her. "Who is Mathilda Harrison and where did she spring from?"

"You don't want to know," she said, in her most discouraging manner.

"If I didn't, I wouldn't've asked. Come on," he coaxed. "Fess up. Tell me all your secrets."

"I don't believe I will," she said, and got up to carry her empty plate to the kitchen. "I'd better be going," she told Juliet, who was sectioning several pies.

"You haven't had dessert yet," Juliet said, looking disappointed. "And since when do you leave before ten o'clock on a Friday night?"

"It's going to take me longer to get home now that you're uptown," Mattie said lamely, at a loss as to how to explain the discomfort Gideon Sylvester had made her feel.

"Come on," Juliet said. "You know Esther'll be going right by your place and she'll drop you off. Don't go yet."

Looking down at Juliet's small, good-natured face, Mattie decided to tell the truth. "It's that friend of Otter's. I don't care for him. He sets me on edge."

"Well, we can't have that. Help me serve up this pie, then I'll come and play bodyguard. I won't have you being chased away by some newcomer." With a sweet smile, Juliet said, "You're a Regular, kid. Regulars have moxie. Now grab a couple of those plates and get in there."

Mattie stayed. Gideon Sylvester made two more attempts to engage her in conversation, but was preempted both times by Juliet, and finally he went to sit with Danny Briggs and Golly Gordon, who were well into a heated discussion on Utrillo's use of block forms and color.

"What d'you mean 'block forms'?" Gideon Sylvester at once asked, and slid right into the debate. "Just because he did a lot of street scenes, with buildings, which just happen to be right angled, generally, doesn't mean he had 'block forms.' "

Off the three men went, arguing more about semantics than about the painter's merits.

"He likes you," Juliet whispered to Mattie.

"Well, that's too bad," Mattie replied, "because I'm not interested."

"How come you don't have a fella," Juliet asked, "a pretty girl like you?"

"I'm not pretty. I'm just very tall, and unusual."

Juliet laughed. "You're unusual, *and* you're tall, *and* you're pretty." Lowering her voice, she asked, "Did you have a bad experience with a fella? Is that why you're so jittery when a new one comes along to the group?"

"Something like that," Mattie said, most reluctant to talk about what had happened with Avery Moon.

"Don't let it turn you off them for good," Juliet counselled. "They're not all bad." She swallowed some blueberry pie, then with a blue-stained smile said, "They're not all good, either, not by a long chalk. But look at my Nickie. He's the dearest fella ever walked the face of the earth."

"That's true," Mattie was able to agree wholeheartedly. "But it seems to me that men like Nickie are either married to nice women like you, or they never turn up where I happen to be."

"You might not know it if one did," Juliet said. "You don't give anybody, least of all yourself, a chance to find out."

"I'm eighteen. What do I need with a man?"

"You've got a point there. Still, they're nice to have around." Juliet looked over at her husband, her expression filled with love.

Mattie took advantage of the moment to glance over at Gideon Sylvester. He saw her and smiled. She immediately looked away. Never mind what Juliet said, the last thing in the world she needed was some man pestering her.

Mattie shifted in her chair, too retrospectively irate to continue, for the moment, with her remembering. If only she'd heeded her own advice, stuck to her guns and to what she'd believed in then, things would have turned out very differently. There was nothing to be gained from that knowledge now, certainly nothing like satisfaction. And were she to be truthful—and why not be, since there was no one to censor or to question her thoughts?—everything that happened had probably been ordained. Somehow, people too often wound up getting the fates they deserved. She'd probably deserved Gideon Sylvester. God only knew it had taken him a hell of a long time to get her, and there was a definite satisfaction in that. She hadn't been one of those frivolous young girls who talked a lot about careers but who secretly wanted to be rescued from the need to support themselves. No, she'd gone after her career, or rather, the pursuit of painting, with everything in her. She'd had little choice really, because her need to capture images, to create some permanent record of her passage through time, drove her like a self-fueling engine without any "off" mode. That engine chugged away inside her, even when she slept. There was little she saw that didn't suggest to her ways in which she might use the light over there, or the shadowplay here, to create a painting that would become part of that permanent record.

Not for a moment did she ever believe her job with Sternholt would be long-term. It was an expediency, something necessary to her survival until such time as her skill as a painter enabled her to live from her chosen work. And she never once doubted her abilities or the intrinsic merit of her work. She was very good. People who would never have lied to her and whose judgment she valued, whose opinions were of paramount importance to her, assured her repeatedly of her value. Nicholas Harvey was one of them; Otter Stoughton, a successful portraitist, was another; and, oddly enough, so was young Hughie Dickinson, her fellow student.

Hughie was a sweet, very shy young man, and an artist of truly exciting potential. The first time she saw some of Hughie's work she literally felt her heart shift. Working primarily in tempera—using egg white as a base—Hughie's paintings were realistic to such a degree that they were almost photographic. Except that they were paintings, and of such a realism and intensity that she had to look again at this young man to be sure there wasn't something about him, some special quality, she'd failed to notice. But he was just Hughie, always in need of a haircut, his teeth always a few days past their most recent brushing, his clothes faintly musty from having been worn too long. Yet twenty-year-old Hughie painted as if he'd been alive from the beginning of time, so aware was he of the way blades of grass bent under a breeze, or of the way light was caught and held in a woman's long hair, or the manner in which an expanse of sand absorbed water. All his life Hughie created portraits of nature wherein people were secondary adjuncts to the elements. If he chose to do a picture of some children on a beach, the children became as necessary to that beach as the sand and the water. If he decided to depict his bedroom window, everything on either side of that window was precisely as it should have been, right down to the flaking paint on the sill, the semicircular crack in one of the panes, and the water stains on the faded curtains. Hughie was a born Master.

Christ! She dabbed at her eyes with a tissue. She should have married Hughie. Heaven knew he'd asked her enough times.

Six

D o you mind if I ask you a question?" Sarah said, approaching Carl who, stripped to the waist, with his trouser cuffs rolled up, was clearing rocks from the beach, setting them in a tidy pile.

"What?" he replied, not lifting his head.

"How did you come to work for Mattie?"

"Why?" he asked suspiciously, his back stiffening.

"I just wondered, that's all."

"You wonder about a lot of things, from what I hear," he said, at last facing her.

She tried a smile. "I'm naturally curious."

He didn't respond to her smile. "Maybe too curious."

"Maybe," she agreed, determined not to let his reticent manner discourage her. "Don't you want to tell me?"

"There's nothing to tell," he said, pulling the everpresent rag from his back pocket to mop his face. "When I came home after 'Nam, I had nowhere to go, wasn't fit for a civilian job. Mattie hired me."

"How did you know her?"

"She and my grandfather were friends. Okay? Is that it? Or do you want to know more?"

"Why are you so angry?"

"Angry? Now why would I be angry?" he asked, his face going hard. "I put in three years fighting for my country, doing things that defy any kind of rational explanation, then come home and get treated like shit. Because it was a dirty little war and we shouldn't've been there in the first place. Even my folks were kind of squeamish having a trained killer in their house. Aside from all that, I had this small problem: I kept thinking everything I looked at was booby-trapped, or there were VC in the trees or outside my windows. My sister called Mattie, and Mattie said something to the effect that there'd always be a welcome in her home for a Harvey. So I came to work for her. Now can I get on with it? Or is there more you're curious about?"

"I didn't mean to upset you," she said softly.

"Ah, lady," he said tiredly. "Will you please fuck off and let me do my work?"

"I'm sorry," she said, and began to back away.

"Shit on your sorry," he said without inflection, and bent to pick up some more rocks.

"Well, to hell with you!" Indignant, she walked away hearing him laugh. The exchange left her feeling inept and unattractive, and she wondered when, if ever, her immediate reaction to any unpleasantness would stop being negative thoughts about herself. Something in her head would start insisting that people treated her badly because she was plain, because she lacked sparkle. She was a plodder, quite content to work doggedly away until a job was done. She'd never had any illusions about her appeal, convinced that when people were kind to her it was because they were able to see past her lackluster surface to the finer qualities underneath. She was confident only of her brain power, her intelligence. Her figure was okay, trim but not spectacular. But she'd always felt more comfortable in clothes that allowed her to move. And makeup was something that defeated her. She never got it right, wound up looking clownlike, and finally removed it.

Her ex-husband, Ray, had been complimentary at the outset, praising the clarity of her eyes and of her complexion. Like a sucker, she'd bought it. His compliments stopped the minute she agreed to marry him; so did conversation. It was as if once she'd given her word he lost interest in her. She became a fixture in his life in advance even of the wedding ceremony. Fixtures, to Ray, were wives, and any members of the immediate family; people worthy only of taking and obeying orders. Why he'd thought she'd tolerate his demands for hot dinners to be waiting the minute he walked through the door of an evening, or sex whenever the mood took him, she couldn't say. The fights started within minutes after the city hall ceremony and lasted right up to the morning when she announced, "Guess what, Ray? You're moving out today." Naturally, his comeback had been, "I was going to leave anyway," which despite its being a patent lie—he'd been happy as a clam with the domestic arrangements—nevertheless galled her. She'd managed to keep silent while he threw his clothes into a couple of suitcases, waited until he'd driven off, then had gone through the apartment in a frenzy, gathering up every last thing of his in cartons she put by the front door. That way, when he returned for the rest of his stuff, all she'd had to do was hand the boxes out to him. He'd made half a dozen trips up and down to his car and then, without uttering a single word, he'd driven off. Six months later her no-fault divorce came through and she was back to where she'd started. In just over a year she'd been married and divorced. And all she had to show for it were some jockey shorts that got left in the hamper (using a tissue, she'd picked them up and thrown them in the trash) and the dregs of a bottle of Aramis cologne (the smell of which, since then, made her gag).

Still, at least she could say she'd been married. She wasn't a woman no one had ever wanted, although having been wanted by Ray was hardly a feather in anyone's cap. Her sister, on the other hand, had never wanted to be married; she liked men well enough but not so much that she wanted one around on a daily basis. "I'll be damned," she often said, "if I'll perform like an indentured servant just for the sake of having someone around full time. Look at Dad! He's a perfect example of indentured servitude, and never mind that he's a man. It's the same thing, except in reverse."

Sarah hadn't yet reached the point where she'd abandoned one hundred percent of her hope that she might, one day, meet a man who'd be sufficiently interested in her to come to some sort of arrangement; who'd have sufficient respect for her to want to make compromises. It didn't seem likely it would ever happen, but she kept a partially open mind on the subject. After all, you never knew what could happen.

"Is Carl the grandson of Nicholas Harvey?" Sarah asked Mattie over dinner that evening.

"So!" Mattie gave her a wolfish grin. "You talked to Carl."

"I'd hardly call it talking. I asked him how he came to work for you and got told off for my trouble."

Mattie laughed—triumphantly, Sarah thought. "But he answered you, didn't he? I told you he would."

"He told me to fuck off," Sarah said, then blushed horribly.

"That sounds like Carl, all right." Mattie drank some of her wine, then said, "Attractive, isn't he?"

"Oh, please." Sarah made a face.

"Whatever his manner might be," Mattie persisted, "you have to admit he's attractive."

"I don't have to admit a thing. What happened to Nicholas Harvey, anyway?"

"What do you mean 'what happened' to him? He got old and died. What the hell do you *think* happens to people? What an imbecilic question!"

"Why is it imbecilic to ask about someone?" Sarah countered. "How would *I* know what happened to him?"

"He'd be ninety-two if he was alive today," Mattie said frostily.

"There's a non sequitur if ever I heard one."

"It most certainly is not. If Nicholas Harvey hadn't died a very long time ago, he'd be ninety-two now."

"Oh, brother!" Sarah whispered, stabbing a morsel of chicken with her fork.

"Seems to me," Mattie said slowly, "Carl certainly got to you."

"I'm not fond of having people tell me to fuck off." Again Sarah blushed.

Mattie laughed. "There you go, being oversensitive again."

"And there you go, being difficult."

"Me? Difficult? Oh, I think not, my dear. You have, I'm afraid, a supersimplified idea of how people should be. I have always refused to behave according to other people's specifications. Learn to adapt, Sarah. You're far too rigid for someone so young."

"I'm not that young."

"So you keep reminding me," Mattie sniffed.

"So, how and when did Harvey die?"

Mattie glared at her for a moment, then laughed so hard she began to cough. When her coughing subsided, she drank some wine and said, "I'll tell you after dinner. Now shut up and let me eat."

Ensconced in the rocker on the verandah with a cigarette and a balloon of cognac, Mattie looked for some time at the color-drenched sunset, then said, "After the stock market crashed in 1929, and after the first wave of suicides, when things settled down a bit, we all thought perhaps life would continue on as before. I still had my job with Stern's Editions, and Mr. Sternholt called the staff together just before Christmas to speak to us."

Every year at Christmas, Mr. Sternholt made a short speech before his secretary, Mrs. Bloom, handed out the bonus envelopes. This year, when everyone was assembled, he said, "No matter what happens, there will always be a market for our books; there will always be well-to-do collectors; there will always be well-to-do people. The demand might decrease somewhat, but I see no need for panic. This company is solvent, and I personally experienced no losses in the market. I think you have a right to know my position, since your livelihoods depend on me. Naturally, some of the orders have been cancelled, but the majority are being accepted and paid for. The bonuses are perhaps not quite so much as I would have liked to give you, but I will continue, as I have always done, to share with you the profits of the company. So," he said, "I wish you all a good Christmas and a happy Chanukah."

There was a round of applause, then Norm Hersh, the foreman, stepped forward to present Mr. Sternholt with the gift the employees had all chipped in to buy, a silver serving dish engraved, "From your friends, the staff at Stern's."

Sandwiches, cakes, and coffee were served, then they closed early for the holidays.

A party was planned for Christmas day at the Harveys for the Regulars who either had no family or couldn't afford to travel home. Mattie spent the morning of the twenty-fourth wrapping gifts, then bundled up and went out in the already melting snow to do a few hours' sketching. Unlike other years, there were no crowds rushing in and out of the stores on Fifth Avenue doing last-minute shopping. There were some people out and about, but nothing like the usual crush. As she trudged up the slushy avenue, she thought about her family, wondering if her father had suffered losses in the Crash. She also wondered if they ever thought of her, or wondered what had become of her. What awful people! For all they cared, she could be dead. Well, for all she cared, the whole family could go broke. In fact, she thought it might even the score a little if her mother and father found themselves out on the street, with only a couple of suitcases and a few hundred dollars. Serve them damned right! she thought, glancing into the store windows to see salesgirls leaning with their elbows on counters, idly picking at their nails.

It began to rain and she returned home without having opened her sketchbook. As she came through the front door, her landlady, old Mrs. Webster, popped out (as if she'd been waiting) to say, "Merry Christmas, Mattie. Care to come in for a cup of eggnog?"

Taken aback by this rare gesture of hospitality, Mattie said, "Sure. That'd be swell. Let me just go hang up my coat."

"You do that, dear, then come on down for a nice cup of nog."

Mrs. Webster's ground floor front apartment was crowded with a lifetime's accumulation of knickknacks, souvenirs consisting of everything from Kewpie dolls to a brass ashtray with a raised impression of the Flatiron Building, fringed satin pillows, and massive pieces of mahogany-veneered furniture.

"Sit yourself down," said the round old woman, presenting Mattie with a chipped mug filled with bright yellow eggnog before positioning herself in what was clearly her favorite chair.

The drink was oversweet but not unbearably so, and Mattie sipped at it as she looked around the room, her eye caught by one thing after another: an enormous leather-bound photograph album, a painted dish commemorating the coronation of George V, and what looked to be a genuine hand-carved ivory fan.

"You've got a lot of very interesting things," Mattie said with a smile.

"Yes," Mrs. Webster said proudly, "I do, don't I? I've had a very good life."

"Have you?"

"Oh, yes, I have. I do miss Mr. Webster, but he was suffering so, it was a blessing he passed on, really."

"How long ago did he die?"

"It's been eleven years now. He was a good, hardworking man, was Mr. Webster, left me well provided for, bless him." She looked at the curio stand for a moment, then at Mattie. "I'll tell you why I asked you in, Mattie. I'm losing one of my best tenants, Miss Perkin. Been with me since Mr. Webster passed on and I started letting rooms. I'll miss her, for a fact. But a woman on her own can't afford to be sentimental, and that's the sad truth. Miss Perkin's flat's the second floor front, right above here. It's got a separate bedroom and its own private bathroom. I thought, seeing as how you're working regular, I'd offer you first chance at the place. It's a sight bigger than your room on the third floor. 'Course the rent's higher."

"How much higher?"

"Well, we'll have to discuss that. Why don't you go on up there and have yourself a look, see how it suits? If you like it, we'll see if we can't come to terms."

Mrs. Webster gave her the key, and Mattie went upstairs.

The minute she opened the door she knew she wanted to make the move, provided Mrs. Webster didn't think she could ask the sun, moon, and stars. The sitting room was well lit by two windows facing the street, and had a working fireplace. The bedroom was small, but adequate. And, luxury of luxuries, off the bedroom was a complete bathroom. If she took over this apartment she wouldn't have to clean other people's scum off the bathtub whenever she wanted to bathe; she wouldn't have to tiptoe down the drafty hall if she had to use the toilet in the middle of the night. With some fresh paint, new curtains, and her own things nicely arranged, the place would be most inviting.

"How much did you think you'd want?" she asked Mrs. Webster upon returning downstairs with the key.

"Sit down, dear. Finish your nog. I want to think about this."

Mattie sat and obediently swallowed some of the syrupy beverage.

"You've been paying me three-fifty all this time and I've never once raised your rent. Now, Miss Perkin's rooms are bigger and altogether self-contained. What would you say to ten a week?"

"I couldn't," Mattie replied. "It's too much."

"Well, what could you pay?"

"I might be able to manage six."

"Oh, dearie me," said Mrs. Webster. "That's really not enough."

"What if I offered to help you out?" Mattie suggested. "It must be a lot of work, looking after this whole house all by yourself. What if I pay you six, but I carry out the garbage cans for you, and sweep the front steps every couple of days? And I'll pay for painting the rooms out of my own money."

"I don't know," Mrs. Webster said doubtfully.

"Look," Mattie said, anxious to take over the apartment. "Let's make it six-fifty, and I'll do the garbage and the front steps, and help you out with odd jobs now and then."

Mrs. Webster gave her a gappy grin and said, "Dearie, you've got yourself a deal."

"When can I move in?"

"Anytime after the first. And if you hear of anyone might be interested in your room, you'll let me know, won't you?"

"I sure will. Thank you for the eggnog," Mattie said, and flew upstairs in a state of great excitement. She'd been planning to spend an hour reading *A Farewell To Arms*, her Christmas present to herself, but was too keyed-up. It was only a week's wait, but she wished she could move downstairs there and then. And wait until she told the Harveys! She'd be able to have guests now. She'd invite Esther, and Otter, and Danny and Hughie and Golly, and the rest of the Regulars.

Things were going wonderfully well. Stern's was paying her twenty-two dollars a week, and she'd been faithfully putting aside seven of that. Unfortunately, she'd run out of new design ideas, but she had come up with a time-saving suggestion for which Stern had given her fifty dollars. "I don't know why I never thought of it myself," he said, and gave her an approving, fatherly pat on the head. "What a clever girl you are, Mattie!" Her suggestion was to shift the locations of the workers so that the books passed in a direct line, stage by stage, through the building instead of zigging and zagging back and forth, thereby wasting valuable time. Now, on top of all that, she was going to have a real self-contained apartment of her own.

She arrived at the Harveys' bursting to tell everyone her good news, but one look at Juliet's face when she opened the door told her something dreadful had happened. The small woman's eyes were red-rimmed from weeping. And, beyond her, Nicholas sat slumped on the sofa with his head in his hands. Esther and Hughie sat on either side of him, looking distraught.

"What's wrong?" Mattie asked anxiously.

"Otter's dead," Danny Briggs told her. "He got cleaned out in the market. He killed himself."

"Oh, no!" Mattie exclaimed, then felt the news travel down through her body from her brain. Her throat seized up, her stomach started to lurch, her knees unlocked, and she had to sit down on the floor, still in her coat and boots. Not Otter Stoughton, she thought. Not that witty, gracious man who'd so generously praised her work, who'd demonstrated such unfailing generosity to all his friends. Quite arbitrarily, she wondered if Otter's friend, Gideon Sylvester, knew of Otter's death and, if he did, how he was taking it. The two had seemed very close, in spite of their disparaging cracks about one another.

"The funeral's set for tomorrow," Esther said.

Nicholas Harvey began to sob. Esther at once put her plump arms around him and drew him to her breast. Hughie gazed down at his folded hands. Juliet stood looking at her husband, as if not sure what she should do. At last, she sat on the floor beside Mattie and whispered, "Poor Nickie. He loved Otter."

"We all did," Mattie said, her mouth gluey.

"He was Nickie's hero," Juliet whispered. "It's so awful."

Not knowing what else to do, Mattie put her arm around the tiny woman's narrow shoulders.

Gideon Sylvester was at the funeral, one of more than a hundred mourners who came. Because of his height, Mattie saw him almost at once, seated in one of the front pews with Otter's family. Esther Loftus made a point of going directly to Gideon after the service to offer her sympathy, which Mattie found a bit odd. She hung back, unsure of the protocol at this her first funeral. To her chagrin, Gideon Sylvester approached her to say, "It's good of you to come."

She didn't know why, but he irritated her, and she thought it highly presumptuous of the man to thank her for coming when he wasn't even a member of Otter's family, but just a friend. It was her understanding that only immediate family members had the right to make remarks like that, and it wasn't in her to let it pass.

"Why are you behaving," she asked in a fierce undertone, "as if you're Otter's widow or something?"

"He was my best friend," he defended himself, thrown.

"I don't care if the two of you took blood oaths when you were eight, you're still a pompous buffoon," she declared, then turned on her heel and went striding out of the church.

On the sidewalk out front a group of the Regulars were making arrangements to go back to Otter's apartment. Mrs. Stoughton had asked Nicholas Harvey to bring along as many of the group as he could in order to have a farewell drink to their friend. It seemed that anyone who'd ever attended one of the Harvey's Friday night open houses had turned up both for the service and to go on to the Stoughton place on Park Avenue, some twenty blocks from the church. Since Otter was being cremated at a ceremony to which only his wife and family were going, the group was expected to convene at the apartment and await their return.

Mattie had no sooner walked through the door of the Park Avenue apartment when Gideon Sylvester came cutting through those assembled, making a beeline for her.

"You've got some nerve, sister!" he said furiously, stopping inches away from her. "Who the hell are you to think you can talk to me that way?"

"I can talk to you any way I damn well please," she said, livid. If he wanted a fight in front of all these people, at a time like this, she'd give him one he'd never forget. "And who the hell are you to usurp people's rights and play at being family? You're an arrogant fool!"

"And you are a big-mouthed, opinionated *child*!"

She glared at his angry face and said, "Do me a favor! Keep away from me! I don't like you one bit!"

"Having said this," Mattie told Sarah, "I turned to go storming off and marched straight into the open closet door. Knocked myself out cold." She laughed, then drank some of her cognac. "What a scene! When I came to, who should be pressing a cold cloth to the egg on my forehead but goddamned Gideon Sylvester. I was positively mortified."

"Then what happened?" Sarah asked.

"You know something?" Mattie said. "You remind me of nothing so much as a newborn bird with its beak open, waiting for its mother to hurry up and drop in another tidbit. You're awfully greedy when it comes to wanting to know things, always got your mouth wide open."

Sarah smiled at her. "It's not my fault if you tell a good story, is it?"

Mattie sighed then swished the cognac around in the balloon, deliberating whether or not to continue. At last, she said, "Let's get back to this on Sunday, after the boys have gone. I'm not in the mood to go on right now."

"Is it my fault?" Sarah asked.

"*Christl! No,* it's not your *fault! Will* you *stop* that? I've talked enough for one evening. *All right?*"

"Why don't I just go away, right?" Sarah said genially.

"That's a wonderful idea."

Sarah got up and then, to Mattie's surprise, bent and kissed the old woman on the top of her head. "You're a miserable old cuss," Sarah said, "But you're growing on me."

Flustered, Mattie had to smile. "Go on now," she said. "I'll see you in the morning."

"I'm sure you'll want to inspect me to make sure I pass muster before your sons arrive."

"Damned right! I won't have them thinking I've got some misplaced hippie working for me."

"Good night, Mattie," Sarah said, and went inside, taking care not to let the screen door slam.

Seven

"Do me a favor," Mattie said. "Go tell Carl to meet the noon ferry. Knowing Giddy, he'll leave the car in the lot on the mainland because he says trying to park on the ferry makes him claustrophobic. Trust Giddy to get sick parking a car."

Sarah had to wonder if Mattie was trying to maneuver her in Carl's direction. In view of the fact that it was Mattie who gave the staff orders, it was most unusual for her to send Sarah off on this errand.

Carl was at the side of the house, cutting flowers and placing them gently in an open-ended basket.

Sarah watched for a few moments, then asked, "What are they for?"

"Oh, shit! You again! They're for the dining table. Okay?"

"Boy!" Sarah said, forcing herself to smile. "You're a real crowd-pleaser, aren't you? Mattie wants you to meet the noon ferry, pick up Giddy and Matthew."

"Fine! Anything else?"

"Not a thing," she said, and held up her hand to silence him. "I know," she said. "Now, fuck off! Consider me gone!" She retreated, muttering, "What a jerk!"

"Hey!" Carl called after her.

"What?" She whirled around to face him. "You wanted to say it yourself?"

Still looking as if he'd be just as happy to kill her, he asked, "You want some of the roses for your room?"

Nonplussed, she said, "Well, sure, I guess."

"Okay," he said, and went back to work with the secateurs.

Unable to think what to say, she returned to the house via the kitchen door. Mattie was seated at the table with Bonnie, going over the menus for the weekend. Sarah poured herself a cup of coffee, then looked over in time to see Mattie consulting her wristwatch, an ancient Whitnauer.

"I'm going up to the attic for a couple of hours," Mattie announced. "Remind Gloria to put fresh linens in both the guest rooms, and tell her to be sure to put the extra-large bath sheet out for Giddy."

"Anything you want me to do?" Sarah asked, as Mattie got up to leave.

Mattie studied her appraisingly for a few seconds. "As a matter of fact," she said, "there is. Come with me!"

Up in the attic, Mattie said, "Go sit there!" and pointed to the armchair.

Bemused, Sarah did as asked.

"Just relax and make yourself comfortable," Mattie said, placing a large pad of newsprint paper on the easel.

"You're going to draw me?" Sarah asked with a smile.

"I'm going to try." Mattie began sharpening a number of pencils, as she did, saying, "What about this husband of yours?"

"What about him?"

"Tell all," Mattie said with a small smile, shrugging on a cotton smock.

Fair's fair, Sarah thought, watching Mattie put the pencils, several charcoal sticks, a bottle of India ink, and some brushes in a neat row on the table beside the easel.

"He was an upscale thug," Sarah said, as Mattie selected a 5B pencil, took a long penetrating look at her, then began to draw. "He was a middle-class, upper-management thug. At the beginning, he talked a great game, made himself out to be very aware, incredibly sensitive. He was about as sensitive as an acid bath. I honestly don't know why he bothered with me. It wasn't as if he couldn't have had his pick of women. I mean, he was handsome, in a Romanian peasant sort of way."

Mattie gave a yelp of laughter. "Was he Romanian?"

"No, that's only the way I came to think of him. We met at a party. It was pretty dark, candles, that sort of thing. Maybe in the dark he thought I was good-looking. I don't know. Who the hell knows what goes on inside men's heads? Anyway, I wasn't particularly interested, and that was probably why he was so damned eager. It seems to me men go crazy over disinterested women. Anyway, he wasn't totally terrible in bed, except he was one of those men who think a woman's brains are in her crotch."

Mattie's hand moving quickly, she laughed again and asked, "And were they?"

"I told you the whole thing lasted about twenty minutes. It started and ended in just over a year. He was the biggest dork I've ever known. It took me longer to figure out why I ever married him than the marriage actually lasted. Men are such jerks."

"I don't know who said it," Mattie said, "but men are just little boys with money."

It was Sarah's turn to laugh. "That's wonderful. I have to remember that."

"It is good, isn't it," Mattie agreed, pausing to take another long look at her. "You've got good bones. Why the hell won't you do something with yourself?"

"I have!" Sarah argued. "I cut my hair, and I bought new clothes. What else should I do?"

"Highlight what you've got," Mattie told her. "Use a little makeup. Do you belong to some kind of religion that prohibits the use of cosmetics?"

"Of course not. I don't belong to any religion at all."

"Did somebody once tell you you weren't good-looking?" Mattie asked incisively.

"Not exactly," Sarah answered, beginning to feel uneasy.

"It's been my experience that attractive women only underplay their looks either for religious reasons, or because somebody, once upon a time, made a point of putting them down. Was it the husband?"

"Partly," Sarah admitted, feeling as if she were edging closer and closer to a forest fire.

"The wicked stepmother!" Mattie looked over to see what kind of reaction Sarah had to this. "I'm right, aren't I?"

"I don't like using her as an excuse for the way I am."

"What did she say?" Mattie asked, going back to her drawing.

"Are you trying to upset me?"

"Not at all. I'm trying to understand why you insist on going around looking like a Carmelite nun."

"Thanks a lot."

"Don't pout! Just tell me what she said!"

Almost inaudibly, Sarah said, "She told me I'd be lucky if any man was ever interested in me, because I was plain. Worse than plain. I was drab."

"And you believed her."

"You would have too, if somebody told you again and again, for years, that no one would ever want you because you were ugly."

"What a bitch!" Mattie said with fire. "Did she treat your sister the same way?"

Warmed by Mattie's sympathetic reaction, Sarah said, "She couldn't. My sister is beautiful."

"So are you!" Mattie said, throwing down her pencil in disgust. "Sit there and don't move! I'll be back in a minute."

It was closer to ten minutes before she returned carrying a small cosmetics bag. "Come over here!" she ordered, summoning Sarah to the window. "Christ!" she swore, her hand turning Sarah's face this way and that. "Drab! All right. Stand still! Are you capable of standing still?"

"Of course I am."

"Good!" Mattie plonked the cosmetics bag on the windowsill, opened it, found what she wanted, and began to work on Sarah's face almost precisely the way she'd worked at the drawing Sarah was most curious to see. It took no more than five minutes, then Mattie held out a tube of mascara and said, "Put this on!" and handed her a small mirror.

"I'm terrible at this," Sarah protested.

"Christ! I have to do *everything*!" Snatching back the mirror and the mascara, she instructed Sarah to look straight ahead, then up, as she applied the mascara. At last, she said, "It would be better if you did it yourself, but it's not bad. Go look at yourself in the big mirror."

Sarah did, and her immediate reaction was to laugh.

"What's so goddamned funny?" Mattie barked.

"Nothing. It's just that I'm not used to myself . . ."

"You start acting like some silly teenager and I'll throw you the hell out of here!" Mattie threatened. "For once, you look like a pretty woman instead of a civil service employee."

"Why do you care what I look like?"

"You're beginning to get on my nerves!" Mattie said gruffly. "I'm an artist, you idiot! I like beautiful things around me. Surely to God you've noticed that all my staff are good-looking people."

That was true, Sarah realized. Bonnie, although overweight, had a lovely face, with small charming features and warm brown eyes. Gloria was a tall, willowy black woman of striking good looks. And much as he annoyed her, she had to admit Carl was handsome in a leathery sun-and-wind-battered way.

"I freely admit to being elitist," Mattie said, going back to retrieve her pencil. "And something of a snob. But if I have to look at faces every day, I prefer them to be *good* faces. Do you think I'd have hired you if I didn't think you were good-looking? And who would be a more qualified judge, your wicked stepmother, or me?"

"I thought you hired me because I had the qualifications for the job, and because I made such a fabulous first impression," Sarah said cheekily.

"Sit down! I haven't finished with you yet."

"Aside from the last six years, have you always kept up your painting?"

"I never stopped. Now be quiet. I'm doing your face."

As if possessed of some kind of psychic radar, Mattie got up and went out onto the verandah a moment before the old Lincoln town car turned in from the main road. Watching from the living room window, Sarah saw the old woman position herself to one side of the stairs. The car pulled up, both rear passenger doors opened, and Mattie's two sons got out. Mattie had warned her, but Sarah still was unprepared for how very different the two men were. Giddy, tall and handsome, his face breaking into a radiant smile, came hurrying up to the verandah.

"You look divine, my darling!" he declared, and effortlessly swung his visibly pleased mother in a circle before planting kisses on both her cheeks.

Matthew, shorter, bespectacled, his good looks soured by an expression of wearied obligation, came up the steps, said, "Mother," and allowed himself to be embraced.

Giddy, as if oblivious to his younger brother, was saying, "I love the dress, my darling. It's heaven. I don't know *how* you do it." Taking Mattie by the hand, he led her inside, saying, "I want to hear *all* the dirt, who's doing what to whom, *everything*. I hope . . ." He broke off, catching sight of Sarah, and at once extending a long graceful hand to her, with another smile, saying, "You're Sarah, of course. What a treat to meet you, finally."

Finding him immediate and accessible, Sarah shook his hand. "I'm happy to be meeting you, finally, too."

Matthew, bringing up the rear, stopped and waited to be introduced. Giddy and Mattie had already settled themselves on the sofa, so Sarah offered her hand and said, "Hello. I'm Sarah."

Matthew's hand was dry, brittle as an old man's. His eyes met hers only for a moment before he went to one of the armchairs, as if to make sure Giddy didn't steal their mother's old Whitnauer when he wasn't looking.

Carl came through carrying the men's bags, made eye contact with Sarah, then went upstairs. Sarah remained by the window, piqued by the family dynamics. Giddy already had his mother laughing, while Matthew looked decidedly sullen. Carl came back down the stairs, again looked at Sarah, and went out to put the Lincoln in the garage. Not wishing to call attention to herself, Sarah slid into the nearest chair.

"So have they found him yet?" Mattie was asking Giddy.

"My darling, it's as if he's vanished off the *face* of the *earth*. And do you *know* what Fiesta Ware *goes for* these days? I really could *kill* him!"

"He made a damned good try at killing *you*," Mattie said wryly.

"You don't know the half of it. I had to use Dermablend to cover the bruises for close to three weeks after."

"What the hell's Dermablend?" Matthew asked.

"Waterproof makeup," Giddy told him, "for people with scars, pigment problems, that sort of thing. They even have some specially for legs, in case you want to cover your varicose veins, dearie."

"I don't *have* varicose veins."

"My, aren't we grouchy!" Giddy flapped his hand dismissively, returning his attention to his mother. "*When* are you going to come back into the city? There are *dozens* of superb new restaurants I'm *dying* to take you to. And at least six shows you simply have to see. Besides, I'm starting to feel guilty living in that mausoleum all by myself. You've been promising forever you'd come stay with me, but you never have, and I wouldn't have bought such a simply *huge* place if you hadn't told me you'd come to stay."

"Hardly by yourself," Matthew interjected. "I'm sure you've replaced the Harley Honey by now."

"How nasty you are!" Giddy said, hurt. "Must you always be so unpleasant?"

"Must you always be so indiscriminate?" Matthew countered.

"Drinks?" Mattie said, looking at Sarah, who at once got up.

"Yes, let me get you something," she said, approaching the testy trio.

"Oh, dearie, I'd adore some Perrier," Giddy said with a sweet smile. "If you wouldn't mind. That *is* a darling little dress."

"Thank you. Mattie, what can I get for you?"

"Something brown, no ice, a double."

"And for you?" she asked Matthew.

"Is there any coffee made?"

"I'll go see."

"If it's not made, don't bother."

Giddy lit his mother's cigarette, then his own. At once Matthew protested.

"You're both going to die of lung cancer, not to mention making me suffer from your secondhand smoke."

"Lighten up, dearie," Giddy told him. "You'll drop dead from stress long before either of us." To Mattie he said, "He bitched all the way up here. If it wasn't my smoking, it was my driving. I'm overcautious, according to him. And if it wasn't my smoking or my driving, it was my choice of radio station, or my suit. I adore this suit. Don't you, my darling? Honestly. Gianni Versace, and I won't *tell* you what it cost!"

"Actually," Mattie said of her oldest son's blindingly white, magnificently cut suit, "I do. The two of us look like missionaries."

They both laughed. Matthew pulled at the sleeves of his white and blue seersucker jacket from Brooks Brothers, shot his cuffs, then recrossed his legs. "I had a call from the accountant," he said importantly. "Since when do you buy more than six hundred dollars worth of art supplies and then have them sent all the way up here from the city by courier?"

Giddy said, "Oh oh," under his breath as Sarah returned from the kitchen with a tray of coffee things she set on the table beside Matthew before going over to the bar to get the drinks.

Mattie put out her hand, her eyes riveted to Matthew, picked up the telephone, punched out a number from memory, then held the receiver to her ear.

"Put your husband on, will you?" she said into the mouthpiece. "It's Mattie Sylvester."

There was a few seconds' wait. Then she said, "George, if you ever again discuss with either of my sons information regarding my expenditures I will fire you on the spot. Do I make myself clear? No, I am *not* interested in your explanation. Do it again, and I'll get myself an accountant who knows how to keep his mouth shut! And you will be working on some small Caribbean island trying to eke out a living by totting up the number of bales of sea-island cotton the natives can chop in one day." She slammed down the receiver, replaced the telephone on the table, then leaned forward, one large hand fastened firmly to the arm of the sofa. "If I drop dead tomorrow, Matthew," she said in a quietly deadly tone, "you still won't have any influence over the disposition of my funds. You will *never* get to call the shots in this family, on any level. In future, leave my accountant alone. I know

damned well *you* called him, and not the other way around. I'm
warning you, either stop interfering or stay away. You're endlessly
trying to play at being your goddamned father, for reasons I cannot
begin to fathom, and I don't like you well enough to tolerate your
sullenness, your meanness to your brother, or your repeated incursions
into my private affairs. I've been through all this crap once, thank
you very much. What, in the name of everything sacred, would
make you think I'd be willing to put up with it again? Do I make
myself clear?"

"Perfectly," he replied curtly.

Sarah brought Mattie and Giddy their drinks, then returned to her
chair.

"Can't you *ever* be pleasant?" Mattie asked her younger son.

"Why don't I just leave?" Matthew stood up.

"Suit yourself," Mattie said mildly. "If you're going to be so tiresome, I'd prefer you went. It's been seven months since you made any
effort to see me. I'll survive your absence."

His bluff called, Matthew wavered. "You never make a fuss over
me," he accused, like nothing so much as a too tall, slightly plump
child.

"That is because you make it so goddamned difficult for people to
like you," Mattie threw back. "Sit down, drink your coffee, and make
an effort to be civilized."

There followed a silence of several minutes while Giddy sipped at
his Perrier, Mattie drank half her Chivas Regal in one swallow, and
Matthew busied himself adding cream and sugar to his coffee. At last,
eager to lighten the mood, Sarah said to Giddy, "I understand you
have a terrific nightclub."

Brightening at once, he said, "You must come, Sarah! If Jessica
Dragonette here will give you a day off once you're back somewhat
closer to the real world, I'd be tickled to death to have you come some
evening as my guest."

"I'd love to," Sarah told him, finding him every bit as irresistible as
Mattie had promised she would. Despite his affected speech, he struck
her as completely sincere and endearingly keen to be liked.

"Nothing too risqué," he said. "But some of the acts are unbelievably good. My darling," he addressed his mother, "do you remember Rita?"

"Which one is Rita?" Mattie asked, working hard to dispel her anger.

"Darling, you *adored* Rita. Don't you *remember*? She's the one who does all the singing impressions." To Sarah, he explained, "She actually sings, my dear. It's not lip-synched. And she's divine. Gorgeous, too. She does everyone from Streisand to Eartha Kitt."

"Oh, I remember," Mattie said with a smile. "She *is* good. I really thought he was a woman," she told Sarah. "He's positively beautiful."

The mood picked up at this point, and they'd just finished their drinks when Bonnie announced that lunch was ready.

Matthew's mood seemed to mellow in direct proportion to the amount of food he consumed, so that by meal's end he'd lost his initial hostility and was quite enthusiastically extolling to Sarah the virtues of low-cost term life insurance. Sarah politely feigned interest, and listened as he switched to describing the ins and outs of some immense corporate takeover in which he was involved. It was hard to follow and fairly boring, but Sarah felt she should make an effort to pay attention, if only for the sake of Mattie and Giddy, who were engaged in close, almost whispered conversation on the opposite side of the table.

After lunch, with a yawn, Matthew said he was going up to take a nap. Giddy at once suggested a swim and Mattie agreed they'd both change into bathing suits and meet on the verandah. Left at loose ends, Sarah, too, went upstairs to change. Upon entering her room, the first thing she saw were the roses. Her eyes kept returning to the luscious blooms as she hung away her dress, then pulled on a pair of loose white cotton pants and an oversized T-shirt. Pushing her bare feet into sandals, she went over to the dresser and, eyes closed, breathed in the perfume of the roses. Then she went in search of Carl, to thank him.

He wasn't anywhere on the grounds.

Back in the kitchen, Bonnie said, "He's probably at his place. Go see."

He lived in the apartment over the garage, and Sarah debated whether or not to disturb him there. He was liable to throw her down the stairs that ran up the side of the garage. She'd try to thank him and he'd tell her to fuck off. Well, she refused to sink to his level. She'd say thank you, then come back to her room, grab a book and read for a while. Or maybe she'd ride one of the bikes down the highway to the general store, and have a Dusty Miller (a local concoction of ice cream with a hot chocolate sauce that formed a hard shell on contact with the ice cream and an overall sprinkling of malt) before riding back again.

She knocked at the screen door.

He came over and talked to her through the closed door. "You want something?"

"I want to thank you for the roses. They're beautiful."

To her amazement, he said, "You want to come in?" and opened the door.

"Okay," she said. "Sure."

"You want a beer or something?" he asked, walking away barefoot over the wood floor.

"No, that's okay, thanks."

He opened a small undercounter refrigerator, took out a Bud, popped the tab, then said, "Sit down," as he came back across the room and dropped into one of the old-fashioned wicker armchairs.

"I'm not sure I should," she said. "How do I know you won't hit me over the head with a baseball bat or something?"

He chuckled and said, "Sit down."

She did, then looked around. There wasn't much furniture: the two wicker chairs, a battered coffee table, and a low bookcase crammed with paperbacks. A large Fisher ghetto blaster sat atop the bookcase, a sizable stack of cassettes beside it. She could see through to the bedroom, and the unmade bed.

"Why have you decided to be friendly?" she asked, watching as he threw a leg over the arm of his chair, then lit a cigarette.

"Why'd you tell Mattie I told you to fuck off?"

"Because you did, that's why."

"What're you, a little kid who goes running to mama? Can't you handle your own problems?" He spoke without inflection, as if he were merely seeking an explanation.

"I don't consider you a problem."

"No? So why tell Mattie?"

"Did you invite me in to have an argument?"

"No. I wondered why, if you had the balls to tell me to go to hell, you felt you had to tell her about it."

"I don't know why. Okay? We talk a lot. She probably asked me. I don't remember."

"Sure you don't want a beer?"

"Quite sure, thank you."

He got up, and she felt arbitrarily alarmed. But he said, "Want to hear something?" and relieved, she asked, "What've you got?"

"Mantovani," he said sarcastically.

"Swell!"

"*Please*! You've got your choice of the Dead, Pink Floyd, Led Zeppelin, Bob Marley, the Eagles, the Beatles, or Phil Collins."

"Phil Collins," she said.

He took the cassette from the stack, dropped it into the machine, adjusted the volume and the graphic equalizer levers, then returned to his chair.

"So," he said after taking a swallow of the Bud, "what're you hiding from?"

"Do I have to be hiding from something? Is that a prerequisite for my job?"

"It usually figures in somewhere. Why else work live-in for an old lady who rarely these days goes anywhere?"

"Is that how you think of Mattie?"

"It's how she is, not how I think of her. That's the reality of the situation. The last six of her secretaries either quit because they were bored, or were fired because Mattie found them boring."

"Really? I'm not bored. And I don't think she finds me boring."

"The makeup looks pretty good," he said, picking up his cigarette from the lip of the ashtray. "You should wear it more often."

"Thank you," she said priggishly, never at ease when alone with a man.

"You always so nervous?"

"I'm not nervous," she lied.

"Fine. You're not nervous. The haircut's decent, too. Another six months and Mattie'll have you turned out like a debutante."

"How d'you know it's Mattie and not me?"

" 'Cause for six months you thought you looked fine, frumping around like a real Granola grinder. Now, all of a sudden, you're into changes. Knowing Mattie, she said something. Probably pissed you off good. So to show her you're no chump, you went for the haircut and the new clothes, the makeup. Am I wrong?"

"No." She moistened her lips, wishing this didn't feel quite so confrontational.

"I'm sorry if I gave you the short end lately," he said. "Women make *me* nervous."

"You don't seem nervous now."

"I'm on my own turf now."

"So, you mean anything outside here is Mattie's turf?"

"Something like that."

"I see," she said, although she wasn't sure she did.

"So," he said, "how long's it been?"

"Since what?"

"Since you made out with anyone."

"God! None of your business."

"Myself, it's been about a hundred and ten years," he said calmly. "I figure it's maybe about a hundred for you."

Even though she was seriously discombobulated, she laughed. "Is there a point to this?"

"Sure," he said. "Why else did you come up here?"

"I came to thank you for the roses."

"You came because you think maybe you'd like to make out with me. And don't have a fit. If you think about it, if you're honest, you'll admit it's the truth. The only problem is you scare me."

"I scare you? Why?"

"Because it's been a hundred and ten years. I might not remember how. I wasn't all that hot at it anyway."

"Maybe," she said, "I should go."

"Nah, don't. We could give it a try, and if it's lousy, we'll forget it and go back to cursing each other out." He stubbed out his cigarette, put down the beer, then stood up and walked into the bedroom. "Come on," he said over his shoulder. "At least we know we're not going to give each other AIDS or some other disease that lasts a lifetime."

"God!" she whispered, looking at the door and thinking she should get the hell out of there. But even as she was thinking it, she'd already started moving toward the bedroom.

Eight

Matthew, why do you do it?" Mattie asked in a fervent tone. "Every time you come to visit you create a scene, do something guaranteed to upset everyone. You're forty-seven years old. Don't you think it's time you not only made an effort to act your age but also about time you started asking yourself what it is that triggers this hateful behavior?"

He gazed straight ahead, framing what he wanted to say, and she could easily see again the boy he'd been. She remembered that child so well it sometimes came as a shock to find this man occupying the place where little Matt should have been. She'd loved that boy without reservation, but even then Gideon Sylvester had been working his insidious way into a permanent place in the boy's brain, encouraging him to be on guard in case his older brother received more than his share of attention or affection.

"You said yourself you don't like me," he said at length. "How do you think that makes me feel?"

"I don't like you when you behave like a rowdy child," she corrected him. "It's probably why Dorothy finally gave up on you."

"I don't care about Dorothy," he said petulantly.

"That may be so, but she cared about you, Matthew. And for far longer than she probably should have, given the way you carried on if she dared even make a telephone call you didn't know about."

He shrugged, still not looking at her.

"I'm too old for this," she said tiredly. "When are you going to grow up and stop hanging on by your fingernails to a past that was *not* what you've painted it to be?"

"When," he countered, "are you going to admit you prefer Giddy to me?"

"Christ, Matthew! Considering the way you behave, I'd have to be a fool not to prefer the company of someone who doesn't walk into every situation prepared for a fight. Whatever his faults, and God knows he has them, Giddy does make an effort."

"Oh, and I don't?"

"You most definitely do not."

"Why should I? You don't trust me," he said bitterly.

"On the contrary, I do trust you. And I'm sure you're an excellent lawyer. I refuse, however, to allow you to control the family finances. If you ever had access to the money, you'd turn into an exact, living, replica of your father, and use that power to bully Giddy and me. I want you to stop all this once and for all. I mean it! And if you can't stop, then either see a psychiatrist, or stay away. I will not allow you to make a misery of whatever time I've got left."

"What does that mean?" he asked fearfully. "Are you trying to tell me something?"

"I'm trying to tell you," she said evenly, "that you're my child and no matter what you do I will always love you. But that does not mean I will blindly accept your childish behavior. I have enough crap to contend with without having to cope with your attempts to manipulate Giddy and me, or with your reprehensible pouting when you don't get what you think you want. You may not care for your brother's life-style—I have to admit there are times when I myself find it excessive—but it's not your place to judge anyone. He's never harmed a living soul in his life; he's kind and generous and even now he's prepared to accept you. Because he's your brother. Why the *hell* can't you stop posturing and accept people for being who they are, and stop condemning all of us because we don't meet your lofty standards?"

"He's an embarrassment," Matthew stated, "and a disgrace to his name."

"Oh, bullshit! If anyone's an embarrassment, it's you. Giddy is sincerely charming and makes a genuine effort with people. You, on the other hand, have turned out to be mean-minded and bigoted. You have, in fact, lived up to your late father's every expectation, I'm sorry to say."

"You're not ill, are you?" he asked.

"Would that make a difference?" she asked, perennially bewildered by the convoluted turns of his thinking.

"Of course! I mean, if there's something wrong, I have a right to know."

"There's something wrong, all right, and I've just told you what it is. My health is excellent, thank you. I want you to think about what I've said, Matthew. That little scene you staged before lunch today was unforgivable. And in front of Sarah! How dare you drag your sordid habits and suspicions out in front of an employee?"

"All I really wanted to know was if you've started working again."

"Then why didn't you *ask* me that?"

He lowered his eyes. "I guess I go about pretty well everything the wrong way."

"I agree. I don't entirely blame you. You and I both know how you came by a lot of your less salubrious tendencies, but now's your chance to stop. As it is, you've had far too many second chances already."

"I know," he admitted. "I tell myself, Okay, this time I won't let Giddy get on my nerves. I won't say anything to upset anybody. Then it all goes to hell."

"I don't want to discuss this any further. For years and years, at some point during every visit, we have this conversation. I'm sick to death of it."

The screen door opened and Giddy stepped out onto the verandah, his eyebrows lifting questioningly. Mattie stood up saying, "Giddy and I are going to take a walk before dinner. You're welcome to join us."

"Thanks," Matthew said. "I think I'll stay here and have a drink, if it's all the same to you."

"Oh, come on, dearie," Giddy said cajolingly. "A walk would do you good."

Matthew looked up at his older brother and saw only sincerity. Why couldn't he accept Giddy and enjoy his company? On a level far below that of his perpetual irritation was an area that housed an abiding affection for his brother. It had always been there. So why did it seem like such a betrayal of himself to show it either to Giddy or to their mother? "Thanks," he said, "but I think I'll take Mother's advice and use the time to think." He managed to smile, and at once, Giddy smiled back, showing his big healthy teeth.

"Maybe later, then," Giddy said, briefly placing a hand on Matthew's shoulder. "We could walk after dinner with two large spray cans of Off."

"Cutter's," Matthew laughed.

"And mosquito netting, dear."

"Don't forget the fly swatters."

"Absolutely," Giddy said, skipping down the stairs to join Mattie.

As Matthew watched, Giddy looped an arm around his mother's waist, and the two of them set off across the lawn toward the beach. Matthew fought down his immediate jealousy, reminding himself he'd been invited to accompany them. He'd chosen not to go. He could hardly blame Giddy for that, yet he wanted to. He'd been blaming Giddy for so many things for so long that it was a tremendous struggle simply to see things in any sort of accurate light. His father had encouraged him to see his older brother as an adversary, and Matthew had bought into it like a hot stock tip. The habit had taken root, had become so well entrenched that he doubted now if he'd ever be able to rid himself of the instinct to suspect every last one of Giddy's words and gestures.

He wanted a drink, but didn't dare to move for fear of losing his train of thought. It felt as if he were closing in on something that had eluded him for decades, and if he sat very still and concentrated hard it would come back to him. He sat, he concentrated, but nothing came. So he let his thoughts drift over his mother's ultimatum. One part of him wanted to say, To hell with it; he'd leave and never come back. That would be one way to rid himself forever of the many and complex emotions aroused in him by his family. Another, more imposing, part of him had to stay. His connection to his mother and brother were all he really had. Yes, Dorothy had been his wife for eleven years. But they had no children. Dorothy had said at the outset that she didn't want them and he'd been relieved to discover this, because in a moment of rare insight he'd realized he never wanted to inflict on a child of his what his own father had inflicted on him— filling his boyhood self with uncertainty, doubts, suspicions, even avarice. He hadn't ever really loved Dorothy. He'd wanted her as a partner, almost the same way he'd wanted his position as partner in the law firm. Love had had little to do with their marriage. It did, however, have everything to do with his dealings with his mother and brother.

That was it, of course. It was because he cared so much that he was forever on the outs with them. He cared, and he wanted them to reciprocate, but he wanted their reciprocation on his terms. He hated the fact that his brother preferred to make love to other men. He also envied Giddy his accomplished ease with and interest in strangers. He had to admit that, to his knowledge, Giddy had never inflicted his preferences on anyone, beyond being obviously, very visibly, gay. It made Matthew sweat with discomfort, but nobody else seemed to mind. Why was that? What did Giddy have that made him so much more acceptable, even as a homosexual, than he, Matthew?

No one in the family was straightforward, not even him, although he liked to think of himself as the only nonconflicted member. With a shake of his head, he had to acknowledge he was likely the one with the most inner conflict. Nothing was clear-cut or simple. All he knew was that he wanted to be able to return, and that he not only should make an effort to visit his mother more often but that he should also apply that to Giddy as well.

He looked up and saw the secretary, Sarah, come hurrying down the stairs at the side of the garage. He hadn't seen her go up, and wondered how long she'd been over there. He sat up straighter and watched her run toward the rear of the house. Was there something going on between her and Carl Harvey? If there was, and a borderline madman like Carl could get himself a woman, it was additional proof that everything his mother had said was true. Because Matthew hadn't been able to get any woman to go out with him more than once in the two and a half years since Dorothy had left. He sighed, badly wanting that drink now. He wished with all his heart he could learn how to do things differently. Even he was tired of Matthew Sylvester.

Feeling shaky, Sarah let herself in the kitchen door, tried to sound casual as she said hi to Bonnie, and continued through to the front of the house and up the stairs to her room. With the door closed and locked, she undressed and went into the bathroom to shower. She had less than half an hour before dinner. Mattie was rigid about promptness.

Once under the shower, she tried to make sense of what she'd done, of why she'd thought she might go to bed with Carl Harvey. She hadn't consciously given him any consideration as a potential partner. She'd reacted to his brusqueness, to his overt rudeness. But obviously other reactions, of which she'd been unaware, had been building. He was physically attractive, and an explicit invitation from an attractive man was clearly something she couldn't dismiss. That damned part of her that still believed people were meant to go off into the sunset in pairs, like passengers on the Ark, had taken her over, and at a time when she'd thought she was well past buying into any of the classic contemporary mythology regarding men and women and their roles. But she'd followed him into his bedroom and promptly lost whatever nerve she had.

He'd taken one look at her face and said, "I know. It's no good. We'll forget it. But I was going pretty good there myself for a few minutes." He gave her an apologetic and self-deprecating smile. "It's all memory work. You know? Stuff I knew how to do twenty years ago." He'd sat down on the end of his bed with his arms folded across his knees.

All at once, filled with sympathy, she'd sat down beside him and said, "That's about the truth of it. I have a better time in my head than I ever do in reality. It's so much easier in your head. You don't have to get into things with people; you don't have to explain anything, or do anything you don't want to do. I keep reminding myself how old I am, but I still keep thinking I'm only eighteen or twenty. I mean, these are the same eyes looking out at the world. I get the feeling, though, that the face surrounding the eyes is like the picture in Dorian Gray's attic; it's old and falling to pieces, but I'm not always aware of it."

He turned to look at her. "You see yourself as old?" he'd asked, his brows drawing together.

"Well, not when I'm with Mattie. With her, I feel about twelve, and fairly stupid. She has a way of making me feel naive and inexperienced. Maybe it's because she's so sure of everything. She knows what she wants and the way she wants it done, and that's intimidating. It probably shouldn't be, but it is. I think it's because, unlike most people, she doesn't futz around being polite. She comes straight out and tells you."

"That's what I like about her," he'd said, slowly straightening. "It's what I like a best about her, as a matter of fact. She's got standards, and she lets everybody know that. You don't seem especially disappointed."

"About this?" She'd looked around the darkened bedroom, then back at him with a slow smile. "To tell you the truth, I'm kind of relieved. You were right about its having been a hundred years. Back when I was fairly active sexually, I wouldn't have thought twice about it. But that was a long time ago, and I'm out of practice; self-conscious, I guess. That's what happens."

"You're pretty truthful," he'd said.

"Sometimes, but it's kind of hard to fake things once your clothes are off." She wrapped her arms around herself as if she had, in fact, taken off her clothes.

He laughed, and flopped back on the bed, folding his arms under his head.

"You want your beer?" she'd asked, looking toward the doorway.

He'd sat up at once. "This make you antsy?"

"Yes and no. I think I want to get to know you, but now I'm afraid we'll start something and I haven't had time to think about any of this."

"And you've changed your mind, but definitely."

"No. I've had a few mintues to think, and with me that's always dangerous."

"Dangerous?" He'd looked skeptical.

"Give me time to think and I'll change my mind for sure. I've been accused before of thinking too much."

"Oh, big sin!" he'd said sarcastically. "Jesus, that pisses me off! How the hell can somebody think *too much*? What the fuck does that mean, anyway?"

"My ex-husband used to say that all the time."

"He probably said it whenever he wanted to get laid and you weren't in the mood. Right?"

She blushed, but had to admit he was right. She liked him for having said that.

"Most guys are such assholes," he'd said digustedly, energetically rubbing his face with both hands.

"Do you still think of yourself as a 'trained killer'?" she'd asked him.

"I'm a little out of practice, but yeah. It's what they taught me to be. And I was very fucking good at it. Take a nineteen-year-old kid, train the hell out of him, then ship him off to a country he'd never even heard of until his friends started getting all gung-ho and enlisting, give him a few days to adjust to the climate, then start sending him into the jungle armed to the teeth and told to shoot anyone, man, woman, or child, who doesn't look right. And never mind thinking twice. Think twice and you'll probably buy it, so get the fuck out there and kill whatever moves. The only good part of the whole thing," he'd said bitterly, "was my being lucky enough not to get an Agent Orange bath, like a hell of a lot of my buddies. Don't know *how* I managed to miss that."

"Did you stay in touch with your buddies after you came back?"

He'd looked at her as if she were crazy. "I thought I'd come home and it'd be *over*. Who the hell wanted to hang out with a bunch of guys who were even more murderous than you were? I figured I'd go back to school, pick up where I left off, no sweat. What a fucking joke! I was on full-time alert. I still dream about looking at the trees and bushes, checking all sides, waiting for the firing to start. Somebody steps on a trip wire, that's the end of that sucker. But how come it was him and not you? Two feet to the right and you'd have been the one blown to shit. I didn't want to be in touch with the few other guys from my platoon who managed to live through it. I figured they were probably okay, living their lives, whatever. My head was fucked, but they were fine. Right? All these years later, I watch TV or read the papers, and I find out most of us are fucked but good. Great! That's very goddamned comforting. I still can't figure out how come I'm not one of the fifty-odd thousand guys who died over there. Bothers the hell out of me, trying to figure that one out."

"You're sorry you didn't die?" she'd asked in a shocked whisper.

"I'm not sorry. I just can't figure it out. It helps, you know, to have some idea why the law of averages decided to exempt you."

She didn't know what to say.

"Your old man didn't go?" he'd asked her.

She shook her head. "He got out of it. I'm not sure how."

"And what about you, sweetheart? Were you one of those long-haired flower children protesting the hell out of the war and spitting on the guys who didn't burn their draft cards?"

"I was in high school," she'd said, as if that explained her position.

"How old're you anyway?"

"Forty-one."

"Wait a minute," he said, doing mental calculations. "I'm forty-four. Yeah, okay. You'd have been, what? Sixteen? I guess that's about right. You don't look forty-one."

"I do to me."

"What the fuck do I know? Right?" He gave her a tight smile.

"You never married, Carl?"

"When? You figure out when I had time to do that!"

Stung, she'd said, "Sorry. But you've—seen women, haven't you?"

"Yeah, I've *seen women*. Not lately. Why'd you come in here?"

"I don't know. I suppose I wanted to make contact. Every so often, I feel totally out of touch. I start thinking other women are living with men, having babies, sleeping every night beside men. But I'm not. Does that mean I'm different, or undesirable? I wonder about things like that, now and then."

"You want a husband and kids?"

"No. I just want to feel wanted, I guess."

He'd smiled. "My intentions were in the right place."

"You have a nice smile. And you can actually talk, when you feel like it."

"Oh, I can talk, all right. Talk your fucking ear off. After a while, I get very goddamned repetitious."

"Not so far."

"You're starting to get to me," he'd said, not smiling now.

"What d'you mean?"

"I mean, maybe you should get out of here now before I put a move on you."

She'd felt all at once overheated. If she stayed, they'd grapple. She thought about how it might be to take off her clothes and lie down beside him and it scared her. "Okay," she'd said, her voice going thick. "Maybe you're right."

"Doesn't mean we can't talk again sometime," he'd said, as she'd got to her feet.

"No, I'd like that a lot."

"After you go, I'll probably dream about taking your clothes off," he'd said as she went to the door. "I'll be kicking myself for not doing it now."

Again she was lost for words. "Maybe," she'd said carefully, "we'll get around to it another time. It's not as if there's a deadline hanging over us."

He walked over to her. "You ask too fucking many questions," he'd said softly, coming right up to her. "But I kind of like you."

"I kind of like you, too," she'd said nervously, looking at his mouth.

He lowered his head as if he were going to kiss her, then stopped, and stepped back from her. She waited a moment, then left, her heart racing.

As she emerged now from the shower she asked herself what the hell she'd been doing. If he'd kissed her, she'd have been out of her clothes and into his bed like a shot. She was going to have to be careful. Things could get very complicated.

Mattie and her two sons were in the living room, finishing their predinner drinks when Sarah came down.

"Sorry," she apologized. "I lost track of the time."

Both men stood as she entered, and she said, "Please sit down. I hope I haven't kept you waiting too long."

"Have a drink, my dear," Mattie said, watching Sarah closely.

"No, thanks." Sarah went to occupy the same chair she'd taken before lunch, noticing at once that the mood tonight was lighter, even pleasant. She saw that Matthew appeared relaxed. What had happened? she wondered.

"I was just telling Mother and Matthew about this utterly *marvelous* movie I saw on the box the other night," Giddy said. "But I can't for the *life* of me remember the name. Maybe you know it, Sarah. Do you like movies?"

"Yes, I do, a lot."

"Oh, wonderful! This was about the Kennedy assassination, and how it had been plotted by all these businessmen."

"*Executive Action,*" she said. "Wasn't it terrific?"

"You're *brilliant!*" he exclaimed. "It's been driving me *wild,* trying to remember."

"I'd like to see that," Matthew said. "It sounds very intriguing."

"You can rent it, my dear," Giddy told him. "I'll give you the name of the place where I rent my movies, if your place doesn't have it."

"Okay, maybe I'll do that."

"Did you and Carl have a nice chat?" Mattie asked Sarah with a meaningful smile.

Brazening it out, Sarah said, "We did, actually. He was telling me about Vietnam."

"Poor Carl," Giddy said. "He's had such a dreadful time. He worked for me briefly after he got home."

"He did?" Sarah asked with interest.

"I had him on the door. I'm afraid it didn't work out."

"Why not?" she asked.

To her surprise, Matthew chose to answer for his brother. "Carl got a bit rough with some of Giddy's 'customers.' "

Giddy shot an angry look at his brother. It was the first time Sarah had seen him look anything but pleasant. "Some of my customers," he said carefully, enunciating every word with deliberation, "got a bit rough with Carl."

"That is *not* the way *I* heard it," Matthew said.

"I don't *care* what you heard," Giddy said, then turned back to Sarah. "We had an element in the club at the time that took political exception to Carl's status as a veteran. They had no right to exercise themselves at his expense. It was most unfortunate, but I had to let Carl go, really for his sake. I *hated* to do it. I've known him all his life, you know. And he's always been one of my particularly favorite people."

"Favorite how?" Matthew asked with an edge to his voice.

"Favorite friend," Giddy said patiently. "*Straight* friend," he added. "I do have them, you know, Matthew, in spite of your belief to the contrary. Some of my best friends are heterosexuals." Once again turning to Sarah, he said, "He was the dearest little boy, wonderfully imaginative, and quite gifted. Wasn't he, my darling?" he asked Mattie for corroboration.

"Very gifted," she confirmed. "I really thought he'd follow in his grandfather's footsteps. But that damned war put an end to it. Carl was never the same after." Her eyes returned to Sarah, but this time she seemed to be inviting Sarah to participate in some covert sort of salvage operation.

In the hope of clarifying her position, Sarah said, "He didn't talk about any of that. We just talked in general."

Bonnie came in to say dinner was ready.

Mattie fell back to walk with Sarah into the dining room. "He's well worth the effort," she whispered, "if you're interested."

Sarah looked into the old woman's eyes. "Are you pimping for him?" she whispered back.

Amused, Mattie laughed. "Don't be such a prude!" she said. "You and I will talk more about this later, my dear."

Nine

Late that night, after everyone else had gone to bed, Mattie sat on the balcony outside her bedroom, wondering if Matthew had actually taken heed of what she'd said to him. There could be no question of the effort he'd made to join into the conversation without jumping viciously on every word that came out of Giddy's mouth. For once, he'd allowed his sense of humor to show. It was his one truly redeeming feature. Her sons had always had the ability to amuse one another, but in recent years Matthew's antagonism toward both her and his older brother had displaced the humor. It was heartening to know he hadn't lost it altogether. There might still be some hope for him, if he could only keep on making a concerted effort.

And dear Giddy seemed forever anxious to have returned to him the little brother he'd so doted on and protected during their childhood. Goddamned Gideon Sylvester had thrived on dissension, had instigated it whenever possible. The man had only ever loved one person completely: himself.

After knocking herself clean out by marching into the closet door, she returned to consciousness to find Gideon Sylvester, of all people, ministering to her with an expression of great concern. It so upset and discomfited her not only to have disgraced herself on such a somber occasion but also to find herself being tended to by a man she loathed that she left the Stoughton apartment as soon as she was able to stand. She stopped only long enough to tell Juliet and Esther she was leaving, then she rushed home.

During the next few days she seethed with embarrassment and anger every time she recalled the incident, and prayed when she went to the next Friday's open house at the Harveys that that hateful Sylvester person wouldn't be there. She was immensely relieved, upon arriving, to find only the familiar Regulars. She didn't know what she'd have done if that man had been there. She wanted nothing to interfere with her friendship with the Harveys and her coterie of new friends. They'd become more of a family to her than her own parents and sisters had ever been, and it made her feel quite desperate to think that poor Otter's introduction of Gideon Sylvester into the Regulars might jeopardize her participation in the group.

Naturally, only a week after his funeral, the talk initially that evening was of Otter and the latest news of his family, who'd given up the Park Avenue apartment. His widow and three children had gone back to Hartford, to live in the guest house on Otter's parents' estate.

"If they have so much money," Mattie wanted to know, "why didn't they help him?"

"Oh, honey," Esther Loftus said, "he didn't want anyone to know what a mess he got himself into. He'd *never* have gone begging to his father. Male pride, you know."

"Well, that makes sense," Mattie said. "I hadn't thought of that. I certainly wouldn't go within a mile of my family with a problem."

"By the way," Esther said, "you know you were telling me about a room that's going where you live? Well, it just so happens I ran into Gideon Sylvester a few days back and he was saying he was looking for a place, so I sent him down to see your landlady."

"You didn't!" Mattie exclaimed.

"Well, sure. Why not?"

"He didn't take it, did he?" she asked. As far as she knew, her former room was still unoccupied.

"Yeah, he did," Esther said. "Snapped it right up."

"Oh, hell!" Mattie muttered. There was no way she'd ever again feel comfortable in that house, knowing she could run into that abominable man at any time. "I wish you'd told me."

"But you said to ask around," Esther said with an expression of bruised innocence.

"I know," Mattie relented. She liked Esther too much to be cross with her. Besides, it was her own fault. She hadn't told Esther not to tell him. "I thought he was well off," she said. "Why would he be interested in my old room?"

"His *family's* well off," Esther corrected her. "At least, they were. Who knows anymore who's got what? All I know is he said he needed to move. I told him about your place and he went right down there and rented it on the spot. That was last weekend. I haven't talked to him since, so I don't know if he's actually moved in yet."

Mattie was so distraught by this news she couldn't eat that night's offering of corned beef and cabbage with boiled potatoes. She did accept a glass of bathtub gin Danny Briggs offered, and despite its foully medicinal taste, drank it down and felt somewhat better.

"What's got you down, kid?" Danny asked, perching on the arm of the sofa beside her.

"Oh, nothing," she said, reluctant to have known her great antipathy for a man she couldn't seem to get away from. She disliked complaining, believing it made people unattractive. Besides, there wasn't much she could do about the situation, except move. And she refused to do that. She'd be damned if she'd let that fool Sylvester force her out of her swell new apartment. She'd simply have to be careful going in and out of the house, and try to avoid running into him.

"Are you all right, Mattie?" Hughie asked her some time later. "You look a little sad."

She suppressed a sudden desire to march him into the bathroom and brush his teeth for him, smiled instead, and said, "I'm okay, Hughie. Just things in general lately. You know how it is."

He nodded. "Going from bad to worse every day," he observed. "But if I can ever help out, just let me know."

From then on, any time she had to do some chore for Mrs. Webster, she worked at double quick time to do the job and get back to her apartment. She lived for several weeks in a state of dread. Every time she had to lug the heavy garbage cans out to the street or sweep the front steps, her heart racketed with fear that she'd encounter Gideon Sylvester. Each day before leaving for work or upon returning home, she scanned the hallways, then flew out of the building, feeling all the while as if she'd narrowly avoided danger in the form of Gideon Sylvester.

The overall effect of this was to make her progressively more furious. It was bad enough that she had to be on her guard every time she went to the Harveys, in case he might be there, but to have to creep in and out of her own home drove her wild. Her outrage built to such a pitch that when he finally did run into her—literally, as she was vigorously sweeping the front steps—she simply exploded.

"WHY CAN'T YOU LEAVE ME ALONE?" she demanded of the startled man. "I HATE you! Don't you UNDERSTAND that?"

He stood blinking at her for a few seconds, then tipped his hat, sidestepped neatly around her, and continued on his way inside.

Incensed, both hands wrapped around the broom handle as if around his throat, she stood glaring at his retreating figure. Well, at least, she told herself, it had finally happened, so she could stop dreading it. She finished the steps, returned inside, stowed the broom in the closet under the stairs, and stormed up to her apartment. She was so agitated, however, she couldn't sit still and, finally, had to get out. She gathered her sketching equipment, threw on her coat, and set off.

She walked for miles, trying to work off some of her irate energy, and wound up near her family's home on Seventy-first Street. Feeling a residual boldness after the confrontation with Gideon Sylvester, she purposefully turned into the street and walked toward the house, fully expecting to run into some member of her family. Nothing happened. The house looked as it always had, the front windows concealed by curtains, the brass knocker and mail slot highly polished. Defiantly she stood on the sidewalk in front of the house for several minutes, hoping grimly that her mother or father might emerge. She'd have loved a showdown, right there in the street. But the door remained closed, and not one of the curtains so much as twitched. She wasn't going to get a blessed thing out of this.

Crossing the street to enhance her perspective, she was all at once taken by the idea of drawing the house. She had, after all, spent the first seventeen years of her life in that dwelling. It was a part of her history and, therefore, a suitable subject to be entered into her permanent record.

Throughout the time she stood on the opposite side of the street sketching the details of the four-story brick building that had once been her home, she expected to see the front door fling open and one of the staff, at her parents' request, come out and tell her to be on her way. Nothing of the sort occurred. What did take place, to her chagrin, was a slow welling-up inside her of a sense of loss. Despite what she considered to be their many failings, and their unforgivable cruelty in evicting her, the people who lived in that house were nevertheless her parents. She didn't miss them so much as she momentarily missed the comfort and security she'd had as a member of the family. They'd fed and dressed her; they'd sheltered and educated her (however grudgingly), and all of that had ended forever, because she'd made one mistake. She didn't regret her experience with Avery Moon. After all, he had, as promised, helped her explore her potential. And now that it had been well and truly explored, she at least knew that no man would ever take better than second place in her life. Her art would always come first, and it might not have been as much of a comfort as once again having her rightful place in the family, but it was a comfort nonetheless.

Her sketch completed, she set off back downtown to Gramercy Park, glad she'd ventured out. The look at her old home had helped confirm her feelings about a number of things. And all she'd really lost in being disowned was money. She had some now, thanks to her own efforts, and soon, according to Nicholas Harvey, she'd be ready to start thinking about attempting to sell some of her paintings.

She arrived home considerably calmer than when she'd left, and didn't survey the street or the hallways but went chin-high straight to the front door and let herself in, then marched boldly up the stairs and into her apartment. Gideon Sylvester had better keep out of her way, if he knew what was good for him.

The next time she saw that impossible man was at the Museum of Modern Art, on an evening in mid-April. She'd gone to see the exhibit advertised as "46 Painters and Sculptors Under 35 Years Old," and was viewing the works at a leisurely pace when a voice from behind her said, "It would seem we're doomed to keep meeting."

She turned to see him, hat in hand, regarding her warily, and at once she asked, "Did you follow me here?"

At this, he laughed and said, "You overestimate your importance, Miss Harrison. Why on earth would I be following you?"

"Well, what're you doing here?"

"I came to see," he said with a languid hand gesture, "what my contemporaries are up to these days."

"Oh!"

"This is my second look," he said with a slight frown. "Some of it's very damned good."

"Yes, it is," she agreed icily, prepared to move on.

"Look," he said. "Could we call a truce? We seem to have started off on the wrong foot. Why not let me buy you a cup of coffee, and let's see if we can't start again."

Her instinct was to say no, but he was making such an obvious effort to be friendly that she had to wonder if she hadn't perhaps been somewhat hasty in her judgment of him.

"I thought you were having financial problems."

"Oh, I am," he said cheerfully. "But my monthly check just came in, so I won't be destitute again for at least another two weeks."

"What monthly check?" she asked, falling into step with him as he headed toward the museum entrance.

"I'm a remittance man. Didn't you know?"

"What's that?"

With a laugh, he said, "I'm someone they pay to stay away."

"Is that a joke?"

"Of course it is," he replied, holding the door open for her. "You are the most serious young lady I've ever met."

"There's nothing wrong with being serious."

"There is if it's all you ever are." He positioned the fedora on his head and took her arm to direct her down West Fifty-third Street. She made a point of shaking herself free of him, which prompted him to say, "Sorry. Merely a habit. You have to remember I'm accustomed to escorting three older sisters and a fairly redoubtable mother. I was instructed from a very early age always to take a lady's arm and, of course, to walk on the outside when on the city streets. Now that I think of it," he said with an amused air, "it must have made quite the picture, stocky little Master Sylvester escorting the ladies of his family along the thoroughfares of downtown Hartford." He launched into another of his wickedly funny family vignettes and she completely forgot her aversion to him, so taken was she by his storytelling skill.

"Our most disastrous family outing," he told her, "was the after-noon Father brought home the new touring car and insisting on taking everyone for a drive. Mother sat up front, proudly wearing the new duster and goggles he'd bought for her, and the four of us children crowded into the back. Somewhere along the way Emily managed to fall out of the car. But since my two other sisters and I were giving Emily the silent treatment that day—she having told terrible tales which resulted in a yet another horrendous Lifebuoy mouthwash—we decided to say nothing.

"It was some time before Mother turned and realized Emily was missing. At which point all hell broke loose. Mother insisted Father turn the car around, and we drove back looking for Emily, who seemed to have vanished off the face of the earth.

"Privately, I hoped she was gone forever. I had plans for taking over her room, which had a window, you see, that overlooked the side porch. From the roof of the porch, it was very easy to lower one's self to the side railing and, from there, merely a three or four foot drop to the grass. A perfect escape route. Besides, Emily was a tattletale and far too chubby to suit me. So while my mother and two other sisters set up a godawful wailing, bemoaning poor Emily's possible fate at the hands of indiscriminate white slavers, I sat back pleased as punch, anxious to get home and start removing Emily's frocks from the closets.

"Sadly, what I got upon arriving home, was a deafening whack across the ear from my father, who accused me—justifiably, I'm ashamed to say—of pushing dear Emily from a moving vehicle. The hapless little angel had been rescued by our neighbor, father's good friend and golfing partner, Scuddy Rowlands, who just happened to be driving along behind us when he saw chunky old Emily come bouncing out of our car. He stopped, made sure she hadn't suffered any serious injuries, and called out to Father to stop. But of course Father didn't hear, and drove on. So good Mr. Rowlands took dear hysterical Emily back to his house, where Mrs. Rowlands commiserated with Emily over her ghastly misadventure and comforted her with lemonade and sugar cookies until we returned home.

"I must say I couldn't hear properly for several days after. And I was enormously miffed at the loss of my planned escape route. But since Georgina and Nancy were also punished, and didn't take it nearly so well as I did, I wasn't as upset as I might have been. Emily did have a few quite wondrous bruises which she displayed for us later that evening, lifting her nightgown to show us the evidence of her injuries marring the perfection of her chubby little thighs and buttocks. All in all," he wound down, "I really did enjoy myself. Although from that day to this, Scuddy Rowlands has referred to me as Bad Little Buddy Sylvester."

"You were a monster, from the sound of it," Mattie said with a smile.

"If you'd been a boy who had to grow up with those four women, you'd have been a monster too, purely in self-defense. You've got to stand up for yourself, or you'll wind up spending your entire child-hood dressed in your sister's clothes, having them tying your hair into rag curls. It was a question of honor."

By this time, they were seated at the counter in a coffee shop with mugs of steaming coffee before them.

"Why," he asked, "were you so het up at dear Otter's funeral?"

"Because I don't think it was your place to thank people for coming."

"You may have a point," he allowed, "but you must understand that Otter and I were friends all our lives. We were as close as brothers. I always felt I *was* a part of his family."

"Well," she said, "maybe I was wrong. I was very upset."

"We all were. I still can't believe he's gone."

"Why did he do it?" she asked.

"I suppose because he didn't think he'd ever be able to recoup his losses. He'd invested a fortune in the market, and drastically overex-tended himself buying on margin. The only assets he had were the apartment and his paintings and some life insurance. I think he thought the only possible answer was suicide. His father would've bailed him out, but Otter couldn't bring himself to ask. I can understand that."

Recalling what Esther had said, and anxious to hear more on this particular theme, she said, "Can you? Why?"

"Because I'd be damned if I'd go begging to my father if I was in trouble. Which, in a way, I suppose I am."

"How are you in trouble?"

"Oh," he sighed. "I hate to bore you with that nonsense."

"Go ahead," she insisted, "bore me."

"It's ridiculous, really. In order not to have to pay Lydia monthly for heaven only knows how long, I agreed to a lump settlement. It fairly well cleaned me out."

"Who's Lydia?"

"My former wife," he said, the corners of his mouth turning down. "My childhood folly. We were married at nineteen. The divorce was finalized early last December. Which was why, you see, I was in fairly desperate need of a place to live."

"How long were you married?"

"Ten years, if you can believe it. I certainly can't. I don't know what possessed either one of us, to tell the truth. I think partly it was because the families expected it. I was still in school, for God's sake. But Lydia was bound and determined, and I never have been good at saying no to women, so we got married. She's rich as Croesus, but insisted on the settlement out of spite. She knew she was cleaning me out, but she didn't care. It was a big mistake. I should've agreed to the monthly alimony payments. My lawyer told me to, but I wanted it over, and I hated the idea of having to write her name on a check every month, possibly for years. Now, of course, I can see how foolish I was. The payments would have stopped if she remarried. And, naturally, she remarried within minutes of the divorce. So, here I am, living on the monthly checks from my grandfather's trust, and trying like hell to get enough paintings together for a show."

"You're going to have a show?" she asked, her interest aroused.

"There's a gallery that's willing, if I can get the work done."

"I'd like to see your paintings," she told him. "Are you any good?"

"Well, naturally, I think so." He pulled himself erect, as if she'd challenged his manhood. "You're more than welcome to come up and have a look anytime you like."

"I might just do that."

"All right," he agreed, "but only if you return the favor. I've heard you're very talented."

"Who'd you hear that from?"

"Otter, for one. Nick Harvey, for another."

"Really?" she said, pleased.

"Yes, really. And do you think you're any good?"

"I am," she stated categorically, "very good indeed. One day, I'll be on exhibit at the Metropolitan, or the Modern Art. And it won't be in a show with forty-five others, either. I'll have my own exhibition, like Charles Burchfield, or Edward Hopper. Did you *see* Hopper's *Lighthouse at Two Lights*? He's wonderful, really wonderful."

"Who else do you think is wonderful?" he asked, again looking amused.

"Are you poking fun at me?" She looked at him with eyes narrowed.

"Not in the least," he said quickly. "Why are you so suspicious?"

"Because I am, that's why."

"You shouldn't be."

"You don't think so, huh?"

"No, I don't."

"Well," she sniffed. "A fat lot you know." She put money on the counter to pay for the coffees, and at once he protested.

"It was supposed to be my treat, Miss Harrison," he reminded her.

"Mattie," she corrected him. "And after that big sob story, you don't really think I'm going to let you pay for my coffee, do you?"

"Big sob story?"

"What would you call it? You're such a rube you get married at nineteen, then get cleaned out so you can end the whole thing. That's a sob story, buster, if ever I heard one. And, say! How much is that monthly check, anyway?"

"A fair amount, really. Sixty dollars."

"In that case," she said, retrieving her money from the counter, "you can pay for the coffee."

With a shake of his head, he reached into his pocket.

That same evening he invited her to come up and look at his paintings. Her curiosity outweighing her reluctance to be trapped alone in a small room with him, she agreed, and climbed the stairs to see if his work lived up to his boastful claims.

Proudly, he showed her half a dozen canvases, and waited for her comments. He wasn't without talent, she thought, but he simply had no eye. The result of this was that his paintings were uninspired but adeptly rendered technical exercises. For some reason, instead of feeling good about this, it made her sad. She wanted to be able to compliment him because he was so manifestly earnest about being an artist, but she was incapable of lying. The most she could do was comment on his use of color, which was effective, and on his sense of perspective, which was very good. But she couldn't, with any honesty, praise any of what she saw.

During those minutes while she examined his oil paintings, she lost her anger with him. It was replaced by sadness and even pity. She wanted to advise him to give it up, to abandon hope of ever being a successful artist, because he lacked a distinctive view that would facilitate that success. The man's vision was so ordinary, so devoid of insight, it was fairly heartbreaking.

"You have good technique," she said quietly.

"Thank you," he replied, complimented.

"Well, it's good of you to let me see all this," she said, and moved to go.

"When will you show me your work?" he asked enthusiastically.

"Oh, sometime," she said, purposely vague, already at the door. "Thank you for the coffee, Mr. Sylvester."

"Gideon."

"Yes." She got the door open, anxious to put some distance between herself and this man she now believed to be lamentably deluded.

"Mattie?" Sarah stood in the doorway, clad in an old chenille bathrobe.

"What?" Mattie growled.

"Are you all right? Would you like some company?"

"I am perfectly all right. Why aren't you sleeping?"

"I will be in a minute, if you don't want company."

"Not tonight, Sarah," she said more quietly. "I'll be going to bed myself when I finish this cigarette."

"All right," Sarah said. "Just thought I'd ask."

When Mattie, as usual, failed to reply, Sarah left and returned to her own room.

Mattie took a last puff on her cigarette, thinking pity was a god-damned perfidious sentiment that led otherwise sensible people to do some remarkably stupid things.

Ten

Before going back to her bed, Sarah stood for a time looking out the window. Mattie's insomnia seemed to be contagious. Ever since Sarah had discovered that the old woman spent most of every night out on the balcony she'd felt a need to keep herself available, in case Mattie wanted company. And even on those nights when Sarah went to sleep at a reasonably early hour she found herself waking at two or three, to tiptoe down the hall to see if Mattie's door was open. If it was, Mattie was sure to be awake and sitting on the balcony. If it was closed, Sarah crept back to her bed. A set of signals was being established.

As she stood looking out the window, she realized with a jolt that Carl was down there at the edge of one of the flower beds. Fully dressed in dark clothing, he stood very still for several minutes. Then he crossed the lawn, his head turning as he scanned the area, to position himself on the far side, near the tall hedge that ran the length of the property line. He stopped, blending into the scenery, then moved on again after a time, out of sight.

He was obviously patrolling the house. She wondered if he did this every night and if it was a holdover from his war experiences. There was something terribly touching about his vigilant surveillance, and she debated the wisdom of going down to talk to him. She decided it would be an invasion, something he wouldn't in the least appreciate. So she threw off her robe and climbed into bed, unable to shake the image of that solitary figure in the dark. She wondered what he thought about out there on his rounds, if he was afraid as he stalked the perimeters, blending with the shadows. It made her lonely to think that while the household slept that sad angry man performed his protective service. Perhaps, she thought, turning on her side and bunching the too-soft pillow under her head, she'd go to talk to him again sometime tomorrow, after Giddy and Matthew left.

Giddy knocked on his younger brother's door, opened it, and entered to say to a groggy Matthew, "Come on. Let's go for an early morning swim, the way we used to."

For a few seconds, Matthew was caught up in a revival of his boyhood, stirred by an excitement he hadn't felt for decades. Throwing back the bedclothes, he said, "Okay. Let's!" and hurried to pull on his trunks.

Laughing, with an unexpected sense of freedom, Matthew went running across the wet lawn with his brother, in exact duplication of a scene that had taken place hundreds of times during their childhood summers. Towels draped around their necks, they pounded across the lawn and down to the beach. Dropping the towels, they glanced at each other then, whooping loudly, charged into the gelid water. The shock of it made Matthew's heart feel as if it might stop beating, but he submerged, then surfaced to see Giddy swimming alongside him as they headed away from the shore.

Giddy looked over now and again at his brother swimming at his side and felt a renewal of the hope he had every time they returned to the island that this time they'd find a route back to the closeness they'd had as boys when they'd shared their every secret and almost every thought. He knew all too well that what lay between them was the corpse of their father, and their very different feelings about the man who'd sired them. Giddy couldn't think of the man without an inner sinking sensation very like despair. But Matthew was given to rhapsodizing about the old shit, as if he'd been the absolute essence of perfect fatherhood. What was pathetic in the extreme about this was that, when pressed, Matt would admit to having hated the man. Only strangers, and possibly Bonnie, had ever really liked Gideon Sylvester. Those who'd known him intimately, including his three sisters, his wife, and his two sons, had tried to maintain a healthy distance from what they knew to be his dangerous charm. Experience had proved to both his sons that a Gideon who came bearing gifts was a Gideon who'd exact a price at some later date for what he'd given.

What had always been best about the summers they'd spent here on the island was that, for the most part, their father had chosen to go to New York while they were here. He'd make occasional appearances, stay for a day or two, then leave on some vague errand or other. Then Giddy and Matt had had the run of the place; they'd spent hours sailing together on the Bullseye, or on the tennis court down at the South End club. They'd been so happy, all those years ago, and Giddy was convinced they could somehow regenerate the closeness they'd had back then, if only he could find some graphic way to induce Matt to remember. He was determined to get it back, and prepared to do almost anything to achieve it.

Alerted by the laughter, Mattie stepped out onto the balcony and stood at the railing, breaking into a smile at the sight of her sons racing into the low breakers. She couldn't remember how long it had been since she'd seen the two of them cavorting together, and it was encouraging to see it again now. Lighting a cigarette, she continued to stand watching as Matthew and Giddy gave up the race and floated in place, laughing, talking. They bobbed about in the water for several minutes, then began to swim back to shore at a leisurely pace, their arms cutting the water in unison. It was an atypically clear morning and she was able to watch as they came running out of the water for their towels. Giddy said something and Matthew laughed so loudly she was able to hear him all the way up at the house. They started back and she returned inside to dress.

She and Sarah were already at the table when Giddy and Matthew came in.

"Enjoy your swim?" Mattie asked. "It certainly *sounded* as if you did."

"My darling," Giddy said, sliding into his chair, "is that meant to be one of your *infamous* cryptic remarks?"

"It was colder than hell," Matthew said.

"Dearie, that's a mixed metaphor," Giddy teased.

"Okay, fine. Colder than . . . what?"

"It was very goddamned cold!" Giddy declared.

"I thought for a moment there I was paralyzed," Matthew admitted. "I had this vision of me sinking like a rock because I couldn't move my arms and legs." He reached for the toast, smiling happily. "Just like the old days, huh, Gid?"

"Absolutely," Giddy agreed. "And I'd never let you sink, dear heart," he said, offering Sarah the platter of scrambled eggs with smoked salmon. "Back in our tawdry youth, I'd start thinking about the island around the beginning of May, counting down the days until school was out and we could come here. We had a whole other life here," he explained to Sarah in a completely unaffected voice as he took two sausages before passing the dish. "There were all the kids we only saw in the summer. Remember, Matt? The Crowell kids, and the Duncans, the Roths, the Jacobs. I have no idea where most of them are now."

"I see Kibbie Crowell every so often," Matthew said. "And I ran into Rudy Roth at the Yale Club a year or so ago. Rudy's on The Street, you know."

"Donnie Duncan married the Jacobs girl," Mattie contributed. "Donnie died in a boating accident, must be five years ago."

"I didn't know that," Giddy said sadly. "He was a hell of a nice kid, Donnie. That's a damned shame. Donnie," he told Sarah, "was this redheaded, freckle-faced kid, and everybody who saw him assumed he was our brother because he looked more like Mattie than either of us did."

"It feels like a million years ago," Matthew said, fairly stricken by what Giddy had said about never letting him sink. It was such a typical Giddy thing to say, heartfelt and brotherly. "We raced back and forth all over the island every summer. We had the boats, and the barbecues, the picnics on the beach."

"And the *games!*" Giddy exclaimed. "The games we invented. Remember, Matt? There was Shipwrecked, and Ace Explorers, and Spy Mission. God! We had fun."

"We sure did," Matthew agreed quietly, gazing at his plate. "I'd forgotten the games. How could I forget them?"

"You were busy doing other things," Sarah said, feeling a sudden sympathy for the man. "You were going to school, getting married, having a career. We all forget a lot of the things we did as kids."

"Mother doesn't," Matthew said, looking over at her. "Do you? You never forget a thing."

"It isn't necessarily a blessing, Matthew," she said, pouring herself more coffee. "There are things I'd be just as happy to forget, I promise you."

"I must make a note to get in touch with some of those people," Giddy said. "We could have a reunion bash. Wouldn't that be *divine*? Why don't we get together sometime this week and see how many of them we can track down?"

"This week isn't good for me," Matthew said.

"Oh! Too bad. Well, maybe next week."

Matthew read the letdown on his brother's face, and wondered why he invariably shied away from Giddy's invitations to get together. "On second thought," he said, and saw the eagerness rush back into Giddy's features, "I may be able to find some time. Let's talk tomorrow after I get to the office and have a chance to look at my diary."

"Wonderful! Even if we don't pull off a bash," Giddy said, "maybe you and I could have dinner. There are so many sensational new places I've discovered."

Watching the interchange between the two brothers, Sarah realized they were two lonely middle-aged men who couldn't quite seem to find their way back together. She wished she knew of something to say or do that would facilitate that. Despite their differences, it was impossible to ignore their underlying affection for one another.

★   ★   ★

"You were very kind to Matthew," Mattie said that afternoon when her sons had gone. "Why?"

"Do you suspect me of having ulterior motives?" Sarah asked.

"I'm not suggesting anything of the sort. I'm wondering why you made such an effort with him."

"I guess because he's so unhappy. I felt sorry for both of them, to tell the truth. Do you think they'll get together?"

"It's doubtful. But at least Matthew made an effort. I just hope he keeps his promise to call Giddy tomorrow. Giddy's such a child about Matthew. He'll be crushed if Matthew doesn't call. Then he'll phone me up to cry on my shoulder and go down the list of every possible sin he might have committed against Matthew. He's always been devoted to Matthew, and Matthew seems to thrive on letting him down. Although, I must say, this time there appeared to be less than his usual brimming measure of antagonism."

"So maybe this time will be different."

"You're an optimist," Mattie accused.

"So shoot me! I believe things will turn out well. What's wrong with that?"

"Tell me! Just how many times, in your critically limited experience, have things *actually* turned out well?"

"Quite a few. Why are *you* such a pessimist?"

"I most certainly am not a pessimist. I've lived a very long time and it's been my experience that most people let you down. That is simply the way things are."

"I don't believe that," Sarah said with feeling.

"In the end," Mattie insisted, "the majority of people you meet in a lifetime will let you down. Some in small ways, and some in critical ways. If you're smart, you learn to treasure the few people you meet who are capable of caring without judging, who don't harbor secret resentments. They're few and far between, the ones with open hearts. The rest of them," she said bitterly, "clutter up your life for a time and then, when you least expect it, they get very red in the face, very self-righteous, and cite a list of grievances they've had against you for years."

"God! That's awful!"

"In time you learn to be philosophical. Otherwise, you die."

Sarah studied Mattie's profile, wondering if Mattie had had the experiences she'd described because of the type of woman she was. She didn't think Mattie had probably changed very much over the years, and most people would, to Sarah's mind, find her hard to take, because she was strong-minded, willful, and only infrequently given to praising others. But these were qualities Sarah was coming to admire more each day. And Carl claimed to like the old woman precisely because she was this way.

Mattie lit a cigarette as Carl drove the town car to the front of the garage, then got out. Removing the cap he wore whenever driving a member of the family or their guests, he blotted his forehead on his sleeve, tossed the cap onto the front seat of the car and came over.

"Anything else need doing?" he asked Mattie, standing with a foot on the verandah steps.

"Not a thing," she said.

"Okay. I'll just hose the dust off the car and put 'er away." He turned and went off.

"He's very definitely interested in you," Mattie said, turning to Sarah with lifted eyebrows.

Sarah laughed. "You're a naughty-minded old woman!"

Mattie gave her a crooked smile and said, "My memory's as good as the next person's."

"I'm sure it is, but what's that got to do with anything?"

"Only everything," Mattie said enigmatically.

"Are you ever going to tell me how Carl's grandfather died?"

"Of old age. I dislike stories out of sequence."

"Does that mean you intend to tell me the whole thing?"

Mattie smartly tapped the ash from her cigarette. "You're playing the newborn bird again."

"I'm probably the best audience you've ever had."

"I don't know about the best. Certainly one of the most argumentative."

"That's why you like me." Sarah grinned.

"Did I say that?"

"Yes, you did, in so many words."

Mattie sniffed. "I don't remember that."

"So much for your famous memory."

"Do you know how few people have green eyes?" Mattie asked her.

"No. How many?" Sarah replied deadpan.

"Jesus!" Mattie laughed loudly. "You can be very funny."

"So can you. As I recall, when we last left Little Mattie, she'd just walked into an open closet door and knocked herself out cold."

"What an exit!" Mattie shook her head. "That has to be, truly, one of the single most humiliating moments of my entire life." She laughed again, then turned toward the beach.

She didn't want to show Gideon Sylvester her paintings. There were a number of reasons, but primarily the idea of showing them to him made her feel guilty. The guilt came as a result of knowing she was a superior artist by far, and he'd be bound to see that. She had no idea how he might react to this discovery, but she preferred not to know. She no longer hated him, and she had no interest in hurting anyone intentionally, even someone whose position on the periphery of her life was not an altogether clear one. He wasn't a friend; she didn't know him well enough to categorize him as one. But he was more than an acquaintance, about whom she knew quite a lot. He, on the other hand, knew very little about her, beyond the fact of her being an artist-in-training, which was how she thought of herself. Her lessons with Nicholas Harvey were ongoing, as were her trips around town in search of subjects to draw. She felt she needed more time and more practice to perfect both her drawing ability and her mastery of oils, her chosen medium.

She'd tried pen and ink, watercolors, tempera, and gouache, but none of them gave her the utterly sensual satisfaction of the oils. Nothing matched the glorious density, the brilliance of the colors of oil paints. It was something of a thrill just to go into an art supply house and linger over the tubes of paint. If there was anything at all for which she had an everpresent and consuming hunger, it was oil paint. She also loved paper, pencils, charcoal sticks, felt shading sticks, palettes, brushes, pans—anything and everything to do with placing images on some surface. And where once she'd been regularly rebuked for her untidiness, she was now fairly obsessive in the tidy arrangement of her supplies. Her clothes might lie in a heap for days, but every art purchase had a specific place.

This same orderliness applied to her work at Stern's. At the end of each day, she left her area spotlessly organized. And every morning, as she walked through the factory toward her space beside the fire door, she anticipated the sight of her dyes and papers and mixing bowls. During her lunch hours she went about with her sketching gear, preoccupied; her eyes roving over every face, each building and tree, taking note of contrast, of color, of texture. The world was crowded with things waiting to be painted, to be incorporated into her permanent record, and her whole body was avidly keyed to approach the task. At night when she slept, she dreamed often of immense vibrant images completed at a demented pace. She painted in a frenzy, applying her visions to expanses of primed and welcoming, tautly stretched, canvases. So exciting were these dreams they were almost sexual, arousing in her similar reactions to the ones she'd had as a result of Avery Moon's lingering kisses in the cabs he'd hired to return her home to Seventy-first Street.

In the weeks following their accidental meeting at the Museum of Modern Art, she ran into Gideon Sylvester a number of times— outside as she was sweeping the front steps, or on the stairs as he was descending from the third floor and she was climbing to the second. He invariably smiled upon seeing her and tipped his hat, but didn't say much more than hello and good-bye and how are you today. He did not show up at any of the Friday night gatherings of the Regulars, which led her to suspect he probably didn't feel comfortable at the prospect of spending an evening with people who had been Otter's friends but never actually his. She really had no idea what the man thought or felt. Since they'd called their truce he seemed to have lost whatever interest in her he'd had.

Relieved, she went about her business. Having relocated her money box beneath a floorboard in the closet of her new apartment, she faithfully added every week to her savings. When banks began to fail, she was glad she'd never been tempted to entrust her money to one of those institutions. A lot of people lost everything as a result of the bank closings, and the idea of losing all she'd saved so diligently horrified her.

In June she looked at the apartment, pleased with its lightness and spaciousness, and decided it was time to invite the Regulars to come for an evening. She limited herself to the Harveys, Esther Loftus, Danny Briggs, Golly Gordon, and Hughie Dickinson. Then, without knowing she was going to do it, the next time she met Gideon Sylvester on the stairs, she invited him, too. And at once regretted her impulse. How would she accommodate eight people? And why had she blurted out that impetuous invitation, to which he'd so promptly responded in the affirmative? A foolish whim, she told herself. But it was only for one evening. Why fret so over extending an invitation to this man?

Fret she did, however. And to ease a nagging sensation very like an itch between her shoulder blades that she simply couldn't reach, she went to great pains to remove every last piece of her work from the living room, hiding it all under her bed or in the bedroom closet. She was determined Gideon Sylvester wouldn't see so much as a sketch of hers. The walls looked terribly bare, with everything hidden away. All she had left were Nicholas Harvey's watercolor and a drawing of her that Otter Stoughton had done one evening, tearing it from the pad and presenting it to her with a wicked grin. She'd asked him to sign it, then she'd had it framed. With only these two pictures on the walls, the place seemed very unfinished. Inspired, she ran downstairs to see Mrs. Webster.

"Would you lend me a few things for one night?" she asked the old woman. "It's hard to explain, but I promise I'll take care of them and return everything first thing in the morning."

"What few things?" Mrs. Webster wanted to know.

"Well," Mattie hesitated, looking past the woman into her apartment. "The Kewpie doll, and maybe that fan. And, if you wouldn't mind, a few of those pennants."

"Whatever for?"

"I've got some people coming for the evening and I wanted to make my place look more—lived in."

"I guess it couldn't hurt. Go ahead. Take what you want. Just make sure they come back in the same condition."

Mattie hurried to gather the things she'd mentioned and a few others as well, thanked the woman profusely, then flew upstairs to arrange her borrowed memorabilia.

She had such fun with Mrs. Webster's knickknacks that she managed to forget Gideon Sylvester and the panic she'd aroused in herself by inviting him to join the Regulars. The evening went well. Everyone commented on the Kewpie doll, the fan, and the pennants, and complimented her on the apartment. Sylvester behaved commendably, and told several highly entertaining tales of his childhood misadventures with his three sisters. The Harveys were the first to leave, because of the sitter who could only stay until ten-thirty. Then Danny Briggs and Golly Gordon left together, after thanking her for a most enjoyable evening. Finally, Esther said she had to go and offered to drop Hughie at his boarding house. Before he left, Hughie handed Mattie a small flat wrapped package, in an undertone saying, "I uhm thought you might like this. You wouldn't want to come out to Central Park after your lesson on Sunday, I don't suppose? We could do some sketching maybe."

"Sure, that'd be swell. Should I open this now?"

"Heck, no! Wait till after I'm gone. I'll meet you uhm at the Harveys at four on Sunday. Okay, Mattie?"

"Toots, you throw a fine bash!" Esther said, swallowing Mattie up in a fleshy embrace.

Which left Gideon Sylvester as the last of her guests. He busied himself collecting plates and ashtrays, carrying them to the kitchen area Mattie had concealed behind a curtain.

"You don't have to do that," she said, as he deposited everything on the small countertop. "I'll take care of it."

"In that case," he said, "I'll bid you good night, Miss Harrison, and I thank you for including me."

"That's all right," she said, going with him to the door.

"But where are all your paintings?" he asked, looking around.

"Oh, they're put away," she said quickly, anxious for him to be gone.

"You will show them to me, won't you?"

She didn't know how to answer that.

"You don't want to, do you?" he said. "Now I find that curious. Why not? After all, I bared my soul to you."

"Hardly your *soul*," she scoffed.

"You don't think my paintings reflect soul?"

"Let's not talk about it. Okay?"

"No, no. Let's do."

"Go home, Mr. Sylvester!" She reached to open the door. "It's been a long day and I'm tired. I want to go to bed."

"Do you know," he said, looking her straight in the eyes, "that you're the perfect height for me? I have to stoop to talk to most women. Most men, too, for that matter."

"I'm the perfect height for lots of people. So what?"

"I don't understand you," he said, looking puzzled. "If you object to me so, why did you ask me in this evening?"

"I don't know why. I just did. Now go home!"

He gazed disarmingly at her for several seconds and then, before she could do anything at all, he tilted her chin up and kissed her on the mouth. Without giving it a moment's thought, she clenched her fist, pulled back her arm, then punched him squarely in the stomach. The air left his lungs in a noisy *whumph,* both his hands immediately covered the offended area, and he began simultaneously laughing and choking, his face turning an ominous purple.

Afraid she'd done him a serious injury, she began pounding him on the back, and he ducked away from her, gasping out, "Christ! . . . Don't . . . hit . . . me . . . any . . . more!"

She stood and watched him regain his breath, the awful color slowly draining from his face. At last, he straightened and held his hands protectively palms outward in front of himself.

"If this is what you do," he wheezed, "when someone finds you attractive enough to want to kiss you, I shudder to think what you'd do to a man who actually dared to make love to you."

"What makes you think I'd ever consider letting you make love to me?" she demanded, very insulted.

"It's inevitable," he said, then opened the door and escaped upstairs to his room.

"You actually punched him out?" Sarah laughed.

"Knocked the stuffing out of him," Mattie confirmed with a contented smile. "It may have been inevitable, but by God I made the bastard work for it."

Eleven

It took her quite some time to cool down after Gideon Sylvester had gone. She tidied the apartment, washed and put away the dishes, then assembled Mrs. Webster's souvenirs to return to her in the morning. She was in bed, about to turn out the light, when she remembered Hughie's gift and got up to get it.

After the arrogant offensiveness of Gideon Sylvester, Hughie's gift was especially welcome. It also highlighted the difference between the two men in no uncertain terms. Sylvester believed it was his right to inflict himself upon people. Hughie sought to make offerings that would speak for him. And what he'd offered was a painting fourteen inches wide by twelve inches high in which he volunteered more of himself than Gideon Sylvester could ever conceive of giving. The very simplicity of the statement was touching. Two mugs of coffee on a tray, one black and one with cream. The shiny checkered oilcloth upon which the mugs sat cast back pale shadows. The whole thing was so perfectly realized that she could almost smell the fragrance of the coffee in the steam rising into the air above the mugs.

She sat admiring the painting, thinking with pride that she now had three original works of art that had been given to her by eminently talented friends. Somehow it represented not only their approval but also their recognition of her right to be among their ranks. Softened and very pleased, she at last went to sleep.

Sunday afternoon as she and Hughie walked from the Harvey's toward the park, she thanked him for the painting.

"You're going to be very important one day, Hughie. I know it. I can't think of anyone else who can do what you do. It makes me very proud to be your friend."

"You know," he said bashfully, "I feel pretty much the same way about you, Mattie. And I know it's kind of pushy, but I was wondering if you'd maybe let me buy that last still life you did, the one of those bottles on the window ledge. I could pay you a little something every week."

"You can *have* it," she told him. "I wouldn't dream of letting you pay me."

"Honest?" He smiled happily, revealing his neglected teeth. "Gosh! That'd be wonderful."

"Hughie," she said, "I want to tell you something and I want you to swear you won't be offended."

"Okay," he agreed. "What?"

"Hughie, you've simply got to invest in a toothbrush and use it at least once a day. You're really not bad-looking, but your teeth are just . . . don't they *feel* funny?"

Crestfallen, he averted his eyes, and she put her hand on his arm, saying, "You swore you wouldn't be offended. If I didn't like you, I'd let you go around with furry-looking teeth. But I do like you, and I think you should know it makes you a lot less attractive. If you're strapped, I'll be happy to stake you to a toothbrush and some Ipana."

"No, that's okay. I guess you're right. It's just that I never remember."

"People judge you by the way you look, Hughie. It may not be fair, but it's the way things are. And you wouldn't want your appearance to interfere with the success you're going to have. I mean, people will come to look at your work and go wild to meet the artist. Then they'll see you with your green teeth and think there's no possible way you could've been the one to paint such exquisite things."

Collecting his courage, he said, "I appreciate your telling me, Mattie. My mother used to remind me, but I haven't been home in a long time."

"Don't start thinking of me as your mother! I was only being friendly."

"Oh, don't worry. That's not at all how I think of you."

"Well, good," she said, satisfied.

Several weeks passed before she had any further contact with Gideon Sylvester. She arrived home from work one evening to find a note that had been slipped under her door. It read: "At the risk of life and limb, I'd like to invite you to see a play. I've got a pair of tickets for tomorrow night's performance of *Uncle Vanya* with Lillian Gish. Kindly reply at your earliest convenience. Yours, Gideon Sylvester."

"Yours, indeed!" she said aloud, tossing the note on the table before carrying her bag of groceries over to the kitchen area. "Pompous buffoon!" She put a pot of water on the hot plate. "It would have to be something pretentious and arty instead of something fun like *Girl Crazy* or *Smiles*." She'd have loved to see Ethel Merman in the Gershwin show or the Astaires in the Vincent Youman's one. But, no. Gideon Sylvester had to try to impress her with a play that would probably put her to sleep. Not that she didn't admire Lillian Gish. The woman was ethereally beautiful and an extraordinary actress. But Chekhov! Really! It was so typical of that man.

While she waited for the water to boil, she found some paper, sat down at the table, and penned a reply.

"Mr. Sylvester," she wrote, "thank you for your kind invitation, but I must decline. I have a previous engagement. Sincerely, Mathilda Harrison."

She opened her door, checked to make sure no one was around, then ran as quietly as she was able up the stairs to stick the note under Gideon Sylvester's door. Just as she bent to push the note home, the door opened and she found herself staring at a pair of highly polished wing-tip shoes.

"Well," he said. "What have we here?"

Rising with the note still in her hand, she said, "I was delivering a reply to your invitation."

"You will come, I hope?"

Instead of giving him the note, she asked, "Why, out of all the nifty shows on Broadway, would you pick that one?"

"I didn't actually pick it. I was given a pair of complimentary house seats. A friend of mine is the stage manager."

"Oh!"

"I take it you're not interested."

"As a matter of fact, I'm not. Thank you anyway." She turned to go.

"Haven't you forgotten something?" he asked.

"I don't believe so," she replied from the top of the stairs.

"You were about to leave me that envelope, weren't you?"

She looked at the letter in her hand, then at him and said, "I've already given you my answer. Good evening, Mr. Sylvester."

"Is it because of the play or because of me?"

She thought for a moment, then said, "Both. From what I've read about Chekhov in the newspaper, I'd probably go into a coma. And from what I know about you, I'd be safer with a gang of marauding savages."

He laughed, then said, "Would you hold on for a minute? There's something I'd like to give you."

"What?" she asked charily.

"Wait! It won't take a moment."

He dashed back inside, and returned with a small brown bag.

"What is it?" she asked, refusing to accept it.

"My God!" he said, exasperated. "It's a killer blowfish! Take the damned thing, will you?" He thrust the bag into her hand.

Distrusting, she opened it and peered inside. "What the hell is that?"

"Will you please just take it!"

She pulled out the cellophane-wrapped package from inside and stared at it. "What's this supposed to be?" she asked, looking at the pair of what appeared to be cakes.

"Something new," he smiled. "They're called Twinkies. Just came on the market."

"Twinkies," she repeated, wrinkling her nose. "They're cakes?"

"Cakes with cream inside. A friend of mine who's in advertising told me those're going to be a very hot item."

"You've got a friend who's a stage manager, and one who's in advertising. Boy, aren't you the lucky one? Chekhov and free Twinkies. Thank you very much." She started down the stairs, then stopped to ask, "Am I supposed to give you a written report on these things?"

"That won't be necessary. I'm sorry you're not interested in going to the theater with me. Perhaps I could tempt you with dinner?"

"Why? Do you have a friend who's a waiter?"

He laughed. "Unfortunately, no."

Having arrived at the second floor, she walked to her door and stood there, determined not to open it until he'd gone.

"Come on," he entreated. "Let's say we forget about the theater, and go out to dinner instead."

"I'm sorry. I have a previous engagement."

"With whom?"

"None of your business!"

"I don't believe you."

"I don't care if you do or not," she said.

"I know a very nice little Italian place. Or we could go to Chinatown."

"Why won't you take no for an answer?"

"Because I don't want to. I can be very stubborn, you know. When I was five, my sister Emily was being especially loathsome one afternoon, refusing to leave me alone. I warned her a number of times. I even made some of my most terrible faces." He demonstrated now, drawing his lips back, baring his teeth, and growling. "She wouldn't desist. She could be quite the little tyrant, Emily. She used to make poor Georgina's life a misery. Georgina," he explained, "is in the middle between Emily and Nancy. Emily, as I've told you, was a chubby thing, and fairly malevolent when she cared to be. Many were the nights I heard the two of them in the next room, Georgina pleading in this tiny voice, 'Emmie, I have to go to the bathroom, please,' and Emily, in this taunting voice, saying, 'Come on! Come on! Try to get past me, I dare you!' She'd be brandishing a coat hanger, whacking it across the palm of her hand and daring poor Georgie, who was on the verge of wetting herself, to try to get past Emily to the door.

"So, as I was telling you, on this particular afternoon, Emily had been after me for hours. Of course she didn't scare *me* one bit, so her threats and her coat hanger were of no use. Finally, I said, 'If you don't go away and leave me alone right now, you'll be very very sorry.' And of course she didn't believe me, so I had no choice but to bean her on the noggin with a silver cup that just happened to be near to hand. As fate would have it, the cup had a nice thin rim and, naturally, the rim caught her on the forehead and cut her. So, there stood Emily, with blood running into her eyebrows, screaming her heart out, while I went off to my room feeling thoroughly vindicated.

"Not five minutes later, Mother came charging in, shouting, 'What have you done to dear Emily, you dreadful little boy?' and without waiting to hear my perfectly valid explanation, she proceeded to whale the tar out of me. Most unfair, under the circumstances, since I'd given Emily fair warning. But at least Georgie was able to make trips to the bathroom for a time without having to get past Emily. Being as good a martyr as she was a bully, Emily retired to her bed for two full days to nurse her wounds."

Mattie laughed. "Are all these stories true, or do you make them up?"

"Gospel," he said, hand to his heart. "I'm not leaving, you know, until you agree to dine with me tomorrow evening. My monthly remittance arrived today," he added.

"Oh, all right," she said and, forgetting her vow not to allow him to see her work, opened the door to her apartment.

Instantly, she realized her mistake, but it was too late. Gideon Sylvester was already staring beyond her into the living room at the walls hung with paintings. And like someone in a trance, oblivious to her, he went right past her to stand in the center of the room, looking at each picture in turn.

Apprehensive, she put the cakes he'd given her on the table, then turned off the hot plate, keeping an eye on him.

He stood for perhaps ten minutes without speaking, holding his fedora in both hands, his eyes moving from one painting to the next, then back again. During this time, as she watched him absorbing her work, the pity she'd felt for him returned. It struck her as very sad indeed that a man of thirty should be living alone in a small room, struggling to do something he believed in yet would never succeed at, while she who was not yet twenty was destined to attain the success he so craved. She had no doubt whatever that she'd have it; it was something she'd always known, something as much an ordained part of her as her left-handedness or her size seven feet. It was a given, and most of the people she'd met since leaving home had sensed it. There was something about her—her talent notwithstanding—that bespoke her destiny. It had never occurred to her to question this nebulous something; she simply accepted it. Always, even at the worst moments, she was able to console herself with the knowledge that her present situation, whatever it might be, was only temporary. All she had to do was keep on going, keep working and learning and, ultimately, she would have everything she'd ever wanted.

But this man, with his technical expertise and his undisciplined eye, would never see the realization of his dreams. And what she found pitiable about that was his failure to recognize his limitations. It would have been infinitely wiser of him to go into some business and be a weekend painter of some small merit, whose paintings would be admired by his family and by visiting friends. There was no shame in that. After all, he was an intelligent man and charming, too, (much as she hated to admit it) and could have had all kinds of success in the business world. He was well-connected and had a wide variety of friends; his background was solid; he was even attractive. He should have had more sense than to pit his meager abilities against those of artists considerably younger and infinitely more gifted. Take Hughie, for example. Gideon Sylvester might live to be a hundred, but he'd never be able to come even a distant second to Hughie's ability to create something profoundly meaningful and evocative out of something so simple as two mugs of coffee.

Finally, Gideon Sylvester sighed mightily and said, "Remarkable. I shouldn't have doubted for a moment that you'd be powerfully talented. Nothing you could have said would have put me in my place as effectively as your work's just done." He took several steps backward, his eyes still on the paintings. "I'll do you the courtesy of leaving you alone, Miss Harrison."

With that, he headed for the door, his demeanor acutely subdued.

"Would you like a cup of tea?" she asked, fairly undone by her compassion for him. "I was just going to make some." Hoping to cheer him up, she gave him a smile. "We could try out your cakes."

He sat down at the table, looked about for somewhere to put his hat, set it on the floor, then lifted his brown eyes to her. "It isn't fair, you know."

"What isn't?" she asked, turning the heat on again under the pot of water.

"You. My big mistake, of course, was underestimating you. Truthfully, I thought Nick and Otter and the others were merely jollying you along. I don't think I wanted to believe you could be this good." As if against his will, his head swiveled and he gazed around mournfully. "I wouldn't want to believe *anyone* was this good. It's too undermining."

"I'm very surprised you'd admit that," she said, reaching for the teapot and some cups. "You don't strike me as someone who likes to admit it when he's wrong."

"You're absolutely right. I hate it. But it's a little hard to argue with the evidence when it's staring me right in the face."

"You've got a very good technique," she said charitably.

"So you said before. Don't you like men?" he asked out of the blue.

"Sure, I do."

"It's just me you don't like. Is that it?"

"I like you well enough," she said. "You get on my nerves, that's all. You've got such—airs."

"What 'airs'?"

"I don't know. *Airs.* Anyway, I'm never doing that again and winding up with another baby."

"I beg your pardon? You have a *child*?"

"It died," she said candidly, pouring the hot water into the teapot.

"You've been married?"

"I never said that," she glanced over at him crossly.

"You really do surprise me. I'd have been willing to bet a fortune you were a virgin."

"Well, I'm not!" she said haughtily. "So there! You'd have lost your money."

"Well, well, well." He smiled as she brought the tea things over to the table.

"*You're* not a virgin, but you don't hear me going, 'Well, well, well.' "

"I'm considerably older than you."

"So what d'you want, a biscuit?" she snapped.

He guffawed, and she thought at least she'd managed to cheer him up.

"I believe I'm going to seduce you, Mathilda Harrison," he proclaimed.

"Think again, buster. You're going to get a cup of tea, then I'm throwing you out on your ear. You're probably the single most fatuous human being I've ever met."

"You're probably the most intransigent," he said quite contentedly, opening the cellophane wrapping and offering her a Twinkie.

She accepted the cake uncertainly, bit into it, chewed, made a face, swallowed with difficulty, and declared, "That's vile! And your friend thinks *that* is going to be a hot item?"

"I rather like them. I've eaten half a case so far this week while I was waiting for my check to arrive."

"Half a *case*? Good gravy! How many is that?"

"Too many. I rather like *you, too,*" he added, leaning with his elbows on the table and smiling at her with his big white teeth on display.

"Well, I can't eat that thing. I suppose you'd like a sandwich."

"That would be kind of you."

"More like necessary. I can't very well sit here eating with you watching me with those cocker spaniel eyes."

"I'd be happy to watch you do any number of things," he said.

"Stop leering at me! I'll wait and eat after you've gone."

"I can't leave yet," he protested. "The tea's too hot."

"I'll tell you what, Mr. Sylvester. You can sit here and wait until it's cool enough to drink. And when you're finished, you can let yourself out. I'm going to take a bath. And I plan to lock the bedroom door *and* the bathroom door. So don't go getting any funny ideas. Please, close the front door when you go."

She took her tea, gave him a nod, and sailed off to the bedroom, locking the door behind her. She stood with her ear to the door listening, and heard him laughing. Laugh all you like! she thought. You can sit out there till the cows come home. It won't do you one bit of good.

First she laundered her undergarments, then she spent a good long time in the tub, drinking her tea and reading *The Maltese Falcon*, which she'd bought herself as an advance birthday present. Then, reluctantly setting the book aside, she ran more hot water, scrubbed herself, washed her hair, and finally climbed out. After applying talc and toweling dry her hair, she pulled on her dressing gown, quietly let herself out of the bathroom, and tiptoed over to the bedroom door. Not a sound. Satisfied that he'd gone, she unlocked the door and stepped into the living room thinking she'd make herself something to eat. She sensed, rather than saw or heard, him and yelped, startled, when he came up behind her, wrapped his arms around her, and whispered directly into her ear, "You knew perfectly well I'd wait!"

So jarred was she by this unforeseen assault she was speechless for several moments. It was just long enough for Gideon Sylvester to untie her dressing gown and apply his large hands to her talc-slippery body. When she was at last able to speak, albeit with difficulty, she demanded to know, in a quavery voice, "What exactly do you think you're doing?"

"Hush now," he crooned into her ear, his hands demonstrating a talent his paintings certainly didn't. "For once, don't say anything at all."

It seemed like good advice. And, besides, she was so hopelessly distracted by his lips against her ear, his hands on her breasts and belly, she couldn't think of a single thing to say.

"You must have known he'd be waiting," Sarah teased the old woman.

"Maybe I did, and maybe I didn't. I certainly have no intention of giving you all the lascivious details. Why," she suggested, "don't you run along and see what Carl's up to?"

"God, but you're subtle!" Sarah said with only a partly offended laugh. "If it's all the same to you, I think I'll go reread *The Maltese Falcon*. Did it actually come out in 1930?"

"Didn't I just say it did?"

"Yes, you did, Mattie. You most definitely did. I take it you plan to stay out here for a while?"

"You take it correctly."

"Fine. I'll see you later."

Mattie relaxed in the rocker, directing her eyes to the beach. She wanted to review in private the details of that memorable, pivotal, evening.

T w e l v e

S arah found a paperback copy of *The Maltese Falcon* among the books lining the shelves on either side of the living room fireplace and took it upstairs to her room where she stood holding it as she looked out the window, expecting to see Carl somewhere on the grounds. He wasn't around.

Gazing out the window, she considered what Mattie had told her about her painting and had to wonder why, if Mattie had had such an overwhelming sense of preordained success, had she never attained it? Yet her husband, whom she'd deemed to be a greatly inferior artist, had. Was it that Mattie had overestimated her abilities? Had she been suffering from an inflated sense of her own worth? Not Mattie. Never. Sarah had never known anyone whose grasp of reality was as unimpaired as Mattie's. She might be obdurate, somewhat intolerant, and critically acute, but she most definitely didn't suffer from delusions. So what did it mean?

Reviewing all she'd been told, there was nothing she could see that indicated Mattie's early work had been anything less than brilliant. According to Mattie, Hughie Dickinson, these days revered as H. Clay Dickinson, had asked to buy one of her still lifes. Surely Dickinson, despite his personal interest in Mattie, wouldn't have wanted—even for purely sentimental reasons—to own a piece of work he considered less than brilliant. The man was still alive, still producing paintings at his Maine home. It would be highly interesting, she thought, to talk to him and hear what he had to say about Mattie's work. Golly Gordon was still around, too. Although Sarah understood that while his mind was still sharp, he suffered from a number of illnesses any of which might take the eighty-nine-year-old fellow at any time. The rest of the Regulars were all dead. And maybe Mattie hadn't cared for Esther Loftus's paintings but a whole lot of other people had. By the time the woman died in 1964, she was being hailed as one of the foremost American abstract expressionists.

These people had, according to Mattie, thought so highly of her work that they'd "parented" her after she'd been thrown out by her family. So what the hell had happened? Sarah wondered, sitting down on her bed with the book. How did this woman, for whom everyone had prophesied greatness, end up being famous solely for having been Gideon Sylvester's wife? It didn't make sense. And how come Mattie claimed never to have stopped painting, except for the six years following her husband's death? Where were the paintings?

Now Mattie had started back to work, and Sarah was overwhelmingly curious to see what would evolve from their recent session in the attic studio. There was something skewed about the oral history Mattie was narrating, and Sarah couldn't help thinking that a look at the work in progress might provide some clues.

There were few events as sharply defined in Mattie's memory as the night Gideon Sylvester caught her sneaking out of the bedroom. She knew perfectly well that what took place that night facilitated everything that followed, blinding her to what, at any other time, under any other circumstances, she'd have been able to spot in an instant. But the man had dazzled her with his one true gift, sending her into an all but hypnotic trance from which she didn't manage to emerge for years. Even now, more than fifty-seven years later, she could feel herself slipping into a trancelike state just recalling that night.

After her initial shock subsided only to be replaced by a jittery sense of overstimulation, she regained herself sufficiently to say, "I refuse to allow you to give me another baby."

Not in the least deterred, he paused. His hands temporarily ceasing their knowledgeable probing, he said, "You have my word I won't do anything that would cause that to happen."

"But how . . . ?"

Again he shushed her, adroitly disposing of her dressing gown so that she was caught entirely naked in his fully clothed embrace. His hands busied themselves once more, skimming over her, halting briefly to press here, squeeze gently there, while he garlanded her neck and shoulders with slow kisses. Held as she was from behind, her arms trapped at her sides, all she could do was twist ineffectually in an effort she wasn't sure was meant to free her or to heighten the pleasure. After all, this was Gideon Sylvester who'd reduced her to a naked state and undoubtedly planned to push himself inside of her, then bounce heavily for a minute or two before groaning noisily and climbing off; Gideon Sylvester, a man she couldn't abide one minute but who had her laughing appreciatively the next; Gideon Sylvester, who was now maneuvering her backward to the armchair. He sat. His arm around her middle brought her down on his lap, her back against his chest. One hand curved around her throat, directing her head back and around so that she could see his eyes glittering with intent before he put his mouth over hers and kissed her so wonderfully well (far better than Avery Moon ever had) that her excitement began to simmer, bubbling away low in her belly and causing her lungs to expand as if she'd never be able to take in enough air to fill them.

And while he kissed her, his hands returned to their investigation, stroking down the length of her body until she lay sprawled in his lap, her legs extended on either side of his knees. She writhed under the pressure of his fingers, her insides dancing madly, and she really wanted to ask him what he was doing, but she couldn't very well talk with him kissing her in that extraordinary fashion. All in all, she really didn't want to converse, especially since his rubbing and stroking was turning her body to white-hot liquid.

Rendered fairly senseless, she returned his kisses, her hands gripping the arms of the chair tighter and tighter until his busy fingers propelled her into an inescapable need to move, to bring about the conclusion she could now feel her body struggling to achieve. In a burst of demented action, she worked and worked until, all at once—just as her body had instructed her to push in order to expel that monstrosity Avery Moon had placed inside it, it now froze her in place for one long heart-stopped moment—she was overtaken by a convulsion of such explosive gratification she thought she might very well expire.

When the last of the tremors ebbed and she'd regained her senses, realizing she was sprawled in Gideon Sylvester's lap like a marionette with severed strings, she at once made to move away. He simply closed his arms around her, refusing to allow her to go.

"Don't fly away," he murmured, nuzzling the side of her neck. "We're nowhere near finished."

Here it came! she thought. Now he'd take off his clothes and lie down on top of her. "You're not giving me a baby, Gideon Sylvester!" she asserted, and was thrown by his soft laughter.

"I've already promised you I wouldn't," he said, the fingers of his left hand idly teasing her nipple. "Tonight is entirely for you," he said mystifyingly. "I intend to make you feel better than you ever imagined possible."

"I already feel perfectly fine, thank you."

"Be quiet, Mattie." He slipped out from beneath her so that she was now seated in the chair and he was kneeling in front of her, his hands covering hers on the arms of the chair. "You are the most utterly incendiary girl I've ever had the privilege to introduce to the finer points of lovemaking."

Having said this, he leaned forward to kiss her again. Like an obedient puppy, she responded eagerly, unconcerned with anything but the moment. She felt decidedly wanton, encouraging him, her one hand in his abundant sandy hair, the other on his shoulder. Again, he made her squirm with the directness and urgency of his touch, his mouth on her breast, his fingers delving between her thighs. This went on for some minutes, and the excitement began to build once more inside of her. Then, to her amazement, he slid his hands underneath her, lifted her forward, and lowered his head.

She closed her eyes to the unbecoming sight of herself with her legs dangling over the arms of the chair, and Gideon Sylvester down on his knees performing an unthinkable act. But never mind how it looked! It was exquisite torture that culminated in another convulsion, this one more pronounced and lasting longer than the first.

When she was finally able to breathe again, she opened her eyes to see him smiling at her, his mouth wet, his eyes still glittering.

"Like it?" he asked, dipping his fingers into the wetness he'd generated.

"I certainly do," she answered. "This is far better than anything Avery Moon ever did."

"Avery Moon, huh? The fellow obviously didn't know a thing about making love."

"Obviously not," she agreed, well past the point of embarrassment. "And obviously you do, Gideon Sylvester."

"It's one of life's great joys," he said beaming, his fingers easing into her. "Next time we do this, it's going to feel even better than it does right now. And this feels good, doesn't it?" he asked, creating a rhythm, his fingers moving in and out of her as his tongue lapped at her breasts.

She nodded, staring, as he took hold of her hand and directed it down, urging her to touch herself, prompting her to bear down against the compelling internal pressure.

"It's starting to hurt a bit," she said, nevertheless driven to move against both their hands.

"Ssshh," he told her, and closed his teeth gently on her nipple.

It took longer this time, but he kept her riding until she went through another series of spasms that left her collapsed half on half off the chair with her mouth open and her eyes glazed and her legs trembling. He pulled her up, draped her over his shoulder like a sack of potatoes, and carried her to her bed.

"You'll sleep like a newborn," he said, setting her down.

Before he covered her with the sheet, he touched her all over a final time, kissed her on the mouth, and said, "I'll lock the door after me."

At the bedroom door, he stopped to say, "We'll spend the evening in tomorrow. I'll be here at seven."

Already falling asleep, she had no energy left to speak.

At work the next day she marveled over the events of the previous night and the things Gideon Sylvester had done to her, the way he'd made her feel. She couldn't begin to think what he might have in mind for the coming evening, but as long as he didn't give her a baby, she was prepared to go along with whatever he decided to do.

At lunchtime she was still hungry after eating the sandwiches she'd brought with her and stopped to buy two donuts before leaning against the wall of a building a block or so from the factory to do several rapid sketches of two workers sitting on the curb eating their lunch. Seeing her, they waved, and she smiled and waved back, feeling exceedingly well.

"You gonna show us what you're drawin', toots?" one of the workmen called over.

"Sure," she called back. "When I'm finished."

They obliged her by remaining relatively motionless. She completed a final, longer sketch, then put away her pencils and went across the street to show them what she'd done.

"Say, kid!" the one who'd called out to her said. "That's a swell picture. Looks just like us, huh, Al?"

Al agreed. "Yeah," he laughed. "That's you, all right, Stosh, stuffin' your face like always."

Respectfully, the men admired the drawing, then handed it back.

"You're an artist, huh?" Stosh asked.

"I certainly am," she told him. "My name is Mathilda Harrison, and one day you'll be able to tell people you met me."

"Mathilda," Stosh repeated. "Some moniker."

"You may call me Mattie," she said. "I have to go now."

"You work over to Stern's there?" Al asked.

"That's right. Maybe I'll see you again, do some more drawings. I'd like to work one of these sketches into a painting."

"No kidding!" Al was impressed.

"So whaddya do with the drawings after you've worked up a paintin'?"

"Would you like them?" she asked the two men.

"Well, sure," they chorused.

"All right. When I'm satisfied and I've got the oil finished, I'll give them to you. I'll even sign them. One day, they'll be worth a lot of money."

"You don't say!" said Al.

She set off back to Stern's deciding she'd try to get a good drawing done tomorrow, if the weather was good, and if the men came out-of-doors to eat their lunch. Then, all being well, she'd start work on a canvas over the weekend.

That night Gideon Sylvester completed her education. He came through the door and took her straight to the bedroom, had them both out of their clothes in no time flat, produced a package of what he called "safes," guaranteed her they'd prevent his giving her a baby, then set about demonstrating even more of his apparently unlimited aptitude for lovemaking.

The night gave way to morning before he was sufficiently weary to sleep. Several hours later, he awakened her, and they started again. She had to ask him to go, finally, on Sunday morning.

"I have my class with Nicholas Harvey this afternoon. You've got to leave now so I can have a bath, eat something, and then do some work before I go uptown."

He sat up, wound his arms around her, pressed his hand into her belly and his lips into her throat, then held her away. "I'm going to have to marry you," he said. "It's the only way I'll be able to have you around all the time."

"Even if I were to consider marrying you," she said, "which I am not prepared to do right now, you certainly wouldn't have me around all the time. I have a great deal to do. I couldn't possibly have anyone around all the time. It would get on my nerves."

"You'll change your mind," he said self-assuredly. "I'm a patient man. I can wait."

"Wait in your own room, if you don't mind." She climbed off the bed, found her dressing gown, put it on, then went around the room gathering up his clothes. Dropping them on the bed, she said, "Get dressed and go home now, please."

With a show of reluctance, he did as she asked. Before he went out the door, he asked, "Will I see you tonight?"

"No. I'm tired. And I have to work in the morning."

"When, then?"

"Not before the weekend."

"If you change your mind, come up and knock on my door."

"I'll do that, if I change my mind."

"Why have you gone so cold, Mattie?"

"I'm back in my right mind again, that's all. I had a very nice weekend, thank you."

He had to laugh. "You're welcome," he said, and left.

The moment he was out of her sight she had to wonder what on earth she'd been doing, spending twenty-four hours in bed with

Gideon Sylvester, of all people. Had she lost her mind? she wondered as she waited for the tub to fill. It certainly felt like a form of craziness, now that she thought about it, flushing at the recall of some of the astonishing things he'd incited her to do. God almighty! She was stiff all over and very sore, but she'd loved every moment of it, and it had taken every last bit of her determination to ask him to go. Never mind the stiffness, the soreness. She'd have been elated at the opportunity to do it all again. As she reached for the soap, she laughed out loud at the recollection of his dismay when he'd discovered he'd used up all his baby-savers. He'd looked like a little boy whose family had forgotten his birthday. But not for long. The man had tricks she doubted most people had ever heard of, let alone put into effect. He'd been, she thought, like a prospector who'd discovered a gold seam and was driven to examine the extent of his wealth. And she'd liked it enormously; she'd even encouraged and abetted him, the result of which was his patiently instructing her as to how she might go about reciprocating the pleasure in quite a number of profoundly naughty ways—all of which she'd also liked very much.

While she dressed, she considered how her newly discovered appetite for sexual experiences might be damaging to her. The risk of pregnancy aside, she had the fairly frightening notion that she might become attached to this man and his artful lust. On the surface that didn't seem such a terrible thing. She was already quite taken with him, and very definitely captivated by his body. But she was a better artist than he and she couldn't see how that could be reconciled. It was bound to bother him sooner or later. Men in general seemed to hate it when women were better at something than they were. Of course, there were exceptions, like Nicholas Harvey, who never hesitated to credit Juliet with being far more practical than he, and much better at handling money; and there was dear Hughie, who could accept criticism with a smile and still go on being friends. But most men, and Gideon Sylvester probably more than most, went peculiar when a woman demonstrated finer skills. And why had he said he wanted to marry her? Did he suppose she expected that, because she was so young and naive? Or because she'd allowed him to make love to her even though it was something supposedly only married people were privileged to experience? She'd have to set him straight on that matter, since she had no intention of marrying anyone for quite some time. Especially not someone who, even jokingly, referred to himself as a remittance man and who had no source of income beyond an inheritance that brought in sixty dollars a month.

No. She'd have to set some rules if they were to continue. She had to be free during the week to work, and she most definitely wouldn't listen to any more talk of marriage. If he chose to accept her terms, she saw no reason why they couldn't spend Friday evenings and Saturdays together. She really did hope he'd choose to accept. He hadn't been gone an hour and already she was craving his touch.

She was so enraged she simply couldn't sit for a moment longer. Snatching up her glasses and sunhat, Mattie marched off the verandah, down the steps, and across the lawn. The bastard! The goddamned bastard! It galled her to think how he'd played her, using her own sensuality against her, luring her into love with him. Oh, he'd claimed to love her! He'd sworn on everything he held sacred that he loved her. But he'd held nothing sacred, and no one who loved her could have done the things he'd done.

He'd netted her so cleverly, charmed her so utterly, that she'd fallen for him. She couldn't possibly have resisted him. He was handsome, amusing, and a sexual wizard. Even while she was attempting to push him away, he was reeling her in without her knowledge. Somehow, he'd been able to see into the very core of her being, and what he'd seen there had given him the weapons he'd needed to ensnare her. He'd seen her vulnerability and her curiosity and her defiance, and he'd been clever enough to see that despite her height and her gruff manner of speaking she was still very young and badly in need of affection. So he opened both his hands and gave her everything she hadn't even realized she'd needed.

Stomping along the sand she wished it were possible to go back in time and slam the door in Gideon Sylvester's face. She could have gone off with Hughie. He'd asked her. Before he left to go to Maine in the autumn of 1930, he invited her out for a walk and said, "I've got a small house in Maine my grandmother left me. I can afford to live there. I can't afford to stay here. There's no work, and I don't care to stand on street corners selling pencils no one needs. I'll be able to manage in Maine and still keep on with my painting. I don't suppose you'd want to come with me? The house is plenty big enough for two people, and there's a vegetable garden. . . . I'd marry you, Mattie," he said, going very red in the face.

"Hughie, I can't," she said, hating to hurt him. "I've got my job here. Everyone I know is here. I like you an awful lot, really, but I've got too many things to do before I think about getting married. I could come up to visit you, though. I'd love to see Maine. And we'll write to one another. I don't want us to lose touch."

"I figured I had to ask," he said, putting on a good front. "I've been brushing my teeth every day, too. See!"

"I noticed."

"And I got a haircut," he added. "And I took all my clothes over to the Chinese hand laundry."

"I noticed that, too."

"Well, I tried, didn't I?"

"Yes, you did."

"We'll write," he said. "And any time at all you want to come visit, let me know."

"You'll probably get back home and find some nice girl who thinks you're the cat's pajamas, and that'll be it for you, Hughie. Next thing I know, you'll be writing to tell me about the wedding."

"Oh, I don't think so," he said seriously.

They'd parted, and he'd gone off to Maine. But he never did marry. There were a few women who came and went during those years before the second world war, but he didn't care enough to want to marry any of them. He was the only man she knew who was able to ignore Gideon altogether. From the outset, Hughie dismissed him as a "fluke" and, later on, as a thief. And every couple of years, he'd ask Mattie if she was ready yet to give in and marry him.

She stopped at the water's edge and looked down at the sand, her rage shifting to sorrow. She'd given herself heart and soul to Gideon Sylvester. In return he gave her two sons and a few years of great passion, during which she believed she'd made the right decision even though she'd had misgivings right up to the moment when the judge began the ceremony in December 1930, some weeks after her twentieth birthday. She'd stood in the corridor at city hall holding Juliet Harvey's hand, whispering, "This is a mistake. I shouldn't be doing this."

Juliet had laughed indulgently and said, "It's only nerves, Mattie. All brides feel that way."

"No, Juliet," she'd replied. "Every bone in my body is telling me to get out of here right now." Holding fast to the small woman's hand, she'd looked down the corridor to where Gideon Sylvester was standing with Nicholas Harvey, and with her eyes on Gideon, and an ominous ache in her chest, she'd said, "I think I'm going to live to regret this."

Thirteen

Sarah hadn't intended to go in search of Carl, but she couldn't concentrate on the Hammett novel and, feeling restless, she went downstairs thinking to sit with Mattie for a spell, but Mattie had gone off on one of her walks. So Sarah wandered over to the garage, peeking into its dim empty interior and, hearing faint strains of Led Zeppelin drifting down from the apartment above, she went to climb the stairs and knock at the screen door.

Carl came, held open the door with the flat of his hand and said, "C'mon in. I had a hunch you'd be by."

"What made you think that?" she asked, again able to see the unmade bed through the open bedroom door.

"We've got unfinished business," he said. "You want a Bud?"

"No, thank you."

He turned down the volume on the ghetto blaster, then invited her to sit in one of the capacious old wicker armchairs. Falling into the chair opposite, he stared at her. "Gave up on the makeup already, huh?"

"I don't have the time or patience to go through all that every day."

He lit a cigarette, dropped the book of matches on the table, and swung a leg over the arm of his chair. "So, what's up?"

"Nothing."

"Getting bored?" he asked with the hint of a smile.

"Not a bit," she answered, thinking it odd that this relaxed, really very attractive man was the same person who spent his nights in camouflage attire stalking the perimeters of the property. "I saw you the other night," she said casually. "I take it you have trouble sleeping."

"What were you doing up?"

"I went to check on Mattie, then happened to look out the window."

"Check on Mattie? What for?"

"To see if she wanted company. I know she spends a lot of nights out on the balcony."

"So what d'you do? Go sit there with her?"

"What's wrong with that?"

"I didn't say there was anything wrong with it. I just asked if that's what you do, Sarah."

"Yes, as a matter of fact. We talk. Or rather, she talks, and I listen."

"You don't think that's a little above and beyond the call?"

"No. I love hearing her tell about the things that happened years ago."

"I'll bet you do," he said.

"Is that a crack?"

"Merely an observation."

"Don't *you* get bored?" she asked.

"My life with Mattie suits me to a T," he said somewhat defensively. "If it didn't, I wouldn't have stayed with her for twenty-two years."

She nodded and sat back, taking him in. He was a big man, muscular, with wide shoulders and a broad chest. He had a workman's tan that ended at the elbows and created fine white squint lines at the outer edges of his eyes. She thought he looked older than forty-four, partly because of the gray that had started overtaking his hair, muting the brown to a lighter, warmer shade, and party because of the seemingly permanent hard set to his mouth and the heavy-lidded incredulity of his eyes.

"So?" he said, catching the long ash from the cigarette in his cupped palm and dropping it into the ashtray.

"So, what?"

"You finished checking to see if I show any overt signs of lunacy?"

"That wasn't what I was doing."

"No? What, then?" he asked.

"I was simply looking at you. You're really very good-looking," she said, then felt herself get overheated. It was such a dumb-broad thing to say.

"You're not bad yourself," he told her, his leg swinging back and forth against the side of the chair.

She thought he now looked about as relaxed as a cobra, coiled and ready to strike. "I'm plain," she said. "You don't have to flatter me."

"I don't do a fucking thing I don't want to do. And you're not plain. You're not Miss America, either, but you're not plain. Nobody with green eyes is plain. And if you didn't wear such godawful baggy clothes, you'd probably show all the boys you've got a nice ass and a decent pair of tits, too."

"You do have a way with words," she said, complimented in spite of his crude manner of speaking.

"I'll bet you thought about what I said."

"Which part?" she asked archly, although she knew exactly what he meant.

"After you left, I lay down in there and took every last stitch of your clothing off you. It was a pleasure."

"You're letting your imagination run away with you. I wasn't bad once upon a time, but it's all turning to shit now."

"Nice way with words." He gave her another hinting smile, then leaned over to put out his cigarette. "You do know you're dicking around here with someone who's playing with a lot less than the full deck, don't you?"

"You seem all right to me. And, besides, how do you know I've got the whole fifty-two myself?"

"I don't. But I'd be willing to bet you've got at least a handful more cards than I do."

"Do you honestly think of yourself as crazy, Carl?"

"I've got the documents to prove it, sweetheart; the stamped and signed papers from Uncle Sam his very self."

"You want to know something?"

"What?"

"You're at least fifty percent more rational than my ex-husband, and all *his* papers say he's a bona fide smart guy with not a problem in the world. And what you said about him was bang on. He only wanted meals and sex on demand, and if he didn't get one or both, he'd start telling me what a dud I was, what a pathetic loser I'd turned out to be. It did wonders for my self-esteem. You don't pretend to be anything you're not. I find that kind of refreshing."

"I think you're one of those chicks who gets off by flirting with things she knows she can't handle."

"I'm not flirting with anything," she disagreed. "I'm interested in you."

"Right. Like a specimen on the end of a fucking pin."

"That's awful! I don't see you that way at all."

"No. You think it's perfectly cool to look out your window and see some guy on night patrol."

"It made me sad."

"Fuck your sad!" he snapped. "Nobody around here needs that shit."

"I'm afraid to have anybody see me without my clothes," she said, looking away. "I find that sad, too."

"Shit!" he muttered. "Did you bring your sorry ass over here looking for sympathy?"

"Don't insult me," she said quietly. "You don't mean it. You just said you made me the subject of at least one fantasy. Your saying that actually made me feel pretty good. I thought about having you do it," she admitted, then swallowed hard.

"Oh, yeah?" He sat up, brought his leg down from the arm of the chair, and glared at her. "What is this, some kind of therapy for you?"

"I've had enough," she said heatedly. "This is giving me a headache. I thought we'd talk, get to know each other, but all we're doing is annoying each other."

"Why the hell would you think you could have a rational conversation with me?" he asked. "Any fool could figure out it's been a lot of years since I made social nice-nice with the opposite sex."

"Is that why I make you so mad?"

"Jesus! Don't you get it? *Everybody* makes me mad, except for Mattie. Bonnie's so goddamned cheerful I'd like to rap my knuckles on the top of her head. At least Glo's smart enough to know I'm a psycho, so she does me the courtesy of staying the hell out of my face. But you, you come waltzing over here like some half-assed social worker, not even knowing what the hell you're after. People like you are why I stay away. You think I give a fuck about your vanity? You want someone to tell you you're not getting old, you came to the wrong place. You *are* getting old, sweetheart. We all are. Big fucking deal! You want a medal? I've got a drawerful of them. Go pick one you like and pin it on yourself. What the fuck is wrong with you?" he ranted, his features going tight.

"Evidently," she said, melting with embarrassment, "quite a lot." She got up and looked over at the door.

"Oh, that's good! When things get heavy, run for the hills!"

"Isn't that what you want?"

"I couldn't give a shit what you do," he sighed, and flopped back in the chair. "One thing's for sure, though. If you think I'm going to do some romantic tap dance because you don't have the balls to be straight about what you're looking for here, you're even crazier than I am. You want to get it on, fine! I'm all for it. You want to play games, take a hike!"

"How am I supposed to respond to that?" she asked, flummoxed.

"Take off your clothes and show some guts," he said tiredly. "I'm only good at stuff like that in my daydreams."

"You don't really think I'm going to do it, do you?"

"Why not? You want me to take mine off first?"

"Yes," she said, shocking both of them. "I'm not going to have you treat me like some charity case. You take yours off, then I will, too."

He gaped at her for several seconds then began to smile. "You're on!" he said, and got up.

She followed him into the bedroom and watched in a dither as he pulled his shirt off over his head without bothering to undo the buttons.

"Come on," he said, starting to remove his jeans.

"God!" she whispered, and began undoing the buttons on her baggy cotton pants, instinctively working in the safest way. Without the pants, she was still reasonably well concealed by her underpants and oversized T-shirt. But she was taking too long. By the time she'd kicked off her sandals, he was standing naked in front of her with his hands on his hips. She glanced furtively at him, then looked away, with the feeling she was about to commit suicide.

"Chicken," he said not unkindly, and came to lift her T-shirt from the hem and drag it up over her head. "This is kind of fun," he said, reaching in back of her to unhook her bra. "It's like being back in high school, except there's no gearshift to get in the way, and you're not saying, 'No, don't! No, stop!' "

She laughed, and all at once it was easier. She crossed her arms over her breasts as he backed away to have a look at her.

"You're no forty-one," he said. "Or else you're the best-preserved old broad I've ever seen."

"Thank you," she murmured, trying to keep her eyes above his waist. "Could you please not refer to me as a broad?"

"I could probably do that," he said, keeping his distance.

"I feel stupid," she said. "I don't know about you, but this is kind of rough."

"Why don't we try to get this show on the road?" he suggested, sitting on the end of the bed.

With her arms still crossed over her breasts, she sat beside him. He put his arm around her shoulders, and again she laughed, letting her head fall onto his shoulder. "You're right," she told him. "It is like high school, only way worse." She lifted her head and looked into his eyes, suddenly able to see that of the two of them he was by far the more frightened. Grow up! she told herself. You wanted to do this, so do it!

She turned and straddled his lap, put her arms around him and pressed her cheek to his, breathing in his scent. "I'm a sucker for good cologne," she whispered. "You smell delicious."

"You feel good," he told her, not moving, simply holding her close. "It's been years since I held a woman."

Did it matter, she wondered, who initiated and who received? Who else would ever know or care except the two of them?

She pulled back her head to look at him again, then kissed him on the forehead, on each cheek and finally, softly, on the mouth. He blinked at each touch of her lips, his hands remaining flat on her back. His apprehension gave her courage, turned her into a new, previously unthought-of, version of herself. The new version wanted to make this man less fearful. She kissed him again, then climbed off his lap, removed her underpants, and straddled him once more. He took in a sharp little breath as she pressed her nakedness against him.

Gradually, as she ran her hands down his solid arms and across his back, he began to thaw. Her hands on his chest, she pushed him back, then took her palm in a sweeping circle over his chest and across his belly. He trembled beneath her fingers, and she became even more determined, kissing the base of his throat, his chin, his mouth again. This time, he took hold of her and returned the kiss.

"Jesus!" he exclaimed, and raised himself to look at her, extending a tentative hand to her breast.

She held his wrist to keep his hand on her breast, gauging his eyes. "I don't know how this happened," she said, "but you're right. I did want it. Touch me," she invited, her hand gliding down his belly. "I want you to." She'd never had a sexual encounter remotely like this. She'd never had to be explicit, to put her desires into words. But he seemed fairly paralyzed with fear, unable to get past it. His touch was hesitant, as if he expected her to disintegrate on contact. And, strangely, because of this, she liked him more and more.

Twisting around, she kissed his hip, her hand smoothing the length of his thigh. Then, overtaken by appetite, she put her mouth on him, and he let out a cry and shuddered violently. Stilling him with her hand on his chest, she continued to taste him, liking the shape and feel of him.

"Jesus, stop! It's too much!" He tugged at her and she sat up on her knees to look at him. He looked as if he'd suffered a mortal blow and might die from the pain.

"Carl," she said quietly, "what do you want?"

He couldn't speak.

"I'm going to do this," she said, lifting her knee across him. "I'm going to do this," she repeated. "It doesn't make a goddamned bit of difference. I'm not going to go away and giggle with my girlfriends, or write this up in my five-year diary. This is between the two of us."

She slowly lowered herself over him, experiencing the old familiar expanding inside and the profound sense of rightness she'd had every time the mood was good and the connection was desirable. Her knees locked tightly to his sides, she came forward to place her hands on either side of his face and asked him to kiss her.

He couldn't. He held her tightly, his hand over the back of her neck bringing her head down into the curve of his neck. His touch was no longer hesitant, but extremely gentle. She found his hand, laced her fingers through his, and began the necessary instinctive motion, her hips rocking against his as he began lifting into her. Their fingers gradually closed together, locked palm to palm, the tempo quickening. She opened her mouth on his neck and ran her tongue up the length of it to his earlobe. At last, he turned and kissed her with surprising sweetness and delicacy as his hand left the back of her neck to close over her hip.

She hadn't thought anything would happen. She'd rarely experienced any cataclysmic pleasure from making love. It had always been an act of accommodation from which she expected very little. So she was taken completely off guard by the first stirrings that prompted her to move automatically toward a peak that was suddenly surmountable. She forgot about him, so caught was she in the grindingly exclusive need to arrive at that promised pleasure. She wasn't aware until those thirty or so seconds of contractions had passed that he'd been helping her, striving with her, holding back in order to be able to see her utterly naked for that fragment of time. When she opened her eyes and looked down at him, having gone arching away in her sightless climbing, it was to see him smiling at her. She gave a triumphant little laugh, turned immediately serious again, covered his mouth with hers, and rode his hips with intent, determined to reach the end of this journey in order to know him as well as he now knew her.

Tears leaked from the corners of his tightly closed eyes and she drank them before they had a chance to escape. "I think," she whispered, "you are the loveliest man I've ever known."

He couldn't speak. She didn't mind. She went on holding him, stroking him, and wondering who'd rescued whom. She felt as if he'd given her something no one else had ever even considered important: the evidence of a vulnerability he couldn't conceal. That he could shed tears at a moment of such intimacy was more real to her than almost anything else had ever been.

"I wish I could cry," she told him. "I forgot how a long long time ago. Maybe that's why I've been feeling so old. I used to cry. I remember doing it. But I don't anymore. It's as if I stopped being human. Or maybe I became like Ray, or my stepmother. Neither one of them were human, at least not in the way I understand being human. But you are."

She could feel him listening, and it was as if her words were small keys that penetrated him to unlock doors that had been sealed shut for a very long time. She saw that, initially, he was ashamed of his emotions and didn't want her to see. Gradually, though, his resistance subsided along with the tears, and he wiped his eyes with the back of his hand before shifting to look at her.

"Where the hell did you come from?" he asked in a hushed voice. "You're not the same woman who came in here before. What happened?"

"I honestly don't know. I think I just fell in love with you. All of a sudden I care about you so much I can hardly believe it."

"You're really getting to me," he told her. "D'you have any idea what you're dealing with here?"

"I think I do."

He sniffed, then smiled at her. "I think," he said, "I'm going to eat you alive, Sarah."

"All right," she smiled back at him. "I can't think of a nicer way to go."

"Don't fuck me over," he said hoarsely. "I don't have any way to handle that."

"I know, and I won't. Anyway, I'm usually the one who gets fucked over. This makes a pleasant change."

"Christ! Miss Sarah said the F-word!"

"Naughty Sarah," she laughed.

"I'll want to start sneaking into your room at night. Mattie'll throw my ass out of here."

"Are you kidding? She's been pushing me at you for weeks. She'll probably give a party, she'll be so pleased with herself."

"It's kind of late in the day to ask," he said, "but are we playing Russian Roulette here with your prime time?"

She kissed him on the arm. "You have the cutest way of expressing yourself. Kiddo, you're looking at the biggest optimist who ever lived. I haven't slept with anyone for almost eight years but I haven't missed a single pill in all that time."

"Christ! You *are* an optimist!"

She looked at her wristwatch, then said, "I've got better than an hour before dinner. Are you tired?"

"You have got to be joking! Eight years is nothing, sweetheart. I won't even tell you how long it's been for me. You'll be very god-damned lucky if I let you out of here at all."

"Fine by me," she said gleefully.

F o u r t e e n

During dinner Mattie kept looking across at Sarah with a quizzical expression. Sarah smiled at her and went on eating, famished after her several hours in the garage apartment with Carl. Mattie quickly gave up on dinner, lit a cigarette, and sat drinking her glass of French Bordeaux. Filled with a lazy sense of well-being, Sarah helped herself to more rice and salad. As she reached for her wine glass, she realized Mattie's eyes had been fixed on her for several minutes.

"What?" Sarah asked, then read the answer in Mattie's eyes, and felt the flush rise from her chest up into her face.

"You look very pleased with yourself," Mattie observed.

"I'm sure I don't."

"*Very* pleased."

"What am I supposed to say?" Sarah asked, carefully setting her glass down.

"You're playing a dangerous game."

"I'm not playing any kind of game at all."

"Oh, but you are," Mattie said confidently.

"Honest to God," Sarah said. "This is like one of those scenes in old movies when the irate father of the girl of the piece confronts the villain who's had his dastardly way with her. You're not his father, and I'm no villain. And, besides, you've been finagling for months, pushing us at each other. Well, it worked. Okay? You pushed us, and things clicked. It's what you wanted. So, what's with the evil glare and the accusations?"

Drawing herself even more erect, Mattie said, "I admit to playing matchmaker. What I want to know is if you're honorable."

Sarah laughed disbelievingly. "What *is* this, Mattie? You can't have it all ways, you know. Yes, you played matchmaker. It succeeded. Now, what're you going to do? Hold me at the end of a shotgun and insist I marry your defiled child?"

"Do you care about him?" she asked, as if the question were painful.

"Yes, I care about him. What do you think I am anyway, some kind of aging trollop? I'm not in the habit of sleeping with just anyone. And in this day and age, that's pretty damned dangerous, to say the least. Of course, I care about him. This takes the cake. It really does. I thought you'd be tickled pink because your manipulating paid off. But, no. You're bent on playing some revamped scene from Julius Caesar, asking yon Sarah if she's an honorable woman! What a crock, Mattie!"

Mattie glowered for a moment longer, then began to smile. "Quite the testy little thing when you're confronted, aren't you?"

"Don't be fooled by appearances," Sarah said brusquely. "I may not be very big, but I know how to defend myself."

"Just verifying," Mattie said with maddening obscurity.

"Verifying what?"

"That you're *not* playing a game with Carl. He wouldn't know how to cope with that."

"I probably know that better than you do."

"Just because you've been to bed with him doesn't mean you know all about him."

"I know what he does every night," Sarah said. "And I know some of what he's been through."

" 'Some' being the operative word," Mattie said. " 'Some' in this case represents only a fragment, my dear. I have a vested interest in Carl's well-being. Delighted as I am that the two of you have engaged in a bit of pleasurable friction, I'm nevertheless concerned that you have more than simple fucking in mind."

Sarah was so shocked she went silent.

"Oh, don't look like that!" Mattie said impatiently. "I was fucking my heart out with Gideon Sylvester long before your parents were born. Why do all you young people believe so egotistically that you invented the world? It's precisely because I engaged so wholeheartedly in that activity that I know how easily it can blind you to other, sometimes more important, things that are going on. Sex can be a venerable weapon, as I believe you discovered with the Romanian thug."

"Mattie," Sarah said softly, "what's this all about?"

"You are taking precautions, I hope?"

"No. I thought I'd get myself pregnant, then leave the baby with you while I go off to seek fame and fortune. Do you honestly think I'm that stupid?"

"Women, my dear Sarah, can be *unbelievably* stupid when it comes to the matter of sex. You're looking at one of them, remember."

"Yes, but nobody ever told you anything about it."

"True. But even later on, when I did know, I was still bamboozled by that ruthless son of a bitch. No one's easier to fool than someone who's willing."

"What," Sarah asked again, "is this all about, Mattie?"

The old woman put out her cigarette, took a fresh one, struck a kitchen match on the underside of the dining table, and puffed away before dropping the match into the ashtray. "I do believe you are an honorable woman, Sarah," she said thoughtfully. "But I think you are in spite of yourself." Once more she gazed at Sarah, and Sarah wondered if it was actually hot in the dining room or if Mattie had managed to skewer her and was slowly broiling her over an invisible charcoal fire. Her instinct was to lower her eyes, but she forced herself not to wilt beneath that heated gaze, and waited. To her intense dismay, Mattie was the one to break the contact, her exceptional eyes filling with tears. It was so distressing to see, that Sarah at once regretted everything: her attitude, the somewhat arrogant stance she'd taken, her disrespect (after all, Mattie was elderly and due appropriate regard), and even having made love with Carl, since it was that which had prompted this contretemps.

"Look, I'm sorry," Sarah apologized. "I overreacted, and I was rude. I wouldn't intentionally say or do anything to hurt you."

"DON'T YOU THINK I KNOW THAT!" Mattie shouted, her

voice cracking as the tears overran the rims of her eyes. "I know that!" she insisted. "You wouldn't be here otherwise. I'm not one of those old fools who's oblivious to everything but her own decaying memories. I've got the *same* goddamned *brain* I started *out* with, and there's not a *thing wrong* with it!"

Her voice gained in volume until the room seemed to resound with it, like the interior of an immense bell, and Sarah wanted to cover her ears with her hands, so dreadful was it to have the old woman bellowing at her this way.

Bonnie pushed open the door from the kitchen, took one look at Mattie, and backed off.

As if deriving physical strength from her outburst, Mattie roared on. "Why do you think that everything has to do with you? You're not as potent as you think! Some things have *nothing* to do with *you!*"

"ALL RIGHT!" Sarah shouted back at her. "There's no need to scream."

Instantly, Mattie regained herself. Her chest heaving, she dabbed at her face with her napkin, took a furious puff on her cigarette, then gulped down half her remaining wine. "You are the most infuriating woman!" she said with considerably less volume. "If you're not asking endless goddamned questions, you're arguing. And if you're not arguing, you're apologizing, and blaming yourself for everything from the Crucifixion to the Children's Crusade. Just be quiet, will you? There are things I'm trying to say, and you keep interfering with my train of thought."

Sarah refilled Mattie's wineglass and her own, then folded her hands in her lap. Having been thoroughly chastised, she felt inept, guilty, and somewhat humiliated. She'd never had an experience quite like this; she'd certainly never in her adult life been the beneficiary of such unbridled fury.

Her tears ended, Mattie sat for a time and smoked. At length, she said, "I know I'm not easy. I never have been. It's doubtful I ever will be. The question is: Don't you think it's time you decided what you're going to be and then stick to it?"

"Is that what you did?"

"I've always known who I am," Mattie said firmly.

"Well, you're very lucky. Most of us don't. Sometimes I think I've got a fix on who it is I'm supposed to be, then an hour later, somebody says or does something, and I have to wonder why I thought I'd finally managed to figure myself out. I'm sorry if you find that infuriating, but there's not a lot I can do about it."

"Of course there is," Mattie disagreed. "Just take a stand, and for Christ's sake, stick to it."

"Every time I do that, somebody comes along and moves the ground I decided to take my stand on."

"I detest self-pity."

"That's fact, not self-pity."

"It's self-pity," Mattie insisted.

"I can't argue with you about this," Sarah said, surrendering. "No matter what I say, I'm going to lose because you only see things from your point of view."

"Don't underestimate me, my dear. I see a great deal."

"That's for damned sure," Sarah agreed, chancing a smile.

"Are you simpleminded or something?" Mattie asked, wide-eyed. "You come in here positively radiating sexual excitement, and you don't think anyone would notice?"

Sarah flushed and looked down at the tabletop.

"I can't begin to imagine what Carl must look like right now," Mattie said. "What a pair!"

"You're enjoying yourself at my expense," Sarah said, looking up in time to see a distinctly mischievous expression Mattie at once sought to hide. "My God! You really are a dirty old woman! And combative as all get out, too. I truly think you thrive on making me feel like an adolescent."

"You do tend to rise somewhat like the flag on the Fourth," Mattie conceded. "It's sometimes hard to resist providing the incentive that sends you on your way."

Sarah shook her head. "Living with you's a little like a roller coaster ride with unannounced stops."

Mattie laughed, then evincing sudden concern, said, "I should warn you. When Carl does sleep, he usually wakes up screaming. It can be very frightening. When he first came to us, I used to go to his room at night and hold him until he was able to sleep again. It drove my late 'husband' wild with jealousy. He was convinced I was making love to a twenty-two year old."

"Were you?" Sarah asked cannily, wondering if this was what Mattie had been building up to confessing.

"Once," Mattie said, and was silent as she extinguished her cigarette. When she looked again at Sarah, she'd undergone yet another mood change. "I felt so deeply, terribly sorry for him. It had nothing to do with my hating Gideon Sylvester. By then I'd been hating the man for so long that very little of what I did had anything to do with him. No," she said slowly. "This had to do with a young man who desperately needed to be held, to feel wanted and of value; who craved normalcy the way certain inmates crave freedom. I've never regretted it. It helped both of us. One night out of our lives when two people each got something they badly needed. Carl got confirmation of his humanity, and I was able to hold in my arms someone to whom I could give unreservedly. What happened that night was something that occurred on another plane entirely, and could never be duplicated.

"Please don't hurt him, Sarah. He's not like other men. Everything he once knew about self-defense, in its most literal meaning, was erased by the war. I love him as much as I do my two sons. Perhaps even more, because he's experienced horrors we can't begin to imagine."

"I would never hurt him," Sarah said resolutely.

"With the very best of intentions you might, because I don't believe you've ever had to handle someone who was even more insecure than you are. And you are quite impressively insecure. If you choose to take umbrage at that, I swear to God I will throw my dinner plate at you."

"What if I told you I love him?" Sarah asked.

"I'd tell you that love can destroy people more effectively than hatred. Pay attention, my dear. There's a great deal at stake here."

"I know that."

"I'm sorry I howled at you."

"Did you howl at me?" Sarah smiled.

"Perhaps you are becoming indispensable," Mattie said with a sad little smile. "I'll miss you when you go."

"I'm not going anywhere."

Mattie sniffed and said, "We'll see."

"Would you like coffee now?" Sarah asked, letting the matter drop. She felt fairly exhausted.

"Outside." Mattie pushed away from the table and got to her feet. "I need some fresh air. Tell Bonnie, then come sit with me. I remember now what I wanted to tell you."

Thrown, Sarah went to the kitchen. If it hadn't been about Carl she'd wanted to talk, why had Mattie gone so berserk? As she was on her way back from the kitchen, she was struck hard by Mattie's confession. There formed in her mind an image of a younger Mattie guiding a youthful Carl into the depths of her long lean body, and it gave her the oddest feeling of loving melancholy. It didn't upset her at all to have been told about it, but her reaction was much the same as when she'd realized that Giddy and Matthew were two lonely, middle-aged men. She felt an empathetic pang for both Mattie and Carl, and also a certain sense of rightness.

She came out onto the verandah, looked at Mattie sitting in the rocker with her eyes, as ever, locked on the horizon, and suddenly had to go over, bend down, and put her arms around the old woman. "I love you, Mattie. I hate it when you get angry with me, because regardless of what you think, I care a lot about you." She breathed in Mattie's fragrance, the warm spicy scent of KL, kissed the woman's soft yielding cheek, then straightened and went to sit in the other chair.

"You're so softhearted," Mattie said, visibly gratified by Sarah's spontaneous affectionate display.

"There are worse things I could be."

"You're also a dolt," Mattie said, "but I'm very fond of you, too." Shifting to cross her legs, she said, "Don't you dare let on to Carl I told you! I've never told anyone about that incident."

"I wouldn't dream of it," Sarah said sincerely.

"The only good thing Gideon Sylvester ever did for me, he did for his own purposes. But he taught me to appreciate my own sensuality.

And the only time I've ever used it strictly for someone else's advantage was with Carl. Of course, I've used it to my own advantage. That's only sensible. Rarely, though, does one have the opportunity to do something that's entirely directed to someone else's benefit.

"I had opportunities over the years to go to bed with quite a number of other men, but I chose not to. It had nothing to do with any kind of loyalty to Gideon Sylvester. I didn't do it—with one notable exception, and I'm not referring to Carl—because it would have diluted my anger with that man. And I wanted to keep that intact. Gideon Sylvester took everything I ever valued, but I refused to permit him to take my anger."

"That's how I felt about Lillian, my stepmother. Not that I equate myself with you, but I do understand how that kind of rage can fuel you."

One of Mattie's kitchen matches flared, then was shaken out and discarded. "I hope," Mattie said passionately, "that nothing even remotely as dreadful as what Gideon Sylvester did to me ever happened to you."

"It's all relative," Sarah said quietly. "But we didn't die."

"What did she do?" Mattie asked.

Sarah sighed and was about to reply when Bonnie came out with the coffee.

"You're not having any dessert?" Bonnie wanted to know.

"Not tonight," Mattie told her.

"You didn't like the chicken, huh?"

"Not a hit, I'm afraid," Mattie answered.

"It was delicious," Sarah put in.

"This is like those guys Siskel and Ebert. One thumbs up, one thumbs down," Bonnie said cheerfully. "I'll leave you a snack upstairs, Mattie, case you get hungry in the night."

Mattie thanked her, and Bonnie returned inside. "Tell me what she did," Mattie said, once Bonnie was out of earshot.

"There's not much point in going into all that."

"Of course there is. It might explain a few things."

Sarah shrugged. "Pru talked back to her once, so Lillian cut off all Pru's hair. She threw me down the stairs because she said I was lying about something. She . . . hurt us, then threatened to hurt us even more if we told our father."

"How did she hurt you?" Mattie asked, turning slowly to look at her.

Striving to sound unaffected, Sarah said, "She hit us with things, made us go without food. We finally ran away when I was seventeen and Pru was twelve. We hitchhiked to Niagara Falls, up to our Aunt Norma's place. She took one look at us, called our father at work, and said she was going to keep us. He was relieved, I suppose. Anyway, we stayed with her for four years, until Pru was twenty-one and I was sixteen. I mean until I was twenty-one and Pru was sixteen. Then we moved to New York and got jobs. I worked as a secretary, and Pru was a file clerk and went to night school to get her high school diploma."

"You're right," Mattie said, her eyes narrowed. "It is a melodrama."

"I told you it was. What did you mean, he took away everything?"

"I spent fifty-one years, six and one half months with Gideon Sylvester, and during that time he methodically stripped me of everything, absolutely everything."

Fifteen

Gideon Sylvester worked upstairs in his small room on the third floor. Mattie worked in her apartment and stored her canvases upstairs so there'd be enough room at her place for the two of them to eat and sleep. It seemed a sensible arrangement, and from time to time when she announced that she wished to sleep alone, Gideon took himself off to the third floor, although not without an argument.

"I *told* you I needed time to myself!" she reminded him often. "Did you think I said that to be coy? I meant it! I see far too much of you. I must be alone sometimes."

"You enjoy being arbitrary," he accused. "You like issuing orders."

"Yes, I do, especially when it concerns my work and my need to get some sleep every so often. In case you'd forgotten, I work five days a week from eight in the morning until six-thirty at night."

"You like to drive that point home with nauseating regularity," he said. "I'm well aware you're gainfully employed. I'm equally well aware that you consider me *un*employed, even though I'm preparing for a show."

"You've been preparing for that show for the last decade! I'm beginning to think it's some sort of fairy tale."

"I find you odious at this moment. I'll be more than happy to sleep upstairs." And off he went, slamming the door behind him.

They had this argument, with much the same dialogue, about once a month. Each time after he'd go slamming off to the third floor, she locked the door, drew a deep relieved breath, and reclaimed her apartment. She execrated the marriage, and refused to do any of the things like laundry or cooking or cleaning that Gideon Sylvester insisted came with signing the license and wearing his grandmother's diamond eternity band. She also loathed his three sisters, his overbearing mother, and almost every last one of his friends. The only member of his family for whom she felt any fondness was Gideon Senior, a good-natured, beleaguered man who'd long since learned that the only way to maintain peace in his household was to acquiesce to the demands of the females. It was from his father that Gideon had inherited his story-telling ability and from him, too, that he'd acquired his height and good looks. In every other way, father and son differed drastically. Gideon was very like his mother, who Mattie discovered at once could not maintain confidentiality. The woman lived for gossip and the least little item could provide dinner conversation for, at the worst, one evening and, at the best, an entire week. Upon hearing some choice new morsel, Adelina Sylvester would begin to smile in a telltale fashion, and her body would actually appear to bloat as if, for her, gossip provided physical nourishment. Since Gideon had no special feelings for any of his siblings or for his parents, it was quite simple for him and, therefore, for Mattie, to stay away.

Each time Mattie reached the point of accepting that the marriage was doomed and that she should take steps to extricate herself from it, Gideon Sylvester seemed to know. He'd pull out his charm like a pocket watch and hypnotize her with it. Having managed to calm her a bit, he'd take her out to dine, or arrive home with some trinket to appease her, and then he'd peel her out of her clothes like a farmer shucking a sample ear of corn to test its ripeness. With unfailing single-mindedness, he'd apply himself to her body like ointment, insinuating himself into every crevice and cranny until she was too satiated to do anything more than plunge into sleep. Peace between them would follow for two or three weeks before Mattie once again felt his presence as an invasion. Then they'd go through their belligerent little minuet one more time. And in this fashion they managed to use up the first two years of their marriage.

Early in 1933 Mortimer Sternholt suffered a heart attack and died in his sleep. The staff, while grieved, were fearful that Mrs. Sternholt would sell Stern's Editions to someone less sympathetic and caring than her husband, or, worse, shut down the factory altogether.

After the funeral, which all the employees attended, Mr. Sternholt's lawyer asked everyone to report to work as usual the following day, at which time he'd make known to them Mr. Sternholt's last requests.

No less grieved and fearful than the others, Mattie arrived early the next day and waited with her co-workers for the arrival of the lawyer. There was much speculation among the staff as to what the disposition of the estate might be, and Mattie tried not to listen. She couldn't see the point to worrying in advance of what might happen.

The lawyer, a longtime friend as well as legal representative of Mortimer Sternholt's, came in promptly at eight-thirty, opened his briefcase, and drew out a legal document.

"We have, each of us, lost a fine friend," he began. "Mortimer Sternholt was a very special man, and one with great foresight. He loved his business and he had faith in every last one of you. To that end, he made an extraordinary bequest. He has left the company to all of you, equally. Since his family has been provided for separately, it was his wish that the twenty-two of you, that is the twenty factory workers and the two office staff, either continue on with Stern's Editions or, should you so vote by a majority, to sell it and divide the proceeds. In the event you decide to continue, his mandate is that any and every issue be decided by majority vote in keeping with the democratic principles upon which this his adopted country is founded. No one employee shall have sway over or exercise undue influence upon another. For better or for worse, Stern's Editions now belongs to all of you. If it is your wish that I continue on as legal counsel, I will be at your disposal."

No one wanted to sell the company. It was unanimously agreed that they would go on as before, as if Mr. Sternholt were still head of the company. The orders would be accepted and filled as they always had been. The quality of the books would be as outstanding as ever. Greatly relieved, the employees went to their work areas and started the day.

Upon hearing of this, Gideon Sylvester stated Mattie had been supremely foolish. "You should have voted to sell the place. You could've made a tidy sum of money."

She looked at him with disgust, feeling tendrils of hatred snaking around her ribs. "I'm not even going to discuss this with you," she told him. "You are completely devoid of sensitivity."

"I most definitely am not!"

"I will not discuss it. My job with Stern's pays the rent and puts food in your mouth." It also provided her with continuing savings, about which he knew nothing.

"You seem to forget my contribution," he said.

"How could I forget your sixty dollars a month?" she asked. "That pocket money you receive regular as clockwork that you use entirely on yourself. That *is* the contribution we're talking about, isn't it?"

He looked as if he wanted to hit her, and she said, "You ever raise your hand to me, Gideon Sylvester, and you'll be going through the rest of your life as a one-armed cripple."

She was so deadly serious that, for once, he decided not to argue. And, as always, when he lost an argument, he had a change of heart and produced his charm much in the way a prestidigitator made bouquets of paper flowers materialize out of the air.

With a wide smile, he said, "We'll forget all about it," and disarmed her by dragging her into a sudden, intense, embrace which culminated in their making love almost fully dressed, and very violently, on the floor.

She was convinced he was using her every time he flung himself at her in this fashion. But she was so irredeemably aroused by his determined mouth and questing hands that she could never sustain her anger with him or her slowly growing conviction that what she was involved in was a love affair not with Gideon Sylvester but with love itself. And not even emotional love, but pure undiluted sexual love. He was so masterly, so inventively dedicated that he could turn her around like a weather vane in a strong breeze. She could point east, and if he didn't care for it, one gust from him had her turning west. Then, too, he had endless stories to tell, and a talent for purchasing items that invariably pleased her sense of whimsy. She couldn't think how he'd done it but he'd gained a knowledge of her that was fairly encyclopedic. Unlike other men who might have sought to ingratiate themselves by offering her roses, or chocolates, or intimate items of apparel, Gideon showed up with half a dozen tubes of oil paint, or several stretched and primed canvases, or a bound sketchbook and half a dozen 5B pencils; he'd reach into his pocket and pull out some sticks of sealing wax and an antique seal he'd found with the initial M engraved on it; or he'd present her with a letter of apology, penned in his perfect calligraphy on the finest parchment. His instinct for what would appease her was, in those early days, infallible. And when he demonstrated his knowledge of her in one of these ways, she'd slide back into love with him, and wonder how she could ever have harbored doubts about him. No one who didn't love her would go to the extremes Gideon Sylvester did to find objects so guaranteed to delight her. So, she'd kiss his well-shaped mouth, their tongues now old acquaintances, and open her thighs to his welcome touch, fired by perpetual-seeming lust. Of course he loved her. Just because their views didn't always coincide, it didn't mean he had some grand design in mind of which she remained ignorant.

And so the marriage staggered along.

In the spring of 1934 the Harveys told everyone they were leaving New York to take up Hughie Dickinson's generous offer to stay with him in Maine.

"Don't forget us, Mattie," Juliet begged. "I'm going to miss you and the other Regulars more than I can say. But what with the Academy closing and Nickie being unable to sell any of his paintings or get another job, we just can't stay. Hughie says Nickie can work part-time at a small girl's school outside Portland. It's the only chance we've got, with four little ones to feed."

Knowing they were in critical need of money, Mattie insisted on buying another of Nicholas Harvey's splendid watercolors. But he wouldn't hear of accepting the hundred dollars she wanted to pay him. In the end, he agreed to take fifty, and hugged her, whispering, "You've always been good to us, Mattie. If you ever need us, we'll come running."

There was a tearful farewell party to which all the remaining Regulars came: Esther Loftus, Danny Briggs, Golly Gordon, Mattie and Gideon Sylvester, half a dozen others, and Hughie Dickinson, who came down by train for the occasion. Upon seeing Mattie, Hughie broke into a huge grin and came rushing over to take both her hands in his, urgently asking in an undertone, "Are you happy, Mattie? I hope you're wretched with that pretentious oaf Sylvester. If you are, I want you to know I'd be proud to take you back to Maine with me."

"Ah, Hughie," she said with an affectionate smile. "I've missed you so much."

"I'm absolutely serious," he told her. "If you ever change your mind, I'll be waiting. I guess you know by now how I feel about you."

To his joy and extreme discomfiture, she kissed him lightly on the mouth, then said, "I'll remember that."

Seeing this exchange from the corner where he was chatting with Esther Loftus, Gideon went rigid with jealousy. Later that evening, when they returned home, he demanded to know just what she thought she'd been doing, kissing another man.

"Oh, good God!" she sighed. "He's not 'another man.' He's my old friend Hughie. Please don't be tiresome. I want to go to bed now."

"I suppose you'd prefer to be going to bed with that dreary little hack."

"That 'dreary little hack' is more of a man and more talented than you will ever be. Don't you dare ever again speak of one of my friends in that condescending fashion. You're not good enough, Gideon Sylvester, in any way whatsoever, to make deprecating comments about other artists. If you were, you'd have had that 'show' long-since."

"If he's so wonderful, why didn't you marry him?"

"I keep asking myself that," she snarled. "God knows, I could have. He asked me enough times."

He went pale, then drew himself up to his full six feet four inches and said, "I think I'll sleep upstairs tonight."

"Suits me down to the ground," she said. "An excellent idea."

"You are a virago!"

"Thank you," she said, pushing the door shut even as he was going through it. "I consider that a great compliment, coming from you!" she shouted through the door as she locked it. "You pompous ass!"

With the departure of the Harveys, the Regulars were no more. It was ended. Every so often Mattie would run into Esther Loftus, but they had little to talk about. The Harveys had been the nucleus of the group and without them there was simply empty air. Mattie felt as if, once again, she'd been disowned. She did receive letters from Hughie and from the Harveys, but the letters came from so great a distance, both logistically and emotionally, that they weren't very consoling. She was left with a husband she too often found hateful, and a job that was no longer rewarding now that Mr. Sternholt was no longer there to praise her efforts. She had precious little time for going out into the streets to draw, and even less time to paint. Gideon Sylvester seemed to sense when she was about to approach a new canvas and he'd make a point, it appeared, of distracting her. He'd either creep downstairs to seduce her on her way to the easel, or he'd come in waving theater tickets that his stage manager friend had given him. She was beginning, by the end of that year, to think she'd have to get rid of Gideon Sylvester. He was impeding her progress. The number of finished paintings going upstairs to be stored was growing less and less, and it worried her. She needed to paint, and it felt as if Gideon Sylvester didn't want her to.

Early in 1935 a number of things happened, one on top of each other, any of which might have prevented her taking flight. Combined, these things bound her to Gideon Sylvester in ways she could never have predicted.

The first thing that happened, soon after the new year, was the death of Gideon Senior. Gideon made a display of pretended grief before, during, and after the funeral, until the contents of his father's will were made known. To Gideon's utter disbelief, he did not inherit the money he'd been counting on but, rather, he became the owner of the family's old summer house on the island.

"It's a goddamned barn!" Gideon railed, furious. "And who the hell's going to want to buy a summer home when half the world's living in Hoovervilles and selling apples? The stupid old bastard! Leaving all that money to those three imbecilic girls!" He went on and on about the lunacy of his father's bequests, and even consulted a lawyer to see if he could contest the will. It was uncontestable, iron-clad. Gideon Sylvester went storming out and didn't return home for three days.

Mattie was happy to have him gone. She was actually saddened by the death of the only member of the Sylvester family she'd genuinely liked. The old man had, on a number of occasions, sent her checks with the firm instruction (strongly underlined) not to let Gideon know about this money. "My son," he'd written her once very soon after their marriage, "has little or no sense when it comes to financial matters. He can be ruthless, but lacks the acuity to use this to intelligent advantage. You'd do well never to allow him control of the family finances."

Gideon Senior had been kindhearted and generous, and his contributions had been promptly cashed, with the larger portion of the money going into the metal box under the floorboard in the closet. The rest Mattie used to pay some of the debts Gideon Sylvester seemed to acquire almost magically. He could go out to the store for bread and thirty days later there'd come a bill for some item he'd purchased en route. The man had no concept of the value of money. He believed it was something designed solely to allow him to realize his least whim. It incensed Mattie, and was the cause of their most vociferous arguments. He so infuriated her with his cavalier attitude that upon receipt, following his three-day absence, of a tailoring bill for a new suit, she went at him with her fists, and succeeded in blackening his eye and cracking two of his ribs.

As he cowered, legitimately fearful in the face of her awe-inspiring ferocity, she told him he'd either have to forfeit the deposit he'd given the tailor, or find some way to pay the man. "I REFUSE TO IN-DULGE YOU!" she shouted. "Your idiotic mother spoiled you rotten! No one in his right mind goes out to buy a custom-tailored suit when he doesn't have the money to pay for it. You take care of this or, by God, I'll care take of it for you! I've had as much of you as I'm going to take, Gideon Sylvester! I want your things out of here. I'm going upstairs now to start bringing my paintings back down here, and when I'm finished you get the hell out, and you stay out! I'm through with you. I knew the day I married you it was a mistake."

Flinging open the door, she stormed up the stairs to the room that had once been hers. It took her better than an hour, making numerous trips up and down the stairs, to clear out her paintings. While she worked, Gideon went off somewhere. She had no interest in where he might have gone. She simply wanted him out of her life for good. She thought she might take a long weekend and go up to Maine to visit Hughie and the Harveys. She could afford it, and not only would it be a relief to be away from Gideon Sylvester, it would also be delightful to spend some time with people she loved who truly cared about her.

As she stacked the canvases against the living room wall, she began to think she must have missed some of them upstairs. There were a number she couldn't find. Another trip upstairs only confirmed their absence. All that remained in the small room were Gideon's works, those arid, visionless, technically adept exercises. Telling herself she had to be mistaken, she returned to the apartment to examine the canvases one by one. No mistake. At least six pictures were missing. She sat down heavily on the sofa trying to think what could have happened to them when her eye was caught by the open closet door.

She was in the habit of keeping that door closed, but it was sitting ajar now. She got up and walked over, suddenly deeply afraid that Gideon Sylvester had discovered her secret cache of money. Apparently, he hadn't. To be sure, she carried the metal box into the bathroom, locked the door, then counted its contents. There was the exact amount there'd been before: eighteen hundred and forty-eight dollars. Almost sick with relief, she returned the box to its hiding place just as there was a knock at the door.

Gideon was standing in the hallway, hat in hand.

"You can't come in! I meant what I said," she told him. "I'm finished with you. But while you're here, tell me something! Where are the other six paintings?"

At once he colored and looked away. "I was going to tell you," he said, trying to smile. "You were so angry, I didn't have a chance."

"Tell me what?"

"I sold them for you."

"You what?"

"I sold them."

"What do you mean you sold them?"

"Exactly what I say. I thought I'd surprise you. I showed them to a dealer I know, an old friend of mine, and he put them on display in his window. He sold them. Naturally, he took a thirty-five percent commission. But he sold them."

"Who to? For how much?" she asked, all agog. "You should've *told* me!"

"Quite a good price, considering the times."

"How much? And where's the money?"

"I used it," he confessed, "to pay some debts."

"You *used* it? You took my paintings, sold them, and you *spent* the money?"

"I was planning to repay you. The thing of it is, I wanted to tell you, but I was so worried, what with the bank failing . . . I honestly didn't know how to tell you."

"What bank failing?" she wanted to know, at last allowing him to come inside so the other tenants wouldn't hear them bickering in the hallway.

"The bank that handled my trust. It failed," he told her, "several months ago. I thought I'd surprise you about the paintings . . . I'm sorry, Mattie. It's all a dreadful mess."

"You mean your checks aren't going to be coming anymore?" she asked, feeling sorry for him as he shook his head morosely.

"I was too ashamed to tell you. And then I thought you'd be so pleased that I found a dealer to take your paintings. Well, one thing led to another, and I thought it best to pay the bills. You have every right to be furious with me. I'm furious with myself."

"People bought my paintings," she said, more to herself than to him. "My first sales. Perhaps your dealer friend would give me a show."

"I could talk to him," he said quickly, setting his hat to one side and slipping down to his knees on the floor in front of her. "I know I've been impossible; I know I've done everything wrong, but I do love you, Mattie. Will you forgive me? Could we try to start again?"

"Gideon, you have no income. Are you proposing that I support you? Do you really think that's a good way to try to start again?"

"I have an idea," he said, his hands on her knees. "I've got the island house. I was thinking we could move there for a while, until FDR gets us out of these hard times."

"It could take *years* before that happens. And what would we live on if I leave Stern's and go to live on some godforsaken island? You're not thinking clearly."

"But I am. I've been thinking about this since Father died. It could work. You'd be able to paint full time, and I'd be your agent, take care of getting your work shown to galleries and potential buyers."

"What about your work?"

"That, too, of course. And don't forget, your share of Stern's is worth something. That would give us some money to live on until we sell more of your paintings."

"I don't know. I'll have to think about this."

"Please think about it," he pleaded. "We wouldn't have to pay rent on two places, the way we do now. We wouldn't have to pay rent at all. We could even grow our own vegetables. Just think! You'd be able to paint day and night, if you wanted, with nothing to stop you."

It was very tempting. "I need time to think," she told him.

"Of course," he agreed. "And you do forgive me, don't you?" He didn't give her a chance to answer. He began a series of urgent kisses that distracted her so successfully that it wasn't until they'd finished and he was pulling out of her that she realized that he'd not only won her over once again, but he'd also made love to her without taking any precautions.

"Just this once won't get you pregnant," he said confidently.

He was, as in so many other matters, completely wrong.

Sixteen

It had gone dark. Mattie stopped speaking and stared in the direction of the beach. Sarah watched the fireflies sparking by the hedges, then saw a rabbit dart across the lawn and into one of the flower beds. A steady breeze came off the ocean. The lights were on in the garage apartment.

"I don't think even Gideon Sylvester was fool enough to think he could make me pregnant on the first try, but I do think he was hoping and praying for it," Mattie said, her voice a catchment where every last drop of bitterness was stored. "It worked out exactly the way he'd hoped it would. Within six weeks, the smell of anything from food to perfume had me heaving. He went prancing about, all puffed up with pride, thrilled at the age of thirty-five by his vision of fatherhood and gloating over his potency.

"Actually," she said, softening, "he was very kind during my pregnancy. He made me endless cups of tea, entire loaves of dry toast. I believe he honestly thought he wanted a child, and for those months he went back to behaving the way he had at the start, before we were married. So, naturally, convinced he'd had a change of heart, I fell in love with him again."

She asked for a meeting of the Stern's employees, and told them she'd be leaving. When it came to the matter of her share of the company, she explained her plan.

"I know you'll have to vote on this, and I want you to," she said. "What I propose is that even though I won't be here you'll go on thinking of me as one of you. I don't think whoever you get to replace me will have the cash to buy me out, and I'd like to stay involved if possible. So what I'm suggesting is that I become an absentee share-holder. That way you won't have to worry about finding the money to pay me; someone who needs it will get a job; and, in time, when the economy improves, you can vote to reimburse me for my shares."

No one quibbled. They accepted her offer, expressed their unhappiness at seeing her go, and wished her good luck with the move and the baby.

She didn't mention any of this to Gideon Sylvester. She simply told him she'd received a fair sum from the company. "It's enough," she told him. "We should be able to manage for a while. And if your dealer friend will take more of my paintings, we'll do nicely. Shouldn't I meet him, by the way?"

"He's out of town at the moment," Gideon said. "When he gets back, though, you should most definitely meet him. He's very impressed with your work."

When they got down to packing, neither one of them had much in the way of possessions. Mattie had the pictures she'd acquired as well as her own, her supplies, and a substantial number of filled sketchbooks. Everything fit into a station wagon Gideon borrowed from a friend, except for a number of both their canvases which he told her he was taking to the dealer. "There's no sense shifting all these to the island, then bringing them back again. We might as well get it done now."

That seemed reasonable, especially when he produced a receipt for the paintings from the Gallery Alexander on Madison Avenue.

Unfortunately, the station wagon's heater didn't work, so their drive was not a pleasant one. Gideon drove directly to the ferry, where only one other car was waiting to go on board.

"It's very quiet on the island in the winter," he told her, as the ferry chugged away from the pier. "Back when I was a small boy, there were a couple of big old hotels, and in the summer there were all kinds of people. The hotels are gone now, and it's quite a while since most of the people we knew have been over. It's six or seven years since I've been here myself."

"You mean no one's stayed in your house all this time?"

"Not exactly. The family pays one of the locals to look after the place, make sure the roof isn't leaking, that sort of thing. But none of us have come over since the summer of twenty-nine. It's a great old house, though. I know you'll like it."

"I thought you were anxious to get rid of it."

"I wasn't thinking clearly," he said. "And I was disappointed there wasn't any cash. But it is a good house."

It was, as he'd promised, a great old house. There was, however, one problem: It had no heating, except for fireplaces in the living room and two of the larger bedrooms. Upon discovering this, she said, "We can't possibly live here through the winter. We'll freeze to death."

"I never even thought about it," he said diffidently. "I'll drive down and have a talk with Tom, who's been caretaking. He's bound to have an idea what we can do."

While he was gone, Mattie wandered through the house, going into each of the six bedrooms, testing the toilets and faucets in each of the five bathrooms, satisfied there was running water, even if it was stone cold. Locating a candle, she went down to the basement, found the hot water heater, and turned it on. If she had to, she thought grimly, she'd spend the next four months in a hot tub.

The kitchen had a huge old-fashioned wood stove and there was still a supply of kindling and wood in the pantry. After testing to be sure the chimney would draw, she fed some of the kindling into the stove and got a fire started. She was relieved to know that at least one room in the house would be warm.

With the groceries they'd bought on the mainland put away, she carried some of the wood from the kitchen to the fireplace in the living room. Down on her hands and knees she held a torch of burning newspaper in the chimney, discovered the flue was closed, got it open, then set about building another fire.

By the time Gideon Sylvester returned some two hours later with Tom in tow, Mattie was half asleep in front of the living room fire.

A surprisingly dapper little man of forty-five or so, Tom offered Mattie a welcoming smile and a hearty handshake, then roundly berated Gideon for being foolish enough to think he could get through a winter in that house. "This place can't be heated!" he stated. "Your only hope is to close off all the rooms, otherwise your heat'll go up the chimney. There's doors to the dining room, if I remember correctly. I reckon they're either in the basement or the barn. First thing to do is put them doors back on. There's a woodpile to the side of the house, but it's probably soaked through. You'll have to move the wood, get it started drying before you can hope to use it. Well, come on!" he said. "Better shift! It'll be dark soon and you'll want to get the doors hung and some wood laid by."

He marched Gideon down to the basement, where they unearthed the doors, then instructed Gideon to start bringing the wood up to the verandah and stack it by the back door. "I'll hang the doors," he told Mattie as Gideon went out through the kitchen. "That one wouldn't know how to hang a door if his life depended on it."

"Would you care for some coffee, Tom?" she asked, taking to this man at once and suspecting they were going to be needing him.

"I wouldn't say no," he said with another friendly smile, prying open the hinges with a screwdriver.

While the coffee was percolating, she asked if there was anything she could do to help.

"You could go up and close every last door on the second floor," he told her. "And shut that one at the top of the stairs leading up to the attic. There's a perfectly good bathroom to the side of the kitchen, so you've got no need to use the second floor at all. Man's a fool," he muttered, "thinking he can live year-round in this old house."

"Could we put in a furnace?" she asked from the foot of the stairs.

"Cost you the earth. You'd have to ship it over from the mainland, for openers. Then you'd have to run ducts everywhere. I could put 'er in for you but I don't see no way to get heat up past the first floor. Unless you want exposed ductwork everywhere. It'd be a fire hazard, too. Nah! It's not worth the bother. You're looking at a heck of a lot of money. Plus there's the expense of the coal which'd have to be shipped over, too."

"How do you heat your house?" she asked.

"Wood furnace. But then, see, I built the place for year-round living."

"Out of curiosity," she said, "What d'you think it would cost to put in a furnace?"

"Oh, you're looking at maybe five, six hundred dollars."

He was right: It would cost far too much. She closed the second floor doors, then returned to the kitchen to get the coffee. While she was pouring it, she listened to Gideon huffing exhaustedly as he stacked the cord wood outside the kitchen door. She smiled and carried Tom's coffee to him.

He finished hanging the doors, then sat with her on the mildewed sofa in front of the fire, sipping his coffee.

"What else should I know, Tom? I think I'd better have all the bad news in one go."

"I saw you found the hot water heater," he said. "You're a smart girl. Every year I used to have to come up here to show Mr. Gideon Senior how to turn the blamed thing on. It's a good heater, shouldn't give you no problems. And I cleaned the chimneys this past September, so you're okay there. The roof's sound, but there was a bunch of starlings up in the attic last summer. I checked around and I'm pretty sure I found the place where they got in. Boarded it over. But they made a hell of a mess up there. You'll want to clean that up come spring, or by summer the smell'll be pretty rank. There's field mice, but they never harmed anybody. Bugs here and there. Nothing sinister, though." He gave her a grin. "Used to scare the dickens out of those Sylvester girls, but I reckon you're made of sterner stuff. Can't see no centipede scaring you."

She returned his smile, then asked, "How can I reach you if I need you?"

"There's a phone," he said, looking surprised she didn't know. "Over to the side of them stairs. All you do is pick up and sooner or later Aggie on the exchange will come on and connect you with anyone you've got a mind to talk to. Even long distance. Course that can take some time. The whole island's a bunch of party lines, so you don't never want to go telling anybody your secrets over the telephone unless you want every last person here knowing your business five minutes after you hang up."

"I'll bear that in mind."

"You want me, you tell Aggie you want Tom, and she'll call around till she finds me. Only so many places you can be on this island. What you want," he said, "is a bicycle, case you need to come down to O'Brian's store for anything. O'Brian brings meat and dry goods over every week from the mainland, unless the weather's foul, which can happen, believe you me. We've been cut off plenty of times for weeks at a stretch. You want to make sure you stock that pantry good, cause you're bound to be cut off at least once during the winter, way up this end of the island. We get some mighty big storms; everything freezes solid; the lines go down, and then you're well 'n' truly cut off, cause there ain't gonna be nobody nearer than four miles away until summer. And even then your nearest neighbor's better than a mile down the road." Lowering his voice, he said, "Mind if I ask kind of a personal question?"

"I don't mind."

"You strike me as a real sensible young woman. How'd you ever let Buddy Sylvester talk you into doing a damn fool thing like this?"

"I didn't know it would be this way," she told him. "If I'd known, I'd have refused to come."

"Just what I figured! He always did have more daring than sense, if you catch my drift."

"I certainly do."

He finished his coffee, then said, "I better go give him a hand with that wood or he'll be out there for a week." Holding his hand out to her, he said, "You need help with anything, pick up the phone. Aggie'll find me and I'll be along soon's I can. Can't say I care much for the idea of you two stuck out here, what with you expecting and all."

"I'm sure we'll be fine," she said, although she wasn't a bit sure of that. "Thank you, Tom. By the way, what exactly do you do on the island?"

"Heck, I thought you knew. I'm the local law. State trooper, Officer Tom Harding, at your service." Chuckling, he went off to help Gideon.

They carried a mattress down from one of the second floor bedrooms and slept in front of the living room fireplace. Gideon would wake up once or twice a night to add more wood to the fire, then hurry back under the blankets to press himself to Mattie's sleeping warmth. He'd build the fire in the stove in the morning before rousing her with a cup of coffee. And, to her astonishment, he revealed that he could cook.

"I don't have much choice, do I?" he said. "Didn't anyone ever teach you any domestic skills?"

"No," she said proudly. "And I have no intention of learning, ever."

The major drawback of being confined to the first floor was the impossibility of painting in the deeply shadowed rooms. The roof of the verandah kept direct sunlight from penetrating through to the interior of the house. This not only made the rooms colder, which was fine in summer, but created a permanent twilight indoors.

"I can't possibly work in here," Mattie complained soon after their arrival, discovering that Gideon had been misinformed or mistaken about everything having to do with this relocation.

"We'll work something out," he said solicitously. "I know how important this is to you."

The master bedroom had not only a north-facing window but a fireplace as well. He made numerous trips back and forth to stock the room with wood. Then, with the help of Tom Harding, he sealed the windows to cut down the drafts, and boarded over the door to the balcony. The two men carried up Mattie's easel, a worktable they found in the basement, and her supplies.

"This will do beautifully," she said, and thanked them both.

Referring back to her sketchbooks, she found the drawing she wanted and made her first project in the new studio a portrait of the two workmen eating their lunch on the curb outside the factory. Gideon stayed out of her way, entering only after knocking, to bring her something to eat or drink, then leaving quickly and quietly.

When the painting was finished, she studied it for a long time, pleased. Her strokes were strong, the colors were lively, the two men were captured forever on their curbside seats on West Thirty-eighth Street. Then, from some instinct she didn't stop to examine, she again approached the canvas. Selecting a very fine brush, she worked her name into the folds at the elbow of one of the men's shirts. She stood back, satisfied. Unless you knew to look for it, the signature wasn't evident. She laughed at what she'd done. There was a cunning element of mystery she'd just added to her work, and it tickled her.

Housebound, with little to do, she hit upon the idea of keeping a log of her work. Using a small bound sketchbook, she sat down and wrote the details of the painting as well as the location of the second signature. After adding the date both of the initial sketches and of the completed picture, she wondered where to keep it. She wouldn't have put it past Gideon to go through her personal things and since nothing was more personal than her work, she decided to keep the book hidden. Creeping up to the feather-and-droppings soiled attic, she placed it behind one of the ceiling support beams.

Thereafter, each time she completed a new piece, she made an entry in the book. It was one more thing to keep her mind off the stark reality of finding herself living out in the Atlantic in the old Sylvester summer house.

Because things were going well with Gideon, she didn't want to say or do anything to upset the smooth course they seemed to be sailing. But doubts had taken root and were sending up shoots she feared might eventually produce some virulently poisonous growth. She did her utmost to make the best of a difficult environment, primarily because Gideon was being ever more lovingly attentive as the baby grew bigger inside her. He cosseted her. Despite his basic laziness, he accompanied her when the weather permitted on long walks up the ice-encrusted beach. He insisted on taking the ferry to the mainland for provisions and accepted the money she doled out without comment. For once he appeared to be doing exactly what he'd said, without making expensive side trips during which he acquired frivolous items that caught his eye. If he said he was going for food, he returned with just food. And he used the car only when it was unavoidable, knowing how much it had upset her to have to pay out the two hundred dollars to buy it. Even though they'd had no choice, his failure to realize beforehand they'd be trapped on the north end of the island without a car had infuriated her. Tom Harding had found them the car, and she'd produced the money.

Somehow they managed to get through the winter without being cut off for more than a few days at a time or experiencing any significant problems. It did, however, cost far more than she'd antici-pated. Had they stayed on with Mrs. Webster, they'd have been much better off. Like the majority of Gideon Sylvester's ideas, this one was not a success. Yet Mattie loved the house and its rugged surroundings. She felt very connected to the island's tempestuous weather, its isolation, and its refusal to be swept away or submerged beneath angry ocean tides. The island was home, and she was determined to find a way to make the place livable. But that required money, and she was too fearful of one day finding the cash box empty to make any but the expenditures needed to sustain them.

When in May the weather finally began to grow warmer and the ice along the shoreline melted, she promised herself that as long as she lived this house would be hers. One day the rooms would have fresh paint and new curtains. There'd be a furnace humming away in the basement, sending currents of warm air right up to the attic. White-painted wicker chairs would sit on the verandah, and the overgrown shrubberies would be cut back and given form. Her child would play on the lawn and run along the beach, splashing in the shallows. More than anything else, she wanted to own this house.

In June Gideon said he had to go to New York. "Alexander wants to talk about a joint showing of both our paintings."

"When did you discuss that?"

"Oh, he telephoned one morning a week or so ago when you were taking a walk on the beach."

"Why didn't you tell me?"

"I wanted it to be a surprise," he said with one of his best toothy smiles. "This could be a great opportunity for us both."

"How can he show thirty of my paintings with the eleven you've managed to do in the last however long it's been?"

"He's not going to hang them all, Mattie," he said, as if addressing someone whose mental capacities were not quite what could they have been. "He'll hang say eight or nine of the best of both our pieces."

"Why hasn't he spoken to me? Why hasn't anyone consulted me? None of this sounds right. What are you up to, Gideon Sylvester?"

"I am trying to sell some paintings," he said patiently. "Since Alexander doesn't know you he can hardly launch into long-distance discussions with you about any of this."

"That's rubbish! If this Alexander person likes my work well enough to want to show it, at the very least I think he'd want to meet me."

"He does! But you must admit we've been just a *little* removed from things for the past three and a half months. Think how many times the power was out, not to mention the telephone line being down, or the ferry service being suspended because of the weather."

"There were plenty of times when everything was working perfectly."

"Mattie, I have to go or I'll miss the ferry. I don't want to be late for this meeting. As it is I've got a hell of a long drive ahead of me. And I'd be more than happy to have you come along, but you're hardly in a condition to be traveling right now."

"When will you be back?"

"I don't want to try to do it in one day. I'll spend the night in the city and be over on the first ferry in the morning."

"I see." She stood with one hand on her lower back and the other on her belly, aware distractedly of the baby's kicking. "Well, I suppose I'll see you tomorrow." She turned and looked up the stairway as if hearing someone calling. Then she turned back to take in this man she'd married, this hopelessly inept liar who really thought she was dumb enough to buy such an absurd story. She wondered if what he actually planned was to see some other woman. She hoped he was. It would be a relief to have him turn his doubtful attention in someone else's direction.

"If you have any problems, just call Tom," he said, moving to kiss her.

At the last moment, she drew away so that his kiss fell on her cheek. He stared at her, then left, whistling as he skipped down the front steps and walked jauntily to the car. She watched through the screen door as he placed his hat carefully on the front seat, then started up the car and drove off.

"Liar," she whispered. "You pathetic goddamned liar."

In the attic, she got out the money box and counted what remained inside. Their few months on the island had cost them almost eight hundred dollars, more than twice what the same length of time would have cost back in New York. At the rate they were going, the money wouldn't last a year. And when it was gone, they'd be destitute, candidates for the poorhouse. Only by then there'd be three of them.

She had to do something but couldn't think what. She was stuck on an island six miles out in the Atlantic, with a husband who was up to no good, and a baby due in less than three months' time. They had a house fit only for fair weather habitation. Not one of her friends was closer than two hundred miles away. She had only one marketable skill that might be of any use and somehow she was going to have to use it to provide the money to see them through the next winter. Moving cautiously for fear of tripping on the steep steps leading down to the second floor, she descended, making her way to the telephone to call Tom Harding.

"I'd like to talk to you," she told him, "if you could stop by when you have a chance."

"Happy to, Mattie. I'll be out after lunch."

And that was how she came to do a number of pencil portraits for those inhabitants of the island who had the money to spare and a yen for something personalized to hang on their walls.

"I was lucky," Mattie told Sarah. "A number of the old summer families came that year, and word spread quickly. I was working from morning to night, from the middle of June right through to the end of August. Gideon was livid when he found out, and forbade me to continue. I told him I intended to have my baby in a hospital and asked if he had the money to pay for that. Of course, he didn't. So he shut up about it. He never mentioned the joint show again, and when I asked what had become of my paintings, he said they were in storage. I decided he'd taken a mistress, which was why his trips to New York proliferated. And for some ridiculous reason, with respect to the paintings, I chose to believe him."

Seventeen

I need you to sit again," Mattie told Sarah the following day. "Could you do that, do you think, without saying a word?"

"I can probably manage it."

"Good. Come up when you've finished your breakfast."

Sarah arrived in the attic half an hour later to see Mattie cleaning brushes. The smell of turpentine lay like plumes across the bands of cool air flowing from the air conditioner. With her hair in an even more haphazard topknot than usual and a cotton smock covering her clothes she looked quite young and purposeful, and Sarah could easily see how striking she'd been years before, when Gideon Sylvester first brought her to this house.

Seating herself in the armchair without being asked, Sarah opened her senses to absorb the sunlight battling the air-conditioning, the dust motes dancing before the windows and beneath the skylight, and the innately elegant old woman whose minor movements before her easel and worktable were balletic by dint of having been performed so many times before.

With the drawing close by as a reference and the model seated precisely as required, Mattie looked for a long time at Sarah before turning her head slightly as her left hand, like that of a surgeon's, reached for a charcoal stick. Then the hand began re-creating Sarah's image in charcoal outlines on the pristine primed canvas. The only sound was of the whish of the charcoal as she worked. A cigarette burned down in the ashtray as again Mattie visually examined Sarah, searching beyond the surfaces to everything underneath that contributed to the composition of the younger woman's face.

It was like being scanned, Sarah thought, by some undreamed-of other-worldly being whose powers were beyond anything ever imagined by mere earthlings. She felt Mattie's eyes peel back her skin to observe the underlying musculature before probing deeper into her bones and their very marrow. She wondered if all the people who'd ever posed for Mattie had felt this same sense of penetration and if they'd felt, as she did now, a burgeoning need for more of the tacit approval that came with having been selected as a worthy subject.

After perhaps half an hour, Mattie put down the charcoal stick, lit a cigarette, and again gazed fixedly at Sarah.

"You're changing," Mattie said mildly. "I'm watching you change. This isn't something that usually happens."

Sarah could only nod in assent.

"Is it Carl?" Mattie asked, smoking intently.

"It's you," Sarah said softly.

"Me?" The cigarette stayed poised in the air.

"I'm beginning to know you, really know you. I'm starting to feel now, when you tell me the things that happened in this house all those years ago, that I was here with you. I feel what you felt; I know why you did the things you did."

"You do, huh?" The cigarette completed its trip to Mattie's mouth. "Maybe so," she allowed. "Be still now," she ordered, and went about the business of selecting her colors the way another woman might deliberate over trays of gems in a jewelry store.

The concentration on both their parts was so intense that Sarah was lulled, drawn into a near dreamlike state wherein she watched the woman watching her, fascinated by everything about Mathilda Sylvester: her large, deep-set eyes, her strong features and beautifully shaped mouth, her long limbs and powerful hands; the bending and flexing of her left arm as her hand moved the brush to the palette secured by her right hand. Judiciously she applied the brush bristles to a daub of paint here, a coil there; dabbing, blending, controlling the tones she then placed on the canvas much in the way she'd put tinted cosmetics on Sarah's face. It was so manifestly obvious that Mattie was in absolute command of this environment that Sarah's respect for her expanded.

For the ninety minutes of silence that held until Mattie said they'd take a short break, both women were supremely happy.

Sarah stood up from the chair to stretch, and Mattie anticipated her. "Yes," she said, "you may have a look."

Mattie stood back from the easel with a cigarette, her right arm across her chest supporting the elbow of the left as she held the cigarette to her mouth and squinted against the smoke, her eyes following Sarah as she walked around to stand before the work in progress.

Sarah stood in front of the easel with the sensation that the earth had suddenly shivered beneath her feet. Her mouth went dry and her heart began to pound as her breathing turned erratic. She drew in a sharp, painful breath, reeled back several steps, then turned to look at the old woman. "My God!" she whispered, utterly shaken. "It was you, wasn't it? You're the one who painted all those fantastic paintings."

"Of course," Mattie said matter-of-factly. "I told you the man had a purely technical skill."

"My God, my God," Sarah said, her head seeming to swell as the implications of this revelation doubled and tripled inside it.

"Do stop repeating that!" Mattie requested.

"But, my God!" Sarah exclaimed. "I can't . . . I mean . . ." How, she wondered, did something like this happen? She wasn't sure she wanted to know. If there were more shocking revelations to come her head might burst from trying to absorb them. *"God!"*

"I do believe," Mattie said with sorely tried patience, "I asked you to stop repeating that."

"Sorry," Sarah apologized, her eyes returning to the canvas. "It was you," she said wonderingly. "You. Everyone believes you were just the wife, someone with a reputation for being exotic and reclusive. And the whole time, you were the artist. You."

"I think we've made that point, my dear. Let's not kick it to death."

"Does anyone else know?" Sarah asked, unable to take her eyes from the canvas.

"A few people. Their knowledge of this, and their quite violent disagreement over it, is in no small way responsible for the rift between my sons."

"I thought I knew what you were going to tell me," Sarah said, "but I don't think I wanted to believe it. I do now." Suddenly outraged, she cried, "How could you let that happen?"

"I didn't *let* anything happen!" Mattie barked. "Haven't you *heard* what I've been telling you? I didn't actively agree; I never gave my consent. It all began more than fifty years ago, and men could get away with things they'd be drawn and quartered for today."

"I'm so sorry," Sarah apologized.

"Shit on your sorry!" Mattie growled, so exactly parroting Carl that Sarah had to wonder what sort of complicity existed between the two of them. "What do I need with that? I don't give a good goddamn about your 'sorry'!"

"Yes, you do," Sarah stood her ground. "You damned well do. Because you know I really care. Maybe I don't quite understand how something like this could've happened, but I want to. I want you to explain to me how all this came about. *I want to understand.*"

"I'm sure you do," Mattie said more quietly.

"Would you like anything?" Sarah asked. "Some coffee maybe?"

"No, but you would. So run down and get yourself a cup. I'm not going anywhere."

Feeling shaky, Sarah said, "I'll be right back," and ran downstairs to the kitchen.

Bonnie was feeding carrots into the Cuisinart and didn't look up but said, "Just made a fresh pot, if it's coffee you're after. And Carl said to say he'd be driving to the south end this afternoon if you want to go, or you need anything."

"Okay, thanks," Sarah said, hearing Mattie say again, Shit on your sorry. One thing was for certain: Mattie and Carl were in very close communication. How else did a seventy-seven-year-old woman come to repeat the precise words of her forty-four-year-old chauffeur/handyman?

Sarah carried her coffee back up to the attic.

"Sit," Mattie said. "I want to get in another hour before the sun shifts too much. You can drink your coffee. I'll let you know when to keep still."

Retrieving her palette and positioning it across the flat on her inner right forearm, she picked up the brush. "It's a great mistake, Sarah," she said, "to assume that anyone merely *lets* things happen. To keep the record straight, I'm going to tell you how that larcenous bastard managed to defraud not only his wife but most of the world population. For once in your life," she warned, "resist the impulse to ask stupid questions or leap to half-assed conclusions. It cannot have escaped your notice that I find it maddening when you do that, so do me the courtesy of restricting yourself to relevant questions. I have great respect for relevancy."

Having completed another of her laserlike visual inspections, Mattie began speaking dispassionately as she resumed her work.

A week before the baby was due, Mattie informed Gideon Sylvester that she wanted to go to the mainland to be close enough to the hospital to get there in a hurry should she need to.

"Where were you planning to stay?" he asked.

"I thought one of your legions of friends might live somewhere nearby and you could use your famous charm to prevail upon him to allow your wife to stay for a few days."

"I don't happen to have any friends in the area."

"Fine. Then I'll rent a room in a boardinghouse."

"We can't afford that."

She laughed and said, "I'll manage."

"What about me?" he asked. "What am I supposed to do while you're on the mainland, waiting for the baby?"

If she'd ever wanted proof of his lack of concern for her, this was it. Any other man would have planned to accompany her, wherever she chose to go, in order to be sure she was all right. But not Gideon Sylvester. He treated her decision as a slight, an indication of her refusal to include him in her plans. Everything, she saw now, boiled down to Gideon's certitude that the world orbited around him. He was the sun and moon combined, and viewed himself as so singularly potent that it was an absolute given that the planets responded according to his personal gravity and magnetism.

"I don't care what you do," she told him. "For all I care you can go down to the harbor with one of your friends, take out one of those little sailboats you're so fond of, and sail off to China. Now, if you'll excuse me, I have arrangements to make."

Right up to the minute she was wheeled into the delivery room she hoped he would have a change of heart and show up. He didn't. With the help of a particularly kind young nurse and the attending obstetrician, she gave birth after seven hours of labor to a hugely healthy infant she intended to call Richard.

When Gideon finally did come to see her the following afternoon, he brought her an antique gold brooch with "Mother" engraved upon it. It made her laugh, which pleased him, as did the sight of his son.

"What a splendid boy!" he proclaimed, entranced by the view of the infant's eager mouth closing rapaciously on Mattie's nipple. "This is marvelous!" he said, then sat down, apparently awed, to watch the infant nurse. He looked more like someone interested in having a go at nursing himself than a proud father, so intently did he follow every nuance of this act. "I've never seen this before," he said, his expression faintly lewd. "I find it very—stimulating."

She could see he'd have been more than willing, had it been possible, to leap on top of her and make love to her right there in her hospital bed. He was sexually aroused by the sight of his son being breast-fed. It seemed to be his only reaction to the entire event. He did not ask about the delivery or how she was feeling. He simply gazed, unblinking, at the baby and her breast. It chilled her and she placed her hand protectively over the baby's body.

When the baby had fallen asleep, and the nurse had taken him off back to the nursery, Gideon prepared to go.

"You have to go down to the office and fill out the birth registration," she reminded him.

"Delighted," he said, and bent to kiss her, slipping his hand inside her nightgown over her breast.

He could catch her every time, she thought, wondering why her body was so inevitably responsive to his touch, even when her mind was recoiling from him.

After promising he'd be back the next day to take her and the baby home, he left.

It wasn't until some six weeks later when she received a copy of the birth certificate that she discovered Gideon had completely disregarded her instructions, and had named the boy Gideon Sylvester III.

"He's *Richard*," she cried, outraged. "How could you do a thing like this?"

"Don't be silly, my dear," he said, undaunted. "There's a family tradition, you know."

"Oh, Christ!" she railed. "Some day, I swear to God, I'm going to kill you. I wanted him to be called Richard Gideon. Wasn't that good enough for you?"

"If he's not happy with it later on, he can always change it by deed poll."

He was insufferable, but there was nothing to be gained by her telling him so. She'd found that arguments with him affected her and the baby. Whatever tension she felt instantly transmitted itself to the baby the moment she sat down to offer him her breast. And since Gideon the Third, as she was now forced to call him, could scream for hours when upset, the wisest course was to try to keep herself calm whenever she held him.

When Gideon approached her some two months after the birth, she went rigid. "You're not coming anywhere near me without a contraceptive," she told him. "I have no intention of going through any of this again in the near future."

"But you love the baby," he said, mystified.

"Of course I do. That does not, however, mean I have any desire to find myself burdened with another one. So until you've had a chance to visit a drugstore on the mainland, you will kindly keep your hands to yourself."

"Don't be so angry, Mattie," he said placatingly. "You know I love to touch you."

"I don't know *what* you love, and that's the God's honest truth. You defy rational explaining. You defy logic."

"Not at all," he crooned, inching closer to her. "I find you fantastically exciting now," he murmured, working his hands up underneath her nightgown to lay claim to those breasts that so intrigued him, exercising his one true power over her. A moment or two and he had the nightgown off her as he touched his tongue experimentally to her nipple. At once a drop of thin, faintly blue liquid surfaced and he caught it on his tongue. Then, his eyes acquiring that meaningful glitter, he launched himself at her with the full force of his concentrated skills.

She could never comprehend why her anger with him in no way interfered with the desire he seemed so effortlessly able to provoke in her. Without fail, he turned her into something very like parched soil that responded with yawning need to his moisture-giving ministrations. He could even rob her of her milk and she'd reward him for it by offering access to any additional part of her he chose to claim. And since it had been quite some time since they'd made love, his timing in this instance was impeccable.

When he'd drained her breasts, he relocated between her thighs, stabbing her with the blunted instrument of his choosing until she reached, twisting, to reciprocate the caress, almost choking herself on his flesh. Something as a result of the birth process had grown more sensitive inside her, so that she reacted violently to his slightest caress. And he seemed to know it. He kept on until she was so inflamed and abraded that his touch became painful. Only then did he allow her to sleep, with his body curved into hers, one hand clamped possessively over her breasts.

In January, when the baby was two and a half months old and sleeping nightly on the mattress between her and Gideon, she decided they had no choice but to spend the money and make arrangements with Tom Harding to install a furnace.

She carried the baby with her up to the attic to check the contents of the money box and knew the instant she set foot on the rickety stairway that something was amiss. The door was open, which instantly alerted her. And there were footprints visible in the dust on the floor. Standing at the top of the stairs gazing in at the space she'd spent several days clearing of bird droppings and feathers during the summer, she could see, with the help of the early morning sun pouring through the windows at either end, the random pattern of the footprints.

Holding her breath, the baby secure in her right arm, she lifted down the box, knowing from its weight that it was empty. She opened the lid and stared into its cleared interior, deeply afraid. Then she thought of the journal and, moving leadenly, she went toward its hiding place, convinced it too would be gone. Nothing was safe from Gideon Sylvester. But, miraculously, the book was still there. She returned it to its place in the rafters, then carried the baby downstairs, maintaining a forced calm until he'd been fed and tucked into a nest of pillows on the sofa near the fire. Then she said, "I want to talk to you, Gideon Sylvester!" and went to the kitchen. He followed, wearing an innocent expression as he sat down at the table.

"Return my money!" she said in a low quivering voice.

"I beg your pardon?"

"My money. You found it and took it. I want it back right now."

"I haven't taken your money, Mattie. I have no idea what you're talking about."

"The money box in the attic," she said, digging her fingers into her palms to stop herself from physically attacking him. "It's empty. You took the money."

"That was yours?" He looked dumbfounded. "I had no idea. Good God almighty!" he exclaimed, realization widening his eyes. "I went up to have a look around. I found the box and thought Father must've hidden it away up there for some reason, perhaps with the idea in mind that I'd find it. It *never occurred* to me that it might be yours."

"I don't care *what* you thought. Return the money and we'll forget all about it!"

"But, I can't!" he said, beginning to look frightened. "I honestly thought I'd found a small treasure."

"*Please!* Spare me this astonishing crap! Just *give* me the *money!*"

"I can't, Mattie! I was so convinced it was found money that I gave it to my broker in New York to invest. It's such a good time to play the market, I . . ." He stopped in the face of her immediate and consuming rage.

"You invested *my* money in the *stock market*? You took *every last cent* we have in the world and used it to 'play' the market?" She could feel herself rocketing out of control. It was as if all the air in the room had been sucked out, leaving her in a pulsing vacuum wherein a little voice whispered, It's all over nothing matters kill him it won't matter go ahead!

"But how was I to know it was your money?"

Giving in to her murderous impulse, she pulled open the drawer in the counter beside her, drew out a butcher knife, and wrapped her hand around it. "I'm going to kill you, Gideon Sylvester!" she whispered, so incensed her vocal cords felt engorged. "I'm going to eviscerate you, you lying bastard!" She raised her left hand with the knife and ran at him. In terror, he leaped from the chair, ducked past her, struggled with the knob on the back door, got it open, and went tearing out, oblivious to the cold and the snow, headed for the car.

"GET AWAY FROM THE CAR!" she screamed, pursuing him with the knife. "GET AWAY FROM HERE!"

He looked back over his shoulder at her as he ran, in fear for his life, turning in midstride toward the driveway. She followed him all the way to the main road, screaming incoherently until he was out of sight. Then, slowly, she allowed her arm to fall and stood sobbing in despair until the cold sent her back inside.

Later that afternoon the telephone rang. When she heard Gideon Sylvester's voice, her fury returned. "When you have my money in your hand, I will consider speaking to you. Until then, as far as I'm concerned, you're dead. Stay away from me or I will kill you!" She slammed down the receiver, then went to pick up the baby, who'd begun to cry at the sound of her shouting.

The next day, when she was marginally calmer, she called Tom Harding and asked if he'd be good enough to come to see her.

When he arrived, she gave him coffee—the only thing Gideon Sylvester had purchased in vast quantity—then sat down with him in the living room and said, "Gideon's used up all our money, Tom. I'm in trouble and I need your help. There's nowhere I can go, and no one I know who could possibly take me and the baby in. I've got this diamond eternity band I can sell, and the car. If you could arrange to sell them, I'd be very grateful to you."

"Mattie, you can't live here without a car. Maybe in the summer, but not now."

"I have no choice. I have exactly eleven dollars and twenty-three cents. There's enough food in the pantry to last for a few weeks, and then I'll be eating snow. If there's any chance at all you could find someone to buy the car, I've got to sell it. I know people don't pay that much for secondhand jewelry, but this ring is supposed to be worth quite a lot. I'll take whatever I can get for it."

"Even if I sell these things, the money's not going to last forever."

"I can make a hundred dollars see us through the winter, Tom. After that, I'll figure out what to do next. Right now, I've got to take things one step at a time. I've told Gideon not to come anywhere near this house until he's got my twelve hundred dollars in his hands." She stopped, fighting down tears. "Please do this for me."

"Okay, Mattie. I'll do what I can. Sure is a shame though, to part with a ring like this."

"I'm more than happy to part with it, I promise you."

At the door as he was leaving, he had to say, "I'll never understand how a woman like you could hook up with a scoundrel like Buddy Sylvester."

"Sheer stupidity," she told him. "Sheer damned stupidity!"

Eighteen

C arl stopped the town car in front of O'Brian's general store and said, "You want to come in or wait here while I pick up Bonnie's order?"

"I'll wait here," Sarah said.

Through the open car window, she could hear people inside the store greeting Carl, calling out hi and asking how was Mattie. The islanders liked Carl. Their voices were filled with friendly interest. She wondered why she'd assumed no one knew or cared about him. As Mattie had pointed out, she seemed to make a lot of assumptions. She really was going to have to stop; it was an appalling habit.

Carl loaded the boxes of groceries into the trunk, then climbed behind the wheel. "What's the matter?" he asked. "You look down."

"Could we go somewhere quiet to talk?"

"Sure," he said readily, and started the car. "I want to drop this stuff at the house before some of it thaws. Okay?"

She said, "Yes," then stared out the window as he drove back to the north end of the island, feeling his eyes as he glanced over at her every so often.

Upon arriving back at the house, he said, "We'll leave the car and walk. Give me five minutes to take this stuff in."

She got out and looked over at the verandah and the empty rocker. Turning, she scanned the beach. Mattie was nowhere in sight. She crossed her arms tightly in front of her and stood waiting for Carl to return, trying to comprehend what she was attempting to contain inside herself. She felt like a small child who'd temporarily lost sight of her mother in a crowded department store. She wanted to see the well-known, much-loved parent moving unfalteringly toward her.

The afternoon air was deathly hot beneath the steady ocean breeze. She could feel the sun singeing her skin, could smell the conditioner she'd put on her hair that morning when she'd showered; everything shimmered before her eyes in the heat haze the breeze couldn't quite dispel. It was like standing at the very center of an air pocket beyond which everything on all sides was caught up in irrevocable motion, swirling, in flux; she was a fragment of jetsam frozen in amber, a pendant dangling from some great unseen chain. If she willed it, she might very well detonate, sending dangerous shards into the space around her. Looking up, she saw Mattie come out onto the balcony and stand by the railing, her eyes, as always, seeking the shoreline. What did she see out there? What did she feel when her eyes monitored the length of the beach? Was there some long-lost part of herself she hoped to spot and retrieve? Did she think she might spy some amorphous yet vital remnant of her former self lying tangled in the clumps of seaweed? If I could, Sarah thought, I'd scour the whole of that beach for you, find what you're seeking, and run to you with it, just to see you happy.

Mattie turned, her eyes coming to rest on Sarah. Even from two hundred or so feet away Sarah could feel the impact of those eyes, an additional heat almost as intense as that of the sun.

Carl emerged from the house and came toward her. Sarah felt him draw near, her eyes still joined to Mattie's, and turned to go with him, reluctantly looking away at last, knowing Mattie would watch the two of them out of sight.

"Let's go the other way," Sarah suggested, indicating the southern stretch of beach where the trees would shield them from Mattie's view.

"Sure, no problem." He stopped to kick off his shoes, leaving them on the grass before stepping down to the sand.

Sarah followed suit, feeling too visible. Mattie's eyes were drilling holes in her spine as she bent to undo the buckles of her sandals, then left them to feel the dry springy grass give way beneath her feet. Carl held out his hand and she looked at it, at its invitation, for a few seconds before entrusting her hand into his. At once his powerful fingers closed around hers, reinforcing the sense she had of having been returned to a childlike state of dependency. Mother stood above, watching; brother/lover took her hand securely in his to guide her.

She looked at Carl's profile as they walked down the beach and with a pang she understood that her silence and her mood had him suspended in a state of uncertainty. "I've never known anyone like you," she said, her voice small against the rush of the waves. The sea was high today, the breakers frothy and clotted with bits of debris. "You're the only man I've ever met whose feelings are visible, who actually says what he thinks and not what he thinks I want to hear."

He turned toward her and she saw for the first time the remarkable color and liquidity of his eyes. This was the first time they'd come out-of-doors together and she was able to see him in natural light. His eyes were almost uncannily like the water in the shallows, predominantly clear gray with hints of blue, then green. They were large and round and thickly lashed and deeply apprehensive. His face altogether was wonderful: a fine tidy nose, a wide well-formed mouth, prominent cheekbones and chin, a broad forehead, and those touchingly pale squint lines fanning outward from the corners of his eyes.

"God!" she said, compelled to smile. "You really are beautiful."

"Oh, Jesus!" He threw back his head and laughed. "That's great! All the boys will be lining up for dates."

"They'll have to get past me first."

"Shit, Sarah," he said, gently remonstrating. "You're not for the long term."

"You want to get rid of me already?"

"It isn't me, sweetheart. You're the one who's not set for the long haul."

"What have I said or done that gives you that idea?"

He shrugged, but the grip of his hand remained firm.

"No, tell me, Carl. What makes you think I'll take off?"

"Just a hunch."

"You get a lot of those, don't you? I'm not so sure all your hunches are right."

"True," he conceded. "Not all of them."

There was a tree-shaded patch of grass about fifty yards ahead just up from the beach. "Let's go sit there for a minute," she said, and tugged on his hand.

They sat on the grass and she looked around. There wasn't a soul anywhere in the vicinity. The afternoon was filled with sound: the surf, unseen insects, birds calling, the rush of the leaves overhead.

"I can see why Mattie fell in love with this island," she said, winding her arms around her drawn-up knees and looking sidelong at Carl. "I never knew a place like this existed. What did you think of Gideon Sylvester?"

"He was a prick," he said unemotionally. "I've met a lot of them in my time, especially in the service. But he was the champ. He charmed the shit out of most people, including Bonnie and maybe even Gloria, although it's hard to tell with her what she really thinks about people. He never fooled me, though. From the time I was a kid and my grandparents brought me over to visit, I knew he was bad news. He got off in a big way on being famous, like it was some drug he had to take. He'd swank it up, playing lord of the manor, patronizing the shit out of us kids, kissing women's hands, bullshit like that. Jesus! What a scumsucker! Thank Christ he was never around much in the summers when we came."

"And what about Mattie?" she asked.

"Why d'you ask so many fucking questions, Sarah?"

"I'm interested in your impressions."

"These aren't impressions, sweetheart. We're talking about *people* here, not photographs in some old album."

"I know that."

"You figure it out!" he said hotly. "How the hell d'you *think* I'd feel about someone who was willing to have me around when my folks were scared shitless of me?"

"You love her."

"I don't talk about love," he said.

"But you do love her," she pushed.

"Yeah, all right. So what?"

"Don't get mad. I'm not trying to get you to tell tales out of school."

"What's with you?" he asked. "It's like you need some kind of proof other people care about someone before you'll give in and admit that you do, too. You have a problem going along with what you feel? You like need a consensus or something?"

"I don't know. Maybe you have a point."

"Yeah, maybe I do."

"I care about you." She reached to put her hand on his arm. "I didn't have to ask anyone else what they thought about you. I figured that out all by myself."

He bent forward and rubbed his forehead against his knees. She wove her fingers into his thick hair, saying, "You don't believe me, do you?"

He shrugged again, sitting upright. She withdrew her hand, sat up on her knees, leaned around in front of him, and gazed close-to into his eyes, smiling. "I care a lot about you. God, you've got a great mouth!"

"You want to watch it," he said, breaking into a smile, "or you'll get yourself laid."

"You have such a way with words," she said, remaining in place, her face close to his.

"Yeah, so you said." The color of his eyes darkening beneath the shadow her body created, he stared at her. "You're a really pretty woman, Sarah. You know that?"

"You're only saying that because I like you."

"No, I'm saying it because you're real pretty. You've got bottle-green eyes, for chrissake, and a nice little nose, and a sweet mouth. And I like the freckles right here." He placed his thumb and forefinger on either side of the bridge of her nose. "You're a goddamned dwarf," he teased, "but you've got a good body, too." His eyes dropped as he opened her blouse, unhooked her bra, and closed his hands over her breasts. "Soft," he said joyously. "And just beautiful, the shape, the color here. I could never duplicate the color of you if I had every shade of paint in the goddamned world and spent my whole life trying. Jesus, look at this!" he said reverently, framing her breasts with his hands, then shaping them with his fingertips before leaning back with his hands planted on the grass behind him to gaze at her. "Makes me feel good just to look at you. You know that?"

She sat with the breeze lifting the sides of her blouse, her breasts on display, and felt his approval bathing her like balm. It simply wasn't possible to be self-conscious when he made love to her this way. She'd never experienced anything like it. All her life she'd wanted someone to declare she was of value simply because she existed. Now it was happening, and it was like entering some arcane place of worship as a full-fledged agnostic only to discover that she'd had a religion all along. It was based on the gospel according to Carl, who quoted from the rustic book of love; chapter and verse in sixties' argot. She remembered years before reading the *Love Poems* of Elizabeth Sargent, and the one line that had drilled itself into a special niche in her brain. *Fuck me again. I'm a poet.* That was Carl, she thought, this man who painted emotions with crude bold strokes designed to conceal a yearning sensibility buried beneath camouflage fatigues, the nightmare remnants of whispered last words uttered by long-dead combat buddies, deadly chemical sprays, and showers of shrapnel.

"I love you," she said, and watched him look for somewhere inside himself to hide. "I love you," she told him, refusing to allow him to fly away to the shelter of his disbelief.

"You're gonna take off and fuck over the both of us," he said, clinging to his doubts. "Me and Mattie, you'll fuck us both over."

"I won't," she insisted, hurt. "I won't!"

"You might be able to fool me, Sarah. But you'll never fool Mattie. She's had the course. Me, I'm easier. Not Mattie, though. And she doesn't deserve that."

"I know that," she argued, undone. From somewhere distant, tremors started up inside her. It was like a visit from a childhood friend, someone she dimly recollected but whom she'd once known well. It started in her chest and caught at her lungs; it turned her throat to fire and burned the lining of her nostrils. She swallowed repeatedly but it was merely dry tinder that added to the fire. The only natural cure was tears. And she was so unaccustomed to that need, so filled with resistance that she fought instinctively, determined to keep a very old promise to herself that nothing ever again would make her cry. But she broke it, that yellow-edged vow. Powdery from years of dry storage, it shook itself like some immense papery ghost that had turned her childhood nights to hours she'd spent quaking fearfully beneath the bedclothes. She opened her mouth to explain how depthless her caring both for him and for Mattie had come to be, to state unequivocally how committed she was to the unexpected feelings she'd discovered inside herself for that ferocious yet lovable old woman, and wept instead, shedding tears that eased the rawness in her throat but in no way soothed her. Hiding behind her hands, she sat on her knees and tried to stop this unseemly display. Grown women didn't cry like babies; they didn't show anyone, men in particular, their weaknesses; they maintained; they held fast and went forward never allowing anyone to know they'd sustained almost crippling injuries that didn't show on the surface of the skin.

"I thought you didn't do that," Carl said respectfully. "I thought you told me you'd forgotten how."

Grinding her fists into her eyes, she said, "I don't. I hate this!"

"I find it kind of endearing, myself," he said, and she could hear the smile in his voice.

She opened her bleary eyes to look at him and he was, indeed, smiling at her. "Don't smile at me!" she ordered, then thought to herself she sounded just like Mattie.

"Aw, lighten up, Sarah! It's no big deal. I cried my fucking heart out when I went a couple of years ago to check out that wall in D.C. Only thing that surprised me was my name wasn't on it. It felt like it should've been. I mean, it seemed to me I was one of the guys who came back in a body bag. I sure as shit feel as if I did. Like they scraped together all the parts of me they could find, dumped them in the bag, and shipped it home to the folks. And I've been trying to reassemble the whole stinking mess ever since, so I can get the hell out of that bag."

She wiped her face on the side of her blouse and stared at him.

"C'mere," he said, smiling again as he held his hand out to her.

She put her hand in his.

"I'm beginning to believe you," he said. "You know that?"

"Well, you *should,* for God's sake!"

He pulled her down onto the grass beside him, saying, "With my luck, the Coast Guard'll come chugging up and arrest my ass for indecent exposure. But what the hell!" he laughed. "Might as well live dangerously. I only wish to Christ you owned a skirt instead of these godawful pants."

Mattie had left a sleeve for transcribing. Pushing her hair, still damp from the shower, behind her ears, Sarah fitted the sleeve into the Dictaphone, muttered, "I wish to God you'd spring for a new machine, Mattie," put on the headset, stepped on the foot pedal, and got ready to type.

The first sound was of Mattie striking one of her wooden matches. It sizzled and flared audibly. Mattie inhaled on her cigarette, then said, "You shouldn't care, you know, what I or anyone else thinks, Sarah. What you do is your concern. In the last analysis, no one else's opinion is ever going to be as important to you as your own. Think about that, please. There's nothing else I intend to dictate. I'm sure you'll be delighted. One less sleeve in the bottomless box. I expect to be in the studio until dinner."

Sarah backpedaled and listened again. Then she turned off the machine.

Mattie was sitting in the armchair in the studio with a cigarette. She appeared to have been waiting.

"You seem very sure of me," Sarah said from the doorway.

"The only thing I am sure of, my dear, is that if I look in the mirror I won't care much for what I see."

Sarah smiled. "That's probably the one thing I know you're wrong about." She started down the room, glancing over at the easel. The canvas was hidden beneath a piece of white cloth.

"When you're in love," Mattie said, "everyone looks beautiful."

"No comment," Sarah said, sitting down on the floor a few feet away. "I plead the Fifth."

"You would," Mattie said, eyebrows lifting briefly. "A comment's as good as a commitment."

"I think a comment's nothing more than an observation. A commitment's something else entirely."

"Not only do you take everything personally," Mattie sniffed, "but you're a literalist, to boot. A lot of people might find you rather heavy going."

"A lot do. But you don't."

"That's true. You seem to be having quite a lot of fun."

"Fun?" Sarah frowned. "I'm not sure I'd call any of this fun. More like a tour of the world's oddest amusement park. Nothing like Disneyworld or Play Land. More like Emotional Express, or Surrogate City. A theme park with a twist."

"What on earth's a 'theme park'?"

"You know. Like African Lion Safari, where you drive through in your car and see all the wild animals."

Mattie laughed. "I adore it! That sounds absolutely right."

"Or," Sarah went on, "there's a place in upstate New York called Artpark. They have jazz, artists, stuff like that. Theme parks," she said. "Get it?"

"Oh, yes." Mattie tapped a finger against her temple. "Everything's still clicking and whirring away up here. I catch on pretty fast."

"What will you do with whatever you paint now?"

"Don't know," Mattie said. "Let them stack up against the walls, I suppose. Then when I'm dead, they'll have a field day discovering all these works by the Great Master they had no idea existed. Who cares? I'll be dead and none of it will bother me anymore."

"It doesn't have to be that way."

"Please, change the subject," Mattie sighed.

"Are you in the mood to tell me what happened after Gideon left you here?"

Mattie laughed again. "It's all the same goddamned subject. Wild animal parks, works of unknown origin, Gideon Sylvester." She reached for a cigarette and her box of matches. "Why not?" she said. "Telling about it helps kill time between meals."

"Does it help at all to talk about it?"

Mattie looked askance at her. "You're no psychiatrist, my dear, and I most certainly am not seeking consolation or an interpretation of events. Help? Christ, no! If anything, it sends my blood pressure through the roof. Or it would, if I didn't happen to have chronic low blood pressure. I remember the nurse taking my pressure just before Giddy was born. Her jaw dropped and she let out this little gasping laugh and said, 'I do believe you're dead. You are, according to your blood pressure.' It was something like ninety over forty, or eighty over fifty."

"Was that from smoking?"

"I didn't take up cigarettes until after Matthew was born. I'd have taken up drinking, but I've never had much of a stomach for it. Three drinks and I'm out like a light. So I took up smoking instead. I could rant and rave and carry on with a cigarette just as well as I could with a drink, and arouse malice in the hearts of all near and far simply by being my inimical self."

"You're not unfriendly or hostile," Sarah said.

"Your command of the language is fairly startling," Mattie observed.

"I read a lot."

Mattie sniffed and puffed away on her cigarette.

Sarah waited. The afternoon sunlight made it appear as if Mattie was wrapped shroudlike in the grayish cloud of smoke.

Mattie looked down at the brown-haired, green-eyed young woman seated cross-legged on the floor who suddenly, very brightly, smiled at her. For a moment, Mattie had the admittedly irrational idea that she could reach down and pick up this woman like a toy. Of course, it was purely illusory. Sarah was of average height, she supposed, and slightly less than average weight. But there was something about her that was so poignantly childlike—the light in those singular eyes, for one thing, and the full bow of her upper lip, for another—that she gave the impression (except when she spoke, thereby revealing a very unchildlike intelligence) of ineffable vulnerability. Mattie didn't think she'd ever met anyone whose physical attributes were so diametrically opposed to her mental ones. Sarah seemed to her, sitting there so diligently waiting, to be the living essence of dichotomy.

The silence grew so lengthy that Sarah finally said, "What do you see?"

Sinking back into the armchair and crossing her legs, Mattie said, "Nothing. I enjoy looking at you. And the more I look at you, the more I seem to see."

"Was Tom Harding able to sell your ring and the car?" Sarah prompted.

"Ah, yes, the ring and the car. Christ, but it was a long time ago! I'd give anything, you know, to have amnesia. Think of the relief of starting all your memories from scratch!" She gave one of her bitter barking laughs, then her eyes drifted away from Sarah, and she traveled back.

Nineteen

Tom Harding was able to sell the car for a hundred and twenty dollars, some eighty less than Mattie had paid for it half a year earlier. She accepted the money gratefully, as well as the hundred and ninety dollars he was able to get for her ring. He came to the house four days later, after delivering the new owner to the north end of the island to collect the car, with her cash and a basket of potatoes.

"You might want to think about putting in a garden to the back of the house," he told her. "By mid-April the ground'll have thawed enough for you to turn the soil, and you can get your seeds down early in May. Tend it, and by the end of June you'll have plenty to eat and plenty to put by for the winter. I'll come by with the seeds when the time's right, help you get started."

"One day," she said, "I'll repay you for your kindness."

"Don't you worry your head about that. If you need me, just pick up the telephone."

Among the mildewing books on the shelves flanking the fireplace she found a cookbook, and in the evenings while the baby slept, she studied it in the light from the fire. It was like learning some esoteric foreign language. It took her a while to get used to the abbreviated instructions, and she kept her initial efforts at the stove simple. Beginning with soups and stews, made primarily with vegetables and a little meat, she was able to feed herself quite well and thereby maintain her milk for the baby.

As the weeks of winter passed, she went on to try her hand at baking bread, and was as proud of her first successful batch of loaves as she'd have been of an especially well-executed painting.

In order to conserve electricity, she used oil lamps at night in the kitchen and living room, and invested in a load of coal which saved on firewood and allowed her to sleep through the night without having to get up to add more logs to the fire. The coal was filthy stuff and quickly turned the living room walls and ceiling a depressing shade of gray, but she was unconcerned with decor. All that was important was surviving the winter.

When the weather allowed it, she bundled herself and the baby in warm clothes, and carried him on her hip for long walks along the beach. It intrigued her to note that with Gideon's departure the baby, whom she now called Giddy, screamed less often and was altogether more placid. He was growing at an astounding rate and seemed each time she carried him out-of-doors to have become much heavier. She rejoiced in him, fascinated by his evolving personality, and spent hours in the afternoons sketching him as he lay cooing on the mattress in front of the fire, grinning toothlessly over at her as his chubby arms and legs pedaled in the air. She made dozens of drawings of her son, finding life, despite the critical circumstances, far more satisfying than she had in the five years of her marriage to Gideon Sylvester.

In the evenings, with the only sounds being the wind howling off the ocean and the creaking of the old house as it resisted the elements, she wrote to Hughie and to the Harveys. She said only that she was for the present living alone with the baby on the island, and made no reference to Gideon Sylvester. She wrote about Tom Harding and his goodness to her, about the other islanders she'd come to know, and about the baby.

On one of his regular trips to the north end to see her, Tom Harding brought along a rusted old bicycle he'd found abandoned.

"Oil her up, pump some air in those tires, and you've got yourself some transportation," he said. "There's an old hand pump in the barn and plenty of rags and oil. Clean her a bit, and you're all set."

She gave him coffee. They sat on the sofa and watched the baby for a time.

"You reckon Buddy's gonna be coming back?" he asked finally.

"Unless his pockets are bulging with money, he'd better not set foot off the ferry."

"I'd feel a sight happier if I knew you had people to go to, Mattie."

"I don't need anyone. I'll manage."

With a slow smile, he said, "I do believe you will. That boy's growing to beat the band, huh? Gonna be a big fella."

She too smiled. "He's good company. Better than his father."

"Probably got more sense, too."

In March there was a severe storm that turned the main road to sheer ice, knocked out the telephone and electric wires, and kept Mattie housebound for nine days. The wind sneaked in through every crack in the big clapboard house, whistled under the floorboards, tore shingles from the roof, and brought down one of the old oaks midway between the house and the barn. She heard a tremendous roaring noise followed by a crash that shook the entire house, and rushed to the window to see the huge tree lying uprooted, its branches obscuring the barn and part of the verandah. Glad it hadn't fallen on the house, she looked at the tree, seeing it as a murdered giant. She went for her sketching gear and spent some time drawing the felled oak, finding it somehow more majestic in death than it had been in life. And aside from being a bonus subject, the tree was a providential source of firewood. It would cut down to several cords of wood, enough to see her through to the end of this winter and even possibly the next. Of course she'd have to talk to Tom about having the trunk cut into manageable sections which she'd then have to chop, but nature had conspired to save her some money.

After the storm the weather remained cold but the road was clear and she was able to tie the baby like a papoose to her back and ride the bicycle into town for as much in the way of provisions as the front carrier would hold: sugar, flour, rice, yeast, salt, lard, washing powder, and soap. Mrs. O'Brian asked with concern how she was getting along alone and Mattie said, "I'm doing beautifully, thank you," as she counted out the money to pay for her purchases.

"Sure is a fine-looking baby," Mrs. O'Brian said, going around to peer at the sleeping boy. "How'd you rig up that contraption anyhow?"

With a laugh, Mattie explained. "It's an old corset I found in the attic. I turned it sideways, lined it with a piece of blanket, and tied the laces around my neck and waist."

"Well, I'll be darned!" said Mrs. O'Brian, impressed. "If that ain't the smartest use ever for one of them mean old contraptions."

Twice a week, Mattie had the luxury of a tubful of steaming water. She'd place the baby on the floor where she could keep an eye on him while she soaked and then, when the water had cooled, she'd lift him into the tub and bathe and play with his sweet slippery body, squeezing him until he squealed, and nipping at his delectably rounded arms and legs. Invariably, the warmth of the water and of the steam-filled bathroom would make him drowsy, and she'd nurse him in the tub, both of them pacified by the rhythmic tugging until he fell away from her breast, his small mouth still open, to sleep in the crook of her arm. Then, both of them clean and dry, she'd carry him down to the mattress in the living room and curl up with him under the blankets.

There were nights when she scarcely slept but lay thinking murderous thoughts about Gideon Sylvester, wishing him obliterated, gone from the face of the earth. There were other nights though when in her dreams he set at her body as he had so often in reality, and she opened to him like some sightless aquatic creature with no brain and totally exposed nerve endings that responded solely by sensory reaction to heat and touch. Coupling, her limbs enclosing him, their mouths duplicated the actions of their loins. She'd awaken from these dreams chagrined at her body's continued hunger for someone so unworthy.

Hughie and the Harveys both wrote often, inviting her to come to Maine if she was able, to visit. Hughie's letters were especially heart-warming. In his typically understated fashion he reiterated his feelings for her, then went on to say how well he was working and that he'd actually managed to interest a gallery in Boston in giving him a show, perhaps in the autumn. He asked what she was working on and begged her not to let anything interfere with her painting. "No one can do what you do, Mattie. I've always envied the confidence of your work, its audacity. My pieces are so *quiet* compared to yours. Kind of makes me feel like a piccolo comparing itself to a whole brass band. I think of you constantly and sure do wish you could come for a visit sometime."

She held the letter to her breast, as if the words written on the paper might travel off the pages and through her skin directly into her bloodstream. He restored her confidence in herself and she sat down at once to write him a reply, saying she planned to begin painting again as soon as the weather broke. "Write more often, Hughie. You cheer me up the way no one else can. I wish I could see you, too, but it's going to be a while, I think. I can't spare the money right now."

She scoured the attic, the barn, and the basement for items that might be of use, and found an old baby carriage in one of the disused stalls of the barn. She guessed one of the Sylvester girls had probably pushed her dolls around in the rather small vehicle. Delighted with her find, she scrubbed it down, oiled the wheels, covered the interior with a clean sheet, then plonked the baby inside and wheeled him around to the back of the house. With the carriage parked in the shade, she paced out the boundaries of what would be her vegetable garden, placed stakes at each of the four corners, ran twine around the perimeters, then set to work with the hoe turning the hard-packed soil. It took a week of strenuous labor to clear the area of rocks and to break down the stubborn clods of soil. But at last she was ready to plant the seeds Tom had bought for her on the mainland.

The garden turned out to require a tremendous amount of attention. Once the seedlings sprouted, she had to divide them and replant. Then there was the weeding and the watering and the discovery that if she didn't take measures to prevent it the wildlife would devour her flourishing plants. So she hammered more stakes into the ground and ran chicken wire around the outside of the plot as well as a foot below the surface to keep out burrowing animals. Her hands were seamed with dirt, cut and blistered and sore. But by June she was able to begin harvesting some of her crop.

Following the cookbook's instructions, she sterilized dozens of old bottles she found in the pantry and turned a batch of wild strawberries into jam. The pantry shelves began to fill as she reaped more vegetables and a second batch of the wild strawberries. She ate her own tiny new potatoes, green onions, carrots, beets, cabbages, bell peppers, tomatoes, runner beans, and lettuce. And the marigolds Tom had advised her to plant around the borders to discourage small foraging animals brightened the dingy interior of the house.

When she wasn't busy in the garden, she wheeled Giddy down to the beach while she cast a fishing line into the surf, not sure she'd know what to do if she managed to catch anything. It was a pleasure simply to stand in the cool shallows with the water foaming around her knees, the sun spangling the waves as she sent her line skimming over the surface. When she did actually hook a fish, it so upset her to see it struggling that she reeled it in, pulled the hook free, and let the fish go, relieved to see it revive after a moment in the water, then twist its body and swim off.

Abandoning her surf-fishing, she lifted the baby from the carriage and walked waist-deep into the waves, to let the baby's feet dip into the water, laughing as his legs churned away.

In the evenings, with the air soft and cool, she sat out on the verandah in the rocker she'd found in the basement, to nurse the baby before putting him down for the night. She felt she had everything she could possibly need, even if less than two hundred dollars remained to see her through the coming winter. She had the house, food from the garden, stacks of wood from the felled oak, and an enormous supply of coffee Gideon Sylvester had purchased from yet another one of his friends. Tom had patched the hole in the roof caused by the storm;

he'd also shored up a portion of the verandah by the kitchen door where the wood was rotting. He refused to take her money, so she paid him with a bushel basket of green tomatoes and two bottles of her wild strawberry jam.

She found time that summer to do several paintings: one of the baby asleep naked on a towel on the beach; one of the house viewed from the beach; and a self-portrait. Her talent was intact. If anything, she was painting better than ever. From habit, she noted the details of her work in the log, and hid a second signature on each of the paintings. It had become something of an amusing challenge to work that secret second signing into the body of the painting, and she'd sometimes spend days deciding where best to place it.

As the summer drew to an end and the leaves on the trees began their color changes, she dug up the last of the potatoes and carrots and turnips and carried them down to the basement to store. The pantry shelves were filled with jars of food she'd put by. It looked to her as if she and the baby could live for years on what she'd preserved. And she'd learned from necessity to put every last thing to good use, even the bread she couldn't eat. She cut it into slices, cut the slices into strips, and toasted the strips in the oven, creating Melba toast for Giddy to gnaw on now that he was teething.

It rained intermittently throughout October and into early November, drowning out whatever remained in the garden. Winter came on so suddenly, so brutally, it caught her by surprise. One day it was cool and rainy, the next the wind turned knifelike, and snowflakes whirled past the windows. It was time to drag the mattress back down the stairs to the living room, time to close all the second floor doors and windows, time to stack plenty of wood next to the fireplace and the stove, time to light the oil lamps early, time to stand shivering first thing in the morning while she got the stove going and the coffee made.

Before winter well and truly set in she went foraging in the attic, looking through the trunks for anything that might be of use to her and the baby. She found a few old dresses that with laundering were good enough to wear, but not much else. She was about to leave when she looked again at the several trunks. Giddy was a year old, already crawling and getting into everything. He'd shortly be walking, and she worried about him creeping away from her while she was sleeping and perhaps hurting himself. One of those old trunks would make a perfect crib. Emptying it, she pulled it down the stairs to the kitchen where, with a hammer and screwdriver, she removed the lid and the hinges. After washing it inside and out, she padded the inside with an old blanket. Then she put in fresh bedding, a small pillow, and took it to the living room.

From the outset, Giddy loved his new bed. When she awakened in the morning, most often it would be to see the baby standing, smiling out at her, bouncing up and down on his still unsteady legs. She could safely leave him in there while she did the laundry in a big tub atop the wood stove, or while she baked a batch of fresh bread, or cooked a meal. He'd do a tour of the trunk, holding on to the sides, or play with the teddy bear Tom had found by the roadside and brought along for him. Periodically, Giddy would take to howling as an incoming tooth pained him, and then she'd rub his gums with a finger wet from the bottle of gin his father had left behind.

By December the number of jars on the pantry shelf had been considerably reduced. Now that the baby was eating soft foods as well as nursing the stock diminished faster than she'd anticipated. She spent her twenty-sixth birthday baking bread and looking every so often out the kitchen window at the ominous clouds blowing in from offshore. A storm was taking shape. Tom Harding called shortly after five that evening to confirm it.

"It's gonna be a bad one," he told her. "Make sure you got plenty of wood in, and keep one of the faucets going just a drip, so the pipes don't freeze and burst. They canceled the last ferry, so nothin's moving. If it's as bad as they're predicting, you're gonna be cut off up there for God knows how long. I hope you've got enough of everything to see you through."

"We'll be fine, Tom," she said, mentally counting the number of jars left in the pantry.

"Long as the phone line's still up, I'll be checking in," he promised. "Stay inside with the baby, Mattie. You don't want to risk going outdoors for any reason. Folks've been known to get turned around in the blowing snow and wind up freezing to death ten feet from their front doors."

By nightfall, the snow was gusting against the windows and the wind was blowing back in the chimney, sending occasional clouds of smoke into the room. Sometime after eight, the snow turned to freezing rain that spat against the windows like buckshot. Mattie sat with the baby, rubbing gin on his gums as he screamed, red-faced, and thrashed about. The gin didn't help, and he refused to nurse, punching at her breast with his fist, drumming his heels against her thighs. In desperation, she carried him into the downstairs bathroom and started the tub filling, pacing back and forth and jiggling him in her arms, trying to ease him. By the time the tub was full and she'd managed to undress them both, she was worn out. Luckily, the instant he was immersed in the water, he stopped shrieking, accepted her nipple and began nursing greedily.

She rose the next morning to absolute stillness. Even the baby seemed awed by the silence, and stood holding on to the side of the trunk, blinking at the brilliant shafts of light penetrating the gaps in the curtains.

The stove fire stoked and the coffee going, she lifted the baby out of the trunk. Drawing back the curtains, she gasped at the sight outside. Everything was encrusted in black ice that glistened darkly under a sky more menacing than that of the previous day. It looked like the end of the world. The power line lay broken and frozen in the driveway; tree limbs with raggedly severed edges were strewn everywhere and frozen solid.

She got the baby fed and had only coffee herself in order not to deplete too quickly their food supply. By the time she had them both dressed and a fire going in the living room, the sky had opened and snow was whipping in frenzied circles, making it impossible to see beyond the windows.

Somewhere along the road between the house and the south end, the telephone line had gone down, too. She was cut off again. For eleven days the storm raged outside and the baby raged inside. Not even a tubful of water warmed on top of the wood stove comforted him. He'd fall into a shuddering fretful sleep and be silent for an hour or so, then wake up screaming. She tried everything she could think of to quiet him, even resorting to a full tablespoon of gin mashed into his potatoes and carrots. It did no good. Neither did rocking him, trying to sing to him, pacing back and forth with him. Not even a spoonful of wild strawberry jam, normally a treat, interested him. He was in pain and could not be distracted from it. She would fall into a fitful sleep when he was silent, then awaken to tend to him like a robot when he roused her with renewed shrieks. He refused to nurse during this time and she had only water to give him to drink.

Seated half asleep over her coffee at the kitchen table on the twelfth morning while he sat on the floor at her feet and screamed nonstop, holding his arms out to her to be picked up, desperation prompted her to lift him onto her lap and offer him some of her now tepid coffee. She held the cup to his mouth. Suspiciously, hiccuping, he tasted the sugared liquid. Then, covering her hand with his, he directed the cup back to his mouth and drank it all.

"Good?" she asked him, certain he'd start screaming again.

"Good," he said distinctly.

"More?" she asked.

Like a happy little parrot, he smiled, showing one fully emerged front tooth and the tiny white ridges of the one breaking through the gum and said, "More."

She poured a quarter cup of fresh coffee, added sugar and some cold water, then watched in amazed relief as he gulped it down. Daring to set him back on the floor, he went crawling around, investigating the corners of the kitchen. She could scarcely believe it, and drank a second cup of coffee while he played with his teddy bear, carrying it around with him for a time, then abandoning it while he pulled himself upright holding on to one of the chairs. He stood, his eyes somewhat doubtful as he let go of the table, managed one unsupported step, then sat down heavily on his bottom. She laughed and applauded, and he beamed up at her.

Later that morning, with the snow continuing unabated beyond the walls of the house, the baby nursed, then fell into a heavy sleep. Too weary even to fasten her dress, she put him into the trunk, then lay down on the mattress and sank into her first real rest in almost two weeks.

A hammering at the kitchen door awakened her about three hours later, and she went drunkenly through the now cold house to open the door to Tom Harding, who'd hitched up a horse to an old two-seater sleigh and made the perilous journey the length of the island to satisfy himself she was all right. She was so glad to see him she threw her arms around him, bursting into tears.

"You're okay, aren't you?" he asked worriedly, looking away from her gaping dress.

"The baby's been miserable with teething, but otherwise we're fine."

"Just wanted to see for myself. I brought a few groceries, some milk, and your mail."

"Sit down, Tom, and I'll put on the coffee."

"Can't stay, Mattie. I don't start back right away, I'll be lucky to get back at all." He put the carton of groceries and the letters on the table and prepared to go.

Having fastened her dress, she turned to say, "I wish you didn't have to go."

"Listen here to me," he said kindly. "I stay and get stuck out here, by tomorrow noon word'll be all over this island the two of us're up to no good. Neither one of us wants or needs that kind of trouble, Mattie. I'll be back again soon's I can."

"At least let me pay you for the groceries."

"If it's all the same to you, I'll say thank you to another jar of those wild strawberries and call it even."

"When all this is over, I promise I'll make it up to you for being such a good friend."

"You just worry about getting through the winter, and don't fuss about making it up to me. Friends help. It's what they're for. Better put some wood in that stove. She's burning low." He pulled up his coat collar and left.

There were letters from Hughie and the Harveys. Cheered, she hurried through the chatty letter from Juliet telling about the children and how much Nickie liked working at the girls' school, and how she hoped Mattie wasn't having too terrible a winter out there on her island.

Hughie wrote, "I have a feeling, reading between the lines, you're not telling me the whole story. Is everything really all right? Please let me know, because I worry and it's been some time since I had a letter from you. I see by the papers the storms have been fierce over your way. I sure do hope you're okay.

"The show was good enough that they want to do another one next September. How about that? We sold some of the smaller paintings for pretty decent prices and after the commissions, I've got some put by to see me through, I hope, until the next show. If you're hard up for money, I could let you have some. So don't be shy about asking. Okay?

"I just finished a new piece I'm really pleased with, and I think you'd like it real well. It's of the woodpile outside here, with an axe jammed into the trunk I use for chopping. The wood grains came out swell. It was slow work, but you'd like it, I'll bet.

"Write to me soon, won't you, Mattie? I'm thinking about you, and hoping all is well, Love, Hughie."

T w e n t y

The winter seemed to go on and on, with one fierce storm after another right up until April. Then with no warning, from one day to the next, the weather broke in mid-April and spring arrived. With only about sixty dollars left, Mattie invested in a small amount of seeds, then went to work on the garden. Once the seedlings had been thinned and replanted, she collected wood from all over the property in order to supplement what remained from last year's oak. She chopped broken branches down to size and stacked them on the verandah, effectively clearing the area of whatever had been brought down by the winter's storms.

Now that the baby was mobile, she fashioned a harness and secured it by a length of rope to a nearby tree so that he was able to run free within a prescribed radius while she made advance preparations for the next cold season. She gathered in everything edible, including more of the wild strawberries, and planted even more potatoes, carrots, and squash. Overcoming her squeamishness, she cast her line into the surf while the baby ran back and forth along the sand, and filled baskets with fish she then cleaned and salted according to the instructions in the cookbook. If she was to keep the telephone line open, she was going to have to forego the electricity, which meant heating all the water for laundry and bathing in tubs on the wood stove. Her only purchases at O'Brian's were flour, sugar, salt, and yeast. Meat was out of the question. She hadn't the money for it, or for anything else other than the cheapest soap.

Throughout the summer as she toiled in the garden and fished on the beach and put up preserves and tended to the baby, she worried what would become of them. With care, they'd make it through one more winter. But after that her money would be gone and she had no way left to get any more. The baby had no clothes that fit and she was spending the night hours trying to refashion the garments she'd found in the attic trunks in order to dress him. On top of that he needed the company of other people, other children. When she rode with him into town on the bicycle, he went wild with excitement knowing there'd be children in the environs of O'Brian's and the post office. And Mrs. O'Brian always gave him a lollipop or a bit of chocolate, which heightened his excitement to such an extent that it was invariably a trial to get him back into the old corset sling to make the ride home. He'd cry most of the way, and she knew he was being deprived of too many things, and most importantly regular interaction with others. She was also feeling critically severed from the world, unable to afford the luxury of newspapers and magazines other residents had sent over from the mainland. For all she knew, she sometimes thought, the rest of the world could have ceased to exist.

Tom Harding came through for her yet again in August, with two customers wanting pencil portraits of their children. This extra bit of money went toward the purchase of some secondhand clothes for Giddy, and an additional store of staples for the pantry.

It wasn't enough. By January most of the wood was gone, and she was eating only one small meal a day in order to have sufficient food to feed Giddy who, at just over two, was the size of other five year olds on the island, and had an immense appetite. He'd stopped nursing altogether and was quite happy to drink coffee, but she fretted that the lack of calcium in his diet might have telling adverse effects on him later in life.

By the end of February she was burning anything she could find in the house or barn or basement that was combustible. There was one bushel basket of potatoes left in the basement, a handful of carrots and onions, and enough flour for one last batch of bread. She tried to fish at the shoreline but couldn't cast her line far enough out past the ice crust to catch anything. The rabbits that occasionally streaked across the property were too fast for her to go after, and she didn't have the heart or the energy to set out snares.

An ice storm early in March cut them off once again, so Tom Harding couldn't get up to the north end with his offerings of groceries and whatever mail there might be. Closed up in the house with her frustrated little boy, Mattie tried to amuse him with stories and drawings; she gave him paper and pencils and encouraged him to draw, but he had no interest. The only diversion she could offer was his bath. She'd sit him in the galvanized steel tub in front of the fire and allow him to splash about in the water until it became too cold. Then she'd give him a spoon and a bowl of mashed vegetables and watch him gobble up the food, then ask for more. She couldn't make him understand there wasn't any more, and that if she cooked anything else for him there'd be nothing for him to eat in the morning.

In the hope of getting him to burn off some of his excess energy, she took him up to the second floor, both of them dressed for out-of-doors, and let him run up and down the hallway, in and out of the disused rooms, playing tag with him and hide-and-seek. He raced about until dark, then grew frightened and clung to her knees as she closed all the doors and, numb now from the cold, carried him down to the kitchen for his bath.

Finally, tucked up in his trunk, he slept, and she sat close to the kitchen stove drinking a cup of black coffee and slowly eating the potato peelings and carrot scrapings she'd saved. She'd burned a fair amount of the furniture from the second floor and was holding the books for last. If she had to she was prepared to take the barn down and burn it board by board. But there was nothing she could do about the fact that all the food was gone.

Before going to bed that night she stood for a time watching the boy sleep. He looked so like his father it often bothered her. Fortunately, he had an intrinsically loving nature and was already demonstrating a kindness startling in one so very young. There seemed little chance he'd grow up to be anything like Gideon Sylvester.

Both she and the baby slept later than usual and awakened in the morning to see the sun shining and to hear the tinkling music of ice dripping from the eaves and the trees. She stood by the window holding the boy, smiling reflexively at the exquisite reflections cast by the sun on the melting ice.

"Isn't it pretty?" she said, bouncing the boy on her hip.

"Pitty," he said, pointing.

"I'll bet you're hungry, aren't you?"

"Hungee," he confirmed.

She got a pot of coffee going, then gave the boy the bowl of bread she'd left soaking overnight in a mixture of water, condensed milk, and sugar. When the coffee was ready, she gave him a cup cut with cold water, sat down at the table with her own, and watched him eat. Now that the weather had broken, she'd take her last few dollars and ride into town to buy some food. She was making a shopping list when she heard a car approaching. Thinking it must be Tom, she got up and went to the window to see a new-looking La Salle pull up. The motor was turned off, the driver's door opened, and Gideon Sylvester climbed out.

She jumped back from the window, ran to the drawer and got the butcher knife. Holding it firmly at her side, she went to the front door, opened it as Gideon Sylvester was starting up the stairs, and demanded, "What are you doing here?"

"My God!" he said, his eyes going round. "You look dreadful. What's happened to you?"

"I said, what are you doing here?"

"May I come in, please? I've got your money."

"Show it to me!"

"Now? Out here?"

"Right now, right where you are!"

"If you insist." He reached into the inner pocket of his expensive-looking topcoat and withdrew a legal-sized envelope. "You'll find two thousand dollars in there," he said, handing it to her.

Leaving him at the door, she went back to the kitchen, where she set aside the knife before opening the envelope.

"Look at this!" Gideon exclaimed, grinning at the boy. "Are you going to say hello, son?"

His face crumpling, the boy clambered down off his chair and hurried to hide behind Mattie's legs, burying his face in the folds of her dress.

"He has no idea who you are," she said coldly, slowly taking in every detail of Gideon Sylvester's attire. "Where did you get this money?"

"I don't suppose you'd give me a cup of that coffee?" he asked. "I've been up for hours so I could catch the first ferry."

"*Where* did you get this money?" she repeated.

With one of his best smiles, he said, "I've sold fourteen of your paintings. There's even more than that," he indicated the envelope she held. "We'll be able to install a furnace, get the house painted from top to bottom. We'll be able to buy you both some decent clothes. You look half starved," he said, losing the smile.

"We could both be dead, for all you cared."

"Don't be that way, Mattie. I've got a carful of groceries, and I've brought you back all your money and then some. I want to come home."

"Oh, no! This isn't your home. It's mine."

"I want to make it all up to you," he said soulfully. "Do you think it's been easy for me since you chased me out of here? I came very damned close to starving myself."

"I couldn't care less. I wish you had."

"Look. Let me bring in the groceries. I'll fix us something to eat, then we'll talk." Without waiting for her to respond, he put his hat down on the counter and rushed out to begin unloading the car.

She sat down at the table with the boy still clinging to her and watched Gideon Sylvester bring in box after box of groceries until the counters were lined and he had to put the last of them on the floor. He'd brought well over two hundred dollars' worth of food, including steaks and roasts, exotic fresh fruits and vegetables from California, and even a dozen bottles of Coca-Cola. When he'd emptied the car, he threw off his topcoat and began stocking the pantry shelves. That done, he said, "I'll fire up the stove and get some food cooking."

"You'll have to fire it up with your smart new coat," she said, "unless you feel like going over to the barn and prying loose a few boards."

"There's no cordwood?"

"You took all my money. Then you went away and stayed away for almost two and half years, leaving me here with an infant. And you're surprised there's no wood. You waltz in here dressed to the nines, driving what looks like a new car, hand me two thousand dollars, and bring in enough food to stock a small store, and you have the gall to act surprised? If I had the strength, I'd take that butcher knife and finish what I started the last time I saw you."

"But everything's going to be all right now. You've got your money, and that's our new La Salle. We've got enough to make this house livable. I've come back, Mattie. I've made everything good again."

"You are unbelievable! I don't *want* you here! Put on your fancy coat and hat and get out! Thank you for returning my money. If nothing else, your timing's good. It'll come in very handy. Now go."

"You can't mean that."

"Gideon," she said tiredly. "I really am very weary, but if I have to, I'll get up from this chair and go for the knife. Get out of my sight!"

Offended, he reached for his hat and coat.

"And I meant what I said about this house. I want the deed. Make sure I get it."

"Why should I sign over my inheritance to you?"

"Because if you don't, I'll go to the mainland and have a nice long chat with the best lawyer I can find. And when the lawyer and I have completed our chat about desertion and theft of my property and sundry other things, you'll be lucky to find yourself left with your BVD's. Do you understand? You owe me a hell of a lot more than what's in this envelope and you damned well know it. Fourteen of my paintings must have gone for a pretty penny, judging from the look of you. You go away to wherever you live these days, find that deed, and have it properly transferred into my name. I figure that should about repay what you've stolen from me."

"Well," he said, "I suppose that's only fair."

"Gideon, most other women would cut off your balls and make soup with them. You should consider yourself extremely fortunate I'm only asking for what a judge and jury would give me anyway. Now, leave! You're making my son very anxious."

At last he went. The moment the La Salle was out of sight, she went to the pantry for the crate of eggs Gideon had brought.

"I'm going to make us something wonderful to eat," she told the boy.

He laughed, stamped his feet, and cried, "Eat!"

"The two of us ate until we both had distended bellies," Mattie said with a smile. "Then we lay down on the mattress and slept it off."

"Did he send you the deed?" Sarah asked, brimming with anger on Mattie's behalf.

"Oh, yes, indeed. Within a week it arrived, duly notarized. He wouldn't have dared to defy me on that. He knew I meant every word of what I said. Nothing would have made me happier than to see Gideon Sylvester go through a few years of what the baby and I had to. It would have killed the silly bastard. He'd never have made it. But we did," she said proudly. "Giddy and I survived it."

"Why did you take him back?"

"There you go again, making assumptions!" Mattie thundered. "I didn't 'take him back.' That wasn't the way it was at all. Do I strike you as one of those moronic women who can't live without 'my Bill?' I most certainly did not just blithely *take him back*. We're not talking about some run-of-the-mill fellow here, my dear. We're talking about the one and only Gideon Sylvester, the likes of whom mercifully come along only rarely. He was very damned clever. If he couldn't get what he wanted one way, he'd keep at it until he found another. He was the most doggedly persistent human being I've ever known, as well as the most ruthlessly conniving. As I've already told you, his sense of timing was one of his greatest assets. He could read the signs like a goddamned astrologer, and he always knew precisely when to make his moves. Perhaps," she relented, "I wasn't as well-armored as I might have been. And perhaps, because I'd been so effectively cut off from civilization for so long, I was somewhat more susceptible than I would have been at any other time."

"So what did he do?" Sarah asked.

Mattie lit a fresh cigarette, recrossed her legs, and went on.

The first thing she did, now that she once again had some money, was to arrange with Tom Harding for the installation of a furnace. Then she took the boy over on the ferry to the mainland to buy them both new clothes and shoes. While over there, she bought a secondhand motor-cycle with a sidecar, reasoning that it would be cheaper to run than a car and better able to navigate the roads in winter. Giddy adored the motorcycle and she had to caution him repeatedly not to stand up in the sidecar while she was driving. She also bought a small radio, a supply of books for herself and for the boy, and some toys.

Tom Harding came to oversee the delivery of the furnace, bringing with him a gift for Giddy, a six-week-old mixed breed puppy.

"You're gonna have to take good care of this little fella," Tom told the boy, who listened attentively. "You're gonna have to feed him and walk him and keep him clean. You understand?"

Giddy nodded several times, clutching the puppy to his chest.

"This is your dog now, boy, and he's your lookout. Word gets back to me you're not taking proper care of this fella, I'll come on up here and take him away. Okay?"

Tearful at the prospect of losing his new playmate, the boy said, "*My* dog!" and held the puppy even more tightly.

Tom stood with Mattie on the verandah, both of them watching the boy tumble about on the lawn with the dog.

"I hear Buddy's back," he said. "He been up here pestering you?"

"Not yet."

"He's staying halfway down the island at the Cooley place. Did you know that?"

"No, I didn't," she answered.

"It worry you?"

"I can handle Gideon Sylvester."

"Have you thought about maybe clearing out of here now that you've got the wherewithall to do it?"

"Tom, this is my house. No one's chasing me out of it."

"You know best, I reckon."

"I'll be coming down to the south end more often now that I've got transportation. It'll give Giddy a chance to play with other children."

Tom laughed. "Your notion of transportation is mighty interesting. All the women are yapping away about you and that 'cycle, convinced you're gonna kill yourself on that thing."

"The only thing on this island that might kill me hasn't got wheels and a sidecar," she said sardonically.

"Remind me never to tussle with you, Mattie," he said appreciatively. "You are sure as hell one tough woman."

"Thank you for bringing Giddy the puppy. He loves it."

"Kids need pets."

"You know that from experience?" she asked.

"Me, I'm an old bachelor. I've got a load of nieces and nephews, though, and I've got eyes and a decent memory. I had me a dog when I was a boy. Best damned friend I've ever had. Told that hound my every thought. Trusted him more than I do most people."

"Why didn't you marry?" she asked, pushing in through the screen door, headed for the kitchen, with Tom right behind her.

"All the women I ever took a fancy to wound up marrying other men. It got to the point where I'd tell a girl, 'You want to get married, step out with me for a time. I guarantee you'll be married to someone else in six months flat.' "

She laughed and set out two cups. "They missed out. You'd have made some girl a fine husband."

"Nah. I'm too set in my ways. And 'sides, my hours'd drive anyone crazy, what with being on call day and night. And," he confided, "I wouldn't want to mess up the situation with Aggie after all these years. Suits us both down to the ground."

That summer she planted flowers in a bed between the house and the barn, in addition to the vegetable garden. She put by preserves and had wood and coal delivered to fuel the new furnace, the fireplaces, and the wood stove. But she felt none of the pressure of the previous years, and took the time to swim with the boy, to run with him and the puppy along the beach. And she fixed him up in his own room adjacent to the master bedroom.

He fell out of the bed the first few nights, then adjusted. In the morning, he'd usually be in the kitchen when she came down, having fed the dog and filled his water bowl. He was a helpful child, and was delighted whenever she gave him something to stir in a bowl. They were making pancakes the morning Gideon Sylvester came by the second time.

He tapped on the screen door to the kitchen and said, "If I contribute, could I join you for breakfast? I've got bacon." He held up a large package.

The boy paused in his stirring to look first at Gideon, then at his mother, asking, "Bacon?"

Gideon opened the door and came inside, almost absentmindedly dropping the slab of bacon on the counter as he made his way to the table. "What are you making, son?" he asked, sliding into a chair as he smiled at the boy.

"Pancakes!"

"You like them, do you?"

The boy nodded enthusiastically.

"And you're helping your mother cook. What a good boy!"

"Good boy," Giddy echoed.

"May I join you?" Gideon asked Mattie.

"He stay, Mama!" Giddy declared, waving the mixing spoon and splattering Gideon with a fair amount of batter.

Pleased by the sight of Gideon dabbing at the batter on his clothes with a handkerchief, Mattie said, "I suppose so. But don't go getting any ideas, Gideon Sylvester. I'm a lot harder to win over than he is."

"But I wasn't really," Mattie said ruefully. "I suppose I did take him back. I'd like to think I put up more of a fight, but I didn't. I'd been alone for too long. He was very determined, and he used his son to get to me. He kept dropping in, bringing gifts, displaying his charm and his big teeth. He bought me this diamond bracelet," she held up her wrist and with a frown looked at it. "I hate to admit it, because it makes me out to be such a mug, but, yes, I took him back. One night he cornered me on the living room sofa, and I guess he found out my brains were still in my crotch—as you so nicely put it, Sarah. Three weeks later he moved back in. I sure as hell didn't trust him, and I had a lot of questions I wanted answered. But for a time things were better with him than without him. He'd signed the house over to me, and he'd returned my money. And he'd told me he'd sold quite a number of my paintings. It was more than three years before I learned the truth of what he'd done. And then it was purely by accident. Gideon's cleverest move had been to gamble on moving me to the island and inducing me to stay, in the hope that I'd grow to like it here. As luck would have it, his gamble paid off in spades. I loved it here. I never wanted to leave.

"What he'd done was, he'd very cleverly moved me away from the scene of the crime, as it were. He put me where I was well and truly out of touch with what was going on in the world. Newspapers, when they did come, were always late, especially in the winter when for weeks at a stretch we didn't get papers or mail, let alone telephone calls. I might never have found out the truth, if it hadn't been for dear Hughie."

Twenty-One

"Would you like it if Carl joined us for dinner?" Mattie asked, changing subjects so precipitously that it took Sarah several moments to make the transition from past to present.

"Well, sure," Sarah said, "if you'd like it."

"Of course *I'd* like it. I've been having meals off and on with him for a great number of years."

"But not lately."

"No, because Carl goes for long periods when he's unable to be what he calls 'civilized.' It enrages him to be confined in a room, at a table, with rows of cutlery lined up on either side of his plate. I suppose it smacks to his mind of military discipline. Mind you, I'm only surmising."

"What makes you think he'll want to come tonight?"

"Ask him! He might leap at the chance to ogle you over the dining table."

"Are we supposed to provide entertainment for you?" Sarah asked.

"I don't find either one of you that entertaining. I'm hoping an invitation coming from you might appeal to him. I worry now and then that he spends too much time alone. Go ask him. Just don't be surprised if he says no."

"I'll give it my best shot," Sarah said, and went off, again feeling Mattie was urging her to participate in some salvage operation. But she wasn't in the least averse.

Carl was vacuuming the interior of the car, and seemed to suffer Sarah's interrupting his work, curtly asking, "What is it?"

It was as if they were back where they'd started, verbally jousting.

"Mattie wanted to know if you'd like to join us for dinner."

He stood holding the vacuum hose, thinking. "Can't do it," he said finally. "Tell her I'm sorry."

"Are you angry with me for some reason?" she asked.

"I'm not anything with you," he said. "I'm working at the moment. And I'm not up for chowing down in the big house tonight. Okay?"

Wounded, she said, "Okay," and walked quickly back to the house.

Mattie was coming down the stairs from the attic as Sarah arrived at the second floor landing.

"He said no."

"Too bad," Mattie said. "We'll try again another time."

"It's as if he goes away somewhere, as if he's never seen you before, and can't figure out why you're bothering him."

Mattie put her hand on the banister and tilted her head to one side, selecting her words with care. "You don't really have the remotest idea what any one of us here is all about, Sarah. Nothing in your life could possibly have equipped you for this particular wild animal safari. I'm not trying to offend you, my dear. I'm simply telling you that no one in this house is as accessible as you might think. Each of us has our confessional moments, our times of seeming rationality. But every last one of us, you included, has secrets we prefer not to share. Not one of us is actually certifiable, and we manage to meet the standards of what's socially acceptable at least fifty percent of the time. In one sense, we're probably quite normal—whatever that might be. We know how to converse, we know how to use money to get what we need, we even have certain skills. But all of us, including Bonnie and Gloria, are here together because we have a fundamental regard for each other's peculiarities. None of this is personal, Sarah, in the sense that you're being vilified in some way, or accused of anything. What I find most ironic," she said, withdrawing her hand from the banister and preparing to go to her bedroom, "is that each of us has accepted you precisely as you've presented yourself. I'm going to rest now before dinner. It's always intrigued me that I can sleep like a baby in the afternoon, but the naps guarantee I'll be up most of the night. I'll see you at dinner," she said, and went into the master bedroom, closing the door behind her.

Disconcerted, Sarah remained on the landing for several minutes, staring at the closed door. Then, sliding down into depression, she went to her room and flopped on the bed. Gazing at the ceiling, she viewed herself as a failure, someone who was graphic in the extreme, looking solely at surfaces and questioning only those things that pricked her interest. It was bad enough to have had her failings pointed out to her, but worse to have to acknowledge the truth of what Mattie had said. She'd viewed Bonnie and Gloria as two attractive, quite pleasant women who worked in the household. But she hadn't thought once about where they'd come from or who they really were.

She rolled over onto her stomach, pounded the pillow flat, and closed her eyes.

Mattie was uncommunicative at dinner. She drank two glasses of white wine, ate a small amount of the swordfish steak Bonnie had concealed beneath a heavy cream sauce, then pushed her plate away and chainsmoked until Sarah had finished eating.

When Bonnie came in to remove the dishes, Mattie told her she'd have coffee out on the verandah, then she got up and went outside.

"You want coffee?" Bonnie asked Sarah.

"I think I'll pass tonight, thanks," Sarah said, debating whether or not to follow Mattie. There wasn't really a choice. She was deeply involved in what Mattie was calling a wild animal safari.

She pushed out through the screen door and Mattie said, "Good. I'm glad to see you didn't let yourself be frightened off."

Baffled, Sarah sat down. Mattie was smiling at her. The old woman was irresistible when she smiled.

"I don't think I'd be able to smile if I'd lived your life," Sarah said admiringly. "I'm sure I'd be a rancorous old witch with not a good word to say for anyone."

"Don't make me out to be Mary Poppins, my dear. I *am* a rancorous old witch."

"I think you're wonderful," Sarah said, a sudden emotional surge threatening to choke her for the second time in one day. "I think you're the most lovable . . ." She had to stop and look away.

"I've never known anyone more embarrassed by her feelings," Mattie observed. "You behave as if they're something on a par with used sanitary pads, as if you're the only one who's ever bled once a month. Why do you do that?"

"If people see you're affected," Sarah said huskily, "they'll take advantage of your weakness."

"On the contrary, my dear. If most people see you're affected, they'll be drawn to you. With the exception of men like Gideon Sylvester and whatever their female counterparts might be. I find you most attractive when your defenses are at their lowest."

"I don't happen to care for myself in that condition."

"Pity. *You're* quite lovable when you stop asking questions and simply react to what you see and hear."

Bonnie came out with two cups of coffee and said to Sarah, "I figured when you came on out here you'd probably change your mind and want coffee after all."

"Thank you," Sarah said. "You're right. I do want some."

"Bonnie knows her apples and potatoes, don't you, Bonnie?"

"Yup, I sure do. I'll leave you a tray for later, Mattie. No go on the swordfish, huh?"

"Sarah enjoyed it."

"Another Siskel and Ebert situation, huh? I'll do up a nice Yankee pot roast tomorrow. You'll like that."

"I'm sure I will."

"You want anything, just holler," Bonnie said, and returned to the kitchen.

"Am I missing something?" Sarah asked.

"For all I know you're missing a great deal," Mattie quipped.

"At least twice a week you leave most of your dinner and then you and Bonnie go through this little song and dance about it. It's as if the two of you are writing a cookbook or something."

"Close," Mattie said, setting down her cup. "We're working our way *through* a cookbook. So far, in twenty-seven years, I think we've done nineteen or twenty of them. We're getting to the end right now of some artsy-fartsy one that hasn't been much of a success. It all started because Bonnie learned to cook in prison and she decided she'd become a chef when she got out. Luckily, when she came up for parole it so happened we were looking for a new cook. I liked her, so I hired her. She's been putting together a cookbook of her own for the last three or four years. It'll probably be a big hit. She wanted to call it *Hard Time Cuisine* but I was able to talk her out of that. So far she hasn't managed to come up with another title."

"What was she doing in prison?" Sarah asked, taken aback.

"Eight years for forgery."

"You're joking!"

"I am not! She worked with another woman, and the two of them made the best-looking checks I've ever seen, naturally on banks that didn't exist. And bearer bonds that were works of art, and sundry other pieces of paper, all of which netted them somewhere in the vicinity of a million dollars. Bonnie was a brilliant engraver, and her friend was a genius with pen and ink and with mixing dye colors."

"My God! That's amazing!"

"Yes, I was impressed," Mattie said coolly.

"I suppose Gloria has some fantastic background, too?"

"Oh, yes, indeed," Mattie said happily. "Quite the little theme park we've got here. Gloria, my dear, was one of the most expensive call girls you'll ever meet. As a sideline, she was Gideon Sylvester's mistress for a number of years. I hired her to cut down on the expense of Gideon's keeping her in an apartment in Manhattan. It seemed more sensible to offer her full-time employment with only one client. And she was beginning to dislike the, shall we say, wear and tear, of the job. After all, she was in her late thirties when I made her my proposition, and she hadn't managed to save very much, what with percentages she paid here and there to a number of unsavory types for various services rendered. I'd known about her for a long time. I telephoned and made an appointment to see her, and offered her a somewhat different form of employment. She was amenable and, in time, volunteered to take over some of the household chores in between her sessions with Gideon Sylvester. The truth was, she was bored. We got along very well. She could see I was busy, so she offered to 'legitimize' her position. I fully expected her to leave after the old snake died, but she told me she'd like to stay, and I was delighted to have her."

"Let me get this straight. You were *both* sleeping with him?"

"Don't be ridiculous! When I found out about Gloria, I was thrilled. He balked, naturally. But it was either Gloria, or going without. And he could never have gone without, so he accepted Gloria on a live-in basis. It's why he was so absurdly jealous when I'd go to Carl at night, and why he was convinced I was having an affair with him. Because to his mind, if I wasn't sleeping with him, I had to be sleeping with someone. And I certainly wasn't about to allow him to find out who I really was sleeping with."

"I'm very confused," Sarah complained. "I mean, back a while when you decided to start talking again, you intimated the two of you were sexually involved right up until he died."

"We were," Mattie smiled evilly. "I played intermediary. Which means I was involved. It all makes perfect sense, if you think about it."

"Not to me it doesn't. There are too many pieces missing."

"We'll get around to the rest of it eventually. Don't worry, Sarah. I planned from the outset to tell you everything."

"What does that mean?"

"It means I decided I wanted to hear myself tell this whole sordid story out loud. And that's what I'm doing." She lit a cigarette, then turned as if driven by some powerful unseen force to look at the beach and the sky, all of it losing its color as the last of the sun faded.

★   ★   ★

Sarah was too jittery to sleep, probably, she reasoned, because of the coffee. She read for more than an hour, then got up and went over to the garage, looking for Carl. He wasn't in the apartment. Returning down the stairs, she stood looking around the dark property, thinking he might be anywhere. It was hopeless to try to find him.

She went down the lawn toward the beach that was only somewhat less dark than everything else. The moon was hidden behind thick clouds and the air was wet and heavy. It would rain sometime soon. She could almost taste it as she trudged along the sand, her hands in her pockets, the breeze leaving a damp residue in her hair.

She walked for quite some time, until she finally felt as if she might be able to sleep. Then she turned and started to run along the beach, anxious to get to her room. She overshot the property in the dark and was almost up to the hedges when she realized she'd gone too far, and swung to the right to cut over the lawn.

Suddenly, terrifyingly, she was stopped, caught by an arm around her middle and a hand clapping over her face. In seconds, she was flat on her back on the grass, the hand over her face holding her locked in place while the other frisked her for concealed weapons. Carl. She made herself go still and covered the hand on her face with her own. Her heart was slamming against her ribs. She could scarcely breathe, let alone speak with that powerful hand closed over her nose and mouth. Something flashed, catching the moonlight, and she saw he had a knife gripped in his right hand as he crouched over her.

She'd lost most of her fear when she'd recognized Carl. It came rushing back now when she understood he had no idea who she was. As far as he was concerned, she was some treacherous Asian female on her way to blow up the house after murdering its occupants. She couldn't think how to communicate with him. Her hand stroking his seemed to have made no impression. He remained crouched over her, the flat of the knife blade resting against the underside of her chin. She tried to talk but could only make indecipherable noises in her throat. They'd both warned her, she thought regretfully, sick with dread. Mattie had tried to tell her this was no ordinary house populated by ordinary people. And so had Carl attempted to explain himself. But she'd ignored all that, convinced she was in control. There was nothing anywhere in this environment over which she had the least bit of control. But she'd stupidly believed she had, and now she was going to die as a result of her assumptions. She closed her eyes and waited for the cold blade to end her stupidity.

Then, incredibly, she heard Mattie whisper, "Carl, let her go, dear."

Sarah opened her eyes to see Mattie standing over Carl, her hand on his head. "Get up, dear," Mattie said very softly, "and put away the bayonet."

Very slowly, he did as she asked, and Sarah watched the old woman take him into her arms, whispering in his ear. Then, still holding him, Mattie said, "Go back to the house, Sarah. I'll be there in a few minutes."

Her trousers saturated with the evidence of her fear, Sarah ran clumsily to the house. Inside, she hurried up the stairs to her room and locked herself in the bathroom. Appalled at having so totally lost control of herself, she threw off her clothes, turned on the water, and climbed under the shower.

When she came out of the bathroom, Mattie was there, standing by the window with a cigarette, waiting for her.

"Please don't say you warned me, Mattie. I know you did."

"You must find me very cruel, if you think I'd come in here to say I told you so." Mattie looked distressed by the idea.

Sarah wrapped her arms around herself and, head bowed, said, "I only think the best of you. I was just so scared."

"Yes," Mattie said. "Of course you were. I should have warned you not to take walks late at night. It was an oversight, for which I apologize. He wouldn't have harmed you, Sarah. In another minute or two, he'd have remembered himself and he'd have released you. We've all had some sort of nighttime encounter with him over the years. His basic sanity prevails every time. But while it's happening, it is truly terrifying."

"You know what I think?" Sarah asked, wiping her face on her sleeve. "I think every last thing you've said about me is absolutely bang-on. And I think I fit right in here." She tried to smile but it didn't come off.

"Is that what you want?"

"I don't know anymore what I want. I thought maybe I did, but I really don't."

Mattie was looking around for an ashtray. Not finding one, she said, "Excuse me," went into Sarah's bathroom to hold her cigarette under the faucet, dropped it into the wastebasket, then came back and stood near Sarah, extending one hand to Sarah's hair.

"You're a lonely, frightened little girl," Mattie said. "We're all just children, really, until something happens to shock us right the way into adulthood. In a way, it's quite tragic. I believe the best of each of us is the child inside, the person we were meant to be, before the world interfered with our innocence."

Sarah turned and put her arms around the old woman, a bit startled by the solid strength of Mattie's body, but eased by her return of the embrace and the almost narcotic fragrance of KL.

Mattie patted her gently on the back and said, "Go to bed, my dear. And console yourself with the thought that you do fit in here, almost too well."

Twenty-Two

Sarah slept badly and was up very early the next morning. She couldn't help thinking of what had happened the night before in terms of an automobile accident. She'd been badly jarred but it was important to climb back behind the wheel and drive again at once. So she quickly washed and dressed and went through the gray mist to the garage apartment.

Carl was asleep in one of the old wicker armchairs, his head at an uncomfortable-looking angle. His dark night-patrol clothes lay in a heap on the floor and he wore only boxer shorts. She hated to wake him but she felt so strong a need to reassure them both that she crept over and laid a hand lightly on his arm. He didn't so much as twitch, but merely opened his eyes, instantly wide awake, and looked at her.

"If I say I'm sorry about last night," she said, "you'll probably say shit on my sorry, which leaves me strapped for some way to tell you how I feel."

"I need to brush my teeth," he said. "Sit down a minute. I'll be right back." He got up stiffly and went off to the bathroom.

Uneasy, she sat on the edge of the other chair and waited for him to return. She'd been energetically bungling since the day Mattie had hired her; there was little she hadn't messed up in her determination to see and hear everything that had to do with Gideon Sylvester and his widow. But it wasn't too late to make amends.

Carl came back pushing the wet hair out of his eyes with both hands. "You want coffee?" he asked, heading for the small kitchen area situated between the bathroom and the bedroom.

"Yes, please."

As she watched, he dumped the old grounds from the percolator, swilled out the pot, refilled it, poured fresh coffee into the basket, set the pot on the hot plate, and turned it on.

"Some fucking night," he said, taking pains to avoid meeting her eyes as he lit a cigarette, then stood looking at the hot plate.

"Yes, it was," she agreed. "Carl, I need to say I'm sorry."

"What've you got to be sorry about? *You* didn't come at *me* with a fucking bayonet."

"I'm sorry because I wasn't listening, because whatever it was I heard was only what I wanted to hear and not what anyone's actually been telling me."

His attention caught, he came over to sit down, looking at her now. "You think people say they're crazy just to be impressive or something?"

"You're not crazy."

"Come on, Sarah! They lock people up for doing the shit I do."

She shook her head. "They'd have to lock me up, too, then. Because if you're crazy, so am I. You know why? Because I've been going around for years believing I'm the only one who was ever tormented by an insane stepmother. I mean, I read the papers and watch TV—just the way you say you do, Carl—and I was still smug about my personal little tragedy. I was the only one who ever had her head held in the toilet while a *really* crazy woman tried to drown me. I was the only one who grew up knowing you couldn't trust anyone because they might smile at you when other people were around but the minute they left you'd be thrown down the stairs, or locked in the cellar, or made to go three days without food. It was nothing!" she said hotly. "Nothing! But it was as if I was in love with that abuse and couldn't let it go because maybe, without it, I was nothing special. I'm offended by myself now for holding on to all that crap like it was a diamond I'd found, or some private treasure. The thing is, after listening to Mattie tell me what she went through, and after what happened last night, all of a sudden I can see that I'm the same as everybody else. There's not one damned thing about me that's special or different. It's all a matter of degree; it's all relative. Mattie's been trying to pound that into my head for weeks, but I didn't get it. Well, I've sure as hell got it now. And that's why I'm sorry. I'm no better and no different than you or Mattie or Bonnie or Gloria, or anyone else. I'm exactly the same, only younger and maybe a little shorter and thinner, with green eyes and not brown, and maybe my feet are smaller. That's all."

"You love to go goddamned extremes, don't you?" he said, stubbing out his cigarette and getting up to turn off the hot plate. Standing with his hands on his hips, his eyes on the percolator, he said, "Don't you know about middle ground, Sarah? Don't you know not everything falls on either one side or the other? If you're not popping up all over the goddamned place asking questions, you're beating yourself up because you think you got something wrong. There's not one fucking thing that's as black or white as that. And I'm not going to sit here and listen and agree with you just because you're feeling guilty, or whatever it is you're feeling. It's not up to me to give you or anyone else absolution, sweetheart. Jesus!" He gave a small tired laugh. "I've got enough problems without trying to take on yours, too. You think I *like* being a psycho? You think I get off on getting ready to slit the throat of a woman I've been making love with? You think I wouldn't like to get my head straight and do all the routine shit normal guys do, like being able to eat with other people, or being able to sleep at night without feeling this fucking worm in my brain that's telling me if I shut my eyes I'll never wake up? It's a goddamn shame some nutso broad stuck your head down the toilet. No shit! That's very damned sad. I hate to hear it. But there's not a thing I can do to change one bit of it. You've got to do that for yourself. Dr. Harvey here has his hands full just pretending to be civilized for Mattie's sake. And maybe a bit for yours, too.

"You're absolutely right," he said, pouring out two mugs of coffee. "It sure is all a matter of degree. And it's relative as hell. The whole thing hangs on what you've got upstairs and how much control you happen to have over your own head and what's stored up inside it." He gave her one of the mugs, then sat down holding his own with both hands.

"Even crazy people need to be loved," she said.

"Damned straight!" he agreed. "You paint the signs, I'll march in that parade."

"I feel the same way about you today as I did yesterday. Only more so."

"You're either stupid," he smiled, "or another true crazy."

"Or both. Does it matter?"

"Hey, babe! Not to me. You're the one chasing her tail. I'm too busy making sure I've still got mine to worry about what matters in the general scheme of things."

For a few moments, she stood outside herself, viewing this scene as if from a corner of the room, or from beyond the screen door, looking in. There was this massively built attractive man sitting in his shorts, talking to a not unattractive woman in a T-shirt and cotton drawstring pants. They were generating energy, both physically and mentally; they were pacing out the perimeters of the arena of their attraction to one another, drawn by emotional undercurrents into a psychological examination. If they stopped talking, they could be touching. And if they were touching, it might prove a more meaningful communication. She could say or do anything and no one would come along and beat her with a rope or drag her across the floor by her hair if what she said or did didn't meet with unanimous approval. She could set down her coffee mug, pull off her T-shirt, then give in to her unendurable need to position herself on her knees in front of him and galvanize him with a shameless display of her encompassing affection for him.

He nearly spilled his coffee, and shakily put the mug aside, hissing, "Jesus, Sarah! What turned your switch?"

She paused and looked up at him. "Don't be stupid," she smiled. "You think I can be scared off that easily? Now, be quiet!" she said and lowered her head again.

After a few minutes he let out a gasping laugh and said, "My brains are going to spill out of my ears if you don't stop that. C'mere," he said, holding her steady to kiss her cool moist mouth. At that moment the rain began. It came drumming down on the roof and sheeting across the windows, bringing the scent of grass and damp soil in through the screened windows as he took her out of the voluminous pants, kicked off his boxers, and put her down on the bare wood floor.

Mattie took a long look at her, then said, "It's a damned good thing I've got the sketch. If I attempted to capture the look of you now I'd be accused of painting pornography. Just sit there and try to be good company."

"Doesn't it distract you, talking while you work?" Sarah asked, tucking her feet under her in the armchair.

"Nothing distracts me when I'm working. This may be a depiction of you, my dear, but it's entirely my statement. The subject is never more than incidental to the medium. Everything is drawn through the filtering process of the artist in question's personal interpreting systems. What makes anyone's work unique is the degree of self that goes into it while at the same time exercising restraint in order not to inflict more of one's self upon a piece of work than is required to provide it with form and substance. Everything I paint is a comment on my cerebral condition and on my ability to render it accessible to the viewer. Just the way a good storyteller will paint you a mental picture without distracting you from the narrative by overloading the tale with gristle or larding the plot with unnecessary details. The essence of all fine art is the artist's talent for distillation, combined with an innate feel for the valid detail." As she talked, her eyes moved back and forth between the palette and the canvas, the brush traveling deftly between one and the other.

"There are one or two things you should know," she went on, "points I want to clarify, so you have no misunderstandings. I could see the wheels turning last night when I told you about Gloria. Neither Bonnie nor Carl has any idea of the details of Gloria's background. And I don't want you thinking that I took an elegant lady of the evening and for my own devious reasons turned her into a housekeeper. I made Gloria what I considered to be an eminently reasonable proposition. She thought about it and decided to take me up on it. It was a business arrangement. But, as sometimes happens between women, we discovered we enjoyed one another. It was Gloria's decision to stay on after Gideon Sylvester died, and her decision to take over the running of the house. She chose to stay, and she chose to do the work she does because it enabled her to maintain her dignity. Like a large number of other women who provide certain esoteric services for men, she has never had any real regard for them. As far as I was concerned, she was someone who did me a tremendous personal favor, and I've always admired her for being able to do something I could never do: She could pretend an interest in that vile old puff adder and make it seem quite genuine. I think she deserves the Nobel Prize for that sustained performance, in view of the fact that within a very short period of time she came to find him almost as repugnant as I did. But she made good her commitment. If you someday take the time to talk with Gloria, I have no doubt you'll find her a remarkably self-possessed woman and an enviably contented one. I'm sure I don't have to tell you that her past is strictly her business."

"I understand."

"Good. You're improving. As for Carl," Mattie went on, "I want you to know I'm proud of you for climbing back on the horse at once, as it were."

Sarah laughed.

"Most women would've been on the first ferry this morning," Mattie said, looking over. "You have integrity. I applaud that."

"I care about him. I'm not going to stop caring because he has problems. If anything," Sarah said, thinking it through aloud, "I probably care more about him because he does. At least everything's aboveboard and I know what I'm dealing with. Which is way better than what I went through with the Romanian peasant."

"You could very well be his cure, you know, Sarah. If you were prepared to put in the time."

"How d'you know I'm not?"

Mattie sniffed, put down the brush and palette, and reached for a cigarette. After it was lit, she looked again at Sarah. "I'd like to tell you about nineteen forty-one," she said. "I think you'll find it very interesting."

With the house winterized and completely redecorated, and with an evidently substantial sum of money in what Gideon Sylvester promised her was a very stable bank, they called another truce, and took up life together again. But now there were certain ground rules. Mattie insisted on a fifty percent share of any revenues generated by the sale of her paintings. Of course she had to trust Gideon's accounting, but despite various mysterious little quirks he displayed whenever the question of money arose—things like reciting from memory which paintings had been sold and for how much, or his insistence that they maintain separate accounts in different banks (which suited her perfectly)—he appeared to be handling matters fairly responsibly. She was admittedly obtuse in her failure to demand written statements from the gallery, or galleries, but he was so adept at sidetracking her when she began asking too many questions that, for a time, she simply went along with him. It seemed that Gideon had found his true niche not as an artist but as the representative of one.

She worked. And periodically he came along to harvest the latest crop of paintings with much the same diligence she put to use on the garden. From time to time she'd insist on withholding certain works— those of the baby, the view of the house, and the self-portrait—and then they'd argue, very nearly coming to blows over her right to keep some of her pieces for herself. She didn't like Gideon Sylvester; she didn't trust him; but she was still somehow in love with him. And he could, when words and all else failed, persuade her with sexual atten- tion. He fell upon her each time as if he'd never touched her before, as if he found her so desirable he wouldn't be satisfied until he'd just about inverted her with pleasure.

To enable her to be free to paint, he took over all the cooking when he was at home, which was perhaps three weeks out of every four, and hired Aggie's seventeen-year-old daughter to live in six days of the week to tend to Giddy. He also hired Mrs. O'Brian's young sister to come to the house twice a week to clean. There wasn't a thing Mattie was required to do, except paint. She had all the time she could possibly want to roam about the island sketching, or order young Jean, Aggie's daughter, to please hold still while she drew the girl's radiant angular face. Mattie gave herself over to her first and best love: her work. But every painting contained a hidden second signature, and each was fully described, from long habit, in the log she now kept hidden in an alcove she'd discovered behind the furnace.

"I was living in a fool's paradise," she told Sarah, "closing my eyes to the fact that Gideon Sylvester was intentionally keeping me ignorant of what he did every time he went off to New York for a week or so, then returned to the island with another fistful of money.

"It's odd, you know, how we'll shy away from suspecting someone we live with of the worst possible crimes. We don't want to believe our judgment is so flawed that we'd take up with someone capable of molesting a child, or of raping a woman on a dark street, or of being a mass murderer. Every goddamned time you read in the paper about someone who's finally gone public with his madness, there'll be fifty people who say, 'But he was such a nice, quiet man.' We just don't want to know. And the only possible reason why is because we believe it'll reflect badly on us.

"I would never have believed what Gideon Sylvester had done if it had been anyone but Hughie who told me. I'd have called anyone else a liar, but not Hughie." She suddenly put down her brush and palette, looking stricken. "I'm sorry," she said atypically, "but I can't stand here and try to paint while I'm telling you about this. I've got to get out. I need air. Come walk with me." She pulled off the smock and threw it down as if it were contaminated.

She was so palpably distraught that Sarah didn't say a word, but just took hold of Mattie's hand and went with her down the stairs and out of the house toward the beach. Arriving at the hard-packed sand, the mist still hovering close to the ground, Mattie raised their joined hands and looked at them.

"There are only six other people who know what I'm about to tell you, Sarah. My two sons, Carl, Bonnie, Hughie Dickinson, and my attorney." Her eyes bored into Sarah's. "Don't presume to judge me!" she cautioned her. "It was another time in another world and things were nowhere near as clearly defined as they are now. People's lives overlapped in ways that simply aren't possible now. It's so difficult, once you're beyond childhood, to believe that the people who come to you come without ulterior motives. Public recognition brings with it some horrifying burdens. I've always loathed the nonsense that goes along with being a so-called celebrity. I can't abide reporters, newshounds, people coming up to you shoving cameras or microphones in your face. Every last bit of it sickens me. Gideon Sylvester, of course, adored it, lived for it, thrived on it." She paused, then carefully extricated her hand from Sarah's, and began to walk.

"Early in nineteen forty-one all the residents were asked to evacuate the island for reasons of national security. The navy had already been on the island for a time. Now they planned to take it over entirely. Barracks were being constructed on the south end for the men who'd be stationed there. Gideon responded to the news by puffing out his chest like a five-star general and declaring he would do his patriotic duty by reclocating us.

"Off he went in his shiny new Oldsmobile, and returned a week later to announce he'd bought the Connecticut house. I was upset at his usual failure to consult me. Until I saw the house. And then it wasn't possible to maintain my anger because he'd found a place that closely duplicated everything I loved about the house here. We made the move to Connecticut, and I found it very easy to make believe little had changed. We still had an ocean view and our own private beach; we had another big clapboard monstrosity with an attic that would convert well to a studio. Aside from the dimensions of the rooms, as you may have noticed, the two houses are remarkably similar.

"Gideon Sylvester arranged for a new girl to look after Giddy, who was now attending kindergarten half days, and for a housekeeper. New house, new faces, different location, same agenda. But now that we were closer to New York, Gideon began to behave like the lord of the manor, ordering the staff around when he was home in a fashion that upset everyone until I had to ask him to leave the people alone or we'd lose them. This dictum seemed to be something he'd been waiting for and he responded by spending even more time in New York. Which suited me fine. The housekeeper was happy to cook when he wasn't around and I much preferred Ina's company.

"Ina was a treasure," she said with a fond smile. "A superb sense of humor, a grandmotherly woman who doted on Giddy and had endless time and patience with him. Which his father most definitely didn't have. Once Gideon Sylvester had succeeded in winning me back, he gave up his feigned interest in his son and scarcely had the time of day for him.

"Well," Mattie sighed. "Everything began to turn sour in October of that year."

Gideon returned home from one of his four-days trips to Manhattan bearing gifts. After dinner on his first evening home, he presented

Mattie with a small blue Tiffany's box, saying, "I had this made for you. I hope you like it."

It was a small golden palette, set with semiprecious and precious stones, each of a different color, representing dots of paint. Across the palette lay a platinum brush with a brilliant cut oval diamond as the head. It was a clever and very beautiful brooch, and she was touched by the trouble he'd gone to.

He produced a bottle of champagne and two glasses and with a telltale glitter to his eyes, suggested they go upstairs to the bedroom.

They drank the champagne and he admired her, saying, "I much prefer your hair long this way. It suits you so wonderfully well. Such a glorious color," he said, his hand gliding into the depths of her hair. "I've never known anyone I have found as endlessly appealing," he told her, commencing yet another jubilant attack on her senses.

But this time it climaxed with his profuse apologies. "I'm sorry. I just couldn't wait. Sorry, sorry. I couldn't hold off."

She lay looking at him, chilled in the same way she'd been after Giddy's birth when Gideon had sat wearing a lewd expression watching her nurse the infant. The chill came accompanied by the certainty that not only was he up to something he was determined to conceal from her, but he was also angling to get her pregnant again. She didn't say a word, but inside her head a door slammed closed with resounding finality.

He was home for two days, during which time he was so comically furtive she was almost amused. When he announced he'd have to go to New York again, she was certain he had a mistress. "Now, why," she said, "don't I find that surprising?" She told Giddy to say good-bye to his father, then took the boy for a walk on the beach.

Three days later she received a letter from Hughie. Leaving Giddy with Ina, she carried the letter out to the back porch.

"I don't know where to begin," Hughie wrote. "I'm still in quite a state of shock and can only hope I'm not telling you something you already know. In my heart of hearts, I can't believe you'd go along with anything like this. Somehow, it's not like you, Mattie. But if you did agree to this, I'm sure you have your reasons."

He went on to say that he'd traveled by train down to New York to discuss mounting a show with a very good gallery. And the talk all over town was of Gideon Sylvester and his brilliant paintings. Having seen some of Gideon's work, and having found it mediocre at best, he was very curious. So he went along to the Gallery Alexander on Madison Avenue to have a look at these so-called brilliant paintings. And to his utter astonishment what he saw was an entire gallery filled with Mattie's paintings bearing Gideon Sylvester's signature.

Mattie read the letter a second time. By the time she finished, her hands were trembling so badly she could scarcely read Hughie's handwriting. She stared into space for a while, feeling horror and disbelief and rage overtaking her. Despite what Hughie had said, she couldn't make herself believe Gideon Sylvester could have done such a thing. She knew she wasn't going to believe it until she saw the proof for herself.

She got up, went inside, and told Ina, "I have to go into the city. I don't know how long I'll be."

"What's wrong, Mattie? You're white as a sheet."

"I have to go," Mattie said. "Look after Giddy. I'll probably be back this evening."

Upstairs, she changed clothes mechanically, then put on her coat, reached for her handbag, and went downstairs and out to the car. Since she'd never driven in Manhattan, and since she was admittedly overwrought, she left the car at the station and rode the train into the city.

Throughout the trip, she gazed unseeingly out the window, with the feeling she was sitting nude and that everyone was staring at her. She didn't dare think about any of this until she'd confronted the truth. Once she'd seen it, then she'd decide what to do.

Upon arriving at Grand Central, she looked up the address of the Gallery Alexander in the telephone directory, then left the station and flagged down a taxi. All the way uptown, she had to keep wetting her lips; her apprehension had dehydrated her. The trembling had overtaken her entire body by now and she had to hold her hands tightly together in her lap.

She paid the driver and stepped out of the taxi in front of the gallery to stand staring at the front window where one of her paintings, magnificently framed and subtly lit, stood on a gilt easel. And discreetly positioned to one side of the window was a small hand-lettered sign that read, "We proudly offer for viewing the works of Gideon Sylvester."

Moving closer to the window, she could see very clearly Gideon Sylvester's signature in the lower right-hand corner. Wetting her lips again, she opened the door to the gallery and stepped inside to see no less than a dozen of her works, all as splendidly framed and precisely lit as the one in the window.

There was a woman in attendance who moved to approach Mattie, and Mattie waved her away, her eyes on the paintings, her heart pounding so hard she was sure it was audible. There they were! Her paintings, her life's blood, on display for everyone to see. For a moment, she forgot the fraud that had been perpetrated; she forgot everything but the rush of pride at seeing her work hung with such care in an actual gallery. For seventeen years she'd lived for this moment. Since she'd first picked up a crayon as a small child, she'd lived for this moment. And here it was: her efforts hung on walls for everyone to see and admire.

"They're really quite remarkable," the gallery attendant observed at Mattie's side. "I get a kick out of coming to work every day, knowing I'll be able to look at them."

Mattie turned to look at the woman and saw she actually was gazing with apparent reverence at the painting of the two workmen eating lunch on the curb. Unable to speak, Mattie merely nodded and moved away, deeper into the gallery.

One after another, she examined her own paintings and the superimposed signatures Gideon Sylvester had placed upon them. She alternated between her feelings of pride and of horror. Gideon Sylvester might not ever have physically harmed her in reality, but he'd savagely raped her. And he'd done it in public, with the full sanction of an unknown number of people.

"Perhaps you'd like a brochure," the attendant said, and pressed one into Mattie's hand, then withdrew to her desk near the entry.

Slowly, moving with difficulty, she looked at every one of the paintings. She was there, at the scene of Gideon Sylvester's ongoing crime, and felt eviscerated. She screamed without making a sound, her eyes almost bulging from the massive effort to keep the agonized howls contained within herself. Yes, she'd thought he was selling her work. But not as his own. It would have been inconceivable to her that he could do what he'd done. But he'd done it. He'd robbed her of the right to accept the acclaim for her efforts. He'd stolen her talent and shown it to the world as his own.

She was able to understand almost everything now, she thought. It sickened her, because by her blindness she'd been Gideon Sylvester's unwitting partner in this crime.

Clutching the brochure, she stumbled out of the gallery and ran into the street, waving frantically for a cab.

"Hughie wanted to know if I was a willing partner in this collusion. He wanted to know if I had agreed to perpetrate this fraud on the artistic community and the general public." Her voice fracturing like shattered glass, Mattie stared bleakly at the horizon and cried, *"Did I know? Had I agreed?* No, I didn't know. I'd never agreed. I would never have given my consent!

"As I rode the train home, I kept slipping back and forth between the tremendous pride I'd felt seeing my work in that gallery, and the revulsion that swept over me every time I thought of how it had all come to be there.

"When I got home, I ran inside and told Ina to pack suitcases for herself and Giddy. We were leaving. I paid off the girl who looked after Giddy and sent her away. Within an hour we were on our way to Maine. I didn't give a damn about anything except clearing myself with Hughie. I couldn't *bear* the idea of him thinking I'd had any voluntary part in what Gideon had done.

"We drove straight up there, arriving early that same evening. Hughie heard the car pull into the driveway and came out to see who it was. As it happened, I didn't have to explain a thing. He took one look at me and said, 'I knew you didn't know! I knew it!'

"That night, after Ina had tucked Giddy in and gone off to bed herself, I did what I should have done years before. I took a good hard look at Hughie Dickinson, saw all the love he'd always had for me, felt the corresponding response inside myself, and got into his bed."

Twenty-Three

Mattie broke off speaking and seemed on the verge of strangling as she stood with the incoming waves flirting closer and closer to her feet, her eyes wide and fixed, one hand at her throat, the other at her breast as tremors overtook her. Sarah went to her, instinctively seeking to offer comfort, but Mattie flung out a hand and cried, "*Don't!* For God's sake, leave me be!"

Feeling horribly inadequate, Sarah stopped.

"I don't want to open this door," Mattie whispered. "I've kept it closed for so long." She shook her head mournfully, as if viewing the remains of someone too well loved whose death would leave her permanently impaired. She drew a ragged breath, then reached into her pocket for her cigarettes. Cupping her hands around the match like an experienced sailor accustomed to lighting cigarettes in a constant wind, she got one going, put the spent match back into the box, and took a hard drag on the cigarette. Perceptibly she regained her control. She looked down, saw the water washing over the toes of her shoes, and took a step back. "I'm not rejecting you, Sarah," she said, her eyes scanning the mist-enveloped shoreline. "I can't accept consolation just now. It would only interfere with my getting this goddamned door open once and for all."

"Maybe," Sarah said, "it would be better to keep it closed."

"I can't," Mattie said, beginning to walk again. "Before I die I've got to get it all out."

"Don't talk about dying! I want you to live forever."

"All creatures have their season," Mattie said. "I've had mine."

"You can't just choose to put a time limit on yourself."

"It has nothing to do with choice. Everything dies."

"This is awful," Sarah said, "really, truly, awful."

Mattie took a final puff on her cigarette, then bent to extinguish it in the sand. Straightening, she dropped the butt in her pocket.

"First you save the match, now you're putting cigarette butts in your pocket," Sarah said.

"Are you actually this stupid?" Mattie rounded on her. "Look around you! Would you want to see all this littered with rubbish? Would you like to have to walk along this beach picking your way over washed-up McDonald's wrappers and thousands of cigarette filters? Use your head! We've already got holes in the ozone layer and acid rain, not to mention an entire generation of women without men because the boys like Carl who went to be soldiers and didn't die in goddamned Vietnam can't quite seem to recover from the things that went on there. One way and another we're ruining everything beautiful about this planet. I refuse to contribute to that!"

"See!" Sarah said. "How can you talk about seasons being over and all the rest of it when you're so involved in what's going on right now?"

"You are being nauseatingly naive," Mattie said threateningly.

"Okay. I'll shut up. I won't say another word."

"Oh, you will," Mattie said. "You can't help it." She held her hands in front of her and studied them front and back, shook them from the wrists, flexed her fingers, then allowed her arms to fall to her sides. "I don't believe I've described Hughie to you, beyond mentioning the things about him that initially annoyed me. He really was a very nice-looking young man, you know. About six feet tall, with deep brown hair and an exquisite peachy tone to his skin, hazel eyes, and good regular features. When he got into the habit of brushing them, his teeth were really very decent. And he had wonderful dimples. To see Hughie smile . . . of course he was always very shy and so didn't smile that often. But when he did . . ."

★   ★   ★

After ten years of sleeping with Gideon Sylvester, making love with Hughie was nothing less than a revelation. She entered his bedroom and automatically went about the business of removing her clothes. It wasn't until she was stepping out of her underwear that she saw that Hughie hadn't moved but was rooted in place by the door, watching her. He looked as if he'd just unwittingly walked into a gallery containing works of art that surpassed all earthly enterprise. She was so accustomed to Gideon Sylvester's urgency that it came as a mild shock to see no sign whatever of it in Hughie. He was beaming as he said, "This is kind of a miracle. I might just stand here the rest of my life looking at you."

"No, you won't," she said, smiling back at him. "Unless you intend to make me very uncomfortable."

"I wouldn't want to do that," he said earnestly. "But I sure do hate to have to stop."

She removed the last of her undergarments, straightened, and walked over to stand in front of him. "Come on," she said lightly, taking both his hands in hers, basking in his visual praise.

"I'm storing up impressions," he told her, "maybe for a whole series of paintings. My memory's first-rate."

"I know it is. I've seen your paintings, remember. Come on," she said again. "It's not very warm in here."

"I've always thought you were a fine-looking woman, but I was wrong. You're beautiful."

"I'm nothing of the sort. All I really am is tall."

"Those are just words. My eyes know better."

Hughie wasn't a technician, or a manipulator, or interested in anything except expressing his feelings for her. His sole aim was to embrace the person dearest to his heart. Once cajoled out of his clothes and into his bed, he lost his shyness. It wasn't that he underwent any sort of startling transformation but rather that his artistry and his obsession with detail were not confined to his work. His sense of wonder had somehow survived intact into manhood and he wasn't ashamed to reveal it as he viewed her body for the first time, finding it a completely captivating landscape.

After more than a decade of cunning assaults by Gideon Sylvester, Hughie's touch confirmed her feeling that she'd been in residence with an exquisite rapist whose technique was so masterfully refined that it wasn't until considerably after the fact that she knew how well and truly she'd been ravaged. Whatever Gideon Sylvester had been doing, it had nothing to do with love. And what she'd felt while he'd been doing it had been a purely primal desperation for release. He'd savaged her nerve endings until she was half mad with a need to have it finished.

Hughie spent a long time stretched out at her side, leaning on his elbow and following the passage of his fingers as they traveled over her. This lingering examination brought her to the inescapable realization that this was the first time she'd ever been touched by someone who loved her.

He was so taken with her, and she was so absorbed in witnessing the unfurling banner of his caring, the contact was doubly revealing. Not only had she misinterpreted Gideon Sylvester's foraging expeditions in her body as signs of love, but she'd been duped by her own sexual responsiveness into believing that what he'd sparked in her during those forays had to be love. What he'd done was to educate her in sexual calisthenics while depriving her of the one thing capable of elevating those endless skirmishes to something beyond merely lusty exercises. He'd withheld emotion, because he'd never loved her. Gideon Sylvester was the champion snake-oil salesman of all time, and she'd been his best customer.

Relinquishing all thought of the man she'd married, she offered herself to Hughie, keeping nothing back. She had to know, finally, how it felt to love without reservation. Concerned only with this kind and gentle man, she put her hands on Hughie's face, brushed the hair back from his forehead, then kissed him. He tasted pleasantly of the pipe tobacco he smoked, and his slow return of the kiss was further proof of his ability to give without making demands. He would willingly collect all the fragments of her scattered self and reassemble them with loving tenderness.

She looked closely at his eyes and said, "If I'd known you could kiss like that, Hughie Dickinson, I'd have done this a long time ago."

He seemed unable to stop smiling, his cheeks dimpled. "The one time you kissed me, at the Harveys' farewell party, I couldn't see straight for days after."

She took her hands down his lean sides to his hips, holding him to her as she shifted under him, aligning her legs with his, lifting to him. He ran a hand over her breasts, said, "We should be using something," and prepared to stop.

"Not this time." She rocked slowly from side to side.

"Is that a good idea?"

"It's a very good idea. I don't want anything, not a blessed thing, to come between us."

He kissed her again and she silently urged him to settle his full weight upon her. She longed to disappear into him, to find herself permanently attached to him. She took his hand, directing it between her legs as she stroked him, their eyes locked. His tongue streamed over her like cool healing liquid. Nothing could have prepared her for the piercing gratification of this meeting. She guided him into her, then enclosed him with her entire body. They set sail together in a fragile boat, caught the outgoing tide, then laughed in spontaneous delight at their fortunate timing.

"I guess you know I love you, Mattie," he said. "Always have and always will."

"I know," she whispered, and held him with great care. "I know."

Hughie was the only man, aside from Tom Harding, who demonstrated true respect for her son as a person. Unlike Gideon, he didn't treat the boy as an unwanted additional contender for Mattie's affections. Hughie had no wish to compete with Giddy for his mother's love. And Giddy adored Hughie from the outset, finding in the soft-spoken man a true ally and willing companion.

While Mattie and Hughie set off to visit the Harveys, who were now settled in a house of their own a few miles away, Ina kept an eye on

Giddy and the dog as they played in the satisfyingly crisp mounds of leaves at the rear of the house.

"Please don't say anything about Gideon to the Harveys," Mattie begged Hughie. "I don't want anyone to know."

"What are you going to do?" he asked.

"For the moment, nothing. I don't even want to think about it. It makes me feel too shattered."

"Eventually, you're going to have to."

"Eventually, I will. But not now."

"I'll just say this one thing, then I'll drop it." He stopped the car on the side of the road, put the shift in neutral, and swiveled on the seat to look at her. "Mattie, he's taken away something you've either got to claim back, or you've got to resign yourself to the loss forever. He's established himself very credibly. Everyone believes those are his paintings. I know if it was me, I'd go after him and kill him. I'd have to. You can't let someone steal the single most important thing in your life and get away with it. Leastwise, I couldn't. But you're married to the man, you've got his child. And it seems to me maybe that puts a different complexion on it. If you decide to make your claim, I'll stand with you. I'll stand with you in any case, if that's what you want. Or even if it isn't. I only know that whatever you decide is going to affect both of us. You want to be shut of him, I'll marry you tomorrow. If you choose to go back, I'll say good-bye and watch you drive off with Ina and the boy, but I'll wait, for the rest of my life if I have to, for you to come back."

Having said his piece, he put the car back in gear and drove on.

It didn't take Gideon Sylvester long to track her down. And then the telephone calls started, along with pleading letters at first, followed by progressively more menacing ones.

Hughie took it all in stride, prepared to cope for Mattie's sake. She refused to speak to Gideon, glanced at his letters, then tore them to pieces and discarded them. She wished she could pretend Gideon Sylvester didn't exist, but he wasn't about to allow that. She longed to be free of him, to live unencumbered by his demands.

It seemed, however, as if fate and Gideon Sylvester were destined always to conspire against her. In the fifth week of their stay with

Hughie, Mattie had to run from the dinner table to be sick. As she bathed her face with cold water she knew Gideon had managed to get her pregnant again. She also knew there could be no possibility the child was Hughie's. This being her third pregnancy, there was an inescapable consistency to the timing of her nausea. It occurred in her sixth week every time without fail. Returning to the table, she dredged up a smile and apologized to Hughie and Ina and Giddy, then forced herself to sit there while the others finished the meal Ina had prepared.

The next day the mailman brought a registered letter from Gideon's lawyer. It said if she didn't return at once to the family home in Connecticut, Gideon was prepared to institute proceedings against her. Just what those proceedings might be was left unstated.

In a rage, she telephoned the lawyer and made an appointment to see him the following afternoon,

"I'll take care of this once and for all," she told Hughie, before leaving for the train station. "I've had as much of this crap as I'm going to take."

Even the lawyer's handshake seemed adversarial. He politely invited Mattie to sit down. She did, and at once said, "I think you should advise your client to stop threatening me."

"Mrs. Sylvester," he said, briefly polishing his horn-rimmed glasses before putting them on and pushing them up his nose with the tip of a forefinger, "my client, your husband, has every right to be making certain demands. I'm not aware of any threats emanating from this office. On behalf of my client, I have requested that you return home. It seems a fairly straightforward request to me, especially under the circumstances."

"What circumstances might those be? I'd be fascinated to hear what lies Gideon has been feeding you."

"No lies, Mrs. Sylvester," the lawyer said calmly. "Would you care for some tea, perhaps, or coffee?"

"No, thank you. Look!" she said impatiently. "Whatever the man has told you, it's a lie. Are you aware of the fact that he abandoned me and his infant son, leaving us penniless? Are you aware of the fact that he stole all my money and left us for two and a half years?"

"He would like you to return home, Mrs. Sylvester," the man said. "He is willing to forget and forgive everything. I would suggest to you he's being exceedingly reasonable, under the circumstances."

"There you go again! What circumstances?"

The lawyer opened one of the drawers of his desk and brought out a file folder which he placed on the blotter in front of him, resting his hand flat over top of it as he said, "It's always distasteful to have to present documentation, but if you insist, I am prepared to go through the contents of this file with you."

"What contents?" she wanted to know, grievously irritated by the man's manner and expression. "I don't believe you have anything in that file that could possibly document one damned thing."

"Very well," he said with a tiny sigh, and opened the file. "I have here two affidavits signed and notarized that attest to acts of yours that constitute reckless endangerment with respect to the minor child Gideon Sylvester the Third."

"What acts?"

"To wit," he read, "allowing the child to stand while riding in an open sidecar appended to a motorcycle driven at high speeds." He looked up asking, "Do you wish to hear it all?"

"That's ridiculous," she said.

"Very well. I have three further affidavits signed and notarized attesting to adulterous behavior by one Mathilda Sylvester with a Thomas Harding . . ."

"That's an outright lie!" she cried.

"Further," he went on, "I have evidence of further adulterous behavior by one Mathilda Sylvester with a Hugh C. Dickinson . . ." He looked up at her expectantly.

"Why is he doing this to me?" she whispered, stunned.

"There are additional documents, Mrs. Sylvester," he said, "having to do with Mr. Sylvester's having been forced to sign over the island property to Mrs. Sylvester while Mr. Sylvester was under extreme emotional and financial distress. Also certain financial statements surrendered by Mr. Sylvester demonstrating his good faith in providing Mrs. Sylvester with fifty percent of the entire income generated by the sale of his paintings . . ."

"Stop!" she said weakly, her head suddenly aching.

"I think you should be aware, Mrs. Sylvester, that it is Mr. Sylvester's intention to seek custody of the child should you fail to agree to return home. In view of the documentation, I doubt he'd have difficulty in proving you an unfit mother."

"I asked you to stop," she said more strongly.

"Sorry," he said curtly, and leaned back in his chair, lacing his fingers together across his chest.

"Why do I have the impression you're enjoying this?" she asked him, trying to locate some small sign of humanity in the man.

"On the contrary, Mrs. Sylvester," he said, coming forward to lean his elbows on the desk. "There are few things I've enjoyed less. May I be frank with you?"

"Please."

"Your husband's a very determined man," he began.

She laughed ruefully. "You don't know the half of it."

"I have some idea," he conceded. "In any event, for reasons not known to me and which are legitimately not my concern, he wants you to return home. Given the lengths to which he has gone to gather and document his facts, regardless of their possible bias, it must surely be obvious to you, as it is to me, that he has no intention of giving up and allowing you to leave him without what I would deem an epic battle. There are two sides to every story, Mrs. Sylvester. I have been retained to present your husband's side, and I must tell you it's substantial and well constructed. If there is any possibility of a reconciliation, I would advise you to make every effort in that direction. Of course you could engage your own attorney and fight it out, but I feel obligated to tell you that, as far as I'm concerned as your husband's counsel, he's got you hog-tied and branded. Why," he said kindly, "don't you go home, Mrs. Sylvester, and save yourself no amount of grief?"

"Thank you," she said thickly, and got to her feet. "I'll think about it."

He offered his hand, saying, "Think very carefully. You have everything to lose and very little, from the looks of it, to gain."

She left the office barely able to navigate the corridors.

During the train ride back to Maine she struggled to bring her rage under control, trying to shake the idea that she had, in taking up with Gideon Sylvester, made an unspoken pact with the devil. If ever there'd been someone truly evil who passed among ordinary people cleverly disguised as one of them, it was Gideon Sylvester. Looking back she could see how, right from the start, it had been his plan to use her in whatever way he saw fit. Nothing she could have said or done, short of killing him with the butcher knife when she'd had the chance, would have stopped him. From the evening he'd caught sight of her paintings through her open apartment door, he'd been determined to superimpose his name upon her work and declare it to be his own.

Hughie had quite correctly pointed out a salient truth with respect to the sanctity of her right to her own work, but there was far more to this situation than he could imagine or that she could reveal. Because to admit her role, regardless of its involuntary nature, was to acknowledge her complicity. She had married the man. By his sights, she and everything about her, including her talent, thereby became his chattels. Even if she were to contest his charges in court, he'd make a so much more credible witness than she that she'd not only lose everything in terms of money and property, she'd also lose her son. On top of all that, she was carrying a second child of Gideon's and she wasn't capable of lying to Hughie and permitting him to believe the child was his, or of asking him to assume the responsibility for the support and rearing of another man's child. Hughie also didn't deserve to find himself smack in the middle of the three-ring circus Gideon Sylvester was bound to make of their lives.

She had no choice, really.

That night, in bed, she told Hughie they'd have to go in the morning. "I want you to understand why I'm doing this," she said, already grieved at the prospect of leaving him. "If I stay here and try to fight him, I will lose. He'll do absolutely anything to destroy my credibility, Hughie. And if that fails, he'll destroy you. He won't be stopped. He *can't* be stopped because he wants the goose back; he has to have the golden eggs. Without them, he's no one; he's nothing. And he has to be recognized, acclaimed, lionized. It's what he's been angling after all his life, and he's halfway there now. He'll see me dead before he'll let me leave and be happy with someone else. He already knows I'll never be able to sell a painting without having people jump up and accuse me of being a clever forger of my husband's finer works. I can't give up Giddy, and I'm pregnant again. I have to go back."

In his straightforward way, Hughie said sadly, "This is wrong, Mattie. Maybe he could find people to blacken your character, but there are plenty of us who'd stand up and defend you."

"Hughie, I'm the biggest fool who ever lived, but I'm not wrong about this. And if he did anything to harm you or to hurt your reputation as an artist I'd never be able to forgive myself for bringing all that down on you. Why," she wondered aloud, "didn't I say yes all those times you asked me to marry you? What could I have been thinking of? I've always cared for you, always held you in the highest regard. Everything I admire most is everything you are. Tomorrow, I'm taking myself and my child back to live in hell."

Hughie reached for his pajama top and blotted her face, asking almost fearfully, "Will I ever see you again?"

"Yes!" she cried, embracing him. "Somehow, somewhere, from now until forever, I'll find ways to be with you, even if it's only for one night once a year. If you want me and can put up with that."

"I'm going to want you, Mattie. There hasn't been a day in all the thirteen years since we met at the Harveys when I haven't thought about you. And if it's one night once a year, you tell me where, and I'll be there."

Everyone shed tears the next morning. Giddy couldn't be made to understand why they had to leave Hughie, and when Hughie lifted the boy to say good-bye, Giddy wrapped his arms and legs around the man and refused to let go, his wet face buried in Hughie's neck. Ina and Mattie had to pry him off, and all the way home in the car, Giddy lay sobbing in Ina's lap.

Gideon Sylvester wanted to pretend they'd been off on a holiday. He'd filled the house with fresh-cut flowers and even had a bottle of champagne chilling in the refrigerator. Giddy came into the house, saw his father, walked straight over to him and kicked him as hard as he was able in the shin. Gideon yelped and raised his arm.

Mattie said, "If you lay so much as a finger on him, you won't live to see another morning. We don't want to be here, and your son has just told you precisely how he feels about you. Ina, please take Giddy up and run him a bath," she told the stalwart older woman. Then she headed for the living room, over her shoulder saying, "I want to talk to you!"

Gideon hobbled after her, sat down and began rubbing his leg, offering up one of his high-grade charming smiles.

"Don't waste it on me," she said, standing by the fireplace, filled with loathing and contempt for him. "Why did you do it?"

"Do what?" he asked, the smile losing some of its voltage.

"Forge your name on my paintings."

"Did you sleep with Dickinson?" he asked with a leer.

"Obviously you already know the answer to that. What did you do, hire a detective to spy on us?"

"Actually," he said, "I have some extremely provocative photographs. I've always wished I could have photographs of myself making love to you. I should be most indignant, but I'll keep the photographs and simply pretend I'm your partner."

"I don't believe you!"

"You should never doubt me, Mattie," he said. "I'll be right back." He left the room and returned a few minutes later with a large brown envelope he held out to her. "I'm sure I needn't tell you there are more copies and, of course, a full set of negatives."

She looked at the envelope front and back, then dropped it into the fire. "Now you'll have to enjoy the copies. Why did you forge your name on my paintings?"

"You've turned the boy against me."

"No, *you've* turned the boy against you. And you'll turn the next child against you, too. You can't stand anything that might impede your progress, and children have a tendency to do that. I want the deed to this house. I also want a signed, witnessed, and notarized document stating that both houses are mine to do with what I like and that their possession can't ever be contested by you or by anyone you appoint."

"Not a chance."

"You'll do it," she said icily, "because you want more paintings. You want to be the biggest bigshot ever, and you can't do it without my paintings."

His eyes went large with something that might have been greed, or even lust. It was difficult to fathom his peculiar and distorted needs.

"You'll do it," she said, "because you want to be famous, and without me that'll never happen. If I stop painting now, your name will just trickle away and in a few years people will be wondering whatever became of Gideon Sylvester, that fellow who used to paint so well. Why did you forge your name on my paintings?"

"Ina has to go."

"Ina stays."

"Giddy should be in boarding school."

"He's staying right here with the two people who love him: me and Ina. Why did you *do* it?"

"I'll agree to the deed and the letter, but I want the self-portrait and the three baby paintings."

"You can't have them. I'll paint four others. *Why* did you do it?"

"Fair enough, four others. I'll go call my lawyer right now."

He was never, she realized, going to admit what he'd done.

Twenty-Four

He had no interest whatever in the fact that I was pregnant again. He'd done what served his purposes, and that was that."

"Did you consider having an abortion?" Sarah asked.

"I considered it, but it would have been playing right into his hands. In order to obtain an abortion it was required I be declared either physically or mentally unfit to bear the child. I was healthy as a horse, so that was out of the question. And if I risked visiting a psychiatrist and managed to convince him I was mentally unfit, I imperiled myself because as someone mentally unfit, Gideon Sylvester could have me institutionalized and leave me there forever, if he chose. I didn't dare give him that kind of power. He was all too likely to use it. And what would have been more perfect for the Great Artist than the tragic burden of an insane wife? Christ! The goddamned press would've eaten it up like candy. They were already like vultures, hovering over him wherever he went.

"Aside from that, I couldn't do it. I already had one child I thought I hadn't wanted, but whom I loved utterly. I knew I'd love the second one, too. I loved being a mother. Next to my painting, it was what I cared most about. I liked my children. So no, an abortion was simply impossible."

Sarah took hold of her hand. Mattie held fast as they continued to walk.

"I became a whore," Mattie said with resignation. "And Gideon Sylvester remained what he'd always been: a whoremaster. I created paintings because at least while I worked I was free. And because people out there loved and admired them, regardless of who they thought had painted them. The paintings were a force unto themselves; they had a life of their own that I gave them, and no one, not even Gideon Sylvester could ever take that away.

"I painted pictures and signed each of them twice, once visibly, once secretly, and all the details went into the journal I kept faithfully. He went off somewhere and painted out my signatures, replacing them with his own. We both knew he did it, but never once would he admit to it. The day he died we were down on this beach having our usual one-sided argument while I tried to force him to admit the truth just once in his rotten life. But he deflected me with his inevitable barrage of bullshit. He was selling snake oil until the last breath left his body."

"What about Hughie?" Sarah asked. "Did you see him again, after all?"

Mattie stopped to light a cigarette, eyeing Sarah over her cupped hands as she did. "Oh yes," she said, returning the spent match to the box. "Hughie, my dear, is the only reason I'm not locked away somewhere in a small padded room." She turned and led the way back to the house.

The mist had lifted a few feet by the time they reached the lawn and Sarah glanced over at the garage.

"He's clearing some brush up near the road," Mattie said, as if reading Sarah's thoughts.

"I think I'll go and change for lunch."

Mattie sniffed, heading for the driveway.

Gloria was coming down the stairs with an armload of bedding as Sarah started up. Sarah said hi and Gloria's eyes flashed with what seemed to be annoyance as she returned the greeting.

"Wait a minute," Sarah said. "Is something the matter?"

"Don't go wearing her out with all your talking," Gloria said, her voice richly deep.

"But she wants to talk."

"Maybe so. But she needs her rest, too, and she's not getting it lately."

"What is it about me that pisses you all off?" Sarah asked seriously. "You don't even know me."

"That's true," Gloria allowed, shifting the load of bedding. "Nobody here knows you. But we all know Mattie, and we care about what's best for her."

"And you don't think I do?"

"Girl, what you care about most don't have a thing to do with that old lady. Or if it does, you sure have one strange way of showing it. Keeping her up half the day and night, getting her to talk about things that upset her."

"You know better than that," Sarah said, her tone conciliatory. "Nobody makes Mattie do things she doesn't want to do."

Gloria looked at her, then laughed. "That's only partway true, and you know it. Leastwise, you ought to by now." Softening, she said, "I've got nothing against you, girl. But I know Mattie, and I care about her."

"So do I," Sarah said strongly. "And whatever you think of me, I haven't made Mattie do anything. She wants to talk. I want to listen. I think my big mistake has been not taking the time to get to know you and Bonnie, and I apologize for that. I'd like to. We live here together, after all. And I love that old woman. I'd never do anything to harm her or upset her. Maybe after lunch, if you're willing, we could have coffee and talk some more."

Gloria smiled, showing dazzlingly white teeth. "Maybe we'll do that. It's about time."

"Yes, it is," Sarah agreed. "I honestly didn't mean to ignore you. I'm just not too good about making the first move. It's a problem I have. I can never imagine why anyone would be interested in meeting me."

"Now why ever would you think a thing like that?" Gloria wanted to know.

"I guess because I'm kind of stupid sometimes. I tend to forget that other people worry about the same things I do, and that one of us has got to take the first step. So, if you have the time, I'd really like to get together after lunch and make your acquaintance."

Gloria laughed and said, "You're on!" and went down the stairs.

In her room, Sarah laid out one of the skirts she'd bought on the mainland and a clean shirt. Then she went into the bathroom to have a go at the eye makeup.

Mattie walked up the driveway, her hands in her pockets toying with the cigarette pack in one and the box of wooden matches in the other. She felt edgy and tired. That door was better than two-thirds open and she found the view of what remained inside unappealing. It was like peering into an abattoir and watching the blood drip from the carcasses suspended from rows of hooks. It was like being forced to breathe in the stink of death and offal, except that in this case, it was the reek of her own remains that so offended her sensibilities. She could see herself hanging from the hook of Gideon Sylvester's devising, hopelessly caught, left to twist and suffer until death finally released her.

With a handkerchief tied around his forehead and his shirtsleeves rolled up, Carl was slashing the undergrowth with a scythe. She stood and watched him, studying the play of muscles in his neck and forearms, the sweat streaming down the sides of his face. She lit a cigarette and he looked over.

"I came to see you, dear," she said.

Raising his arm, he wiped his face on his sleeve, then came over to her, pulling a cigarette from the pack in his breast pocket.

"Are you all right?" she asked.

"Yeah." He drew on his cigarette, then looked down the driveway toward the house. "I'm hanging in."

"Any better?"

"Maybe, yeah. In fact quite a bit."

"And you'll be able to deal with it if the worst happens?"

"Shit, I don't know. I won't know that until it happens. But I'll give it my best shot, Mattie. What about you?"

"I'm just tired. I'll rest after lunch."

"Anything you want me to do?"

She put her hand on his cheek and smiled at him. "Not a thing," she said. "I'm proud of you."

Like a small boy, he grinned bashfully, lowering his eyes. "Yeah, well. I'm trying."

"I know you are, dear." She withdrew her hand, then turned and walked away.

He stood smoking, watching her retreat into the mist.

"I take it the cookbook experiments are only offered at dinner," Sarah said, helping herself to lobster salad.

"It's a good thing. Otherwise I might develop malnutrition." Mattie buttered a piece of a whole wheat roll, then bit into it. "As it is, cigarettes tend to kill off my appetite, but I do like good food."

"Have you seen Hughie since Gideon died?"

"Yes, I have," Mattie answered. "I saw him last in March, shortly after you came."

"But the longest you were away was for an afternoon."

"Keeping a clockwatch on my movements, are you?" Mattie asked slyly.

"No, but since you've only left the house a few times, I was bound to notice."

"We've been meeting for years at a point midway. He drives down from Maine and before Carl came, I used to take one of the cars and drive up to a place outside Worcester. I lived for those days. We had to plan so carefully and often, at the last minute, something would come up and I'd have to cancel. Then it would be weeks, sometimes even months, before I'd have another chance to be with him. Not once in all those years did he ever complain or make a fuss because at the last minute I had to go out to a pay phone to call him and say I couldn't come. He'd just say, 'Let me know when you can get away,' then ask if I was all right, and how were the children.

"Giddy quickly learned never to mention Hughie's name in front of his father. Gideon turned demonic hearing Hughie's name spoken— by anyone. We might be in New York to go to the theater or to a concert—Gideon Sylvester adored making public appearances and I was expected to accompany him, like a large-sized boutonniere—and by chance someone might comment on Hughie's latest exhibition or the prices his pictures were commanding, and by the time we got home, he'd be in a complete frenzy of rage."

She came back to him because she had to, but she refused to allow him to touch her. When he came to get into bed with her the night of her return, she leaped out of the bed, demanding, "What do you think you're doing?"

"I'd say that was obvious, wouldn't you?"

"There are three unoccupied bedrooms in this house. Pick one of them and sleep it in from now on, or else I will. It doesn't make a shred of difference to me which room I sleep in, just so long as you're not in it."

"I know you," he said smugly. "This won't last."

"It'll last until one or the other of us dies."

He laughed and went off to one of the guest rooms. But he was unconvinced and nightly thereafter appeared in the master bedroom until she took to locking the door. Then he began making sexual remarks during dinner, until she said, "If you don't stop, I'll eat at six o'clock with Giddy and Ina and you can have the dining room to yourself. It's bad enough I have to look at you and try to eat at the same time, but I'll be damned if I'll sit here and listen to you, too."

They dined in silence from then on.

For almost five months she managed to freeze him out. Then she was roused in the middle of the night in early April by a body pushing against hers and hands groping her body. Once past her fear, she lay without moving as he mauled her. "If it gives you some kind of satisfaction to molest a woman who's almost seven months pregnant, by all means go ahead. Just hurry up. I'm tired." She raised her nightgown over her protruding belly and opened her legs. "Hurry up!" she repeated.

"You bitch!" he hissed. "You castrating bitch!"

"Get yourself another whore, Gideon. You've got one who'll work for you. Now find one who'll sleep with you."

"You'll regret this!"

"I already regret this. I've *always* regretted this. Are you finished? If you are, please leave the way you came in. Otherwise, get this over with. It'll be the last chance you have because first thing in the morning I'll be on the telephone to a locksmith and the only way you'll be able to get in here from now on is with dynamite."

"You'll regret this," he said again, retrieving his dressing gown from the floor.

"Oh, good! You're finished." She pulled down her nightgown and drew up the bedclothes.

"I could ruin him, you know."

"I will ruin *you* if you so much as *think* about it."

He came closer to the bed. "What is it you think you could do to ruin me?"

"Don't ever push me, Gideon Sylvester! I do have a few cards left up my sleeve. And I'm sure I don't have to remind you that without me, you cease to exist. Go away now. I'm very tired."

He sputtered for a moment more, then left, looking somewhat worried.

What worried her was her unshakable idea that she'd fallen from grace in Ina's eyes. Ina was there; she lived in the house and she knew everything that had gone on.

When Gideon Sylvester next took himself off to New York, Mattie invited Ina to sit down with her in the morning while Giddy was at school.

"Ina, I think you deserve some kind of explanation."

"I don't, not really, Mattie. I'm just hired help, paid to see and hear nothing."

"That's not what you are here, Ina. You're far more than that, and your opinion of me matters."

"I explained everything to her," Mattie said. "I had to. I couldn't live in the same house with the woman and feel her becoming contemptuous of me because she and I both knew that what was going on was morally wrong, dishonest, and probably illegal, to boot.

"There was more to it than wanting to clear myself with Ina. There was a philosophical fine point I considered more important than anything else. And that was this: Even if Gideon Sylvester did take my paintings and forge my name on them, he would never be able to do what I could. At best, the most he'd ever be was a thief and a genius at public relations. It was my work that was garnering praise from all quarters; it was *my* vision, *my* skill, *my* technique the critics were raving about in the press and in art magazines. Yes, he might be able to deprive me of the credit, but he could never have the true satisfaction of knowing he'd been the one with the talent. He had to steal to attain the status he so craved. But the one thing he couldn't steal was my ability.

"However, to be completely candid, I have to admit that I have no doubt his talent for promoting himself, his public demeanor, his love affair with the media, were in no small way responsible for the overall success. And you see, I could never have done that. I hated having people hound me, even playing the peripheral role I did. I hated dressing up, playing out a part for the public. I loathed interviews, and journalists, and photographers. I hated every last aspect of everything Gideon did with perfect ease and unrelenting charm. He was always ready with a smile, a good quotable quip; always ready to sit down and give a two-hour interview. It was never too early or too late for those newshounds to disturb him, asking their endless irritating questions. He loved the attention and he was brilliant at manipulating everyone, including the people who thought they were manipulating him. He was the grand master of self-promoters. And while the paintings were unquestionably good, Gideon Sylvester, by the sheer force of his personality, gave them the stature of greatness.

"Credit where credit is due," she said, aligning her knife and fork on her plate before reaching for her cigarettes. "The old fart may have been selling me snake oil, but he got the general public to buy the real McCoy. And every time some new gallery came along wanting to pay astronomical sums for two more pieces, all I could feel was the thrill of knowing that a few thousand people in Minneapolis or Dallas or Phoenix were going to go to the gallery and stand in admiration before another painting of mine. In that sense, at least, it was worth it."

"God!" Sarah said. "Didn't it kill you to do it?"

"I became a master at rationalization."

"I don't know if I could be philosophical about someone stealing my work."

Mattie sniffed and drank some of her Chablis.

"So, what about Hughie?"

"What about him?" Mattie asked.

"Gideon Sylvester's been dead for six years. Why aren't the two of you together?"

"Hughie and I agreed in nineteen forty-one never to discuss my arrangements with Gideon Sylvester."

"So?"

"So don't you think the subject might rear its ugly head were we to spend long amounts of time together?"

"Are you ashamed of what you did?" Sarah asked, and knew the instant the words were out of her mouth that Mattie would go wild.

"What do you *think?*" Mattie roared. "Would *you* be comfortable going about your business knowing every time you turned your back the other party was wondering about your morals?"

"But from everything you've said, Hughie isn't like that."

"There are limits, my dear, to everyone's tolerance. The last thing I need is to see myself as a failing light in the eyes of the only man I've ever loved. *I will not be judged!*"

"He would never judge you," Sarah argued.

"Please!" Mattie warned. "Don't speculate on things you know nothing about."

"All right," Sarah backed down. "So you meet with Hughie some-where outside Worcester. What do the two of you do?" Sarah asked the question and winced at how ineptly she'd phrased it.

"We invite in half a dozen strangers and play pinochle! What a moronic question! What the hell do you think two creaking senior citizens do, for Christ's sake?" Mattie's face went very dark. "I can't talk to you anymore right now. I'm going to take a nap."

"I'm only trying to understand. Don't be angry with me. I know I put that question to you all wrong."

"*I'm not angry with you! When will you get that through your head?*"
With that she rose from her chair, knocking it over in her haste to
escape.

Guiltily, Sarah got up and righted the chair, then went out to the
kitchen to tell Bonnie they were finished. Bonnie looked accusingly at
her, and Sarah said, "I didn't do a thing. Okay? Don't look at me that
way!"

"Don't get your shirt in a knot," Bonnie said placidly. "Glo says if
you want to she'll have coffee with you on the back verandah. Said to
tell you she'll be down in about fifteen minutes."

"Thank you."

"You wanna try'n calm her down, take this here tray up to her."

"She'll murder me," Sarah said. "Are you kidding?"

"She'll be nice as pie. Don't you know yet she yells when things
start hurting too much? I'd've thought you'd've figured that out by
now. Just ticks her off to have people start apologizing. That's why I
was givin' you the look when you come in just now. I thought you
knew enough to let her blow off instead of tryin' to smooth things
over."

"You've been with her what? Twenty-seven years?"

"That's right."

"And you want me to have figured her out in seven months?"

"Just go on and take her the tray. There's some of her favorite dark
chocolate from Godiva. She'll have herself a piece and calm right
down. You'll see. But don't get her talking again, Sarah. Let her have
her rest, and you come on down and set a spell with Gloria."

Grateful, Sarah kissed the woman's cheek.

Bonnie smiled and said, "Go on and get that tray up to her now."

Sarah knocked at the door. Mattie growled something indecipherable, and Sarah opened the door to see Mattie stretched out on her bed
with one arm folded under her head, the other shielding her eyes.

"I've got some goodies for you from Bonnie," Sarah said, setting
the tray on the bedside table.

Without moving, Mattie said, "Thank you. I'll get to it in a minute.
Would you mind closing the curtains?"

"Not at all." Sarah did as she'd asked, then said, "Is there anything else I can do for you?"

Mattie sat up and swung her legs over the side of the bed. "Yes, there is," she said. "Come here."

Sarah went back across the room.

Mattie said, "Give an old lady a hug, would you?"

Sarah was happy to do it and embraced the woman, luxuriating in the closeness. "It's coming to an end," Mattie said mysteriously, "and I am so very fond of you."

"I'm very fond of you, too."

Mattie stroked her hair, and Sarah let her head rest against the old woman's shoulder.

"You're like that puppy Tom Harding gave Giddy."

"I thought I was like a hungry newborn bird."

"That too," Mattie said, releasing her. "Off you go now."

"Don't you want him, Mattie?"

"That's like asking someone if air is really necessary to sustain life."

"Then why not do something about it?"

"It's far too late. Now, run along."

Obediently, Sarah went.

Twenty-Five

Mattie looked at the tray, smiled, then took off her dress and shoes, and in her slip lay down on the bed. The room was pleasantly dim, the curtains lifting with the breeze. If she listened, she could hear the roar of the breakers. For a time she watched the shadow play on the ceiling, the odd shaft of light fencing with the darkness created by the drawn curtains. She lit a cigarette and folded her right arm under her head.

In a lifetime brimming with mistakes, Hughie was the one right thing she'd ever done. And yet she felt she'd deprived him of all he should have had—the children he'd have fathered with such tender courtesy, the wife who'd have shared with him on a daily basis. Never mind his protestations, he'd have found someone. A man like Hughie could have had any number of women. But he'd given his word to her, and he'd kept it. It was frightening to think she'd fostered such abiding loyalty in someone that he'd live alone for months and years on end in order to be free when she called to say she could get away a week from tomorrow, or in three days' time—for a few hours of conversation, mixed in and around lovemaking. Sometimes they simply talked. They kissed hello and good-bye and, in between, they held hands and looked into each other's eyes, and talked. But beneath everything they said or did lay what they'd agreed not to discuss: her husband, his ongoing fraud, and her role in that.

Hughie evinced no rancor; he accepted her terms and never quibbled. Each time she saw him it was more difficult to leave. She was returning to Gideon Sylvester and dreading it like someone on a day pass from an institution with incomprehensible rules that had to be obeyed, whether or not the inmates understood them. Every time she saw Hughie she felt more strongly the shame of her alliance with Gideon Sylvester. But she couldn't stay away from him because Hughie was her reward for weeks and months and years of battling with someone determined to see her lose at all costs. If he didn't acknowledge it, the crime, so far as Gideon Sylvester was concerned, did not exist. She wasn't lucky enough to have so convenient a conscience that allowed her to be selective about her worries. She was chained into marriage with a man who had no morals, who wasn't above tormenting his children in order to punish their mother for her refusal to let him make love to her. And to compound her own felony, when she made love to Hughie she did it without benefit of contraception, in the hope that she'd become pregnant and be able to give this man she so revered something tangible. She loved the irony of that possibility almost as much as she loved Hughie. Were she to become pregnant, Gideon Sylvester would be compelled to accept the child as his simply because he'd never risk the loss of face attached to being a cuckolded husband. She longed to have Hughie's baby, but it didn't happen. And she had to face another, different irony. Gideon Sylvester had been able to impregnate her almost at will, but when she desperately wanted it to happen, she and Hughie couldn't make a child. Not that Hughie was aware of any ulterior motive to her lovemaking with him. He was far too impeccably ethical ever to countenance anything like that.

He was altogether the antithesis of Gideon Sylvester: scrupulous in his dealings with everyone from the man who ran the nearby general store, to the curators and gallery owners and dealers who sought him out; he was shy and self-effacing and uninterested in money; his needs were simple, and he lived within them, in the same small house he'd moved into early in his twenties. The only complicated thing in his entire existence was his love affair with Mattie. And he didn't question it, but went along with her like the seasons, changing to accommodate her requirements, elated at the opportunity to spend one hour or ten, so long as he could be with her.

Dear Hughie, with his one good go-to-town suit, his collection of pipes, and his aromatic tobacco whose scent clung to every garment he owned; Hughie who would set down his brush to go out and chop firewood, or to rake the leaves; Hughie who would take the time to think before expressing an opinion; and who smiled with his cheeks dimpling and his eyes shining. Hughie, who, at seventy-nine, looked years younger and still took rambling walks along the back roads, stopping to exclaim over the way the light penetrated the leaves, or the discovery of a wild fern, or the pungent smell of woodsmoke.

Doting Hughie who could stand and marvel over the sight of her removing her clothes, not in the least bothered by what she viewed as the ravages of time and he considered to be enhancements of her beauty; Hughie who had painted her from memory and who gazed at her every night when he got into bed, having positioned the painting on the wall opposite in order that she'd be the first thing he saw in the morning and the last thing he saw at night. She'd never seen the painting, but he'd told her about it, talking about the little ceremony he'd made out of selecting just the right place and then hanging the picture. "Right between the bedroom windows, so it glows with reflected light, but won't get faded."

Respectful Hughie who had never in his life taken anything for granted, least of all her, and who approached her every time with a degree of uncertainty, never assuming he had a right to her body but awaiting her invitation. And once she extended the invitation he responded as if she'd given him the gift of his dreams and he didn't have the words to tell her how greatly he valued it. So he illustrated his appreciation through acts of love, paying homage in countless ways, sighing with pleasure at the feel of her skin beneath his fingers or marveling over her hair and its unique fiery hue, or watching with fascination as her body lifted to his caress. There wasn't any part of her he didn't praise and find worthy of his admiration.

And in turn she fell more and more deeply into the chasm of her love for him, wondering what dreadful flaw in her vision had prevented her from seeing so much sooner his many rare and lovable qualities. The more she cared for him the more convinced she became that she possessed a fatal weakness and it was this weakness that had caused her to pass over Hughie in favor of someone so inferior in so many ways.

It was a classic double bind. As her attachment grew for Hughie, so did her remorse. He admired her, and she was unworthy. She had allowed herself to be blackmailed into an ongoing partnership with someone she despised and who would never release her. On the half dozen or so occasions over the years when she declared she intended to leave him, Gideon Sylvester reminded her of the twenty-four incriminating photographs he wouldn't hesitate to use against H. Clay, as Gideon and everyone else now referred to Hughie. And if that didn't succeed, why he'd simply invite the two boys in for a chat one evening and show them the photographs of their beloved mother engaged in acts that would undoubtedly shock them witless. And if by some chance that failed to have the desired effect, perhaps she might be interested in seeing some very interesting photographs he happened to have of their older son, engaged in acts that would undoubtedly shock her witless, or would certainly cause young Matthew to view his brother with somewhat jaundiced eyes. On and on.

Gideon Sylvester had his mistresses, and his several clubs, and his entourage of doting collectors; he had his custom-made suits and shoes, his monogramed silk shirts, his cashmere topcoats, his three expensive cars, his wife, his sons, his staff, his fame. And if she chose not to work, it was of no consequence. The absence of new pieces would only heighten the demand and make the prices skyrocket. "So take as much time off as you like, Mattie. It's probably a wise idea."

She didn't want to think about him; she'd been trying for the last six years not to think about him, but she had to. If there was an afterlife, she'd have so goddamned much explaining to do she'd most likely create a traffic backup at the gates of hell that would take centuries to clear. She could see herself standing at the portals to a blast furnace the size of the Grand Canyon, calmly detailing her many follies to a red-suited, quite handsome assistant devil, complete with horns and pointed tail. Bored beyond measure, he'd lean on his pitchfork, trying to conceal his yawns, as he listened to her tedious recitation, visibly wishing she'd hurry up and get finished so he could process the several thousand people behind her volubly protesting the interminable wait.

With a dry laugh, she dropped the burned-out cigarette in the ashtray and lit another. She could think endlessly about Hughie, with great fondness and amusement, but she couldn't make herself believe it was her right to have him. It was too late; they were both far too old; neither one of them had any real idea how the other lived. She was prone to temperamental outbursts Hughie would no doubt find shocking. It was what came of fifty-odd years of barely sublimated fury. She'd always reserved the best of herself for Hughie, putting on display the positive side of her nature that had, over the years, disintegrated until there was precious little of it left. She didn't really have much of an appetite for death when it came right down to it, but she had a nearly insurmountable need to put an end to the era of Gideon Sylvester. Unfortunately this end she'd been seeking had taken far too long. She'd never thought she'd get to be very old and still be tangled up in tentacles extending beyond Gideon Sylvester's grave.

She recalled her disbelief at his death, and how she'd stood gazing at his lifeless body on the beach before running up to the house, not for help because the deceitful bastard was well beyond that, but for confirmation of his having left her permanently stalemated with no chance of the truth being aired in her lifetime. She'd knelt on the sand looking at that vile old man's vacant eyes while she'd swallowed down the bile of a rage that no longer had an outlet. Getting to her feet, she'd had to overcome the desire to take a rock and deface the body, to pulverize it beyond recognizing. But what would have been the point? He'd bested her, and she hadn't surrendered to the impulse to maim him while he'd lived, so there seemed no sense to doing it after his death. Gideon Sylvester had sucked her dry, then left her to try to function as the husk he'd left behind, the Great Man's widow. He'd been the living essence of cruelty; he'd placed a blight on everything he'd ever touched. And her only regret, even now, was that she'd never looked up Lydia, his first wife, to talk to the woman who'd had the good sense to pick the man clean on her way out of his life. Lydia would, no doubt, have had engrossing tales to tell. But Lydia had died in 1946. Mattie had read a small obituary notice in *The New York Times* and was sad at having missed a singular opportunity to trade horror stories with the woman.

Back near the beginning she'd railed now and then at the gross unfairness of the turns her life had taken. But as the years went by, she came to believe she no longer had the right to complain. Despite the fact that all her decisions had been made under duress, she'd nevertheless chosen to fall into line with Gideon Sylvester's demands. In part, she'd done it to protect the people she'd loved, but she'd also done it in order never again to have to watch a child of hers scream with hunger. And she'd done it, finally, for the paintings, those other children of hers, those adopted foundlings who now lived in hundreds of homes around the world.

There had been a few occasions when she'd got her own back, and the most memorable of those had been the occasion of Matthew's birth. Gideon had, of course, been away during the final weeks of her pregnancy, and had little interest in attending while a child of his was pushed from her body. At Mattie's bidding, Ina had gone out to a pay phone and telephoned Hughie to tell him Mattie was alone and that the birth was imminent.

Hughie had come at once. He'd checked into a cabin court nearby, and had been waiting at the hospital some twelve hours later when Ina brought Mattie in. The hospital staff was encouraged to believe Hughie was the father-to-be and he'd been allowed to stay with her in the labor room. For more than six hours he'd sat at her side, holding her hand, talking her through the contractions and massaging her belly as it undulated beneath his fingers. He'd remained with her until she was wheeled off to the delivery room. Once assured by the staff that mother and newborn son were well and that he'd be able to see them both in an hour, he ran from the hospital, jumped into his car, and drove off to buy gifts.

He'd come into her room with an armload of flowers and a beribboned teddy bear for the baby. Most solicitously he'd asked how she was and if there was anything he could do, and she'd wound her arms around his neck to kiss him, the flowers crushed between them.

"I went to the nursery," he'd told her, "and this nice young gal held up the baby and for a minute there, I felt like he was something we'd made, you and me. It's the greatest privilege of my life, being here with you for this."

He'd meant it, too. Until Matthew was well into his twenties, Hughie asked after him. And whenever they met, he was disappointed if Mattie failed to arrive with snapshots of the boys. He had more interest in and affection for Giddy and Matthew than their own father did.

She leaned over to put out her cigarette, then lay back with her eyes closed, eased by her memories. They, at least, were safe. They couldn't rework themselves, couldn't be tampered with, or have someone else's identity superimposed upon them. She sighed, her bones crackling like a brushwood fire.

Gloria was sitting on the top step at the rear of the verandah, her eyes hidden by large mirrored sunglasses.

Sarah came out and sat beside her, giving Gloria a mug of coffee.

Gloria thanked her and set the mug down. "I never will get used to the weather on this island," she said. "Wake up every morning and swear it's bound to rain, but it never does. By afternoon it's clear as glass. I'm a New York City girl. When I see a gray morning, I go out with my umbrella." She gave a slight shake of her head.

"I'm always freezing," Sarah said, "and Mattie has fits over my sweaters. She hates the way I dress."

"It's pretty bad," Gloria said, with a smile. "What you got on now don't look half bad, but them pants and those T-shirts! Girl, you've got the worst taste! How come you wanna go making yourself look so lame?"

Sarah laughed. "God! Do you all get together and crack up over my clothes?"

"Say what?"

"First Mattie, then Carl, now you. Maybe I should pop into the kitchen and get Bonnie to make it unanimous."

"She's not exactly fashion conscious. Unless you were wearing something edible, there's not much chance she'd notice what you had on."

"How did you come to work for Mattie?"

"How did you?" Gloria asked.

"I heard through a friend of a friend who knew the second-to-last secretary. It sounded good to me. I was sick of paying nine hundred a month for a studio apartment in Manhattan and dipping into the cash line on my Visa card to make the rent every month. So I asked around, found out which agency the second-to-last one was hired through, called them up, and applied. I've finally paid off the Visa card. Anyway, Mattie's not at all what I expected."

"What'd you expect?" Gloria picked up the mug and drank.

"Oh, crowds of the rich and famous, lots of glitz and little substance, glamour."

"You sure picked the wrong job for that!" Gloria grinned. "Mattie hates all that shit."

"Tell me about it! But it doesn't matter. Mattie's wonderful. She's got a phenomenal temper, but I'm getting used to her now. So what about you?"

"How come you're asking when you already know?"

"You talked to Mattie?"

"We all talk to Mattie, Sarah. It's why we're here. I talk with the woman most every morning of my life. Bonnie gets the coffee going and I come on up with two cups and we talk while I make the bed or set out fresh towels or collect the laundry. For years now, we been talking mornings. Bonnie and her, they talk doing the menus and after dinner sometimes. Carl she talks with in the night. And you, you fill in all the other hours. You've got her going like nobody ever has. I figure Mattie has that much to say to you, you sure must be something special. But I can't say I've seen any sign of it, until this morning."

"That's my fault," Sarah said quickly.

"Maybe. I've been thinking some about what you said about making first moves. I think I've got me an aversion to them, too, just like you say you do. Hard getting together when nobody's willing to be first to say hi."

"You're really very beautiful," Sarah said, then flushed with embarrassment.

Gloria took off her sunglasses and looked sidelong at Sarah. "Bet you didn't know you were gonna say that," she said with another smile that showed her exceptional teeth.

"I didn't," Sarah admitted, "but it's true."

Gloria shook her head. "One time, Sarah, I was hot, and didn't I know it. Most conceited girl in Harlem is what I was. But if I say so myself, thirty years ago, I was one very good-looking high-assed black girl. Didn't have too much in the way of sense, mind, but for a time I rode mighty high on my looks. I had men lined up, waving their money in my face. And I had such contempt for those fools. If I could've banked that, girl, I'd be a millionaire today."

"How did you meet Gideon?"

"Through another client. Man was an ass! I took one look at him and knew right off he thought *he* was hot. Hunh! You know how come I got such feeling for Mattie? I'll tell you why: Cause she let that nasty man put his hands on her and she never once squawked about it. It didn't matter to me, understand, 'cause he was just another job. But how she could do it, I'll never know. He had himself all these ideas what a woman was good for, and they weren't none of them nice. Course he was old by the time I come along. Could be he wasn't so bad when he was young. But I've got my doubts. Anyway, when he dropped dead nobody was happier to be rid of him than me. I know it's wrong to speak ill of the dead, but it was good riddance, I say.

"My mama was gone by then, and I lost touch with my baby brother better than twenty years ago. All of a sudden the old man was dead and I was scared, you know. I was too old to go back into the life, and besides I didn't want to. I was happier with Mattie than I'd ever been. She never once made mention of what I'd been, or what I did in her house. She treated me like a friend. So after the funeral, when I asked her if I could maybe stay on and run the house like I'd been doing, I'll never forget what she said, the way she said it. 'Gloria,' she said. 'I'd be honored.' Imagine that! Imagine her saying such a thing to me! Oh, I know she's crotchety now and then, but if it was me, I'd be a thousand times worse. Mattie's the best woman I know, and that's the truth. You like to dance, girl?"

Thrown, Sarah said, "I guess so. I haven't in ages. Why?"

"There's a dance down to the club on the south end tonight. You oughta get Carl to take you. He's one helluva dancer. Mattie's a member, so you can get in."

"What about you?"

Gloria laughed wickedly. "You been looking at this face while we been talking? You noticed it's a black face? You want them high-payin' nonresidents having heart attacks?"

"I don't think I'm interested in going there," Sarah said. "I'd rather get Carl to bring his ghetto blaster down here and we can all dance."

"Now, there's an idea. Go on over and ask if he'll do it, and we'll maybe have ourselves a little activity."

Sarah put down her coffee and ran over to the garage apartment to knock on the screen door.

Carl appeared from the bedroom saying, "Come on in. What's up?"

"Gloria and I were talking and she thinks—we both do—we should have a little bash after dinner. Will you bring over your ghetto blaster and some tapes?"

"Shit! We haven't had one of those in far too long! I'll dig up some dance mixes. Yeah! Great!"

"Okay," Sarah laughed. "This'll be fun."

"Bet your ass! Wait'll you see old Glo shake her buns. The woman can *dance*! And Mattie always had a good time when we used to do this. Hey!" he said, looping his arms around her waist. "This is good, Sarah."

She gave him a kiss, then said, "I'd better get back. Gloria's waiting."

He released her. "I'm just gonna grab some zees."

"This is when you sleep, isn't it?" she asked from the door.

"You got it in one, sweetheart."

"In that case, maybe I'll come over here tonight. Late."

"I'm not gonna give you any argument."

"I love you, Carl."

He nodded.

She opened the door and went out.

Twenty-six

Mattie sat in the rocker and watched the young people dance, reminded of weekends years before when, while Gideon Sylvester was off on the mainland, the Harveys and their brood, and she and her boys would hike up the volume on the record player and dance on the verandah. That was back in the fifties, after Ina had retired, when Matthew was still a teenager and Giddy had just finished college. She could remember wishing she had the courage to invite Hughie to come with the Harveys, but she'd always had the feeling that Gideon Sylvester's radar would signal him some warning, and he'd turn up to make an ugly scene—about which he'd have had no compunction because he had no regard either for the Harveys or for their children, and he despised Hughie because he knew without her ever having said so that Mattie preferred the nonflamboyant dullard to him.

Carl had been a young boy then, and Giddy had taken him under his wing, going off sailing with the boy or driving him down to the South End club to introduce Carl to the summer kids. Matthew, who was only three years older than Carl, wanted nothing to do with him. Matthew, encouraged by his father, believed the Harveys to be socially inferior. It had hurt Giddy, softhearted Giddy who couldn't bear to see anyone left out. So he'd taken charge of Carl, and Carl had responded to Giddy much in the way Giddy had, as a small child, responded to Hughie.

They'd had bonfires on the beach, and roasted hot dogs and ears of corn. They'd sat around the fire on itchy gray blankets and sang old songs while the smallest of the Harvey grandchildren fell asleep across their laps. Mattie would turn every so often to look at the house, its windows glowing golden in the night, thinking how perfect everything would be if only Hughie could be there too. He was her unseen partner through the years, the voice on the other end of the pay telephone, the bedmate in her dreams.

Occasionally she'd look out over the water, charting the course that led across to Maine. She'd picture herself setting off in a boat with a good motor to plow through the waves and step ashore only a few miles from Hughie's house. Having the Harveys there, though, was almost as good as having Hughie himself. They always came with messages and letters he'd written and saved up until they could be hand-delivered. Pay phones and messengers, untraceable communications so that Gideon Sylvester could never amass more ammunition against them than he already had.

Sitting by the bonfires, she'd imagine those incriminating photographs growing yellowed with age, possibly even disintegrating. But the only thing that was suffering the effects of time was her own body. Monthly, yearly, she could feel hope dwindling away, taking with it all traces of her youth. Rather than mellowing with the years she could feel the fire of her disappointment spreading, churning inside her volcanically. She'd wanted to be gazing into the dying blaze on the chilly beach with Hughie beside her on the itchy blanket, his arm around her waist, the pleasant smell of his pipe tobacco mixing with the fishy tang of the sea at low tide.

Now it was too late. She'd never find a sturdy boat and travel that well-charted diagonal course to the coast of Maine. The hull lay splintered and bleached by the sun and she'd forgotten, if she ever knew, how to read a compass.

Carl was putting another cassette into the machine, saying, "This one's for Mattie." Then he came over and held his hand out to her. "May I have this dance, please?" he asked, as Glen Miller's orchestra played the opening chords of "Sunrise Seranade."

"You know all my weaknesses," she accused with a smile, getting up to feel the solid warmth of his hand closing around hers.

"Only some of them," he grinned. "Make believe we're on a date."

"I never had enough of them to recollect the protocol."

Sarah and Gloria sat side by side on the verandah railing; Bonnie was seated sideways on the top step; all of them watching with automatic, gentle smiles as the music transported them to another era and Carl led Mattie in the dance.

"You used to dance with me out here when I was a kid," Carl said. "Remember? And Gran and Grampa used to cluck and coo. Remember? You were always so nice to me, Mattie. And Giddy, too. All those times he'd take me out in the L-16 and make sure my Mae West was on properly, then we'd go sailing off. It seems like so long ago, but sometimes, like tonight, it feels like yesterday. I'd get so worked up when my folks would say we were coming. All the way over on the ferry, I'd stand by the railing waiting for the first sight of the dock and your red hair. I'd see you from way out and start waving. Remember? It's a shame we ever have to grow up."

"When each of the boys was a baby, I'd look at them and wish I could keep them tiny forever, like hamsters." She laughed softly.

"Christ! Remember the hamsters? Remember when they got out and we hunted high and low for them? And Matthew—he must have been about twelve then, I think, because I was about nine—finally found one in the pantry, and he was out there talking to the hamster, asking it, 'How did you get out? I want to know how you got out!' " He laughed. "Christ! That was hilarious! Matthew with this little hamster in his fist, asking it to *tell* him how it got out of the cage."

"And the other one made a clean getaway," Mattie laughed. "It was the female, and I used to imagine it bred with chipmunks; I pictured hundreds of oddly marked chipsters living happily under the house."

"Chipsters," Carl chuckled. "Damn, that's good."

"You were the dearest boy. You'd come racing off the ferry, whooping and hollering, and dodge the other passengers, to be the first to get to me. If I close my eyes, I can still remember the little-boy smell of your hair and feel those wiry arms hugging me so hard. Of all the Harvey children, you were my favorite."

"And of all the Sylvesters, you were mine. Still are. And the best dancer, too."

"When did you ever dance with any of the others?" she teased.

"I've seen Giddy dance," he reminded her. "I put a few months in at the club. Jesus! What a zoo that place was! But it was fun, too."

"He says he'll probably have to close. The homosexual population's no longer quite so gay as it was. He says he'd like to take things easy for a while."

"Did he call this week?"

"I called him. I wanted to know if Matthew had kept his word to meet with him."

"Did he?" Carl asked doubtfully.

"As a matter of fact, he did. They had dinner the other night. Giddy was fairly ecstatic. It's the first time in years they've gone out together. He said Matthew was a bit nerved-up, but he had a couple of drinks and calmed down."

"Will wonders never cease! I can't see Giddy taking things easy. He'd lose his marbles."

"That's what I told him. We'll see. Perhaps he'll meet someone decent and take up a new business."

The number ended and Mattie said, "Go dance with Sarah or Gloria now."

He escorted her back to the rocker, made a little bow, then went to change the tape.

Sarah came over to sit beside her, picking up the box of kitchen matches to light Mattie's cigarette.

A Joe Cocker tape started and Carl lifted Gloria off the railing to dance with her. Gloria gave one of her melodious laughs, and all of them smiled in response to the wonderful sound of Gloria's pleasure.

"That was nice," Sarah said, watching Carl and Gloria dance. "You're a good dancer."

"I've still got a few miles left on me."

"More than a few, I'd say."

Mattie turned to look at her, eyebrows lifted, eyes amused. "Don't grease my skids, Sarah."

Sarah laughed loudly. "Don't be cantankerous. I'm on the home team, you know."

Mattie sniffed and turned back to watching Carl and Gloria, as she did saying, "That woman moves like nothing on earth. I've been intending to have her sit for me for ages."

"She can be your next project," Sarah said.

"Possibly. Quite possibly."

"I'm going to miss this place when we leave."

"When we leave, or when you leave?" Mattie asked without turning.

"When *we* leave."

"I always miss this house," Mattie said. "But I'm too old to handle the winters here."

"Whatever happened to Tom Harding?"

"He and Agnes retired and moved to Florida in fifty-five. He died in seventy-two and Agnes went in seventy-five."

"Did they ever get married?"

"Agnes was never divorced from her first husband," Mattie said, taking a thoughtful puff on her cigarette. "She couldn't find him to have him served with the papers. And they were better off, Tom and Agnes, financially, that is, remaining unmarried. Social Security, you know. I did repay him, in case that was going to be one of your next questions. When I received my Stern's money, I made Tom take a cashier's check for five thousand dollars. Aggie had to talk him into accepting it. Women are always more sensible than men, especially when it comes to things like taking money from a woman. Not that he was offended, understand. It was more that he didn't feel he'd done anything so important that I should give him so much money. To my way of thinking, what he did was keep Giddy and me alive. Five thousand was nothing, a token. If I could have, I'd have given him two or three times that amount. But it was the best I could do at the time. The rest went into trust for the boys, because I could never be sure Gideon Sylvester wouldn't pull some stunt that would leave us penniless again. Giddy used his money to buy the club. And Matthew, being his father's son, lost most of his on the stock market. He did quite well for a time, then the price of oil skyrocketed in the early seventies, the housing market fell apart, and Matthew took a beating. He's always been resentful of the fact that Giddy invested in something Matthew considered sleazy, and turned it into a fortune. Gideon Sylvester and Matthew both looked down their noses at Giddy. Gideon, of course, encouraged Matthew's disparaging view of his older brother, and I've spent years trying to undo some of the damage. Gideon's influence on Giddy was nonexistent, but it was substantial with Matthew who, being five years younger, didn't have his older brother's memories. Matthew can't quite relinquish his hold on anything his father ever gave him, even though he knows that whatever Gideon Sylvester did give him had a blight on it.

"Interestingly enough, Matthew's the one most bothered about his father's theft, as it were, of my paintings. I think Giddy sees my point. But Matthew would love to debunk the whole myth. He has the idea that it might somehow free him once and for all from any filial obligation he thinks he has to respect the thieving old bastard."

"I think your sons are fortunate to have you for their mother," Sarah said. "If we got to choose, I'd pick you to be mine."

"That's a kind thing to say." Mattie gazed at her appreciatively.

"It's the truth. With you as my mother, maybe I wouldn't be so messed up."

"It's difficult to know when to stop using survival tactics," Mattie said. "Sometimes we have trouble seeing we've already won and there's no need to keep on fighting."

"Is that how you feel?"

"No," Mattie answered. "In my case, it's a matter of admitting I lost and laying down my arms because the goddamned war's been over for years."

"Maybe it doesn't have to be that way."

Mattie put out her cigarette, saying, "Go dance with Carl. He's waiting for you."

In spite of her promise to herself to stay awake, Sarah fell asleep. When she awakened at just after three a.m. she was alone. If she got up and made a dash for the house, the chances were Carl would materialize out of the darkness and come at her with his bayonet. But she felt ill-at-ease staying in the garage apartment alone. So she got up and pulled on her clothes, then opened the screen door, and looked around. Carl was not to be seen, but he was undoubtedly somewhere close by, concealed by the shadows and his camouflage garb. She stood for several minutes afraid to go down the stairs and make the walk over to the main house.

This is ridiculous! she told herself, closing the screen door and slowly descending the stairs. She couldn't go on being afraid of some-one she cared for. Carl wouldn't kill her. It would never go that far. She got to the bottom of the stairs and had to stop. All she had to think about was how terrified she'd been, how she'd wet her pants, convinced she was about to die. She sat down on the next to the bottom step, wrapped her arms around her knees, and waited.

For almost an hour she sat there, her eyes roaming over the prop-erty. This was one of the nights when Mattie wasn't sitting outside on the balcony. The house was dark. Nothing moved. Ridiculous! she told herself again, getting to her feet. Nothing was going to happen.

She'd walk the few hundred feet to the house, go inside and up to her own room, and sleep in her bed.

Stepping down onto the grass, her heart racketing, she shivered, feeling the cold now that she was out of the lee of the garage. She didn't dare run, even though her every instinct was to bolt for the safety of the house. One foot placed in front of the other, her whole body pulsing in syncopation with the antic tattoo of her heartbeat, she headed slowly for the house, its darkness looming larger as she got closer, moonlight reflecting off the windows. Night birds called, crickets whined, the wind sighed in the trees. She was halfway there. She paused and turned to look around. Carl was standing by the hedge, about the same distance from her as she was from the house. Had he seen her? She tried to think if she could make it to the house before Carl could make it to her. Should she keep going? Fear immobilized her. She was certain that if she moved, he'd somehow fly through the space separating them and throw her to the ground. He'd crouch over her, holding his knife to her throat, and she'd be unable to identify herself to him. What they needed was a password. Why hadn't she thought of it sooner? If they had a password, she'd be able to move about the property at night without fear. But she hadn't thought of it and now she was caught out here, with Carl standing sentry by the hedges and the house just a bit too far away.

Her whole life was like this, she thought wretchedly, standing out in the cold like a statue. She never considered beforehand the possibility that she might require some specific means of identifying herself in order to make safe passage through potentially dangerous territory. Everything she wanted was always separated from her due to some oversight on her part. It was the same with people. She never took quite enough time or made the right amount of effort to determine in advance what might be needed. Like her failure with Gloria. Like all her failures with so many other people.

Here she was, still sticky from the lovemaking she'd engaged in only a few hours earlier with the man over there, of whom she was now utterly afraid. Was she going to stay out here shaking like a trapped rabbit, or was she going to do something? She wanted to take some action. But what? What the hell was she supposed to do? Her brain felt as if it was closing down, swamped by fear. Her hands and feet felt numb; her chest pained slightly from the continuing frantic action of her heart. *Do something!*

She whispered, "Carl?"

Nothing.

Slightly louder, "Carl?"

He heard her. He stirred.

"Carl, I'm not going to move," she told him as he approached, the knife held down by his leg. "It's me, Sarah, Carl. Please don't be afraid!" She was telling *him* not to be afraid. That was good. She was scared witless, but she was telling him not to be afraid.

As he came closer, she whispered, "Do you know who I am?"

He didn't make a sound, but came gliding across the lawn.

She felt she might wet herself again as she whispered, "Carl?"

He came right up, put his arms around her, and she started to cry, noisily in gulps, like a child.

"It's okay, babe," he said. "It's okay."

"I got myself so worked up. I'm such a moron."

"Hey!" he said softly. "You did the right thing. Don't go beating yourself up all the time. Okay?"

"Could we work out a password or something? I don't want to be afraid of you, Carl. It makes me feel so defective, so damned inadequate."

"Why should you feel that way?" he asked, perplexed.

"Because I'm not doing everything I could to make this work. I haven't been using my head about this."

"A password's good. It's very good. We'll work something out tomorrow. How'll that be?"

"Good, yes."

"Go on in," he told her. "Get some sleep."

She kissed him several times, then broke away and ran to the house.

Mattie was in the kitchen with Bonnie and Gloria when Sarah came down for breakfast the next morning. The three women were seated at the kitchen table and all looked up as Sarah came in saying, "Good morning."

Mattie stood, collected her cigarettes and matches from the table, and said, "Feed us, Bonnie. I suspect Sarah's probably very hungry."

Sarah smiled and held open the door, allowing Mattie to precede her into the dining room. Mattie seated herself at her usual place and looked expectantly at Sarah.

Bonnie came bustling in with a large tray and began putting platters on the table. Eggs scrambled with chives, crisp bacon, sliced beefsteak tomatoes fresh from the garden, toast, homemade croissants, a large pot of coffee, and a good-sized jug of cream.

Mattie took several strips of bacon and a croissant while Sarah poured the coffee.

"I was right," Mattie said, watching Sarah fill her plate. "You did work up a hearty appetite."

Sarah blushed but smiled through it. "Carl and I are going to work out a password."

"That's resourceful. Your idea?"

"We both thought of it."

"Magnanimous."

"What's wrong?" Sarah asked.

"Not a thing, my dear."

"No, I can tell. What is it?"

"You know, you're a most intriguing young woman," Mattie said. "Someday, I'd very much like to meet your sister Sarah."

"But I . . ." Sarah froze.

"I've met any number of journalists in my time," Mattie said, "but never one I've liked as well as you. I liked you when you came for the interview. I hadn't expected to, of course. I was all set to let you carry out your silly charade and then bounce you on your head. But I liked the look of you, and you said something that was so true, it forced me to reconsider. Your comment about working for men who were only half as competent but made twice the money. I agreed with that. You made a few crucial errors, however. Your biggest was in assuming that usurping your sister's identity would be sufficient cover. No good,

Sarah. For years I've kept people on retainer simply to investigate prospective employees. And when the first report came in, it didn't feel right. I called and told them to go deeper into Sarah Kidd's background. And, lo and behold, what did we find? Sarah Kidd had a younger sister Pru who was, is, a journalist."

Sarah felt as if all the flesh had evaporated off her body, leaving her exposed skeleton propped up in the chair. The fear she'd felt the night before was minor compared to what she experienced now as Mattie's eyes remained on her and she tried, in her instantly overwrought state, to think what to say. Seeing that Mattie didn't look especially angry but appeared only to be awaiting some sort of explanation, Sarah shakily put down her knife and fork, wet her lips, and whispered, "Do you hate me?" then tried to hold herself together, fervently wishing she'd never had the idea of going after this job in the first place and, at the same time, weakly praying Mattie wasn't going to demand she leave at once. Never in her life had she wanted anything less than to have to leave here.

"Not at all," Mattie said, as if taken aback by the question. "You were really very clever, assuming your sister's identity. With anyone else but me, it might have worked. But as you've undoubtedly realized by now, I have a strenuous aversion to members of your profession, and therefore I'm triply cautious. The biggest giveaway," she continued, unfazed, "was your face. It simply isn't the face of a forty-one year old. You scarcely look thirty, let alone thirty-six. Although your impossible taste in clothes did lend a degree of plausibility to the pretense."

"Mattie, please, you've . . ."

"Then," Mattie rode over her, "there were certain other things that didn't jibe, even if I hadn't already known about you. Your knowledge of painters, for one thing, is not that of the average secretary. There was also the matter of your most charming habit of editing my correspondence and producing grammatically correct, properly punctuated letters—something no secretary of mine's ever managed to do before. I found it most amusing."

"But I don't understand," Sarah said, almost wailing. "If you knew, why did you hire me? And why aren't you sitting there screaming at me? I mean . . ."

"If you don't mind," Mattie said, "for the moment I'll go on calling you Sarah. Pru—not even Prudence, mind, but *Pru*—is a singularly unappealing name. Of course, if it were my choice, I'd call you something more appropriate, like Laurel, for example. I always planned to name a daughter of mine Laurel. Such a pretty name." She sniffed, lit a cigarette, and went on, unconcerned with Sarah's very obvious distress. "As I said, I quite liked you when you came for the interview. It was the last thing I expected, but there you are. Life's filled with surprises. I'd been thinking for some time about telling the whole slimy story to someone impartial. It did, however, take me far longer than I thought it would to get my nerve up. But I liked you, Sarah. You're far more engaged with people than I think perhaps you realize. And you've been most sympathetic, which has helped enormously. Imagine how dreadful it would have been to reveal everything to someone who didn't give a damn but was solely interested in getting a story. No. I made a wise decision, and I'm not at all displeased. I've read a number of your articles and you write very well. I believe you'll do a good book."

"Wait a minute . . ."

"There is, though," Mattie swept over her, "one condition."

"But, Mattie!"

"Ssshh! I'm not finished. I will, of course, give you the log and whatever else you need to document and substantiate what you write. You will, though, have to wait until after I'm dead to write this book."

"Mattie!" Sarah's voice rose sharply. "God! Wait a minute! I'm very confused. Wait!" She held up both her unsteady hands to silence the old woman. "I'm not sure I'm actually hearing what you're saying. Are you telling me you want me to write about what you've told me?"

"I dislike it intensely when you're obtuse."

"You want me to write about it," Sarah repeated dumbly. "I can't believe this! I'm sitting here having a coronary, convinced you're about to tell me to be out of town by sundown, but you're saying you planned the whole thing. I think I'm getting a headache."

"Don't be self-indulgent!" Mattie warned.

"Oh, God!" Sarah said, as if to herself. "This is too bizarre!" She looked again at the old woman, whose eyes were fixed unwaveringly on her. Sarah could have sworn Mattie was amused. "You think this is funny!" she accused.

"It is," Mattie said. "I've had a good deal of pleasure watching you put your toe over the edge of a hole, realize you were about to step in, and pull back. You're to be commended. You've performed very well."

"But I haven't been performing. That's the point. Mattie, I changed my mind about doing the book weeks ago. Yes, it's why I took the job and why I lied about being Sarah. I *thought* I could do this. I thought I could sign on as your secretary and find out all about Gideon Sylvester, then go away and write a big juicy unauthorized biography. But I can't do it. I don't *want* to do it!"

It was Mattie's turn to look distressed. "But you have to!" she declared. "You must! I realize there's an indeterminate wait involved, but I'm prepared to make some kind of financial arrangement to tide you over. I'm counting on you."

"Don't you *get* it?" Sarah cried. "*I can't do it!* First of all, I couldn't, absolutely could not, hang around like some kind of vulture, waiting for you to die. I don't even want to *think* about you dying. And in the second place, it's totally wrong. The truth should come out now! Not in fifteen or twenty years, but *now*. No, wait!" She stopped Mattie from interrupting. "I know every single one of your arguments, and they're all lousy. You are *not* too old; you are *not* too tired. You're not one damned thing that would prevent you from seeing it through. And there'd be no need for you to be swamped by the media. It could all be done like a presidential press conference. It's your *right*, Mattie," she said passionately. "You can claim back everything he took from you; you can finally have the credit you deserve."

"*It is too late!*"

"*It is not!* " Sarah asserted, beginning to shed angry tears. "I know I'm on very shaky ground here, but I'm not wrong."

"You are utterly, totally, wrong!" Mattie maintained hotly. "You will respect my wishes in this matter!"

"You can't force me to do something I don't want to do!"

"NEITHER CAN YOU!" Mattie shrieked.

They sat glaring at each other.

Sarah mopped her face on her napkin and said, "I can't believe we're fighting about this. You want me to do what I came here to do in the first place, but I don't want to do it. This is the nuttiest thing ever! Here I thought you were going to throw me out on my ear, but it turns out I've been the one operating in the dark all along. You're as guilty as I am. Why didn't you say you knew who I was and that you were willing to go along with it?"

"It would have spoiled things. You'd have lost your impartiality."

"*God!*" More tears gushed from Sarah's eyes. "This can't be happening!"

"I honestly don't see why you're carrying on and making such a fuss, when really I ought to be the one doing that."

"You want me to wait around for you to *die*, and you don't know why I'm upset? Jesus, Mattie! Whether you believe it or not, I love you. It would be obscene for me to agree to that. That would be living up to exactly what you believe all journalists really are: vampires!"

"Well, what do you propose to do?" Mattie asked briskly.

"I suppose you want me to pack up and get out," Sarah said.

"I don't recall saying anything like that."

"You mean you don't?" Sarah asked wide-eyed.

"Well, I mean to say, I just assumed you'd go, once we got to the end." Flustered, Mattie lit a fresh cigarette.

"But do you *want* me to go?"

"I simply haven't thought . . ."

"Let me stay!" Sarah begged. "Please, let me stay. I really want to. I want to be here with you and Gloria and Bonnie and Carl. There isn't anywhere else I want to be."

"We seem to have ourselves a dilemma," Mattie said.

"You want me to go," Sarah said, sinking.

"Not at all. I mean, if you want to stay . . . it's just that I hadn't given it any thought . . . I suppose you could. I can't see what harm would come of it, and you really are a first-rate secretary. But will you be content with that?"

"I already am content with that. And I could still do articles. It wouldn't interfere with the household."

"You astound me," Mattie said. "I didn't expect any of this."

"Well, you astound me, too. And I didn't expect any of this, either. Can I stay?"

"Of course, if you're sure it's what you want."

"It is!" Suddenly, everything clicked into place and Sarah knew exactly what she had to do. "The only thing is," she said, "I need a few days off to go to the mainland, if that'd be all right with you."

"I suppose you need to tie off some loose ends."

"That's just what I need to do." Sarah got up and went around the table to drop down on her haunches beside Mattie's chair, taking hold of her hand. "I know it's a bit presumptuous of me under the circumstances, but will you trust me?"

"Sarah . . . Christ! We must rename you! I cannot abide these biblical names. Yes, I trust you. Now eat your breakfast and then go off and do whatever it is you have to do."

Sarah kissed the old woman's hand, and Mattie swatted her on the top of her head. "Stop that!" she ordered. "Behave yourself and get back in your chair!"

"Yes ma'am," Sarah said and did as she'd been told. "My middle name is Holly."

"Holly? Were these people mentally balanced when they named you children?"

"Very possibly not."

"Holly," Mattie repeated, reaching for her coffee. "It's better. I think Holly's a name I can live with."

Twenty-seven

Is this a polite kiss-off," Carl asked, "or are you really coming back?"

"I'm coming back, I promise. Why would I lie to you?"

"Jesus, be serious! I don't even know your real name."

"Call me Holly. And what's happened between you and me has
nothing to do with anyone but the two of us. I'll be back the day after
tomorrow. If I don't turn up, it's because I'm dead. Okay? Come hell
or high water, I'll be on the five o'clock ferry. If things work out, I
could be back as soon as tomorrow, Carl. The only reason I'm going
is because I've got something very important to do."

"Like what?"

"Unless I hit a snag, you'll know the day after tomorrow. Now,
give me a kiss and let me go. The cars are already on board. I don't
want to miss this boat."

"You know how I feel about you," he said awkwardly. "It's hard
for me to say these things."

She kissed him, then smiled. "It's okay. I know."

He stood on the dock, hands in his pockets. She waved and finally
he raised a hand to wave back.

She went to the first pay phone she could find on the mainland and
put in a call to Matthew. Keeping her fingers crossed, she waited to be
put through to him, hoping his feelings were as Mattie had said.

After reminding him who she was, she told him what she had in
mind.

"That's wonderful!" he exclaimed. "Has Mother actually agreed
to it?"

"She's putting up a fight. That's why I'm calling you. I thought if you could maybe come up for the weekend, and bring Giddy, the two of you could help convince her. It's the right thing to do, Matthew. It truly is."

"You don't have to convince me, Sarah. Nothing could make me happier than to have the truth finally come out. But Giddy's another question. He tends to agree with Mother that they should just maintain the status quo."

"But you could persuade him, Matthew, if you tried. He's your brother and he loves you. The two of you combining forces would make a big impact on Mattie. And if she knew you'd both stand behind her on this, she'd give in. Just think how good Giddy would be at dealing with the press! He'd have a field day."

"Good point. He would."

"Will you call him and try?" she asked.

He deliberated for a moment, then said, "All right, I will."

"And you'll come up for the weekend?"

"Yes. We'll both be there. By God!" he said, catching fire. "If you can pull this off, you're a genius. And I get the feeling if anyone can do it, you can. I'll call Giddy right now."

"Good for you, Matthew."

"Thank you, Sarah. You know," he said, "I think this may solve a lot of problems, for everyone."

"I sure as hell hope so. Thank *you*, Matthew."

Lowering his voice as if fearful of being overheard, he said, "I love my mother and brother, you know, Sarah."

"I know you do. I'll see you at the end of the week."

Forty minutes later, she was in a rented Buick, headed for the interstate. She spun the radio dial, found a station playing Van Morrison's "Moondance," thought of Carl, and left it on.

She was nervously excited and had to concentrate hard not to floor the accelerator. This had to work. She'd never done anything remotely so bold, but she had every intention of giving it her best shot. With luck, she'd make it to Maine in about five hours. She'd book into a motel for the night and first thing in the morning she'd phone H. Clay Dickinson.

Until things had come to a head this morning, she'd been feeling progressively more rotten, considering herself yet another person planning to defraud Mattie. The fact that she'd changed her mind didn't alter the reality of the motive she'd had upon applying for the job. Now she had a chance to do something that could only benefit Mattie, in every way, provided Hughie Dickinson was actually as Mattie had described him.

She was checked into a motel by twenty past five and couldn't see the sense of wasting any time. She found the number she'd copied from Mattie's address book and picked up the receiver with a suddenly damp hand. She dialed. The ringing started and she held the receiver to her ear with both hands, well aware she was about to do some God-playing with other people's lives on a fairly major scale.

On the sixth ring, a cheerful-sounding male voice said, "Hello. You've got me, so speak your piece."

She had to laugh, then asked "Do you always answer the phone that way?"

"Most of the time. I can't stand these machines. Someone's forever calling up trying to sell you something you don't want, or wanting you to part with something you don't want to sell. Those *TV Guide* people are the worst. They just won't quit. You're not one of them, I hope."

"No. My name is Sarah Kidd and I've been working for Mattie since last February."

"Oh, yes. Mattie's talked about you. How are you, Sarah?"

"I'm fine, Mr. Dickinson. How are you?"

"Right as rain. Mattie's all right, isn't she?"

"She's great."

"Say! Where are you calling from, anyhow?"

"About three miles down the road from your house."

"Well, now, you don't say! Thought it was a mighty clear connection."

"Would you mind if I came over to see you, Mr. Dickinson? I'd very much like to talk to you."

"How d'you feel about chili?" he asked.

"It depends on how hot it is. I can handle medium, but I pass out on hot."

He chuckled and said, "You know how to get here, or you need directions?"

"Maybe you should give me directions, just in case."

"Get yourself a pencil, and I'll tell you the way."

She put on the dress Mattie had said was rather sweet, then stood in front of the mirror in the badly lit bathroom and applied some makeup. Then she brushed her hair, checked to make sure she didn't have lipstick on her teeth, and set off to meet Hughie Dickinson.

He came to stand in the front door as she pulled into the driveway, and it touched her to note that he and Mattie both had the endearing habit of waiting close by to open the door before expected guests had to confront bells, buzzers, or knockers.

Like Mattie, his spine was very straight. And like Mattie, he looked younger than his years.

She got out of the car and walked over to him, saying, "Hi. It's very good of you to see me on such short notice."

His hair had gone white but there was still plenty of it. His hazel eyes were remarkably clear, and his skin did indeed have a lovely peachy tone to it. He exuded well-being standing there in jeans, with a red plaid shirt, and L.L. Bean Chukka walking boots.

He gave her hand a gentle shake, smiling as he said, "Trust Mattie! She always had fine-looking women working for her. Come on in, Sarah. I figured you'd probably be thirsty after that long drive, and I've got some apple cider here that'll give you a good little buzz."

"Since you've been talking to Mattie, you probably know my name isn't Sarah."

"Uh-huh," he said, pouring two glasses of golden brown liquid and handing her one.

"She and I have agreed she'll call me Holly. It's my middle name."

"Come sit down," he invited, heading for an old armchair with worn upholstery positioned to one side of the fireplace.

She sat in its twin and tasted the cider. "This'll definitely give me a buzz," she told him.

"So, are you gonna do the book for Mattie?"

"Mr. Dickinson—"

"Call me Hughie, please."

"Hughie, I've told Mattie I don't think it's right that people won't learn the truth until after she's dead. Aside from the fact that I find the idea of waiting around for her to die morbid as hell and twice as upsetting, I feel she deserves to have the recognition now. The gods willing, she's going to live for a good long time still, and she ought to be able to enjoy the accolades she'll get for her work. Which is why I'm here. From everything Mattie's told me about you, I can't help believing you'd feel the same way I do about this. People should know."

He nodded solemnly. "Unfortunately, dear girl, whatever you and I might feel, nobody's ever been able to make Mattie do something she didn't want to do."

"Except for Gideon Sylvester."

His features creased with distaste. "Except for him."

"Hughie, I love that woman with all my heart, and I want her to be happy. I know, regardless of what she says, that once the truth came out she would be happy. And I think this is one time when somebody else has to make the decision as to what's in her best interest, because she flatly doesn't want to see or admit it."

"And you're presuming to do that?"

"Yes! Yes, I am. There are two things I believe it's her right to have. They happen to be the two things she thinks she no longer has any right to: her work, and you. Hughie, don't you want to be with her, to be together?"

"Now, that's not such a simple question."

"Yes it is. Wouldn't you?" she repeated.

"You always this forceful with folks you've only just met?"

"Hardly ever, as a matter of fact. But she's never going to send for you, even though she wants to more than anything else. And you know why? Because she's convinced Gideon Sylvester would always be an issue between you. Is that true?"

"Not so far as I'm concerned. Mattie's feelings are something else, of course. And she's got a right to them, whether or not you happen to agree with her."

"But the two of you are apart for no good reason. I mean, here you are in Maine, and she's over on that island six miles out in the Atlantic. Doesn't that seem a little extreme to you?"

"You ought to be in a court of law," he said admiringly, "fighting for some noble cause. I'll bet you give Mattie a good run for her money."

"We argue like crazy," she admitted, "and we tease each other. She makes me think, which is something no one has done in a very long time. Hughie, she'll listen to you. If you tell her to go ahead and do this, she'll go along with you. I could make up a press release and call a news conference, maybe in September when we get back to Connecticut. It'd be the sensation of the century!"

"And what's my role in this supposed to be?"

"You come back with me to the island and you stake your claim on the woman you love. Then you hold her hand while she tells the world the truth about Gideon Sylvester. It's the only way she'll ever agree to do it. Do you honestly want to see her live out her last years alone, frustrated and defeated, famous only as the great painter's widow?"

"Can't say I care for the picture," he said, setting down his glass and picking up an old briar pipe. As he began scraping the bowl with a small penknife, he said, "I'm going to have to think about this. I've never been one to make impetuous moves. It goes against my nature."

"I realize that. And I know I'm trying to manipulate the situation, but only for Mattie's good. You have my word my intentions are strictly honorable."

"I believe you. Let's talk some more over a bowl of chili." Putting aside the pipe, he got up and headed for the kitchen. "Come on, young lady. It's your choice. You can grate the cheese, or dice the onions."

"I'll do the onions."

He turned back to smile at her. "I like you. You've got no compunction about getting the dirty jobs done."

"I like you, too," she told him. "And I think journalism is the fraternal twin to the doing of dirty jobs."

"You do, huh? I'll have to think about that, too."

They sat together in the old-fashioned kitchen at the oilcloth-covered table with bowls of chili, a plate of Saltines, and the bottle of cider.

"This is good," she complimented him, eating heartily. "Is it your specialty?"

"I've got a couple of them. The chili's one. Beef stew's another. I can fix a decent spaghetti sauce, too, and a tolerable meat loaf. But the chili and the stew are my best. Mattie tell you about Ina?"

"Yes, she did."

"It was Ina taught me the recipes for the chili and the stew. I think she figured I'd starve if I didn't learn how to cook a few things I could make in quantity that'd last a few days. Awfully nice woman, Ina was. Just crazy about Mattie and the boy. The boy," he chuckled. "That boy's gotta be fifty now. A good little tyke he was, Giddy. Never have met another child so eager to please. By all sights, he's still the same."

"He struck me that way. I liked him a lot."

"Holly, huh? How'd you come to be calling yourself Sarah?"

"Sarah's my older sister. I used her résumé to get the job with Mattie. Sarah's secretary to the president of one of those executive head-hunting outfits in New York. She's been there about fifteen years, and I figured if anyone checked, I'd come up sounding solid and reliable."

"Doesn't your sister wonder where you are?"

"I write to her regularly. I told her I was researching a project, which wasn't entirely untrue."

"What exactly was your plan?" he asked interestedly.

"I didn't really have one. I thought I'd work for Mattie indefinitely. Somewhere along the line I'd find out what Gideon Sylvester was really like, and when I had enough material I'd quit the job and start working on the book."

"What prompted your interest?"

"Oh, the paintings. I saw my first one when I was about fourteen, in an art book I borrowed from the library. It was a collection of modern American artists, and I liked quite a few of the paintings. But when I got to the one of Grand Central Station with the people in the foreground, I was bowled over by it. It was so real, so strong, I had the feeling I was standing over on Vanderbilt Avenue watching the whole thing. I'd never seen anything that gave me such a sense of place and character and mood. Looking at that painting, I felt I knew exactly what New York was like in the late twenties. After that, I was hooked. I went back to the library to find books with more paintings by Gideon Sylvester. I thought he was a genius. Now, of course, I know who the real genius was. The thing that really kills me is knowing Mattie was only seventeen when she painted that picture. She's amazing!"

"Yes, indeed," he agreed.

"And yours were the other ones I loved. Honest to God! I'm not just saying that to flatter you. It's wonderful to meet you and be able to tell you how much I love your work."

He wiped his mouth with a paper napkin, then smiled. "Compliments always sound so much better when they come from the mouths of pretty young women."

"It's the truth, Hughie. It's incredible to think I'm actually sitting here with you, eating chili."

"With onions."

"I won't be able to breathe on anyone for a month," she said happily.

"Someone you want to breathe on?"

"Someone you know, as a matter of fact."

"Carl Harvey, huh?"

"Right in one," she said, and hearing herself quote Carl, she had to laugh. "That's one of his expressions," she explained.

"I thought it sounded familiar."

"Hughie, will you please come back with me tomorrow?"

"You want to finish that food before it goes cold, and I want to think on this some more. I wouldn't want to go doing something that would upset Mattie."

"Look, there's one thing I absolutely have to say, and it's this: You two belong together. Mattie feels too guilty, and she thinks it's too late; she's too old to ask for what she wants. And with all due respect, I think because of the long-standing terms between you, you don't want to inflict anything on her she doesn't seem to want. But, don't you see? You both want the same thing, but neither one of you is willing or able to take the first step. So I'm doing it for you."

"If you write as well as you talk," he said with a slow grin, "I'll bet you're one heck of a writer."

"Lately, I've been a better talker than a writer."

"And a better talker than an eater. Now get that food into you, Miss."

She finished, then sat back from the table with a groan, saying, "I may very well explode."

"Don't you worry. It's my custom to walk after dinner. If you're planning to explode, you can do it out-of-doors. I'm not much of a housekeeper, as you may have noticed, and I'd hate to have to be picking bits of a pretty young woman off the furniture for days and weeks to come."

She laughed loudly. "You're very funny, H. Clay."

They left the house and started down the road. Hughie had his pipe lit and looked about as he walked, apparently pleased by everything he saw. "You know," he said, talking around the pipe stem, "I started asking Mattie to marry me after the second or third time we met. I never have experienced anything before or since like the feeling I got the first time I saw her. She was sharp as a tack, smart as a whip. And she couldn't walk down a street without turning heads. You should've seen her," he said with wistful pride. "The most arresting face and figure, tall and slim and straight as an arrow, with that flaming hair and those don't-you-dare eyes."

"Don't-you-dare?"

"She'd look you straight in the eye and defy you to try to get away with even the smallest white lie. I never could; never wanted to, in any case. She tell you about the time in the park when she threatened to march me into the nearest drugstore and buy me a toothbrush if I couldn't afford one myself?"

"She did."

He grinned and shook his head. "Damnedest woman ever lived, but kindhearted, too. If she'd gone and married anybody else in the world

296 CHARLOTTE VALE ALLEN

and been happy, I'd've been happy for her. But for my Mattie to take up with that scum Sylvester, well, it about broke my heart. You can't tell people, though, Miss Holly. They won't hear; they won't listen, because they can't. I'm the same. I'd never countenance anyone saying so much as one bad word about Mattie. I wouldn't hear, and I sure as hell wouldn't listen. But in my case, it'd be because I'd know they were wrong, you see. Oh, I know she thinks she's had me fooled all these years, being on her best behavior whenever we'd meet up. But she forgets I was there. I've known her since she was seventeen. She always was feisty and given to stating her opinions out loud and clear. Since I had a problem speaking my mind, it only made me admire her all the more. I like an outspoken person who's not afraid to say what she thinks and's willing to take the consequences. She forgets, too, that I've seen her when there wasn't any chance for her to be anything but herself. I was there with her when Matthew was born, and she had a rough time of it but she never fussed or complained. She got on with it and never even raised her voice. I've known men couldn't take what life's dished up to Mattie." He stopped, saw his pipe had gone out, and relit it with a kitchen match. "So you've taken up with young Harvey, huh?"

"I care very much about him. I'm hoping we'll be able to work things out. He still has some serious problems. Once upon a time, I'd have jumped in with both feet, positive I could cure him simply by caring. I don't believe I'm that potent, but I intend to help, if I can."

"Terrible what happened to him," Hughie said soberly. "Me and Mattie both were students of Nicholas Harvey, you know, Carl's grandfather. Carl was my student for several years and I had the highest hopes for him. He inherited Nick's talent for watercolors but with a boldness and a feeling for color. He was on the way to being even better than Nick. Then he went off to that Vietnam thing and came back with his head and his heart in pieces. It was a genuine shock to see what that experience did to the boy. And his folks, you know, they were sick with upset at having to turn him out, but they were afraid of him. He still sleep during the daylight?"

"Yes."

"Damned shame. I was against that war from the start. Mattie was, too. We went twice to D.C. to march. Did Mattie tell you? We met up there, and the two of us marched with thousands of other folks. First time was in sixty-five when it wasn't so popular to be against that war. She was worried maybe she'd turn up in some newsreel, so she wore this hat covered all her hair and big dark glasses. Second time, we went for the night march in sixty-seven. That time, she said to hell with Gideon Sylvester, and didn't bother disguising herself.

"It was a matter of principle, and nobody was gonna stop her making her feelings known. Then poor Carl came back and had all his troubles, worked a time for Giddy in the big city, but that seemed to make him even worse. Mattie made up her mind and wasn't taking no for an answer. Carl was coming to her, and that was that. Between you and me, Miss, I think the only reason that boy's alive today is thanks to Mattie. She's got a good heart."

"You know you're coming with me tomorrow, don't you? If I have to kidnap you to get you there, I'm taking you to the island."

He laughed and said, "You sure do tickle me. Big as a minute and mean as a bull moose, threatening an old man."

"You could probably swat me like a fly," she said with a smile. She'd rarely met anyone she'd liked so immediately and so well.

"Well," he said with a sigh, "I guess I'll have to dig out my traveling bag, and see what kind of condition the suit's in."

"I think you could wear what you have on now and Mattie would be thrilled to see you. This is going to make her, and you, very happy."

"She might just shoot the both of us."

"Well, then we'll die trying."

"I guess we will. You sure are the most powerfully persuasive young woman I've ever met."

"I didn't really have to persuade you at all, did I?" she said, linking arms with him. "I think I'm only a kind of letter you've been waiting a long time to receive."

Twenty-eight

She turned to smile over at Hughie, who fussed periodically with the seat belt.

"I never have liked these contraptions," he said, giving the belt a tug. "I know they keep you safe but it's like having someone you don't specially care for keeping an arm draped over your shoulder."

"Hughie, what do you think of Matthew?" she asked.

"He's not the worst man I ever met," he said, cradling the bowl of his unlit pipe in his right hand as he gazed straight ahead through the windshield. "I've seen him maybe twice in the last twenty years, you understand. But I don't care one bit for his disrespectful attitude to Mattie and his brother. Not that his heart's not in the right place, but that Gideon Sylvester turned his head around and poor Matthew's been trying ever since to get it back on straight. You're a good driver," he observed. "Mattie was the worst. Made my stomach go into knots driving with her. Nobody was happier than me when she gave it up and let Carl take over. She was too impatient. And she'd curse out everybody on the road." He laughed softly. "It was a true test of my affections, getting into a car with her."

"Did she think she was a good driver?"

"Oh, naturally. Me, I've never cared much for automobiles. Gotta have one to get from point A to point B, but I prefer to walk if I can. I only started driving after double-u double-u two. I'd see another car coming along the road I'd try to drive on the shoulder to get out of its way. I'm what you'd call a nervous driver. I figure most folks are aiming to get themselves killed and take me with them while they're at it. I'm the one always drives the young folks crazy on the road, pooping along at forty-five and holding up the show."

"I intend to get you to the island in one piece. Okay?"

"Suits me. I never have been to the island, you know. Ought to be really interesting to see that house, finally. From the way Mattie's talked about it, I kind of picture it like the House of Usher, dark and Gothic."

"It's nothing like that. It's very light and airy upstairs, and shaded downstairs. And Mattie has a wonderful studio in the attic."

"She started back working yet?"

"She's painting my portrait."

"Well, now, you don't say!" He looked at her again. "That's a mighty encouraging sign."

"I think so, aside from the fact that I'm insanely flattered."

"Funny she didn't mention to me she was working."

"When was the last time the two of you talked?"

"Oh, a while now," he said. "Must be a month or more. We're both a couple of old night birds these days. She'll phone me up now and then at two or three in the morning and we'll talk for half an hour, an hour. But she hasn't called lately. So when you phoned last night, I was worried maybe she was taken sick or something. Not like her to let so much time go by without calling."

"It may be because she and I have been talking a lot at night. It's so funny. I never once caught on that she was telling me about her life on purpose. I mean because she wanted me to write about it." She smiled. "She really put one over on me."

"If it's any consolation, Miss, she wouldn't have said a word to you if she didn't think very highly of you. We talked quite a lot those first few months after you came, and I could hear in her voice how much she was growing to like you."

"It's completely mutual. Please let me know if you want to stop for any reason."

"I surely will."

"And if you want to smoke your pipe, I wouldn't mind at all."

"Thank you," he said. "I appreciate the consideration."

★　　★　　★

While they were waiting on the dock for the ferry to come in, Hughie looked out over the water saying, "This is quite an adventure, Miss Holly. I sure hope you know what you're doing."

"Hughie, there's no way on earth she isn't going to be ecstatic to see you. She might not be so thrilled with me for doing this, but after she insults me for a while she'll calm right down."

He chuckled. "That sounds about right. That's my Mattie." Turning, he asked, "You got anything else planned I should know about?"

"I've talked to Matthew and he and Giddy are going to come up for the weekend to lend their support. Otherwise, no sir. Getting you to the island was my last and only plan."

"She might make you swim back, you know. Have you considered that?"

"Are you kidding?" she laughed. "I'm risking my life with this. But I'll never believe it's not worth it. Just to be on the safe side, though, I'll walk behind you, in case she pulls a gun."

He looked down at himself. "She's not going to be crazy about these clothes. Used to accuse me of looking like an elderly lumberjack."

"You're fine," she told him, putting her arm through his. "Here comes the boat."

They had to wait half an hour while the cars were offloaded and the passengers disembarked. Then Hughie said again, "Some adventure," as they were allowed to board. "I like boat rides. I like water. Never could paint it worth a damn, though. Hard as hell to paint water. Only a few people do it well. Nick Harvey could paint water. And so could Carl. Mattie's got some of Carl's sketchbooks. You might ask her to let you see them sometime."

"I will. Maybe, between us, we could encourage him to try going back to it."

"Don't know about that," he said thoughtfully. "But it would be worth a try. I don't mind telling you, Miss, I'm a mite nervous about this."

"So am I. It'll be fine, I'm sure."

"If it isn't," he said, "there'll be two of us dog-paddling back to the mainland."

★   ★   ★

Mattie sat out on the verandah, her eyes, as usual, on the beach. This morning a group of rowdy teenagers had discovered what they thought was heaven in the form of a deserted beach. They'd left their bicycles parked under the trees, then gone splashing and shouting, in and out of the water. Mattie had enjoyed watching them until they began littering the beach with soft drink cans and chocolate bar wrappers. She then had to send Carl down. Carl had stood, hands on his hips, while they picked up every last bit of their trash. They'd looked as if they'd wanted to argue, but they'd been wise enough not to try, and had left peacefully enough.

After they'd gone, Carl had come to stand with his foot on the first step of the verandah. "Anything special you want done?"

"Yes, dear. I'd like you to join me for lunch today."

He looked down for a moment, then returned his eyes to hers. "Okay, Mattie," he'd said. "I'll go clean up."

"Carl, dear," she said, stopping him. "I know you'd prefer to be devoured by flesh-eating African ants, but I would like your company."

He smiled and said, "I think I can handle it," then he'd gone off to shower and change while she got up and went to tell Bonnie to set two places for lunch.

"What about dinner?" Bonnie wanted to know. "How many?"

"Two."

"Sarah's coming back, huh?"

"Holly," Mattie corrected her. "I loathe the name Sarah. Thank God, it's not her real name. Imagine having to live with that for the rest of your days! I'd be living on tenterhooks, expecting some type with dirty bare feet in sandals and a lot of unkempt facial and other hair to show up spouting radical sixties rubbish."

Bonnie had snickered. "The things you say, Mattie!"

"Whatever. Try to remember to call her Holly. It's too cute for words, but it's infinitely preferable to Sarah. Or Pru, which, if you can believe it, is her real name."

"Pru?" Bonnie made a face.

"Precisely!" Mattie had said, and swept out.

★   ★   ★

Carl had arrived with his hair wet-combed, in a white shirt that set off his tanned face.

"This is very nice," Mattie said, as he held her chair for her.

"Not quite as bad as flesh-eating ants."

Bonnie came in with bowls of gazpacho garnished with shavings of green onion.

"If you don't want to eat it, I won't mind," she said.

"I'll tough it out," he smiled, then stared down at the cold soup as if small fish might be swimming beneath the surface. He couldn't get himself even to put the spoon into the bowl.

"Have a cigarette," Mattie suggested, setting down her own spoon and picking up her pack.

Grateful, he lit her cigarette and then his own. "I'm sorry, Mattie. I don't know what the hell happens to me, but I start thinking there's all kinds of weird stuff in the food."

"It must be very difficult," she sympathized. "You'll be relieved to know I asked Bonnie to fix some chicken sandwiches. And, just for you, a platter of her French fries. With ketchup," she added.

He said, "Thanks," and, relieved, untensed his shoulders.

Mattie stepped on the buzzer under the carpet beside her chair and Bonnie came in and, without a word, removed the soup. In five minutes, she was back with the sandwiches and French fries.

"Go ahead!" Mattie had urged. "Help yourself, dear! I know you're hungry."

He stubbed out his cigarette and filled his plate with sandwiches and fries. He started to eat and Mattie watched, smoking her cigarette. Satisfied he was all right now, she said, "There's something I'd like you to do for me, dear."

He paused in dipping one of the fries into a pool of ketchup. "What?"

"Holly's being very obstinate about this matter of the book."

"Oh yeah?" He popped the potato into his mouth and reached for another.

"It seems we're at cross-purposes. I want her to do the book, but she's changed her mind and says she won't do it."

"No kidding!" He picked up half a sandwich and bit into it.

"It rather defeats the whole point of this exercise if she won't agree."

"I guess so," he nodded. "And you want me to try to talk her into it. Right?"

"Something like that. You do have a certain influence with her."

He finished chewing, then said, "Much as I love you, Mattie, I have to tell you I tend to agree with Sarah, or Holly, or whatever the hell she's calling herself."

"Why?" she asked stiffly.

"Don't go all frigid on me," he said nicely. "She's got a couple of very good points. It would be seriously sick of her to hang around waiting for you to croak so she can publish a book. Jesus! I mean, if she was capable of doing that I wouldn't want to know about her. You know? And maybe you could explain to me why you shouldn't go ahead and dump on the old prick now, have yourself a field day trashing his dead ass. Christ, I would!"

"I am not you," she reminded him.

"No shit!" he said with a smile. "Nevertheless, sweetheart, I think your idea's a crock. And there's no way I'm going to try to talk Sarah, Holly, whoever the hell she is, into going along with you. If you can change her mind, swell. It's between the two of you. If it was up to me, though, I'd say get your big boots on and tromp all over that mother."

Her face falling, she puffed on her cigarette. "I'm very disappointed. I was so sure you'd want to help me."

"Mattie, there's nothing I wouldn't do for you. Except that. I won't use a woman I care about as a favor for another woman I care about. That's dirty, not to mention dishonest. I've got about as much as I can handle just getting by. I start trying to move people around and I'll go nuts for sure. Anyway, you're wrong. I don't see why you won't just go for it, go public."

She didn't answer but sat gazing past him into space.

"Come on, Mattie," he'd cajoled. "You knew I'd never buy into that. Why even try?"

Her shoulders lifted a little, then fell.

"Listen," he said. "I know you're pissed off with me, but you'd be even more pissed off if I went along with you on this. And you know it."

With a sigh, she'd said, "I suppose you're right."

"Have a fry," he suggested, pushing the platter toward her. "They're damned good."

She sighed again and took one, saying, "Give me the goddamned ketchup!"

He laughed and handed it to her.

After lunch Carl had gone to the garage apartment to sleep for a few hours, and Mattie had climbed the stairs to the master suite to stand contemplating the bed, wondering if it was worthwhile to try napping. At last, she decided she was tired, and stretched out on the bed.

At four-thirty, she got up and came down to the verandah where she now sat, her eyes on the beach, anticipating Sarah—Holly's return. She was by no means finished with that young woman, and had one or two cards still left to play.

Carl threw his arms around the old man with a laugh, saying, "This is too much!" Turning to hug Sarah, he said, "You've got big balls, sweetheart. I can't *wait* to see this!"

"You're looking very well, Carl," Hughie said, as Carl held open the passenger door for him.

"You look damned well yourself, Uncle Hugh. Man! This is too incredible!"

From the back seat, Holly asked, "Are you Carl's uncle?"

"Honorary, dear girl. But I've always encouraged it," he said with a wink. "I'm so looking forward to seeing the house. Mattie, too, of course. But I've been hearing about the house for better than fifty years."

"Jesus, Uncle Hugh," Carl said, as they headed for the north end, "how did Sarah, I mean, Holly, talk you into this?"

"I'm not sure I know," he replied, looking around. "Pretty place, isn't it? Some splendid old houses. My goodness! Look at that one! Isn't that something? Gingerbread trim and shutters. Haven't seen houses like this since I was a boy."

Mattie's head turned as the car pulled up in front of the house. Holly jumped out and waved as Carl hurried to open the passenger door for Hughie. Watching, Mattie went very still. Upon seeing Hughie step from the car, she shot to her feet.

"Uh oh!" Carl said under his breath, taking Holly by the arm to hold her back as Hughie started toward the house.

Rigid with shock, Mattie watched Hughie come toward her.

"Hello, Mattie," he said from the bottom of the stairs. "Made up your mind yet how you feel about this?" he asked with a smile.

"You silly old bugger!" she cried, hurrying down the stairs. "You're trying to give me a heart attack."

"Oh, now," he said, his hands on her shoulders as he studied her face. "I wouldn't want to go doing anything like that."

"Hughie, damn it!" She was unable to keep from smiling. She hugged him, saying, "It must be you. You smell like that foul pipe tobacco."

"You smell just fine," he said contentedly.

Breaking away from him, she turned to shake her finger at Holly and Carl. "Don't think you're getting away with this!" she said, then laughed and spoiled the effect. "Just because I look amused doesn't mean I approve of your sneaking around, Holly Kidd!"

"No, ma'am," Holly replied. "Ten lashes after dinner. Right?"

"Go away, the two of you! Can't you see I've got a guest?" Turning back, she linked her arm with Hughie's, saying, "Would you like to see the house, my dear?"

"I believe I would."

They started up the stairs together. "Will you be staying?" she asked.

"I thought I might, if that sits well with you."

"You silly old bugger," she said again, "letting yourself be horn-swoggled by a pretty face."

"I was fixing to come for you anyway," he said. "She got me moving, that's all."

She opened the screen door and stood aside for him to enter. Then while he looked around, she went to the kitchen door to say, "Bonnie, there'll be three for dinner." Returning to Hughie, she said, "Come upstairs. I want to show you what I'm working on."

"This is some impressive place," he said. "Back to work, huh?"

"Well, it's about time. Wouldn't you say?"

"I surely would. You know, Mattie, I've been thinking, and that Miss Holly's right. It's time you let folks know the truth about Gideon Sylvester."

She paused on the landing to look at him. "I swear to God," she said. "I will murder that young woman."

He chucked her under the chin and gave her a kiss. "Now, now," he said soothingly, "don't go getting your drawers in a twist. It's an idea whose time has come and you know it."

"I refuse to have the press crawling all over me."

He kissed her again and said, "Only one around here's going to be crawling all over you is me."

"Dirty old man!" she laughed.

"Show me what you're working on," he said. "Which way?"

He took several steps down the hall, looking into open doorways. She watched him, her heart fluttering. "It's this way," she said after a moment. "You know, Hughie, we really must get an L.L. Bean catalog and order you some new things."

"You think so?"

"Maybe a few more shirts and two or three new pairs of jeans."

"No new suit?" he asked, following her up to the attic.

"Why would you need a new suit?"

"For when the press come wanting to crawl all over you."

"Damn it!" She stopped just inside the studio. "I won't discuss this any further."

"That's fine," he said. "Isn't this wonderful!" He looked around eagerly. Spotting the easel, he headed straight for it.

"Hughie? Do you think you'd be able to work here?"

"I can't see why not. It's got good light. And you're here."

"Jesus!" she said softly. "This better not be an old lady's daydream or I'm going to be sick with disappointment."

"If you're dreaming, Mattie, I'm in an awful lot of trouble," he smiled. "Cause I just dreamed I came over to this island on a ferry. And I've been dreaming about doing that for half a century."

Taking his hand, she said, "Let me show you the new piece. I'm very pleased with it. It had been so long, you know, I was afraid I'd have nothing left. But everything's still there."

Over in the garage apartment Holly and Carl were sitting in the old wicker chairs.

"She'll do it," she was saying. "I know she will. Especially when Giddy and Matthew show up and tell her they think she should."

"You are one astonishing broad. You know that?"

"Please don't refer to me as a broad."

"Woman. Okay?"

"Yes, thank you."

"One of these times," he said, his leg over the chair arm swinging rhythmically back and forth, "I might hit on Mattie for some paper and stuff, and take a shot at some sketches."

"One of these times," she said, "you and I are going to sleep together in that bed for an entire night."

"Don't push it," he said. "Let's aim for an hour. Okay?"

"I'll settle for that."

"You're gonna have to, sweetheart."

"That's fine," she said. "I'm very happy."

"Yeah," he grinned. "Me, too."

Charlotte Vale Allen was born in Toronto, Canada, in 1941. After more than ten years as a singer, actress, and cabaret/revue performer, she began writing in 1971, and has been a full-time writer since the publication of *Love Life*, her first novel, in 1976. She has published twenty-five works of fiction, as well as the award-winning autobiographical account of incest, *Daddy's Girl*. She emigrated to the United States in 1966, and since 1970 has made her home in Connecticut. *Painted Lives* is her twenty-sixth novel.

TELL A FRIEND

Dear _____,

I just finished reading *Painted Lives* by Charlotte Vale Allen and wanted to tell you about it because I think it's a book you will love too.

Sincerely,

_____

Painted Lives is available at all bookstores.

(seal here)

TELL THE AUTHOR

Dear Charlotte Vale Allen,
I just finished reading *Painted Lives* and wanted to tell you how much
I enjoyed it.

_____

_____

_____

Sincerely,

name _____

address _____

city, province, postal code _____

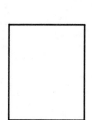

Charlotte Vale Allen
c/o Random House of Canada Limited
Editorial Department
1265 Aerowood Drive
Mississauga, Ontario
L4W 1B9

(seal here)